A Voice

That

Thunders

A Voice That Thunders

Book One

Cully Mack

Copyright

ISBN 978-1-9160970-0-1

Dedication

For my daughters.
In life, let the voice that thunders be your own.

Epigraph

For to the thunder resting places were given,

as it awaits its voice,

and the thunder and the lightening are not separated.

And (although) they are not one,

by the wind the two of them go and are not separated.

(1 Enoch 60:11 L14)

Part 1

Prologue

Thunder reverberated through the small cave. Gabe stood at its entrance watching a carpet of forest green treetops swishing in the breeze. He often came here with Eran and Tam where they tossed stones or sparred with practice sticks but mainly it was a place to sneak off from their chores.

In the distance, gripped in the mist which pulled the sky down into the sea, dark shadows swayed in the swell on the horizon. He strained to make out their form, imagining a fleet of sailing ships or a congress of leviathans, but they were too far away.

An uneasiness settled in his gut as he sensed their lure summoning him.

Thunder grumbled its last lament.

Gabe entered the cave, collected the empty sack and his cloak drying by the fire pit.

It had been Tam's idea to stock the cave with firewood. A ritual they now carried out whenever they ascended up through the forest.

Dried earth dusted into the air as he shook out his cloak. Nuri lifted her head and sneezed.

'Time to go,' Gabe said.

Nuri yawned and stretched out her front legs. Rising, she circled around searching for the warmest spot to lay back down.

'No you don't,' Gabe said, ruffling the black fur on Nuri's neck whilst shifting loose dirt with his foot over the tawny embers.

For a young hound, she was oversized. Her eyes, one blue, one golden studied him. She considered the warmth of the fire and the icy chill outside before padding out of the cave.

They descended under the forest canopy until they stopped at a small clearing. A wealth of spindling mushrooms had erupted from the damp soil around the edge of an empty boar pit. Gabe's sack was almost full when Nuri froze. She lowered her lean body, raised her front leg and sniffed the air.

Gabe searched the sound of the forest. Raindrops dripped and bounced off the curling leaves before joining the sizzling chorus of snaps and crackles whispering their secrets along the ground. Bird wings fluttered taking flight. Nuri's fur raised and quivered on her neck.

'Stay close,' Gabe said.

He reached for his sack and a tall man stepped into the edge of the clearing. He leaned against a tree and scraped dirt from under his nails with a quartz stone knife.

Others came from the tree line. Gabe counted seven, but he was sure more stayed hidden in the shadows.

The tall man, he recognised, Lestas. One of Naphal's latest brigand leaders who came all the way from Radad. He'd recently passed through the rock shelters of Barakel where Gabe lived with his crew demanding a tenth of everyone's stock.

It had angered Gabe that his Elders surrendered so easily to their demands. They'd loaded a small cart with furs, crab pots, salted fish and pottery, then tethered several goats and sheep to the cart before leaving.

'What you got there?' Lestas said, not veiling his conceited judgement as he bobbed his head towards Gabe's sack.

Gabe scanned the group. If he'd carried a knife, he would have displayed it. Not even a branch on the ground looked strong enough to use as a weapon.

'Just Shrooms. My Ma is a healer.'

'I don't care about your Mother,' Lestas cut in. 'Hand them over. We can have fun with them later, right lads.'

He laughed and the others, in a chorus of cackles joined in. Lestas flicked his eyes to a member of the group who stepped forward to grab the sack. Nuri growled, and he halted.

'Nice sturdy pup you got there. What's its name?'

'Look, take the Shrooms,' Gabe said, lifting the sack.

'Oh, we will,' Lestas said, walking towards him. He unhooked a rope from his shoulder, placing it over Nuri's head. Nuri recoiled, shaking and thrashing against the rope. 'And we'll take the pup too.'

Gabe lunged for the rope. An obese lad, body slammed him to the ground. His weight forcing the air out of Gabe's lungs. With his face pinned to the ground, Gabe watched Lestas struggling to reign in Nuri. Her back now arched as she swayed her neck back and forth against the rope.

'She's got some fight in her, I'll give her that,' Lestas said, as he kicked Nuri in the ribs. 'Come,' he said, turning to leave, 'we don't have time for this.'

The lad pushed his knee into Gabe's back. 'What do you want us to do with him?'

Lestas scanned the clearing and pointed towards the boar pit.

'Throw him in there.'

⁂

When Gabe came around rain pelted in thick icy droplets, soaking him to the core. Lestas, his thugs, and Nuri were gone. He ran his hands over his body checking for wounds. Blood tipped fingers confirmed what he expected as he felt above his left ear. The severity of the gash was difficult to assess, but it throbbed and ached as much as his ribs, thighs and shoulders. To his relief, nothing appeared to be broken.

A layer of uninhabited crustaceous exoskeletons covered the ground beneath him, and small animal bones crunched under his feet as he stood. A quick assessment revealed protruding tree roots escaping from mud slick walls. He tried to climb out, but the roots snapped, taunting him with their betrayal. If he could get back to Barakel and find help, he'd have a chance at saving Nuri.

Thunder voiced its agitation, and the ground slipped out from underneath him revealing the skull of a Repnar. He snapped off the lizard's hook-shaped snout and dug out hand and footholds. But each time he tried to climb the rain washed the holds away. He shivered, sinking down into the muddy pool now forming in the base of the pit and wondered how long it would be before whoever set the trap returned. If he hadn't sought shelter in the hideout, none of this would have happened. He'd be home, his belly full, Nuri lazing by the fire pit, Ma and his sister Mirah tending their herbs.

Stars emerged in the night sky and nocturnal insects crept from silent tombs searching for sustenance. Something nipped him. Gabe stood, skin prickling. He swiped his hands over his body flicking off any bugs.

A deluge of rain now poured from the heavens and the water filled the pit up to his ankles. Too exhausted to shiver, he huddled in his sopping wet cloak and sobbed until he didn't have the energy to sob anymore.

'I'm sorry Nuri,' he mumbled.

⁂

Hours later a shadow swept over the top of the boar pit. Gabe at first thought it a cloud but it glided too fast. It reappeared, disappeared and reappeared again. With each passing a cold gust of wind swept down into the pit. Whatever it was, it was flying, and it was massive, blotting out the stars as it passed.

A lightning flash lit the sky long enough for Gabe to make out the silhouette of a figure, followed by an oil light hovering over the edge of the pit.

A deep voice asked, 'Are you all right down there?'

Gabe stayed silent waiting for the thunder to pass. Veiled behind the light, he couldn't discern who this stranger was. He sat still as if feigning death.

'Don't worry, we'll soon have you out.'

The oil light vanished and squelching footsteps retreated from the boar pit. His low rumbling voice was overtaken by the sound of rustling leaves and the creaking and splitting of wood.

'Stand back now Son.'

A sturdy coniferous branch lowered into the pit and Gabe resolved himself to the fact that friend or foe he would have to take his chances. As he climbed, he tried to remember the layout of the clearing and the fastest route towards the tree line.

Any chance of escape diminished when he reached near the top and came face to face with a monster. He couldn't force his eyes away from its elongated bill, filled with rows of conical razor-sharp teeth. A maroon sail-like crest was mounted on its head, and below, two golden eyes studied him.

Gabe hesitated, he considered climbing back down but was too afraid to move. In the darkness he didn't notice the Hermit until he stepped closer to the edge of the pit, offering his outstretched hand towards him.

'This is Terra,' the Hermit said, patting her on the shoulder. 'She might look terrifying but she's quite tame for a Dactyr.'

Moonlight reflected off shiny hooked talons that arched over gripping into the soil. Gabe was not convinced.

The Hermit sighed and turned towards the Dactyr. 'Thank you Terra," he said. 'I'll meet up with you later.'

The Dactyr let out an indignant snort, stretched out her leathery wings and ascended into the air.

'Don't mind her, Terra can get a bit testy when she feels under appreciated. You'll get used to it. Let's get you back to my shelter and cleaned up.'

'I can't my Ma will be worried and I have to find Nuri.'

'Son, this forest at night is too dangerous, you know that, and besides no one will be out searching for you in this storm. You need to eat and dry off those clothes. Leave at first light if that's what you want.'

The growl in his belly double-crossed him at the mention of food. He analysed the Hermit, of whom he'd heard rumours that he lived somewhere near the borders of Barakel, watching, waiting but never crossing the boundary lines.

Some of the older lads once went to confront him but they'd never found him. Standing here, drenched by the rain, he didn't seem so mysterious anymore. Something about his seasoned face reassured Gabe that he meant no harm.

'Until first light,' Gabe said.

⁂

In the morning, Gabe awoke to find himself in a rock shelter similar to his own. The bed he lay on was situated in a recess carved out of the rock and he nestled between a straw mattress and goat skins.

Etched into the limestone walls were unfamiliar symbols and rows of small lines and triangular wedges moving and breathing in tune with a flickering orange glow. The source of which was obscured by the Dactyr curled up on the floor, its neck bent over its immense frame like an elegant bird.

Her dark grey skin was thicker and tougher than any leather he'd seen and he wondered if there were a blade sharp enough to penetrate it until he saw a long scar running down the length of her ribs.

She reminded him of Nuri, relaxed, absorbing the warmth from the fire. But this wasn't Nuri. This beast could eat him whole.

Off to the side, an old wooden table bowed under the bulk of stacked clay tablets. The Hermit, seated with his back towards him, busied himself by pressing a reed into soft clay.

He turned. 'Good, you're awake, and no fever I see.'

Placing the reed on the table he meandered across the shelter and poured water heated within a fire pot into a bowl. He placed the bowl, a torn piece of cloth and a small round cut piece of glass next to Gabe. Gabe examined the glass but wasn't sure what the Hermit expected him to do with it.

'I call it a reflector. It's like looking into a pool of water.'

He lifted the glass. It shocked him to see so much mud mixed with blood covering his face. After rinsing his skin, he inspected the wound above his ear. It was deep but no longer than his thumbnail and would heal in time.

The Hermit picked up a small ladle. 'I presume you are from the rock shelters at Barakel?'

Gabe placed the reflector onto the goat skins.

'Would you like some stew? My own recipe, onions, garlic and red deer. Terra caught the deer. She is a wonderful hunter, you know.'

'I don't doubt it.'

'It's rare, I have the fortune of company.' The Hermit placed a bowl in Gabe's hands. He stepped back and frown lines appeared on his shallow forehead, framed between bushy brows and matching silver hair. Hair which had been cut short and revealed larger than average ears. 'Good, isn't it?'

'Yes,' Gabe replied between slurps.

Not wanting any of the stew to go to waste, he tipped the bowl and sipped at the last remnants before wiping at the juice trickling down his chin.

The Hermit's face lit up with appreciation. 'Would you like more?'

'I need to go.'

'Oh yes, of course.' The Hermit collected together some apples, dates and a water skin. 'I was thinking I should come with you. We don't want you falling into another boar pit.'

'I didn't fall someone pushed me.'

The Hermit darted towards the table shuffling through clay tablets, putting some into a sack, discarding others. 'Pushed?'

The events of the storm, Lestas, and Nuri, poured from Gabe in frenetic waves, each one more heartfelt than the one before. The Hermit listened whilst brushing his fingers through his thick trimmed beard.

'I see. And Nuri, she is the one for which you seek help?'

'Yes. I can't leave her with them. She is my responsibility… more than that she's my friend.'

The Hermit's fingers slid over his mouth and he tapped them against his lips. 'I know an underground passage that will lead us north of Barakel. It will take a good few hours off your journey. I can show you if you'd like?'

'What about her?'

'Terra?' he said, glancing over at the Dactyr's heaving body curled up on the floor. 'She'll follow above the canopy. You won't even know she's there. If we're journeying together, I should at least introduce myself. I am Meciel.'

‘My name is Gabe.’

‘Here take this,’ Meciel said, passing a parcel of food.

He reached for his rod. Terra rose and sauntered towards an opening in the rock wall. The exit opened into a larger cavern.

After they passed through, Meciel turned and raised his rod towards the opening, whispering, ‘Sathar.’

A corona of flaxen light surrounded the void, shimmered, and then the opening disappeared.

Amazed Gabe felt along the cavern wall where the entrance had been. ‘What did you do?’

‘It’s still there. Everything hidden from the eye has its blessing. I wouldn’t want anyone snooping whilst I’m gone.’

‘But how?’

‘I told it to conceal, and it did so.’

‘Like magic?’ Gabe asked, following in Meciel’s footsteps.

‘Not magic. Magic requires tapping into a force other than yourself. When you view physical matter as I do, it’s easy to move it around. One day after you’ve retrieved Nuri, I could show you.’

‘I’d like that.’

Meciel led Gabe through a series of tunnels and they emerged midway along a ravine. They’d been following the Apaqi River downstream for some time when Meciel stopped.

‘Before we go any further, there is something I need to tell you. But first, you need to promise that you will hear what I have to say, all of it, and not run off?’

‘Run off? Why would I?’

‘Promise me,’ Meciel urged, his voice unsettling.

Gabe stared at him, trying to discern a clue, but was met with a face of stone. Meciel refused to say another word until he agreed.

‘I promise.’

Meciel scratched above his ear, making Gabe uneasy.

‘Yesterday during the storm, ships entered the bay. I saw them on the horizon and travelled down the ravine to investigate. I presumed they came seeking shelter. Your people must have gone to assist them unaware of the danger.’

‘Danger? What do you mean?’

'If only I had realised the size of the ships but they looked so small on the horizon.'

'What are you saying? You're not making any sense.'

'They weren't ships from around here. If I had known, I would have sent Terra to warn your people. You have to realise; I could do nothing.'

As Gabe listened a gust of wind carried a haunting death stench up his nostrils. The smell of burnt flesh lingered in the back of his throat. As much as he tried to expel it, he could taste the essence of humanity.

'When I reached the cliffs the attack had already begun. I searched for you but you were not there. So I sent Terra to find you. I couldn't let you go back last night. It was too dangerous. You would have been killed.'

Leaning over, he urged and vomited the half-digested residue of red deer stew.

Meciel rushed forward.

Gabe ran.

Over his footsteps, he heard Meciel shouting, 'Stop, you don't know what you're running into!'

He did not stop but raced the surging river down the ravine. He sped past the deep reservoir of water, vacant of the usual bathers and joined the trail which led to a narrow rock plateau running alongside the entrance to the rock shelters.

The sky hung low, the colour of dirty snow. All around, embers fell like red ochre leaves, dancing in the currents of the breeze. As they touched the soft earth in front of the plateau, the ground smouldered.

And there, stacked in a monstrous central fire pit, were the bodies of his fellow clan members—piled high as if on an altar to the gods, still burning. Horrified, he bolted towards the rock shelter entrance and raced through tunnels until he came to his family's shelter.

'Ma, Mirah,' he cried.

No one answered.

He darted through a series of interconnecting tunnels, searching each shelter until he reached a large circular cavern. The cavern revealed intricate charcoal paintings of lions, oxen, and bears.

Beneath them were crocodiles and hippopotamuses submerged between undulating lines.

On the far side, stencilled handprints traversed the wall reaching up over the ceiling creating the form of an ancient tree. Each print represented the younger members of the clan's transition into manhood.

Instinct made Gabe look over at his own, as he always did on entering the circle, but he expected no overwhelming sense of pride today. Beneath the blood-spattered wall lay the bodies of many of the elder women, his Ma among them.

Throwing himself on the ground beside her, he cradled her in his arms. He glanced around for Mirah but she was not among the dead. After kissing his Ma on the forehead he lay her down, gently taking the shard of green glass hung on a leather string around her neck. He slipped it over his head and retraced his steps to return outside.

Without letting his gaze fall on the smouldering mound, he headed for the bay. He passed charred remains of the goat and fowl pens which he'd spent the previous spring erecting and stepped over discarded wooden spears.

The body of an Elder lay on the ground, the back of his head crushed in. On the beach, more bodies, younger, fitter were scattered around. It was clear they had rallied together when the first line closer to the shoreline fell.

Blood oozing from corpses ran in rivulets towards the shore and merged with the splintered remains of the dock and small fishing vessels. He searched the beach, no one had survived.

Carrion birds descended to gorge themselves on flesh and drink blood. Gabe screamed and flapped his arms to shoo them away but there were too many.

He wretched again, but there was nothing left inside him. Everywhere death's aroma sought him out, so he walked to the far edge of the beach, sat on a rock and focused on the horizon.

Crunching bones, ripping flesh, and squawks from bickering carrion ceased when a shadow emerged and emitted a piercing screech. The carrion made a rapid ascent. Terra flew over Gabe's head and landed on the rocks behind.

A short time later Meciel came and sat beside him. Neither spoke. They watched the sun dip lower and violets and blues swam across the sky.

'Who could have done this?' Gabe asked, in tears.

'Nephilim.' Meciel pointed towards huge indented footprints pressed into the sand. 'They are giants, a hybrid offspring of the Watchers who descended from the sky.'

'But why?'

'They take women for wives and to build their armies.'

'My sister?'

'Taken, I expect.'

'I have to find her.'

'That's impossible. Even if you could find her they would kill you before you got close.' Meciel stood. 'Before it's too dark, I should take care of your people. I'm sorry I can't offer them a proper burial but I can at least purify their remains. Don't step off the rock.' Meciel lifted his rod and faced the dead bodies of the clan. 'Puroo,' he called out.

On the beach each corpse, in turn, engulfed in a fiery blanket, burning quickly to ash.

'My Ma and others are inside.'

As they made their way back to the rock shelters they heard sobbing coming from the latrines. Gabe lifted the lids one by one until he found, crouching in the waste, a lad with his face tucked down deep between his cradled legs.

The lad lifted his head. 'Gabe? Is that you?'

'Tam?'

Gabe helped him climb out and led him down to the shoreline to wash.

He picked up a discarded slingshot, selected a handful of rounded stones and began launching them out to sea. In the darkness, a plopping sound confirmed when they landed.

He wondered how he was going to save Mirah. He didn't know where she'd been taken. All he knew was he'd need the one thing he didn't have, a boat. And what of Nuri? He wouldn't be able to find her now. In his heart, he refused to let her go.

'I will come for you soon, I promise.'

Frustrated, he walked further along the beach kicking at clumps of seaweed. He was about to return when a shimmer in the sand caught his eye. Brushing sand away exposed a long length of metal he'd never seen before. He dragged it along the beach towards Meciel and Tam who was now dressing.

Meciel stepped forward to get a closer examination. 'It's a sword. It reminds me of a sword I once saw—' He stopped himself from disclosing anything further. 'Can I see it?'

Gabe passed him the sword.

'Look at the glyphs carved into the blade. If you give me some time I will decipher them.'

'It's death, Gabe, that's what it is and I don't want it anywhere near me,' Tam said, storming off to sit on the rocks.

Gabe chased after him wondering if Terra would descend. She was more than he thought Tam could handle right now. As Gabe sat, Tam lifted his rusty coloured cap and replaced it.

'Did anyone escape?'

'I don't know, maybe.'

'What about Eran?'

'The last I saw he ran forward with the others.'

'Your Ma?'

'We were by the goat pens when they attacked. I've never seen anything like it. They were huge with long rusty coloured hair. Their faces, fierce like lions but not. I can't explain it. They even stalked like lions, stealthy, chasing their prey before they struck. Ma told me to hide. As I ran towards the latrines, I heard her screaming. I would have stayed, you know I would, but she'd told me.'

'It's all right Tam.'

'No, it's not. She's dead because of me. They all are. And I'm only alive because the stench of shit masked my scent.'

'Whatever this is. It's not because of you.'

Meciel hefted the sword onto his shoulder and walked over.

'From what I can tell it reveals the history of the blade. See this symbol here?' Meciel pointed to a series of small dots and dashes, above them were two vertical lines, and above them a half crescent. 'This represents its owner, someone named Bishnor. And this symbol here, the circle within a circle is a symbol for oath bearer. The dots and dashes to the side read Shemyaza. The glyphs reveal that Bishnor is a son of Shemyaza. The other symbols will take time to translate. But what is of importance is the name Shemyaza. When he came down from the heavens, he created an empire to the north east in the mountains of Hermonial. They will take your sister there.'

'I'm going back to my shelter to sort supplies,' Gabe said. 'In the morning I'm leaving. Will you both help me?'

'Are you insane? They are giants. You see what they did here,' said Tam.

'I don't care. It's Mirah. I won't abandon her.'

Gabe stood and stared at Meciel.

'I can see you will go whether I assist or not,' said Meciel. 'Tonight let's sleep. It's a long journey. We had better rest until morning.'

❊ 1 ❊

Mirah concentrated hard until she timed her breathing with the rhythmic rotation of the ship's oars. Though she succeeded in slowing her pounding heart, memories of yesterday pushed themselves to the surface panicking her to the point of dizziness.

Several other girls from her clan sat huddled with her in silence, listening beyond the sound of creaking beams and drips of salty water to the footsteps on the deck above.

'Where do you think they are taking us?' Neviah asked.

'Shh,' Mirah whispered. 'I don't know.'

Neviah lowered her voice, 'Do you think they mean to—' She glanced around at the others and decided not to continue.

'I don't think so. They would have done it by now.'

'But what do they want then? Some of them, the tall ones, they didn't even look like men. Did you see them? Where do you think they come from?'

'Please be quiet, Nev, let me think.'

She glared at Neviah, her pleading green eyes willing her to stay silent, fearing the sound of their voices might alert the men above.

Neviah threaded slender fingers through her long auburn hair and tugged it to the side. It was a habit she'd done since childhood whenever she became agitated.

'Of course, you are right, we need to figure out a plan,' Neviah said.

Mirah rubbed her forehead.

A voice above them hitched onto the wind and sent a howling reverberation into the hold. The dialect was unfamiliar, but the tone was clear, the sound of mastery, influence and power. The oars picked up speed, and the vessel tilted. They were turning.

Damp from the wooden beams had seeped through Mirah's skirts and her legs ached when she stood. Unbalanced by the vessel's surging and swaying, she took tentative steps forward and peered through an oar-hole. She could see another level below them with oars propelling the vessel through the swell.

From beyond the stern of the ship, the sun dimmed and rested from its labour, and the deep black sea merged with the darkening sky. Speckles of starlight sparkled to life as Mirah breathed in the salt air.

She wondered if Gabe had returned from collecting shrooms and seen the devastation. Would he realise they were missing or presume them dead with the rest?

She suppressed the screams, the horror and brought her mind to the present. She needed to focus on the now. Neviah was right to question their motives, but she contemplated questions Mirah didn't know how to answer. Why were they taken and not slaughtered along with their clan? She returned to the others. At least nestled together she didn't feel so alone.

The gentle rise and swell of the ship brought little sleep. Throughout the night most of the girls broke into whimpering cries of grief.

After sunrise, Abela doubled over wheezing and gasping for air. Mirah rushed to her side and brushed golden strands of hair from her face.

'Abela, Abela, focus on me,' she said, as she leaned over her.

Abela was now arching her back, flipping and gulping for air like a fish pulled from a stream.

'Relax, try to breathe, slow and easy.'

Ayla hurried over and with her skirts, she gently stretched a layer of fabric over Abela's gasping mouth. 'Look at me, Abela. Steady breaths, remember?'

The other girls stood and fanned their skirts, sending a cooling breeze towards Abela who now laid on the floor; her faced flushed drawing on the air through the fabric. Mirah rummaged in a pouch tied at her waist. She pulled out a root of ginger and snapped off a small piece, offering it to Abela.

'Don't swallow it, just chew. It will help.' Turning to Ayla, she said, 'We need water and we need to get out of this damp, stuffy hold.'

The rasps in Abela's breathing became less frequent. So they assisted her beneath one of the ship's oar-holes and let the coolness of the sea breeze open her airways.

They had been sitting there for hours, each lift of the waves drawing them further from the rock shelters they once called home when a latch scraped overhead. A hatch opened and a channel of light illuminated the hold.

A silhouetted figure descended the cedar beamed stairway. He stopped at the base of the steps, black calf-length boots secured his footing with practised ease. He glanced around, his head nodding as though counting they were all in attendance. Satisfied, he beckoned a second man who carried a bucket of water.

He placed the bucket on the deck and gestured for them to drink. The girls needed no further convincing. They gathered around and drank from the ladle. Each gulp cleansing the fiery ache in their throats.

'Give me your names and I'll arrange food,' the first man said.

It wasn't a question. He expected them to fulfil his command.

He was tall and broad-shouldered but nowhere near as tall as the giants Mirah presumed were on the deck above. Sunlight filtering down the stairwell magnified the sheen on his wavy, onyx hair.

He wore a raven black jacket, buttoned up to the collar with an emblem stitched in gold peeking out from underneath a deep blue cloak. The emblem's stitching was eloquent but too concealed for Mirah to make out its full form. He studied them as they drank. As much as she resolved glare back at him, she had to glance away.

'You,' he said, pointing forward, 'name?'

'Dara,' replied the eldest of the group, a slender girl who until yesterday had cared for the clan's chickens.

'I've heard of Dara,' he mused, 'it means pearl of wisdom. Does it not?'

Dara shrugged, not sure how to answer.

'And you. What is your name?'

'Huldah.'

The man smirked. 'Well, I hope you don't put that to the test. I can assure you, you won't get far.'

Huldah meant quick as a weasel and although she resembled one with her mink coloured hair and button nose, she had not been favoured with the gift of speed.

His focus turned towards Abela leant against the side of the ship sipping from the ladle held out to her.

'My name is Ayla, and this is my sister Abela.'

'What's wrong with her?'

'She suffers from the Shaaph.'

He studied Abela with a hint of compassion and Mirah took the opportunity to explain.

'She means she has wheezing breath.'

'I understand what it means,' he said, tilting his head towards her.

His eyes, the colour of pale blue sea glass searched for any sign of her thoughts.

'And you are?'

'My name is Mirah. She needs fresh air. All of us do. And some hot water for ginger tea.'

'Does she now? And what do you know of ginger tea?'

'I understand a few things. My Ma is the heal—' Mirah stopped herself realising her Ma was no longer the healer of anyone. The hull closed in around her, with nowhere to find solace and no way to escape these men, she pushed back unshed tears, refusing to let them see.

Neviah stood, clenched fists on hips, before pulling her fingers through her hair. 'What is the purpose of this? You slaughter our families, tear us from our homes and you want to know our names. Why? Why do you care about our names?'

'I will throw overboard whoever does not give me their name… that's the only 'why' you need to know.'

The muscles in his sturdy physique tensed as he dropped his hand and rested it upon an ornately carved lion head protruding from a sheath at his side. He stepped forward.

Neviah's eyes narrowed, the only sign she seethed inside. She glanced at his sword. 'Nev, my name is Nev.'

Victory gained, he turned to leave. The other man went to retrieve the bucket.

'Leave it,' he ordered. When he reached the top of the cedar steps he said, 'If you didn't already know, there's power in a name.'

The hatch closed behind them.

'There's power in a name,' Neviah mimicked. She flopped onto a bedroll. 'Who does he think he is?'

Huldah pushed her hand against her stomach. 'I wonder if they'll bring food soon?'

They were starved but thankful at least for the water.

An hour later the hatch reopened, and an arm waved from above ushering them to follow.

As they made to climb the steps Neviah whispered to Mirah, 'Whatever they say, whatever they ask, don't tell them about Gabe.'

'Why would they ask about Gabe?'

'I don't know. I have an uneasy feeling. What if there really is power in a name?'

They assembled in a cluster on the ship's deck. Land had slipped off the horizon and left nothing but ocean. The sun hung low in a hazy blue sky and Mirah guessed it would soon be mid-morning.

The crew on board busied themselves adjusting ropes or washing down cedar beams and near the bow, some of them dangled overboard grappling with nets. Every now and then one of the crew gave sly glances in their direction. Mirah had to give them credit the vessel was spotlessly clean.

A man with dark hair tied tight in a bun ushered them forward to a set of barrels and told them to sit. Two men arrived, placing a jug of water and a tray of fruits on an empty barrel and gestured for them to eat. Their stomachs grumbled in protest as they stared at the fruit, each one hesitant to go first.

'It's not poisoned,' said the man who'd asked for their names, coming up behind them.

'We didn't think it was,' said Neviah. Her tone defied him even though she dared not meet his eyes.

Dara rubbed the bridge of her nose and flashed her a warning glare. 'What Nev meant to say was thank you.' She turned towards Neviah who stood with her hands on her hips. 'Isn't that right?'

Neviah stayed silent, longer than Mirah believed his patience would last, before mumbling, 'Thank you.'

He unfolded his arms and dismissed her. 'I've come to tell you there are no prisoners aboard my ship. When we reach our destination… well, let's just say that's up to you. You are free in daylight hours to come above deck as you please. At night you will go below for your own safety. My men won't harm you in any way. I just don't want anyone falling overboard.' He pointed across the length of the ship. 'At the stern is a makeshift area for your private affairs.' He focused on Mirah, 'We don't have any ginger but if you give what you have, I'll make sure one of my crew brews some ginger tea.' Turning back to the rest he said, 'For now, eat and enjoy the sunshine.' He turned to go but hesitated. 'My name is Nate,' and then strode away.

Mirah thought she caught the glint of warmth in his eyes but it disappeared and so did he towards the ship's bow. She'd had no expectations other than being trapped below deck for her foreseeable future and after that, what then?

No one dared speak for fear of being overheard and one by one they ate. Halfway through sucking the juice out of a chunk of pineapple, Mirah remembered the giants. Attempting to not draw attention, she scanned her eyes over the vessel and found it larger than expected.

The hatch opened up roughly in the centre, and behind her, further along, was a small wooden structure with a door which she presumed led down into another section of the ship.

On the bow of the ship sat one solitary giant. His back towards them as he gazed out over the sea. His frame resembled an ox, muscular as though he'd spent his days on the plough. Strands of his long, red hair had escaped its binding and whipped around in the breeze.

Nate stood beside him, his head and shoulders rising above the seated giant. From what Mirah discerned, he showed the giant no fear, and he gestured with an air of confidence which Mirah knew she would never gain.

She caught Neviah's eye and flicked her own in the giant's direction. Neviah and the others followed her gaze.

'I need to go to the privy,' Ayla said.

Not wanting to separate, the girls made their way to the ship's stern. They found a private area sectioned off by a makeshift tent hung over wooden beams. Inside, sat a barrel of water for washing and a smaller pail, light enough to carry and throw its contents overboard.

Ayla entered as the others waited outside and she retched up the fruit she'd just eaten.

'Did you see the giant?' Dara asked.

'Of course, we did,' Neviah said. 'Who could miss that hulking monstrosity?'

'Where are the rest?' asked Huldah.

'Maybe they're on the other ships,' Abela said, casting her gaze over the ocean. 'I wonder where they have gone? I can't see any.'

Neviah's lip curled into a feral snarl. 'I don't know. Who cares? We only need to concern ourselves with this one. You're not prisoners aboard my ship,' she recited, doing an accurate impression of Nate's accent. 'I don't understand what game he's playing but I'm not buying it. They have just murdered our families. Ripped us from our homes. And who knows what is waiting for us when we reach their destination. I hate them.'

Neviah's pale blue eyes became glassy, and she blinked back the tears she refused to let fall.

Mirah understood she should hate them. What they'd done was justifiable enough to warrant such hostility. They terrified her and she didn't trust them. But the hatred didn't come, her emotions were too numb. Seeing the tiny fractures forming in Neviah's mind, she was at a loss of how to help her. She couldn't even fathom how to help herself.

Neviah relaxed her shoulders and let go of her hair. 'Look, let's keep quiet, watch their routine and try to find a way off this ship.'

For the rest of the day, they stayed near the makeshift tent at the ship's stern. The day's heat battled with a gentle breeze, neither surrendering to the other.

They watched as the crew shifted around attending one chore or another. Twice men above deck retreated to the lowest deck to relieve those on the oars. The giant never moved from the bow and Nate traversed the deck, giving orders and keeping a constant eye towards its stern.

Before sunset, the lingering odour of cooking fish mingled into the salty air. They were requested to return to the barrels to eat before returning below deck. This became their routine for the next few days. At night, in the inky blackness of the hold, they thrashed out and dismissed ideas of ways to escape.

⁂

Towards the end of the week, wrathful clouds raised a shadowy protest and lightning cracked forked tongues against the choppy waves. They spent the day below deck clinging to anything fixed in place as the ship creaked and groaned. The storm broke just before sunset and they ascended from the hold to the usual smell of fish.

Mirah stood leaning against the side of the ship as the others finished washing in the tent. She noticed hints of starlight awakening in the dimming sky and turned to go.

'Stay,' Nate said.

She hadn't heard him come up behind her. The others filled out of the tent and paused.

'Go below,' Nate ordered them. 'I won't keep her long.'

They hesitated and Neviah stepped forward but Dara wrapped her arm around her waistline drawing her away. Their footsteps padded towards the hatch and then they went silent.

He didn't say a word as they watched the constellations sprinkle to life and spread their sky map across the heavens. Mirah thought of her brother Gabe, alone, with only spectacles of celestial beauty to breach his darkness.

'How old are you?' Nate asked, his confident tone a little softer.

She considered staying silent, but she was too afraid to make him angry, besides knowing her age didn't appear too much of a risk. 'Seventeen.'

'And the others?'

'Dara, the slender one with the waist-length dark hair, is the eldest. She's nearing twenty.'

'And the blonde ones, they're twins, right?'

She glanced down to see his fingers tapping on the ship's rail. 'Ayla and Abela are the youngest. They're fifteen.'

'And the stubborn one?'

'Neviah is seventeen and so is Huldah.'

'How is Abela?'

It surprised her he'd thought to ask. 'The tea is helping, thank you.'

She was aware he judged her responses, testing them for truth. What else did he see other than her slight frame? She let the waves of her messy red hair fall over her face, creating a shield between them. Through her hair, she watched the universe as it expanded until she felt herself fading. She wished she could walk across the waters or sink into the ocean. If only she could slip into a dream where none of this was real.

'Do you know the constellations?'

Mirah shrugged.

'Come, let me show you.'

She followed as he walked to the stern of the vessel.

'The sky is divided into three parts. To the north is the way of Enlil, the south is the way of Enki and in between is the way of Anu, their father.' He pointed ahead, 'That is the star of Anunitu, goddess of childbirth. She stands in the path of the moon and behind her is Dumuzi, the hired man. Over that way is The Seven Stars—the seven gods, and that is The Snake—Mastema lord of the netherworld.'

As Nate pointed them out Mirah tried to remember their locations. She recognised none of their names but their positions mapped out a carousel of incandescent beacons which could light her way home.

'Some believe Anu created the stars as soldiers to destroy the wicked.'

She peeked through her hair and found him watching her. 'What good are soldiers seated in the heavens?'

She wanted to say if that were true then surely they would have destroyed you but those thoughts were safer kept to herself.

'What good indeed,' he said.

His tone stung with an undercurrent of resentment. She considered pressing him further but his white-knuckled fingers gripped the wooden beam so hard she decided to remain silent.

'I'm sorry about your mother. Was there anyone else you cared for at Barakel?'

Her mind flashed back, and she remembered that it was him who'd dragged her away from the central cavern and how she'd thrashed against his tight hold to return to her Ma. He'd snapped at her saying, you don't need to see this, and his repentant, furious glare had urged her to move faster.

She couldn't work out his agenda as he regarded her now waiting for an answer.

'My Pa died in a hunting accident a few years ago.'

She recalled Neviah's warning not to mention Gabe, and it wasn't a total lie. Gabe, to her relief, had not been there. If Nate noticed her omission, he gave no indication.

'You have to know. I never raised my sword against any of your Kinsmen.'

'Why then? Is the giant in charge?'

His eyes burned like a blue heated flame, expressive and full of contradiction and for a moment she suspected he'd stay silent.

'Who Bishnor? Don't be ridiculous.' Nate sighed. 'What happened at Barakel, it shouldn't have gone that way. We came for a tithe but your Elders refused.'

'So you let the giants slaughter them?'

'Your Clan drew blood first, leaving me in no position to stop Bishnor.'

She knew it was pointless explaining that the one who'd thrown the first dagger wasn't from her clan. He'd been a trader who'd injured his leg and for reasons unknown hadn't moved on.

None of what Nate was saying made sense. The giants could force anyone to do anything as far as it concerned her. The men were Nate's, they responded to his commands without hesitation. If the giant, Bishnor, didn't outrank him then why hadn't he stopped them?

A well of emptiness in the pit of her stomach filled with angry emotions. They clashed together, spitting sparks of fury, scorching her, consuming her.

'I'm tired, I need to go,' she said and turned to leave without waiting for his dismissal.

He followed. If he noticed the unquenchable fire threatening to erupt in her, he didn't show it.

As they reached the hatch, she couldn't even bring herself to face him. 'Good night,' she said, dipping her head into the darkness.

He leaned into the hold and whispered, 'When we get to Hermonial, I will make sure the Azu heal Abela.'

By the time she reached the bottom step, burning tears coursed down her cheeks. She wiped them away, so as to not alarm the others and fumbled in the darkness to her bedroll.

'What happened?' Dara asked.

'I'm tired.' She pulled the blanket tight under her chin and wiped her nose.

'What did he want?' Neviah pushed.

'I don't know. He didn't touch me Nev, if that's what you're thinking. Although he did ask about Abela. He mentioned something about sending her to the Azu. I think they might be healers.'

Abela sat up. 'Do you think they can help me?'

'That's what he said.'

Ayla shuffled on her bedroll. 'How?'

'I don't know.'

'What else did he say?' Neviah demanded.

'He taught me some of the constellations and from what he showed me, we may be heading north but I can't be sure. He said we are going to Hermonial.'

'Never heard of it,' said Dara.

The others shook their heads in agreement.

'If you flash your pretty green eyes at him, you may be able to glean more information. Something which might be useful,' Neviah said.

Mirah considered telling them he'd mentioned he was sorry, but she knew they'd never believe it. She wasn't even sure if she did.

'He said they came for a tithe.'

'What sort of tithe?' Dara asked.

'I don't know. I think maybe it might be us.'

❊ 2 ❊

They had been sailing for several days and Mirah was beginning to understand the layout of the heavenly hosts. Nate had told her the stars were not just used for navigation and announcing the cycle of the seasons, but they were also a symbolic representation of deities and heroic figures of renown.

He'd said for those who could discern them, they mapped their adventures out across the heavens, from the beginning of time. She had never given much thought to deities but of the ones he mentioned, none of them sounded appealing. He didn't seem to prefer one over the other and she often caught a resistance to something simmering within his eyes.

Their routine stayed the same. Up at first light, fruit for breakfast, watching the endless sea as it escaped over the horizon and later spitting out fish bones before the others retired leaving her to gather more information.

The one thing of interest to report was the giant, Bishnor, was Nate's younger half-brother and although the strength of his muscled frame didn't show it, he was only nineteen.

On the ninth day, land came into view. They followed parallel to a weathered white cliff face until it receded into a sizeable cove. In its basin were the remaining ships of Nate's fleet. She saw eight in total and like the one they were on, all boasted three levels. The vessels hung low in the lapping water, weighted down by a congregation of battle ready giants on board. Nate's vessel didn't enter the cove and soon after the other ships followed.

They'd been travelling along the coastline for much of the day when in the distance, several spirals of smoke rose from beyond a headland. Nate ordered his oarsmen to cease, and the vessel slowed to a halt.

The other ships continued on until they reached the headland. Giants and men lowered boats into the water and rowed towards what she presumed was a hidden bay.

Mirah waited and watched as seabirds launched themselves from the cliff face. They dove into the rhythmic sea, emerging to return to their nests with silver fish.

It must have been a few hours before the boats returned, one breaking off from the rest and heading towards them. As it neared Mirah could see six girls around her age seated between two hulking giants.

Bishnor got up and with heavy thudding footsteps crossed the deck. It was the first time she'd seen him move from the bow. Her stomach drained with dread as he towered above her. His face had underlying feline features with a broad ridged nose set over flaring nostrils. Charcoal-black vertical slits slashed through his blazing, fire opal eyes. They pierced right through her without acknowledging her existence. She took a deep breath but the warm breeze felt like it would never sustain her and did nothing to prevent the rise of overwhelming fear.

He leaned over the side and the whole ship dipped into the wave. 'Was there any trouble?'

His voice was as expected, similar to the dreaded rumbling of rocks during a cavern landslide yet she hadn't anticipated the hitch in his tone as though any trouble sent him shivers of excitement.

'No. They agreed to our terms,' replied the bulkiest of the two giants seated in the boat.

'Return to your ship. There is another bay not far along the coastline. Tell Balashi we'll collect tithes from there before nightfall.'

Bishnor pushed his hands off the rail and retreated to the ship's bow. Nate coordinated the transfer of the girls aboard and then ordered two of his men to lead them below deck.

'You are monsters the lot you,' Neviah yelled and tore off after the new arrivals.

Horrified by Neviah's outburst, Mirah and then the rest followed after her.

'If you don't shut your mouth, I'll cut out your tongue,' Nate's voice echoed from behind them.

So shocked, Mirah spun on the spot and glared at him. Every moment of doubt fled when faced with the vision of him standing before her. Nothing, not even a hint of what she thought lay beneath remained. She heard the others' footsteps distancing behind her but couldn't move.

Nate came over, gripped her hand and tugged her after the others. 'It's not safe for you here right now,' he whispered.

It was as though his manner revealed one thing and his words pleaded something else. She didn't dare look back at Bishnor for confirmation.

The new girls gathered together in a corner of the hold. They were all blonde with long braided hair and wearing fine woven, goat hair skirts, decorated with tiny blue beads.

Dara and Ayla tried to give them solace as best they could. All Mirah could do was offer smiles of reassurance whilst at the same time battling the conviction she had no assurances to give.

When it was time to eat, they declined to come up on deck. Nate instructed the crew to take food down into the hold but the new girls still refused.

'I don't blame them,' Dara said. 'We'll be growing gills if we eat fish for much longer.'

After dark, they ushered another group of six down through the hatch. The girls spread out over the hold, huddled in their own groups on bedrolls in the darkness.

It was the first night Mirah didn't spend time gazing up at the stars. She was wondering if Nate had noticed her absence when Neviah's voice rose above the new girl's whispers.

'You were right. We are a tithe. That giant confirmed it.'

Mirah sighed. She imagined the new girls' Elders had handed them over out of fear. She'd heard no screams or sounds of fighting. Was Nate telling the truth when he'd claimed what happened at Barakel wasn't supposed to go that way? She knew the others assumed the worst but how could she tell them? Neviah wouldn't hold her temper. She'd never believe it even after insisting he confess. Mirah didn't understand his motives but somehow knew to expose him risked endangering them more.

'I think I may know a way to escape,' Dara said.

'How?' Huldah asked.

'We are near the shoreline and far behind the other vessels. There are more of us now and maybe we could slip off the ship's stern one at a time without notice.'

'What and abandon the new girls?' Mirah asked.

'We have to leave them.' Dara continued. 'Too many of us going missing will draw their attention. We'll need to make small distractions. Nothing too obvious. If we are lucky, we can swim to shore before they even see we've gone.'

'What if they come after us?' asked Ayla.

'I don't know, let's get off this ship before we worry about that,' Dara replied.

They all agreed Huldah, Dara, Ayla and Abela should leave first as they were less likely to be missed. Whispered debate arose over who should go next. Due to Neviah's latest outburst, they presumed she was being watched and Neviah pointed out that Nate never took his eyes off Mirah for long. After much debate, they decided Mirah would go last and if needed distract Nate.

All their planning was to no avail. When they rose above deck the following morning the coastline was a distant shadowy grey. It was a good plan, and they agreed to follow it through at the next opportunity.

❊

At dusk, Mirah lingered near the hatch but Nate was nowhere in sight. She was about to retire when he marched across the deck.

'You never came for your lesson last night,' he said, his gaze settling on her lips.

She darted a glance at him and what she saw there made her shift. 'Is that what it is?'

'What else would it be?'

'I was busy,' she declared.

He took a deep breath and after a heartbeat, said, 'You can't help them you know?'

'Well, I can at least try.'

'What can you offer them?'

She didn't let her voice waver. 'I'm a healer.'

She figured he didn't need to know she was still in training and besides she understood enough to get by.

He searched her, his piercing blue eyes possessing her as she tried to hold his stare.

'I see you, you know.'

Mirah blushed. Feeling a fraud and outmatched by his intense new attitude, she walked over to the side of the ship.

A moment later, Nate came up beside her, his manner more controlled. 'You would do well with the Azu but I suspect you wouldn't like their appearance.'

She turned from facing the ocean. 'Why? What's wrong with it?'

'You'll see,' he said his face breaking into a knowing smile. 'Where I come from we have a rare plant. It's a little like a lily, but larger and has the most exquisite silver tubular flowers rising above glossy green leaves. In the sunlight, the petals open to reveal a cluster of golden stamen.'

'It sounds beautiful. What is it used for?'

'It's one of the deadliest poisons I know.'

He grinned and although Mirah resisted she couldn't help but smile.

When it was dark, he pointed out more constellations. 'See up there, that is The Old Man. He's an ancestor of Enhil and over there is The Crab, the seat of Anu. And that is The Lion— he's called Latarak, the protector, although I believe he has another name which I do not know. It's my favourite constellation. The star which stands in front is The Abundant One and behind is The Star of Dignity.'

The Dignity Star shone brighter than the others and twinkled with an icy blue glow.

'Is there a star up there called Cruel Deliverer?'

A surge of pain drifted across his face and she regretted how her words cut him even if they were true. Hoping to catch him unguarded she asked, 'How many tithes do you need?'

'Six lots of six.'

She made a quick mental calculation. The total was thirty-six. They needed another eighteen. They still had time to make their escape when they drew closer to the shoreline.

He stood stone rigid, and she knew if she didn't appease him he'd say no more. 'I didn't mean to be so cruel just now.'

'I deserve it. You must hate me.'

His tone was urgent, testing to see if his assumption was true. Why did he care what she thought?

'Who is the tithe for?'

Nate sighed in resignation. 'I don't suppose it matters anymore, you'll find out soon enough. The tithe is for my stepfather. When I was a babe, my father died. My stepfather married my mother, but she died giving birth to Bishnor.'

His sadness was dipped in anger and she could see him resisting, forcing his feelings deep within.

'Anyhow. I have little memory of her and none of my father.' Shaking his head as if to shake off the fragments of his past, he turned to her. 'My stepfather is a god. That's why Bishnor and the others are so formidable and mighty.'

He glanced over his shoulder at Bishnor still sat on the bow. As if in answer to his statement, Bishnor rose and stretched out his powerful arms.

Mirah swivelled her gaze back from the muscles bulging across his shoulders and asked, 'Are all the giants his sons?'

'No, not all. Five gods descended together from the heavens.'

'What does your stepfather do with the tithes?'

'The tithes go into service.'

Mirah couldn't believe what he was saying, and she was sure loathing laced his tone. She wanted to ask more about these gods and what kind of service they expected but Nate shifted into a stiffened posture which she recognised as conversation over. He wouldn't be divulging anything further.

As if in confirmation, he sighed. 'It's getting late. You should go now.' He walked her over to the hatch and opened it.

As she descended into the hold, she paused, the softness of her voice whispered on the breeze. 'I'm sorry about your mother.'

⁂

At breakfast, Nate stood on the bow of the ship next to Bishnor.

Neviah fiddled with the band on her braid. 'We need to find out their intentions and I for one, will not wait until tonight. God or no god, I refuse being forced into service by anyone.'

She picked an apple from the platter on the barrel and making sure none of the men were paying attention, rolled it up the deck. The motion of the apple caused crewmen to lift their heads, and she feigned being clumsy and set off to retrieve it. She soon came rushing back, apple in hand and hurried past them towards the stern. As discretely as they could they meandered after her.

'What did you hear?' Dara asked.

'That giant accused Nate of spending too much time with her.' Neviah sneered at Mirah. 'He's not your friend, no matter how much you think he favours you. He's lying. I heard him say, back off brother. It's my ship, my rules and if I single out one girl to keep the rest in line, it will be one of my choosing.'

Neviah's words dropped like a rock in the pit of her stomach and she restrained herself from doubling over. Their voices blended into an inconsistent hum of syllables which held no meaning. He was using her. He wasn't sorry.

She rushed for the hatch, her vision blurred, dizziness sending her with a thud to the deck. Nate was soon at her side. He lifted her up, took her to his quarters and laid her on the bed. The sandalwood and cinnamon scent of him clung to his blanket. That she recognised it made her recoil into a place deep within.

'What's wrong?' he asked, pouring her water.

Mirah rolled over and faced away from him.

'Are you ill?'

'Just go. Leave me alone.'

He hovered for a moment before the door creaked shut. Drawing her knees up into her chest, she rocked herself until she fell asleep.

Faceless gods and monsters chased her through her dreams. She kept running, faster and faster, never looking behind as they breathed the heat of their disgusting sickness on the nape of her neck. Exhaustion gripped her and then Nate was there. Would he save her? He snarled in her face. I was wondering how much you could take before you break? Her body recoiled at the sight of him and she awoke.

Nate hadn't left. He sat on the floor, leaning against the door with his arms resting on his bent knees, concern written on his face. He's such a good liar she thought.

'What's happened?' he asked.

'Bad fruit.'

He didn't believe her and she didn't care.

❊ 3 ❊

A sedating fog brooded over the ocean for most of the morning until bringing peace to the choppy waves. Once calmed its unsullied whiteness crept away leaving them under the far-reaching scope of blue sky. By the afternoon they rowed towards a foreign shore.

Mirah suppressed Nate's betrayal. If he wanted to use her to keep the peace, she'd let him. It wasn't as though their goals differed in that regard.

The girls were waiting by the tent watching the distant forest of green spreading along the cliff tops. They'd agreed as soon as the tree's brown trunks became visible Mirah would make her move. She hoped Nate would leave Bishnor's side soon. If he didn't what then? They couldn't slip off without notice, he glanced over too often for that.

Her belly ached with apprehension. There were so many ways their escape could go wrong. She ducked into the tent and patted water on her face.

'It's time,' Huldah said, popping her head inside.

Mirah clasped her arms around her. 'Don't take any risks. If you're not sure, wait. There will be another chance.'

Huldah gave her a slight smile. 'Go. I'll wait for you on the shore.'

Mirah brushed her skirts and flicked back her hair. Crossing to midway up the vessel, she halted. Nate frowned and through gritted teeth argued with Bishnor. For the first time, she didn't care why and positioned herself to obscure their view. Too focused on Bishnor, he didn't peer her way.

After some time, awkward glances from the crew made it impossible to stay. She had nothing, no idea how to gain Nate's attention without raising Bishnor's as well. Reduced to a failure she turned to leave.

'Did you want something?' Nate asked.

He'd moved fast and the sound of his quickened breaths matched her own. If she played this right, they might escape after all.

'I lied to you yesterday. It wasn't bad fruit.'

Nate walked away from his crew and she followed, keeping to his right so his back faced the ship's stern. She kept silent for as long as possible without his gaze wandering. Let him think she struggled to confess the truth. Now he was here, she didn't know how to distract him. She gripped the ship's rail. It seemed like the right thing to do. Conscious that she needed to buy them time, she switched tack.

'Did Bishnor say something you didn't like?'

'So it wasn't bad fruit?'

He let his question hang in the air with a sense of amusement. That he'd ignored her question and got straight to the point like he'd won some kind of achievement gnarled deep within.

'Nev accused me of giving you the wrong impression.'

His eyes widened. 'And what impression is that?'

So he intended to drag the truth out of her and if his blue-eyed gaze was anything to go by, he appeared more focused than ever. She could play along if it gave the others more time.

She recalled the times she'd seen Dara flirting with Liron, luring him closer by saying one thing and meaning another with the grace of a beautiful deer. The sheepish look she attempted fell short, so she opted for a small smile.

'Well, you know.' Her cheeks heated, and she berated herself for her lack of skill.

'I'm not sure what you mean?' he goaded.

'Just because Neviah says we spend too much time together. It doesn't mean anything. I wouldn't want you thinking I like you in *that* way.'

'What way exactly?'

His grin was the complete opposite to the snarling face she'd seen in her nightmare. So much so, she struggled to remember who he was and why she was playing along. She closed her eyes to prevent herself from glancing at the others and alerting him to their departure.

'You know.' She shrugged.

'No, I don't. What are you trying to say?'

'I just want to make it clear, I don't like you *that* way.'

'So you do like me?'

'What?'

'By you saying you didn't like me *that* way implies that you like me in another way. I get it. It happens, there's no need to be shy about it. I just had no idea.'

'No, you're mistaken. I didn't mean—'

This was all going wrong. How could he believe she liked him in any way after all that had taken place?

He laughed, and she looked up more confused than ever.

'I understand why you would never like me in *that* way,' he confessed. 'I just found your behaviour amusing. By the way, I can see what you're plotting. Don't.'

She fixed her focus on the boats rowing towards the shore and held in the horror that he'd somehow overheard their plans.

'You think my vessel will be too slow and if you swim fast enough, you could reach the shore in the next bay before the others return with smaller boats. It's true. What you've yet to realise is Dagani circle beneath us.'

'Dagani?'

'They are servants of my stepfather.'

Mirah peered into the ocean. She observed nothing other than darkness breached by the cresting of foaming white waves.

'What are they?'

'Monsters of the deep.'

'You're mocking me.'

'See for yourself.' Nate let out a whistling shrill.

She surveyed the ocean, half expecting to see nothing.

Did he believe she'd succumb to this nonsense? He sounded like Gabe teasing her about Leviathans. Still, it grated on her that he'd thought of her in such simple terms. Even if in her heart she knew it was true.

Beside the vessel, the swell sank into a whirling depression and an arc of scales the colour of clotted blood breached the surface. They curved like a red crescent moon as its eely form arced out of the water. The scales rippled up and over before descending back into the deep with graceful ease.

Mirah wondered at the extent of the sea dragon when a ribbed dorsal fin broke the surface. The beast paused its motion, revealing scaly skin, stretched taut between each of its dorsal fin's ribs. In the central fin was a hole covered with a glossy membrane. It slid up and an amber serpentine eye blinked open. She jumped back. Whether this was the only one or hundreds of these beasts lurked below, she knew leaving this vessel was not an option.

'No,' she cried and shot off to the stern of the ship. Neviah's face blanched as she ran towards her with Nate's thudding footsteps following behind.

'Nev, stop them,' she screamed.

By the time she reached the stern, it was too late. Huldah had already jumped overboard, each stroke of her arms bringing her closer towards the bay. Mirah called after her but she didn't turn.

'What's going on?' Neviah asked.

Before she could answer, two ribbed fins rose out of the water. One on either side of Huldah as though guiding her towards her fate.

'You must do something. Call them back,' Mirah begged.

'There's nothing I can do. I can't stop them.'

The fierce current pushing against Huldah slowed her progress. Hunted by an unseen hunger, she was oblivious to their existence. The Dagani sliced through the swell racing in front of her.

'Are they leaving?' Neviah asked. 'Maybe they haven't seen her.'

'No. They rarely hunt on the surface, preferring the depths of dark waters. They'll swim ahead and turn, so the sunlight is behind them before… If I was you, I wouldn't watch.'

Huldah had almost reached the waves breaking against the surf when one of the Dagani coiled around her and dragged her under. Everyone stood stunned gaping at the ocean but not even the fins rose again.

'You should have warned us,' Dara snapped.

'If I were strong enough, I'd rip your head from your shoulders,' Neviah yelled, 'And your god's after that.'

The shadow of Bishnor fell over them like an ominous cloud and Nate clenched his fists. He ignored their sobs and whimpering.

'Do you realise what you've done? Did you believe I hadn't noticed you scheming away in your huddled whispers? I knew you'd try something foolish, but I thought you'd have at least had the sense to wait until my men reached the shore. She will need to be replaced.' He glared at Mirah as if she was to blame. 'You know nothing,' he said and stormed off towards his cabin.

No one spoke. No one noticed the shadow fading away. They stood facing the ocean. Hoping for a hope that would never come.

⁂

They'd travelled another three days before the smaller boats went ashore to retrieve the next six girls. At night Mirah replayed over and over the events leading up to Huldah's death. It wasn't her fault. Whatever Nate thought of her, she could never have known about the Dagani. Her mind betrayed her, trying to convince itself of what she refused to accept. Nate had tried to warn her. He'd just been too late.

To her horror when the boats returned she counted not six but seven girls on board. Neviah had told her to stop torturing herself but she couldn't help wonder which of the seven girls replaced Huldah.

They had an aloofness about them which mirrored Nate's most recent disposition. He hadn't acknowledged any of them other than to recite his, there are no prisoners aboard my ship, speech to the new arrivals. Even when he spoke it in a foreign tongue, Mirah was sick of hearing it. She'd knotted her hands in her skirts. How could she ever have been so foolish to consider trusting someone who even if he hadn't done it himself, had stood by whilst giants murdered their families?

The night was warm, the air stuffy and Mirah struggled to sleep. She was deliberating asking to use the privy just to get a moment's reprieve when an oil lamp lowered through the hatch.

'Mirah, I need your help. One of my men fell out the crow's nest, and he's injured,' Nate said.

She sucked in the air above deck, disappointed to find its mugginess clinging to her airways. Nate led her beyond his quarters to another cabin. She heard the muffled screams before she entered. Two men pinned a man on a table, one holding his shoulders, the other his legs. Above his elbow, a sharp splinter of bone stuck out of his flesh. As soon as she saw it she knew she was out of her depth.

'I can't help with this. The arm can't be saved.'

'If I cut it off, can you stop the bleeding?' Nate asked.

'But he'll need it in the next life.'

'For now, all I care about is this one.'

She thought back to the times she'd helped her Ma. Nothing came close to this. She remembered when a boat maker chopped off his thumb and how her Ma used heated copper from the potter's kiln to staunch the blood flow.

'Can you heat something copper so I can sear the wound? And do you have some animal skin and sesame oil?'

Nate gestured to the crewman holding the injured man's legs. 'Go, I'll take over. There are pigskin maps in my quarters.'

'We will also need something for binding,' Mirah said, 'and clean hot water.' The man nodded and left.

From illuminated oil lamps, she took in her surroundings. Apart from the man on the table, the cabin was a sparse wooden shell except for a single chair and a mattress laying on a raised timber frame inhabiting a space underneath a porthole. She had little time to think of the cabin's purpose because the man returned with a pigskin map and a tunic.

'The copper is being heated,' he said to Nate. He set to work shredding the tunic into strips.

The shuffle of footsteps and a bucket of hot water being placed on the ground brought her out of her desperate thoughts. She dipped her hands in the water.

'Before you touch him you'd better wash your hands.'

Nate's hands and everything else was drenched in blood. His brow creased confirming his confusion.

'Do as I ask,' she said, 'I'm the healer.'

She grabbed a torn strip of tunic and bound it around the man's arm below his shoulder.

While she waited, she glanced at the pigskin map. Dark ink outlined landmarks, rivers, mountains and forests. In strategic places, someone had marked territories with a seal. She wondered if any of them was Barakel.

The door opened and one of the crew handed over a jar of sesame oil. 'The copper is ready.'

'Keep it heated until I yell,' Nate replied. He released the injured man's legs and asked the man shredding the tunic to take over.

Mirah set to work soaking the pigskin in sesame oil.

The man on the table shrieked, so high pitched, she almost jumped. He thrashed around and then passed out.

Nate unsheathed a blade. 'Are you ready?'

She wasn't ready, not even close. 'I don't know if this will kill him.'

'If we don't try, he'll be dead before sunrise.'

He lifted the injured man's arm away from his body and the man roused. The scream as his spine arched ripped into her soul and she knew she'd never forget it.

'I need more men,' Nate yelled.

Two crewmen rushed into the cabin.

'Hold his shoulders,' Nate said, 'and you grab his legs.'

When they were ready, Nate repositioned the arm to the right angle and yelled, 'Bring the copper.' He waited until a man entered the room holding a copper bowl in tongs. 'When I finish cutting, pass the tongs to her.'

The man nodded and came around the table.

Nate lifted his blade. Mirah turned away but she couldn't escape the sound of crunching bone. When she knew it was over she took the tongs and brought the copper bowl to the man's fleshy stump. The vicious hiss of sizzling flesh and the stench of burning blood and skin seared into her nostrils. She wrapped the pigskin map around what remained and bound it in place before releasing the ligature.

She stared at the man unconscious on the table, willing him to survive as Nate's men busied themselves clearing up the blood before making a hasty departure.

Nate dried his wet hands on his thighs. 'You did well,' he said studying her.

'If he dies, will I be in punished?'

'Of course not.'

She glanced around and spotted a blanket hanging on the back of a chair. Folding it into a pillow she placed it under the unconscious man's head. As she did so, she kept a close eye on the man, waiting for the moment he might exhale his last breath.

'Do you mind if I sit with him for a while?'

Nate dragged over the chair, gestured for her to sit and then slipped out of the room.

Her stomach contracted threatening to purge itself of the fish she'd eaten. She could almost smell the fishy odour mixed with the tang of blood. She tried to focus on the motionless man. He was older than most of Nate's crew. His receding dark hair greying above his ears.

Nate returned with two jars of beer and she gulped the cool liquid washing away the bitterness clogging her throat.

'You should rest. Use that bed behind you. I'll watch him.'

Did she look that ill? Did he assume the sight of blood made her nauseous? Out of her depth as she was, once she'd started searing and binding the gruesome wound she'd recalled every piece of advice her Ma had taught her. No, not the blood, not the gore, not even the man's screams distressed her compared to the thought of what might happen if he perished.

She lay on the hard straw mattress, eyes closed until fish remnants no longer threatened to splatter the decking. When she reopened them, Nate was removing the man's leather boot.

'What is his name?'

Nate reached for a remaining piece of ripped tunic and dabbed it across the man's damp brow. 'He's called Jabril.'

'Are you close?'

'No. He only joined my ship this year.'

That surprised her. She thought by the way Nate determined to save his life, the man must be a member of his family.

'If he's not close, then why do you care?'

'Why wouldn't I?'

She could think of a multitude of reasons, starting with her Ma. Anger rippled inside her and she snapped. 'I know you only use me to keep the peace.'

'Girl, I don't know what you think you've heard, but you're wrong.' She heard the door click as he left.

⁕

With each day the sun blazed, and the climate became warmer. Nate ordered his crew to erect shaded canopies for them. He never mentioned Jabril. She'd considered asking but feared he'd died and didn't want to know.

They'd been travelling for over a month before they collected the last of the thirty-six tithes. Mirah had never left the borders of Barakel, she'd never witnessed such dark and beautiful skin and gazed in awe at the tithes standing in the smaller boat. They were physically stronger than every female aboard Nate's vessel and all of them adorned in jewels and gold the likes of which she'd never seen.

Shayla boarded the ship like she owned it followed by her entourage of five. She surveyed the tithes, pausing for a moment on Dara, as though assessing her own competition before fluttering her lashes over flighty brown eyes at Nate.

He was about to begin his speech when she announced, 'It is an honour to be chosen. When do we arrive?'

Not fazed by her interruption, Nate said, 'So you've known someone selected before. Then I presume you need no introduction,' and walked away.

The other tithes took little time in gravitating towards Shayla as she sat under the canopy, one of her consorts sliding a comb through her thick glossy dark hair. Fixed in her ears were dazzling pendants like small chunks of ice and Mirah watched on in amazement as they sparkled in the sunlight.

Shayla told them there was nothing to fear and that she, and her companions, had been preparing for this their whole life. As she spoke, her full lips glistened as though covered in moisture though Mirah never saw her lick them, not even once. Some of the tithes attempted to question her, but she raised her hand to her silky brow and closed her eyes.

After another three days Nate's ship veered off from his fleet and a few days later they reached a river inlet. The river narrowed at first before opening into a wider expanse.

Along the riverbank, a forest of leaning golden populous trees reflected their honeycomb hues over the water. Intermittent trees with orange shades like carotene and turmeric, rippled across the surface, blending in with the glow of gold. They crossed over the river's fiery threshold towards Nate's home.

Mirah watched fishermen sat in long reed canoes, casting nets overboard before dragging them back through the water and knobble knee storks and mole rats foraging on the marsh riverbank. She turned as she heard his familiar footsteps.

'We'll arrive at Hermonial soon.'

'And what then?'

'You will be presented before my stepfather and the testing will begin.

❊ 4 ❊

The oarsmen rowed for a further two weeks up the river, keeping to the deeper channels with practised ease. Shayla spent most of that time between encouraging her now expanding entourage, telling them they would soon be adored and revered and offering seducing smiles at Nate.

Neviah had threatened to confront her, saying her lies were as deceptive as her demeanour. Fake or not, her charisma was very real. Seeing the tithes' hopes flicker Mirah asked Neviah to keep her thoughts to herself.

She descended through the hatch earlier that night due to Nate making preparations for their arrival. Two of the tithes had dragged their bedrolls over and were talking with the others.

'This is Ninsun and Ninkurra,' Dara said.

'They don't like Shayla much either,' Neviah whispered.

'We are sisters,' Ninsun said. 'I am eighteen and Ninkurra is sixteen.'

As she moved the golden beads woven into her braided hair clinked together on her shoulders. The sound of which blended with the musical twang in her accent. Her sister, Ninkura, leaned into Ninsun, her fluffy spiralled curls pressing against Ninsun's shoulder. A golden band with a row of tiny dangling raindrop beads sat high on Ninkura's neck just beneath her hairline.

'You arrived with Shayla, isn't that right?' Mirah asked.

'We did,' Ninsun confirmed.

'Ninkurra has been explaining that Shayla is the granddaughter of their tribal leader and they have been ordered to escort her,' Dara said.

'We had our spears taken from us before we boarded the ship,' Ninkurra moaned.

'So are you her protectors?' Mirah asked.

'We are warriors and have trained all our lives to protect our tribe's future heir,' Ninsun said.

Mirah studied them as best she could. In the moonlight their dark, silky skin shone, illuminating their toned muscles, and as they moved golden bracelets jangled on their wrists.

'Is it true what Shayla says, that being chosen is an honour?' Mirah asked.

'I suppose if you have come far from their borders you have much to learn,' Ninsun said. 'The ones' you call giants, to us are known as the Nephilim, the sons of Shemyaza. Shemyaza is worshipped by those around him, it's an honour to be going in

to his service.'

'What's he like?' Ayla asked.

'We have not seen him but we know he has blessed all who bow before him with wealth and unimaginable wisdom,' Ninsun answered.

Mirah lay on her bedroll and contemplated what she'd learned. No matter how she tried to see things in a positive light she couldn't shed her sense of trepidation.

⁂

As they neared Hermonial, the riverbank marshes receded, and the trees diminished to make way for irrigated fields. She watched a chain of mountain peaks rising in the distance. Towering high into the cloudless sky, one mountain stood above the rest, clothed in a crystalline, sapphire blue. Unlike the others, its summit had no peak but a level plateau.

'The tallest is Mount Hermonial,' Nate said, as he came over.

'It's beautiful.'

'Impressive isn't it?' he said glancing at her.

Mirah sighed. The weight of anxiety pressed down on her like waves dragging over beach shingle. 'Is it true what Shayla is saying, she seems ecstatic about being a tithe.'

'For most, it is an honour.'

'Why won't you tell me what will happen?'

'Because until the testing begins, I do not know.'

'What is the test?'

‘That is for my stepfather to decide.’

‘Whatever Shayla says, I am not honoured.’ She searched him for something, anything that would save her but what she found were eyes as lost as her own. ‘I feel betrayed,’ she said and left him to be with the others.

They came to a section on the river bustling with industrious activity. Everywhere, men were in boats rowing to unknown destinations or completing bewildering tasks on the bank of the riverbed.

Bishnor caught a rope thrown to him from a bare chested man standing on a wooden pier. The rope pulled taut as he heaved until Nate’s ship came flush up against the pier with a bump. Without a word, he secured the rope, transferred from the ship and left Nate’s men to moor the vessel.

Nate oversaw the arrangement of the girls back into six groups of six and assigned several of his men to each group. His men led the first five groups off the vessel and disappeared across the pier.

To her relief, she spotted Jabril being assisted off the ship. He never acknowledged her and she presumed he didn’t know she’d been there that night. Mirah and the others, along with a short girl with dark shadows under her eyes waited for Nate to give final orders to his crew.

On the other side of the pier a long boat stacked high with trunks of cedar wood, minus their branches hung low in the water. Men wailed and gestured with their arms as one trunk lifted from the ship and swung in the air.

A small boy running up and down the length of the swinging wood made her uneasy. He appeared to be doing something to the ropes attached to the trunk but she couldn’t fathom why.

Whoever his parents were they should be ashamed, she thought as she watched him drop with both grazed legs wrapping tight around the trunk. He smiled as the trunk swung out over the pier towards the riverbank. Whatever his purpose, success and joy beamed on his confident little face. Still, his parents should know better, she thought.

Nate beckoned them to follow and four of his men escorted them along the pier. The lingering effects of constant motion left her off balance. How much of the nausea was due to land-sickness or the apprehension of what was to come she couldn't tell.

'Welcome to Hermonial,' Nate said, as they stepped from the pier onto firmer ground.

Everything she observed was unfamiliar and a far contrast from her home in the rock shelters of Barakel. Instead of a small beach, the pier led onto a levelled area, busy and thriving with all kinds of industry. Workers, flecked with sticky black bitumen, leaned over waterproofing upturned reed boats by the riverbank.

They reached men and women singing a harmonious chorus whilst tying marsh reeds into bundles and stacking them on carts. The women smiled, and the men dipped their heads at them as they passed.

They then came across a dusty track and on either side rows of clay bricks were drying in the sun. Men wearing nut colour skirts with sweat glistening off bronzing skin occupied themselves tamping straw into clay or pouring the clay into wooden frames.

She hadn't known what to expect but industry on such a mass scale hadn't been it. The whole affair sent powdery cloud plumes into the air and Abela started wheezing.

'I thought this might happen,' Nate said, tracking back to them. 'My stepfather is building an empire and with it comes a lot of dust.'

He paced up and down, running his hands through his hair whilst waiting for Abela to recover. Mirah wondered if he cared or was more worried about losing another tithe.

They followed him, pausing now and again for Abela to catch her breath until he stopped outside a grandiose white building.

Painted gold cuneiform symbols covered the high walls. A brass doorway loomed at the entrance and to each side stood two bronze rising serpents, coiled around even higher bronze rods.

'Wait here,' he said and shot off inside.

The way the serpents coiled around the buff bronze rods reminded her of the Dagani and she glanced at the short girl, guilt rising. If they hadn't attempted to escape Huldah would still be alive and the girl wouldn't be here. The least she could do was to let her know she wasn't alone.

'What is your name?'

The girl's eyes flicked from Nate's men to the bronze door and then back to her.

'I've tried,' Neviah said. 'I assume she doesn't understand.'

After a few moments, Nate returned with a woman enriched with several coloured jewel amulets tied around her neck. She was slender and wore robes with layered fringes, dyed in varied shades of pastel greens.

Under her eyes, black powdered antimony lines made her face pallid. But most startling of all was her elongated cone-shaped head. From the ridge of her hairline, her skull flattened and tilted backwards, the shape somewhat like a large marrow. She'd fastened braided mahogany coloured hair wound in a spiral around it with a golden pin.

'This is one of the Azu. She will take care of Abela,' Nate said.

'We're not leaving her here,' Neviah replied, staring at the Azu's head without even attempting to hide her revulsion.

'I'll stay,' Ayla offered. 'If I can?' She pleaded her case at Nate with silent urgency.

'Fine,' he said. 'You can stay. But you alone.'

Dara took Abela's hand. 'Stay safe and we'll see you soon,' she said, trying to encourage Abela and offer some relief against the uneasiness which comes with the unknown.

Turning to the Azu, Nate said, 'I expect them both returned by this evening.'

The Azu acknowledge his demand and beckoned Abela and Ayla inside with her hand.

'She will be, all right? Won't she?' Mirah asked.

'The Azu understand Abela's purpose here. They serve my stepfather and would never dare defy him. Come, we need to go.'

He went to walk off but Mirah refused to move. 'What will they do to her?'

'I told you. They are healers.'

'Yes, but how?'

He exhaled a long breath. 'What does it matter? When she returns, she will be healed.'

Mirah crossed her arms over her chest. 'It matters to me.'

Nate's impatience made it clear he would not give her answers or maybe he didn't even know. He dropped his fist over the pommel of his sword and his men standing behind them stepped closer. Ready to herd them on if they continued to resist.

'Mirah asked you a question,' Neviah pressed.

Nate ignored her and guided them on through a network of sandy cut stone roads, some of which ran adjacent to what he called canals. They passed by rustic homes shaped like rounded towers created from clay bricks with reed and bitumen thatch roofs.

Now and then they came across vast decimated spaces filled with substantial sized boulders. Stonecutters nearby chipped and cut angled edges into the stone. The sound of their labour tinkling to a rhythm similar to the pattering of rain. When they reached an even wider area of devastation, labourers with arms stretched wide carried boulders away.

Mirah put her silent protest to the side and caught up to Nate. 'What happened here?'

He kept walking as he explained, 'Those are the remains of the temple of Enki, the god of sweet waters. He used to be the keeper of the decrees of the gods. When my stepfather arrived, he gave the order to tear down the temples. He said, he had pushed back the powers of chaos and there is only one we must serve now.'

She had a thousand questions but didn't know how to phrase them. She didn't understand these gods or the loss of them or about the changes his stepfather had made.

'It's simpler now with just one.' Nate said to himself.

'And you serve him?'

He couldn't look at her, couldn't meet her eyes. 'I brought you and your friends here, didn't I?'

They moved towards a more populated area where homes were covered in white plaster. Small slits for windows were set high in the walls but through their large open doorways, she spied exotic courtyards with fruit-bearing trees which the homes appeared to be built around.

They came up behind a procession of people meandering down a sloping passage. The women dressed in vibrant coloured sleeved dresses with fitted bodices. Lapis lazuli beaded necklaces and bracelets in silver and gold jangled on their wrists.

Dara adjusted her skirts and Mirah noted she wasn't the only one to realise how dull they were in comparison. They had never seen such a display of coloured fabrics.

'Look at their eyes,' Dara said. 'They've painted their faces.'

They watched in awe as women paraded, smiling and chit-chatting with eyelids painted in shades of lilac, pinks and greens.

The men, dipping their heads or averting their eyes wore wraparound garments, decorated with tiered petal-shaped fringes and around their waists, rounded belts fastened the fabric in place. Musicians with sistra, lyres, and cymbals manoeuvred through the crowds with children dancing around their feet.

The passage opened onto a wide square plaza paved with sandstone slabs cut to precision. Stationed around the edges were horse drawn carts and from the carts, men were selling an array of produce, from corn and grain to pottery and ornate carved figurines. They weaved through the parting crowds with ease.

Surrounding the mountain up ahead a deep blue boundary wall ascended towards the sky. It towered so high it was difficult to determine where the wall ceased and the heavens began.

On nearing its arched gatehouse, Mirah saw a mosaic of lapis lazuli gems covered the wall and two inlaid winged golden bulls rising on each side of the gatehouse. It was the most spectacular creation she had ever seen.

'I guess this is it then. We finally meet our destiny,' Neviah mumbled at her.

They crossed under the gatehouse into a mammoth square courtyard with barrack houses surrounding it. The clatter of wielded swords and pear-shaped maces echoed around the courtyard as sparring warriors, soaked in sweat, fought with ferocity as though their souls were on fire. Off to the side, others with slingshots launched small clay balls into bales of straw with deadening thuds.

Beyond them, the mountain cloaked in crystalline blue mediated between the heavens and the ground. She wondered as she craned her neck what hidden secrets it held within and dreaded the thought of them being revealed.

Nate dismissed his men and turning to the girls, he said, 'Follow me.'

'We've been following you all day,' Neviah grumbled under her breath.

Nate refused to wait.

On the far side of the courtyard, a gaping chasm opened at the base of the mountain. As they approached, two men in raven black with high buttoned jackets in the same fashion as Nate's stood to attention. The light shimmered on curved, steel blades sheathed across their backs and as they drew closer Mirah saw jagged-edged daggers strapped to their black calf-length boots.

Nate stopped in front of a tall, broad-shouldered man with an adventurous gleam in his brown eyes and asked, 'Is he here?'

'Not yet,' he answered.

The man attempted to stay on his guard but a held back smile betrayed a flicker of friendship.

'It's good to see you, Zeev,' Nate said, patting him on the shoulder. 'Anything I should know?'

Zeev surveyed the girls, giving a brief pause on Neviah. He shrugged off his thoughts and smirked. 'Nothing you can't handle.'

'Report to me in an hour. You can update me then. And bring beer.'

'Yes, Captain.'

Nate led them through a wide rough cut tunnel which opened into a circular chamber. The far side housed an unusual wooden contraption. Set against the chamber wall, its base was made of long planks of wood and all around a lattice of reeds fixed to a wooden frame. From somewhere above, thick ropes suspended and attached to its base. He made them squash together on its platform and then stepped on board.

The platform rose into the heart of the mountain. Thrust into darkness, it jolted and Mirah grabbed onto the person closest as they swung and jerked their way upwards. Water drips and the sound of stretching ropes masked their shallow breaths as they climbed higher and higher. In the pitch black Mirah couldn't see her hand as she waved it across her face. Time felt eternal as every second extended beyond her reach.

Nate's voice echoed up through the shaft when he announced, 'There are two ways off this mountain. One exit is back the way we've come. The other is to descend from outside. I warn you now, there are worse things than Dagani roaming on this mountain.'

When they were nearing the top, torchlight filtered into the shaft. Mirah blinked, adjusting her vision to the brightness. She spied Nate with a self-assured grin on his face.

'A captain never kisses and tells,' he whispered, admiring her hand on his arm.

Mirah blazed red and released her hand. She didn't know what was worse that he implied they'd been intimate or that the others would believe him. She was about to defend herself when she spotted Neviah's bared white teeth which told her all she needed to know. She glared at Nate who chuckled under his breath.

He raised his hands in mock defence. 'What?' he said. 'It was funny.'

When they reached the top, three women dressed in pastel fabrics, with elegant gold butterfly pins holding back their hair greeted them.

'Take them to their rooms,' Nate said. Without looking back, he left.

❊ 5 ❊

Nate reprimanded himself as he paced through the tunnels leading to his chambers. The first opportunity without his men or Bishnor's eyes watching his every move and he'd been foolish enough to reveal a small part of himself. Mirah had looked mortified. He rebuked himself for repeating a familiar joke, of course, she'd never heard it.

He reached his chambers uninterrupted and closed the door. Everything appeared as he'd left it. Cut out of the mountain rock his first room was filled with rolled-up scrolls and pigskin maps of territories, some captured and some Shemyaza still itched to claim.

He regarded weapons stacked against the walls, making note they needed attention and dipped under an archway leading into his bedchamber. Throwing his sword on the bed, he unsheathed a dagger from his boot and another from a belt at his side. He stripped and bathed. He'd not long finished when a knocking thud interrupted his thoughts.

'Beer,' Zeev said, holding up a clay jug as he entered.

Zeev had grown up with Nate. He was the youngest son of Nate's old nursemaid Sumer. They were both twenty-one and Nate trusted no one as much as Zeev. Without waiting, Zeev pushed through the door and grabbed a cup from Nate's table.

After pouring, he waited until Nate swigged on his beer and said, 'Zamani's been slain.'

Nate choked and spluttered.

'I thought that would get your attention.' Zeev's grin spread so wide crease lines formed on his tanned cheeks.

Wiping his mouth, Nate asked, 'What? How?'

Zamani was Shemyaza's firstborn. He had been the largest and strongest of all Shemyaza's sons.

'A few days after you left, we heard a rumour of warriors arriving in Anat from across the sea. We don't know where they came from. Shemyaza ordered Zamani to take reinforcements up through the desert plains to see if the rumour was true.'

He grabbed a chair, gesturing for Zeev to take the other and sat. 'If they were that far north, they wouldn't have been a threat unless they passed into the desert. Why didn't Shemyaza wait until then?'

'He said he didn't want them gathering in numbers and to tear down any threat before it arose.'

'And Zamani's men?'

'One returned, rambling on about how a dark haired woman with a crossbow had killed Zamani. He was sent to the Azu for his injuries but died the same night. We haven't seen Shemyaza since the news first broke. He's been in council on the mount since then. No one is sure when he will return for the testing.'

Nate gulped down his beer. 'What woman?' He held out his cup to Zeev for a refill. 'I can't believe one woman could kill Zamani.'

'No one knows. People are saying she's a rogue Chashmalim.'

A rogue Chashmalim. He'd never heard of such a thing.

From what he knew only three of Shemyaza's offspring had ever been slain and the others had been weaklings, like runt pups in a litter. What would this mean? How would Shemyaza's enemies interpret this if word spread?

Cutting into his thoughts, Zeev said, 'I guess Bishnor could become a Chieftain now.'

Nate let out a hefty sigh. Bishnor had always been jealous because Shemyaza accepted Nate as one of his own. Until now Nate outranked him, maybe that will soon change.

As if reading his mind, Zeev asked, 'How was he?'

'As bloodthirsty as always. I refused to let him ashore after what he did at Barakel.'

'Did you find him? The one Shemyaza sent you after?'

'They're all dead except for the six we took for the tithe, Bishnor made sure of that.'

Conviction flashed through his mind as he remembered bending the truth in his favour. In truth, Mirah's clan had drawn blood first but even if they hadn't, the outcome would have been the same.

Shemyaza had instructed Bishnor to leave no survivors at Barakel and he'd been powerless to do anything about it. Nate knew Shemyaza selected someone there for destruction, he just didn't know who, or why.

Nate offered a sly smile. 'If it's any consolation Bishnor lost his sword. During his bloodlust, he dropped it and somehow it got covered in sand.'

'You never.' Zeev said, sitting back and squaring his ankle over his knee.

'He spent the rest of the time sulking on the bow of the ship.'

'I'd loved to have seen his face.'

Nate wasn't sure if anyone survived to find it but knew where the sword would lead if they did. He'd known before leaving the middle deck which girl to select to find out answers.

Abela had been sat, leaning up against the side of the ship, cast pale, any colour, any remnants of life washed clean away. He knew if he pressed her, she'd start wheezing and be unable to provide anything useful. He'd considered her sister Ayla but her concern was for her sister, she had no thoughts for anyone else. Huldah had been so overwhelmed with shyness, she'd reveal nothing and Dara, had a wisdom about her, enough to hold on to words and select what to say. He'd taken an instant disliking to Neviah and the thought of spending any time with her undesirable, besides she was too guarded. After discerning them all, he knew Mirah would be the best choice.

He admired that, despite her fears, she had risen above them, requesting he consider her friends' needs. Her eyes reminded him of spring meadow green grass, glossy and watered. Even though she avoided his gaze, he'd seen in her a gentleness and innocence so rare he'd had to push down the urge to protect it.

From afar, he admired her sensitivity towards the others and the way they gravitated around her, relying on her for support. It touched him how she'd brush her graceful hand along her brow, inhaling a deep breath to rejuvenate what she'd depleted.

He knew he could lean up against her naivety, teasing out whether she'd known if anyone was missing that day. It hadn't even been difficult. Her slight hesitation when he'd asked if she'd lost more than her mother told him what he'd needed. Someone survived. Someone who for whatever reason had not been at Barakel. If not her father, then possibly a sibling or a lover. He'd studied her often as she stood beneath the stars, hiding behind her hair. The thought that she protected a lover, built into a crescendo of resentment inside him.

'Esha has been testing the boundaries,' Zeev said.

He didn't want to know but found himself asking, 'What has she done now?'

'Whilst you were gone she took it upon herself to dominate a few of your men. Ordering them around as if they were her own.'

'You let her?'

'Of course not. But she has an art of persuasion too difficult to decline.'

Nate understood full well how persuasive Esha, the Fire Wielder could be. He still remembered the warmth of her heat, the way she would wield her fire over his flesh in bed, not burning but holding the balance so finely between the embers of pleasure and pain. She'd used him to gain her position then flicked him aside, a hot coal dying without the intensity of the flame. It had taken all his strength to rise out of the ash that remained. He was stronger for it, a lesson well learned.

'I'm glad you're back,' Zeev grinned.

A knock at the door saved him from Zeev's jibes at how foolish he'd been.

'Come,' Nate said.

Sumer rushed across the room and swept her arms around him. 'I'm so delighted to see you returned.'

Nate let her hug him and whispered in her ear, 'I've missed you.'

Any memory of his true mother had been nurtured through her. She retreated to brush her gaze over him, scanning for injuries. Deep lines crossed her brow. 'You've lost weight,' she observed. 'I'll go fetch you something to eat.'

'No, don't bother. You have enough on your hands.'

Nate stayed silent for a moment tripping over the question he resisted asking.

'Out with it,' she prompted.

He glanced at Zeev's, quizzical expression. 'Among them is a redhead with long flowing wavy hair. Mirah. I'd like it if you took care of her personally.'

'As you wish,' Sumer replied. She never forced the issue or pushed him for more. 'I'll send someone else with food.'

She smiled at her son before retreating.

After the door clicked, Zeev wasn't as considerate. He shifted in his seat and leaned forward. 'Well?'

'Well, there's nothing to tell.' Nate shot Zeev a warning stare urging him to back off.

'Are you mad? You know why the tithes are here.'

Nate knew. He'd spent the previous year and the year before that collecting Shemyaza's tithes.

Sumer still believed the earth was as flat as bread without yeast but she'd never left Hermonial's borders. To reach Barakel, they'd travelled further than he'd gone before and though Shemyaza insisted the world was shaped like an orb, he couldn't help keeping his eye on the horizon.

He hadn't wanted any tithes on board longer than necessary so after Barakel they'd returned via Talamu, Palasu, Nadanu and Kasadu, all habitations along the coastline of Alme, a territory closer to Hermonial conquered long ago.

Before reaching the river Buranuna they'd collected the final tithes from Ana Sepiya, a small city reaping the rewards of Shemyaza's favour. As with each conquered territory, Shemyaza renamed it. Ana Sepiya meant at my feet and he'd wondered how long it might be before someone enlightened Shayla.

Regardless of how he felt, the tithes would first be tested, then trained and this time, now Shemyaza's sons were old enough, they'd become their brides.

'Of course, I know,' Nate snapped.

They sat in silence, taking swigs of beer that no longer refreshed Nate's thirst. 'I'm sorry, Zeev,' he said, stifling a yawn. 'Maybe you should check on the guards. I'll catch up with you tomorrow.'

'It's good to have you home,' Zeev said, before leaving.

Nate picked at the food delivered to him before laying on his bed. He could see through the cut hole in the rock wall, the Star of Dignity, shining bright in the darkening sky.

After that first night with Mirah standing under the stars beside him, he'd craved to be near her again. She hadn't even realised she'd shone brighter than them all.

Many times on dark ocean nights he'd dreamed of helping her escape, he'd even dared to dream of escaping with her. His heart had leaped at those dangerous dreams but the morning light always delivered the obvious truth. They might have escaped Bishnor, but he'd never escape Shemyaza.

Several footsteps echoed up through one of the tunnels. Not the sound of guard boots but of soft padded slippers. Their quickening pace and hushed whispers told Nate that Shemyaza had returned. Tomorrow the testing would begin.

He turned and pulled the covers over his bronzing skin but sleep refused to come. Worry spread its tendrils from the pit of his stomach, winding its way up through his tightening chest until it reached his mind. He saw Mirah's mortified face as she stood on the platform, horrified that he'd implied they'd been intimate in the darkened shaft.

A horror, he realised, which would only come from someone who'd never been kissed.

What had possessed him to do that? He thought back to how she'd watched in awe at the women in the city with their loose fitted garments and painted faces. He remembered how her full lips had parted and how he'd imagined the sounds she'd make if he ever parted them more.

He turned and stared at the star gleaming through the rock hole and wondered how she'd managed to slip through his defences.

❊ 6 ❊

Mirah's room was the last in a row of six along a tunnel carved out of the rock. Plaster, painted light blue and decorated with a range of colourful flying birds covered the walls. Someone had cut a circular hole in the rock and a pink glow of evening light flooded into the room over a royal blue rug.

She looked out of the opening, the city of Hermonial spread as far as she could see. Opulent houses clustered around fruit-bearing trees, their white boundary walls now covered in a rosy pink light, and beyond, the reed-covered tower houses were no more than ruddy red mounds.

From here she could see many areas of devastation where temples once stood dispersed between dwellings and stony canals. How many gods had Shemyaza destroyed?

In the distance, coursing streams sliced through marshes and fields crisscrossed in shades of gold, greens and browns and to her right, the winding river shimmered like the colour of washed away blood.

She leaned through the opening and found a level plateau jutting out from the mountainside beneath her. How was it possible to create a whole city? So overwhelmed by its design and sheer size, she retreated from the opening and focused on her chamber.

Her bed was not cut out of the rock as at home. This bed had a wooden frame, and a mattress made from straw. A blue robe lay over silver silk fabrics with blue embroidery draped over the bed.

On the far side of the room, she found a recess. Mirah peeked inside and saw on a lower level a pool of water. She tested it and found it warm. Rushing back, she picked up the robe, returned to the recess and after stripping off her clothes, lowered herself into the blissful pool.

As she lay there, she realised this was the first time since boarding Nate's ship she'd been alone. She closed her eyes and drank in the silence. A lonely tear ran down her cheek and was soon joined by an uncontrollable flow. Her sobbing brought forth memories of her Ma and Gabe.

Her Ma was gone. She would never see her joyful smile and those adorable dimpled cheeks or watch her graceful hands as she attended to the sick. What would become of Gabe? Older sisters were supposed to be there for their brothers and she was on the other side of the world.

She cried until her eyes stung and her throat dried. She'd never known such brutality existed. Why would they do such an evil thing? Why steal her innocence and immerse her in a world that isn't her own?

Emptiness, mind numbing emptiness filled her soul. She lay there watching goose flesh pimple on her sunburned skin until her fingers whitened and crinkled. Something within her clicked, a change which she didn't yet have a name for.

She cupped water in her hands and washed away her tears. They wouldn't help her survive.

Laid out by the pool was an array of small green perfume jars with black geometric designs. She inhaled their scents, preferring one smelling like violets. After washing the salt and dust from her hair, she found a fine ivory comb adorned with pearls and lapis lazuli gems.

When Mirah re-entered her room, someone had left a jug of sweet water and food. The fruits and cheese she recognised, but the meat was unfamiliar and covered in spices. She ate it anyway, at least it wasn't fish.

When she finished, she wasn't sure what she should do. She considered going to see the others but anxiety prevented her from opening the door. After tidying her clothes into a pile in the corner of her room, she dripped a few droplets of oil from one of the least complimenting perfumes over them to cover their stench.

Giving her room a closer inspection revealed another smaller recess filled with a choice of gowns and bodices in various colours like the ones she'd seen the women wearing when she'd arrived.

The garments were all beautiful, and she sat studying the fabrics and their exquisite embroidered designs.

Darkness crawled across the sky and no one had come so she climbed on the bed. The soft, silk fabric felt smooth against her sun-beaten skin. She lay staring out through the hole in the rock at the world outside until the stars burst into existence along with thoughts of Nate.

Who was he?

In his eyes, she often saw elements of contradiction but he guarded his truth so tightly. Neviah accused him of lying but what if Neviah was wrong?

There had been glimpses of kindness, of another person held deep within. He'd cared enough for Jabril to risk the wrath of death in the next world and he'd tried to warn her about the Dagani. Surely it wasn't just for the sake of the tithe. And why when she'd asked about him serving Shemyaza had he refused to look her in the eyes?

Tired of listening to her doubts, she curled up her knees, cradling the weight of confusion. In the darkness, the silence sent nothing, and she reminded herself that even thorns die in the dark.

Discarding her puzzled thoughts of Nate, she thought back to their arrival. The people she'd seen were joyful and filled with celebration. They didn't look like an oppressed people, even the labourers seemed passionate as they prepared to rebuild the city, erasing memories of the gods she didn't know. A flicker of hope ignited as she drifted into the place of dreams.

Whatever it is which gives the awareness of being watched, forced Mirah to awake. Disorientated, she was alarmed to find a shadow cast across the floor of her room.

'It's me,' said a voice she recognised. 'I came to make sure—Well you were already asleep.'

His silhouette hovered in the doorway.

'I should go. I just wanted to apologise for earlier. The kiss and tell thing. Here, it's a familiar joke.' His shadow bounced across the wall and he turned to leave. 'I just want you to know that if I could have found a way, I would have… I mean…' He sighed.

'Wait.' She flew off the bed and the scent of perfumed oils and a hint of beer filled her senses on reaching him. 'What is it? What are you afraid to tell me?'

He reached up to brush away straying strands of her hair but hesitated. 'Whatever the outcome of the testing tomorrow, please remember to hold on to yourself.'

As he slipped from the doorway his words lingered. She'd once heard something similar from a dying man to his whimpering son. Desperate words, filled with regret, no time, not enough, never surrender. That man had been her father.

⁂

Mirah awoke to sounds of hoarse grunts and snarls which erupted into an escalating deep-throated roar. She threw herself off the bed and ran to the hole in the rock. Four enormous beasts now occupied the arena below.

One crouched low in a submissive pose, its head turned at an angle with fur-lined lips curved upwards displaying serrated edged fangs. Another standing rigid over the first, veins in its thick neck expanding, as it let out another roar.

They looked like lions, except instead of a fiery mane they had black-tipped quills and protruding from their ribcages were two golden feathered wings. Feeling satisfied it had won, the victor stalked away exposing a flesh piercing spikey tipped tail. There would be no attempts to descend the mountain.

Over the arena, the distant sun breached a peach streaked sky, lavishing the city's red mud-bricked buildings in an amber glow. She could see the river rippling like silk as it meandered past Nate's ship still tied to the pier. Today would be a warm day.

Mirah walked to the recess and gaped at the garments. She wasn't sure what she should wear. She opted for a silver fabric which reminded her of the flowing water.

'Good choice,' said a woman coming in through her door with flat raisin cakes on a tray.

She was about the same age as her Ma with silver streaks blending into her long dark hair. Hair which curled around her plump, round face and warm brown eyes. She placed the tray on to the table.

'Here let me help you,' she said, taking the garment from Mirah. 'First, eat and then we'll get you ready.'

To Mirah's relief, the woman helped her into a matching bodice which overlaid the draping fabric. The woman laced up a blue ribbon at the front and proceeded to brush Mirah's hair. Her efficiency, softened by her gentle touch.

'I can do that,' Mirah said, reaching for the comb.

'Don't you worry. You have such beautiful deep red hair and lovely golden highlights. It's the colour of autumn,' she declared, sliding the comb through Mirah's hair. 'We'll have you fit and ready in no time.'

She pulled mussel shells from a pouch tied at her waist. They clinked together as she opened tiny silver hinges. Each one contained powders in different colour shades. She found one she favoured and discarded the rest on the ledge of the rock's hole. 'This will suit you best,' she said.

Before Mirah could object the woman brushed the gold powder onto her eyelids with a carved ivory pin.

'There,' she said, stepping back to assess her creation. 'The gold enhances the golden flecks in your pretty green eyes. My name is Sumer. Come, we need to leave.'

'Where are we going?'

'Trust me. There's no need to be afraid. Nate won't let anyone harm you.'

She found that hard to believe. This woman obviously didn't know Nate had allowed the giants to slaughter her clan.

'You know Nate?'

Sumer gave her a reassuring smile which lit up her face. She was about to ask what Sumer meant when she opened the door. Outside her room, Abela and Ayla stood in shades of optimistic lemon.

Mirah rushed over to Abela, checking her over as she did so. 'Are you all right?'

'I'm fine, better than fine actually,' she said, smiling.

'What did they do to you?'

'They gave me some mixed herbs which tasted awful and a group of Azu chanted something I didn't understand. I doubled over coughing, one of the worst fits I've ever had and then it lifted and I knew they had changed me.'

'That's all?'

Ayla put her hand on Abela's shoulder. 'I saw the whole thing.'

'I wonder what those herbs were? I would love to know.'

Neviah's door opened, followed by a woman with her face flaring and frantic.

'I can't believe they won't give me my skirts back,' Neviah grumbled. 'I feel like I'm naked.'

Neviah had chosen a crimson pink which clashed with her auburn hair and she had no eye powder. Mirah guessed she'd won that round. Seeing Ayla and Abela, relief washed over Neviah's face.

'I'm fine,' Abela said, before Neviah pressed her with a thousand questions.

They congregated in the passageway until Dara exited her room. Dark purple powder shaded her eyelids and her smooth dark hair flowed over a complimenting lilac fabric which somehow made her appear even taller.

'You look wonderful,' Mirah said.

Dara swept her hand over her dress in appreciation. 'Thank you, so do you.'

Sumer ushered everyone together. 'Follow me,' she said, as she rolled on her heels and took off.

They reached the end of the tunnel and came face to face with some of Nate's guards. Sumer busied herself giving instructions and sending the women who helped dress them on their way.

Neviah whispered to Mirah, 'Have you seen those beasts?'

Observing Neviah's tension, she smiled mischievously and said, 'The loudest one reminded me of you.'

The guards became chaperones as Sumer cut across a network of tunnels winding their way deeper into the mountain.

Crystalline blues and silvers sparkled in the walls, highlighted by suspended torches and as pretty as it was an uneasiness coursed through Mirah's body. She tried to calm herself but a gripping tightness, cramped against the muscles in her stomach. Were they being taken to Nate's stepfather? A god, he had called him. And they were his tithe. She didn't even know what that meant. What did a god want from them? What were his intentions?

She wanted to run, to escape, be anywhere but here. Still not believing it, she recited Sumer's words over and over, Nate won't let anyone harm you. It was pointless and stupid but the only thing she could think of to do. She studied Abela, a blaze of golden sunshine, filled with apprehension but no longer gasping for breath. Surely they wouldn't heal her just to bring them to their deaths but what about the testing?

They rounded a bend, and the floor sloped upwards and further along, the tunnel opened out into a cavern. Shards of lapis lazuli covered the walls and all around tiny golden discs glistened. Their patterning seemed familiar and Mirah realised she was looking at a replica of the night sky. So taken back, it was a while before she noticed Nate and an assembly of giants stood further inside. The other tithes were waiting nearby in their groups of six.

Neviah whispered, 'Where is the girl they paired with us?'

'She is no longer needed and has been removed,' Sumer said.

'Removed. What does that mean?' Neviah asked a little louder. Her voice echoed around the chamber and some of the giant's heads swung around.

'Shh, no time for questions,' Sumer said.

Sumer ushered the girls forward, leading them past the giants and Nate. She made them halt before an elevated golden throne. Three pairs of golden wings were mounted on the throne. They were positioned as if in flight, rising higher than the chamber ceiling with their wing tips folded over to fit in the room. Seated on the throne was Nate's stepfather.

He appeared of human likeness but he was not human. In the light emanating from him, he had a man's face and a flicker of something else, something feline.

Mirah could hear gasps coming from those around her but she couldn't take her eyes off him. He rose and golden feathered wings spread out above him. He seemed to expand, rising taller than even the giants. The brilliance of a fiery furnace flared in his eyes and his outstretched arms gleamed like polished bronze. He was the most terrifying and the most beautiful thing she had ever seen.

No one dared to move. He smiled a warm knowing smile and lowered himself back onto his throne. The light dissipated around him, his wings now folded, unseen. If it were not for his eyes Mirah would have thought him just a man.

His voice broke like the ocean waves.

'I came through the clouds like a whirling storm and held back the powers of chaos. While Anu slept, I alone defeated the raging ones. I am Bel Shade—Lord of the mountain. I am Sahar—Day Star, Son of Dawn. My name is,' he paused, waiting for effect before, 'Shemyaza' flowed like rushing water from his lips.

At the mention of his name the giants, Nate and everyone else in the chamber bowed their heads. Mirah and the others quickly followed if only to capture a moment of quick relief before Shemyaza continued.

'It is I alone who brought mankind out of confusion. I offer to you the mysteries of my heavenly kingdom. I extend my mercy and offer you peace. My oath will not be broken.'

His eyes scanned over them purifying any doubts simmering beneath the surface. She couldn't deny a god sat before them.

'Welcome to my kingdom.' Shemyaza said, before turning towards the giants. 'Tonight we celebrate the gift of the tithes.'

The giants let out a ruckus of cheers, raising their arms and shoving into each others' shoulders in a similar way Gabe messed around with his friends Eran and Tam.

As Mirah and the others were led away, she didn't feel as though Shemyaza delivered her out of confusion. She'd just been sent deeper into a world which was not her own. Even Neviah was speechless.

❊ 7 ❊

'I will show you back to your rooms,' Sumer said, 'and for the next few days, I will escort you until you are familiar with your surroundings. After that, you are expected to find your own way.'

Mirah noted the lack of guards on their return. Beast or no beasts were they foolish enough to leave them unattended?

'You are free to go anywhere where no guards are posted. That is mainly this level and the one below. You may wonder at the lapse in vigilance. I can assure you it is not necessary.'

By midday, everyone had congregated in Dara's chamber. No one dared venture further. Her chamber walls were light pink and her silk bedding silver. A comfy grey rug with red floral patterns covered the floor on which Mirah sat kneading her fingers into its thick pile. Dara pulled out most of the garments from her recess and draped them over the bed.

'What do you think is appropriate to wear to the celebration?' she asked.

I have no idea,' Ayla said, brushing her hands along a golden gown. 'This one looks nice though.'

'They're all elegant,' Mirah said. 'I can't imagine how they are made.'

Neviah huffed and tore her attention from whatever she viewed outside. 'I can't believe you're all worried about clothing when we should be discussing Shemyaza, what his test will be or how to escape this place.'

Mirah realised she was right. They'd picked a safer option as though focusing on something so harmless would be a comforting distraction.

'You are right,' Dara said. 'But what else can we do other than fret all day over things we can't control?'

A loud roar reverberated around the chamber. Neviah leaned her head out of the opening. 'What do you think they are? They look like a mixture of animals, like a lion, a bird and some kind of spikey thing, not one kind or the other.'

'I'm not sure but we are far from home and I'm positive they won't be the last strange thing we encounter,' Mirah answered.

'I don't think anything could be stranger than Shemyaza,' Abela said. 'He is both ugly and beautiful at the same time which I can't quite understand.'

Out of all of them, Abela was the last person Mirah expected to make a comment about Shemyaza. She often avoided stressful topics and kept her own council for fear of the Shaaph taking hold of her or relied on Ayla to make her wishes known.

As usual, Ayla intervened and changed the topic. 'My feet are sweltering. Do you mind if I soak them in your water pool? I don't think I'll ever get used to the soaring temperature here.

'Of course not,' Dara said. 'I'll join you.'

Before long they all had pulled their garments past their knees and sat with their feet dipped in the pool.

'This reminds me of home,' Ayla said, 'paddling in the rock pools.'

Mirah remembered when they used to sit on the edge of the rock pool sharing their secrets. The lads in the clan ran and jumped off a ledge into the deeper end of the pool and they'd sit and watch dreaming about who they'd one day marry.

Dara being older had been promised to the blacksmith's son, Liron. She hadn't been brave enough to ask Dara if she had seen his battered body by the pyre. Abela and Ayla both liked Gabe and even though he was a year older, he was still young and foolish and no one had stolen his heart.

Every one of them had their favourite, except Mirah. Her clan expected her to one day marry Eran. He often arrived on the pretence of meeting Gabe, only to hover around her Ma's herb garden. As much as she'd wanted to relax around him, she'd always kept her guard up for fear of leading him along. She wondered if she'd somehow missed seeing his butchered body and if that was an act of grace.

Before her mind wandered into the place of death remembered she changed her focus and a whispered, 'What do you think of this place?'

No one spoke for a while.

'For what it's worth, the Azu seem to care for the people. When we were there yesterday, a child arrived with an injured ankle, they fixed him up and didn't even ask for a payment,' Ayla said.

There was a knock on the door and then light footsteps.

'I thought you'd all been foolish enough to attempt an escape,' Sumer said. She chuckled. 'What on earth are you doing?'

'We're cooling our feet. Would you like to join us?' Dara asked.

'Well, that is tempting but no, I've brought your food.'

Sumer darted away and they heard her giving instructions from the tunnel. When they returned to Dara's chamber an array of fresh fruit, cheeses and flatbreads lay on the table.

'I'll be back later to ensure you are ready for the celebration,' Sumer said, turning to leave.

Another roar erupted from the plateau beneath them.

'What are those beasts?' Neviah asked.

Sumer pivoted. 'I suggest you don't go near them. They are Shemyaza's personal guards.'

❊

Later that evening, Mirah traded the silver garment for a radiant jade fabric embroidered with little green birds. This one had a woven green band stitched under the breast and needed no bodice. She wrapped a darker green shawl over her shoulders.

'Sumer, what did you mean this morning when you said Nate wouldn't let me come to any harm?'

Sumer gave her such a look of remorse, Mirah felt a sob rise in her throat.

'I heard about what happened at your home, not from Nate, I doubt he'd ever speak of such an atrocity to me. I raised him as my own, along with my son Zeev. They are like brothers and never separated for long. Nate is a good man. I don't understand what happened, but I'm positive someone forced his hand. I have my suspicions concerning who but of that, I will never speak. He's my son and mothers see things their sons do not. Come we need to collect the others. The celebration will begin soon.'

The sound of timbrels, lyres and harps carried down the tunnel as they made their way to the celebration. Mirah watched Sumer's skirt swishing against her strides and wondered what it was she'd seen. She'd been adamant Nate was a good man but how much of her affirmation was blinkered by a mother's love.

'You're quiet,' Neviah said.

'What? Oh, I was just thinking about what's to come.'

If the throne room had been a representation of night, this chamber represented day. Lustrous gold lacquered the walls with tapestries draped all around depicting gardens and water scenes.

In the centre, people and giants were dancing. A rainbow of colours spiralled and swirled as women were guided around. Watching giants dancing seemed strange. They smiled and trod with such feline grace that it was difficult to picture their ferocity.

A raised dais at the far end hosted two life-sized golden replicas of the beasts in the arena beneath her room. In-between them, sat Shemyaza with Bishnor seated to his right and Nate to his left.

'Go,' Sumer said. 'This is all for you.' She dropped her hands from her hips, walked off into the room and disappeared in the crowd.

'What should we do?' Ayla asked.

'Well, I for one will not stand here looking like a tangerine, ripe and ready for picking.' Neviah said. 'Let's get lost in the crowd.'

They meandered through the room and Mirah spotted some of the Azu, dressed in their garments of green, amulets glistening in the light. She considered going over to thank them for assisting Abela but they weren't interacting with anyone. She decided to wait for another opportunity.

Some men in the same raven black uniform as Nate's, ogled at the women. She recognised the one Nate had called Zeev from the day before and as soon as she saw his eyes she knew he was Sumer's son. He chuckled and sipped on beer, his wavy, acorn brown hair framing his handsome face.

Mirah glanced over to find Nate watching her. She wondered if he wasn't allowed to leave the dais. Some of the tithes who'd travelled with them were already dancing, and to Mirah's surprise even laughing.

'Will you dance?' a soft-spoken man asked Dara. She hesitated, and he reached out his hand. 'Please?'

Relenting, she permitted him to lead her to the floor. She stumbled at first but soon slipped into his guidance with graceful ease. Mirah studied her beautiful lilac swirls as she danced. A giant, a head shorter than the others clasped hold of Ayla's hand and before Mirah could do anything they were dancing. Neviah snorted in disgust.

'Maybe they're too unsure to decline,' Mirah offered.

She noted Abela dip her head to one of the Azu who showed a hint of recognition but nothing more. Only Neviah and Mirah had not danced. Neviah glared at anyone who dared approached her and she was never asked.

The music lowered and Shemyaza came to the edge of the dais. 'It's time for the testing. Whatever I decide shall not be altered.'

Sumer arrived and arranged the girls into their groups of six.

Mirah's group was the second to approach the platform. As they were waiting, she spied a group of women standing to the side of the dais, wearing silhouette-black leather pants and deep blue silk shirts. The shirt's fabric crossed over across their chests and wrapped around their bodies. They were strong and foreboding and nothing passed by their discerning eyes.

The first group of six stepped forward. One by one the girls stood before Shemyaza. He held out his hand over their bowed heads and without touching them recited words she didn't understand and the girls were led off.

'What is he doing?' Abela asked Ayla.

'He said it was a test.'

With her eyes fixed on the dais, Neviah said, 'It doesn't look like any kind of test I've ever seen. I thought we would have to do something. What is he even saying?'

Mirah leant her chin over Neviah's shoulder. 'Well, at least it doesn't appear painful. Shall I go first?'

'I'll go,' Neviah offered. 'It's not like there's a way out of this, is there?'

When the first six had been tested, Neviah clasped her hands together and walked up and stood before Shemyaza.

'Taphas,' Shemyaza said.

A woman with long, henna-dyed hair, standing by the dais, dressed in the silhouette-black pants and deep blue shirt gestured for Neviah to come to her. Ayla stepped forward next followed by Abela.

'Azu' he said over them each in turn.

At least that was something Mirah recognised and she began to get a picture of what he was testing. Gifts. Somehow he could see beyond into the essence of a person.

Dara advanced next and when Shemyaza declared, Chashmalim audible gasps echoed around the room. Shemyaza's skin gleamed, and she was led off.

As Mirah approached, Nate leaned forward in his seat. His face became a picture of anxiety. Shemyaza held out his hand, and she waited.

'Taphas,' Shemyaza announced.

Nate's eyes widened. Whatever Taphas meant, Nate didn't like it. Mirah retreated and stood with Neviah. She surveyed the Taphas women and had the suspicion she wouldn't like it either.

Shemyaza completed his testing, retired from the chamber and the music returned.

The henna-haired Taphas woman announced, 'Soon you will be summoned and your training will begin.'

Mirah looked up to find Nate had left the dais and the Taphas women turned and left as well.

'What do you think Taphas means?' she asked Neviah.

She glanced around for Nate but couldn't see him anywhere.

'I don't know but they look deadly,' Neviah said, watching the Taphas leave.

After Shemyaza had retired, the celebrations shifted up a notch. The music tempo increased, and the dancing became more sensual. Mirah had not seen such provocation. She felt torn between intrigue and wanting to leave.

She focused on Ayla and Abela who were busy talking to some of the Azu. A sense of rejection overwhelmed the appreciation she'd experienced before. Not that it was their fault, but she'd been sure Shemyaza would have recognised her skills in healing. What did he see in her?

Neviah scoffed, and she turned to see attendees drifting past, their indiscreet glances falling on the mystery that was Dara.

Mirah left them and circled around the edge of the room to find a quieter area. She stopped to observe the detailed stitching of a lake surrounded by conifer trees in a tapestry. She followed the patterns of its weave and wondered how it had been made. She didn't hear Nate as he came up behind her.

'Walk with me.'

'What about the others?'

'It's all right, they'll be fine. Sumer will escort them back soon.'

She hurried to keep up with his pace through the winding and bending tunnels.

'Sumer told me you're her son.'

'She was my nursemaid and the closest person I have to a mother.'

'She said the girl paired with us has been removed. Do you know where?'

He stopped mid-stride and glanced down both ends of the tunnels. 'Before I brought her here, she prepared fish, so I found work for her in the kitchens.'

'Why did she have to leave?'

'She's in the safest place I could think of.'

It wasn't the answer she was looking for but he picked up his pace with a look which told her not to press for more.

They emerged on a veranda hanging over the side of the mountain. Nate leaned against a grand, ornamental wooden balustrade, its parapets carved into peacocks with trailing feathers fanning out and touching the adjoining parapets. He silently studied the darkness.

She came and stood beside him. 'You could have warned me about your stepfather.'

He gave her a sidelong glance. 'I told you he was a god. What more could I say.'

The sky flecked with stars and it reminded her of when they'd watched them on the rise and swell of the ocean. There was no swell here, no rocking motion, Nate stood stone still, whatever was eating away inside him threatened to unleash. She'd seen that look before, once when he'd torn her from her Ma's arms and after Huldah. She wondered if she had done something wrong.

His eyes intent and weighty beheld hers and in a voice filled with determination he said, 'Tomorrow before you begin training with the Taphas, I want you to meet me an hour before dawn.'

She ignored his gaze as it roamed over her body, there was nothing sensual there. It was like he was assessing her, taking in every detail, before giving her an order.

'What for?'

'You're not strong enough,' he said flatly. 'You will need extra training.'

The hair on her arms rose, and she tightened her shawl across her shoulders. 'Not strong enough for what?'

'Taphas—they're Wielders. They go to the front lines.'

Even though she dreaded the answer, she asked, 'Wielders of what?'

In the second he took to reply, the whole world stilled, the stars didn't twinkle, the trees gave up their sway, even the river went silent and seemed to hold its watery breath.

'Some wield one element and others another. That doesn't matter.' He sighed, confirming she was resigned to a fate she didn't understand. 'Magic, Mirah. I'm talking about magic and I don't trust it. I've seen it fail. Do you understand what I'm saying? It means you're going to have to learn how to defend yourself.'

'You're scaring me.'

'You don't need to be afraid. If it comes to it, I'll be standing by your side.'

'What about Nev?'

Nate let out a low groan. 'I'd rather not. She's too hot headed.'

'Well, I'm not going if she doesn't.'

He didn't answer. She waited, trying to reassemble what he'd told her into something she could understand. The Azu made some sense, they were healers and that she could grasp. Although the shapes of their cone-heads were revolting.

'What will happen to Ayla and Abela's heads?'

Nate rolled back his head and laughed, his tension dissipating in his bellow. She couldn't be sure if it was a reflection of starlight or actual light in his eyes but whatever it was, it released the sound of the river flow and she relaxed a little.

He held onto the balustrade and leaned backwards. 'They won't turn them into cone-heads if that's what you're thinking. Although I suppose they could. The Azu were once chosen at birth and their heads were strapped to boards to encourage that shape.'

Seeing a bench covered in deep pink cushions perched against the mountainside, she went and sat down. 'Why would they do such a terrible thing?'

He turned, leaning on his elbow. 'The practice was ordained by the old gods. So they could retain more knowledge and wisdom. It's not necessary anymore.'

'What will happen to Dara?'

'Tomorrow Dara will journey into the desert to the fortress of the Chashmalim. You don't need to worry about her. She will learn to draw power from the fiery pillars on which the world rests and become stronger than any of us. Except for my stepfather of course.'

The thought of Dara being taken away overwhelmed her. 'I'd like to return, to say goodbye if she's leaving.'

'Of course, I'll take you back.'

Nate traversed along a maze of tunnels. As she grew closer to her chamber, some of the tunnels were becoming familiar.

'Will you help Nev?'

He exhaled a long heavy breath. 'Fine. As long as you tell her she is to keep her mouth shut. I'll arrange for Sumer to fetch you both in the morning.'

On nearing the tunnel entrance which led to their rooms she mustered up the courage to ask, 'Why are you helping me?'

'Because if there's one bright star in the darkness it would be a shame not to see her light shine.'

❊ 8 ❊

Mirah was up and ready before Sumer arrived. She came into the room soon after and appraised her.

'You'll not be wearing that,' she said. 'Quick change into these.' She passed Mirah black leather pants and a loose-fitting deep blue tunic, the same as the Taphas had worn. 'Hurry. Nate's not good at waiting.'

Neviah was rushing around in her room when they arrived.

As they crept down the tunnel, Mirah heard movement coming from Dara's room. When she'd returned the night before, the girls had congregated in her room and she'd told them everything she'd learned. Dara had studied her in sombre silence until Mirah hugged her and promised that whatever happened they would see each other again.

Abela and Ayla mirrored each other's movements, rubbing their hands together, keen to meet with the Azu. They reasoned by becoming healers they could at least make a difference to others who needed help. Mirah understood and a tinge of regret overcame her at the thought of what she was leaving behind.

Neviah had said if Nate was foolish enough to teach her any skills which she could use against them, then she'd savour the opportunity and one day use it to kill them all.

Mirah believed her. She knew in her heart she could never bring herself to cause intentional harm but she had no justifiable reason not to learn how to defend herself.

Mirah and Neviah followed Sumer as she led them towards the shaft which would take them to the courtyard of sparring warriors. When they emerged from the mountain, in the murky light, no warriors were in sight. Nate paced back and forth and Zeev stood nearby. Sumer had left them at the top of the wooden platform saying she didn't have time to descend and come straight back up again.

As they approached, Mirah ran her fingers through her hair, letting it fall over her shoulders.

Nate stopped pacing. 'This is Zeev,' he said, gesturing his hand towards him. 'He's my second.'

Zeev appraised them both his gaze fixing on Neviah. 'I hear you have a temper?'

Neviah shifted her weight on one hip and played with the ends of her hair. There was nothing seductive in her pose, fury simmered beneath. Mirah leaned in closer and nudged Neviah's shoulder so gently she wondered if she felt it at all.

Zeev missed nothing, his mouth twitched at the corners, his deep brown eyes sensing in Neviah a challenge. 'Well, we'll soon sort that out of you.'

Neviah knew full well she needed to be on her best behaviour but still, in the dim light, Mirah saw her nostrils flare.

'We'll see,' Neviah muttered under her breath.

Zeev's smile beamed. 'Bring it.'

'Enough. We don't have time for this,' Nate said, coming up to Zeev and turning his broad shoulders to face the girls. 'The first thing to teach you is how to get out of a grab hold. Like this.'

Zeev swung his arm around Nate's neck, gripping him in a tight chokehold. Nate grabbed Zeev's forearm and whilst turning his body, dipped his hip and pulled Zeev over his shoulder. Zeev landed on the floor with a thud and laughed. Mirah had seen Gabe tumbling with his friends Eran and Tam but this was nothing like that. These were battle-honed men trained in fighting, their strength and technique overwhelmed her.

'I'm not letting that filthy man put his paws on me,' Neviah said and darted off towards the chasm leading back into the mountain.

Mirah rushed after her and caught hold of her clothing. 'Nev, please. You might need this one day.'

Neviah paused, pulling her fingers through her hair, calculating how much she would tolerate and what she'd lose or gain. 'Fine, but if he touches me in any other way, I'm leaving.'

As they walked back, Zeev lifted his hand beckoning Neviah towards him.

'Throwing you in the dirt will be a pleasure,' she snapped.

Nate ignored them and focused on Mirah. 'Come, let me show you.'

He came up behind her and gently reached his arm around her neck, tightening it enough so she couldn't slip through his grip.

Apart from a hug from Gabe, she'd never had a man touch her, except when she'd fainted on Nate's ship but even then she'd been semi-conscious. She could feel the warmth of his chest and the conquering strength in him as he held her.

'Dip your hip, turn and then pull me over your shoulder.'

As much as she tried his feet wouldn't lift from the ground. 'I can't do this. You're like a solid block of muscle.'

He shifted closer. 'Yes, you can. Don't over-think it. Let the momentum take me over. When you drop your hip, lift the other one,' he patted her other hip with his hand, 'and push it back into me.'

Embarrassed he might notice the heat emanating from her face and quickly spreading down her neck towards his arm, she drew a deep breath and tried again. He heaved over her shoulder and thudded to the floor. Guilt overwhelmed the rising thrill of success, she reached down and held out her hand. 'I'm sorry. I didn't mean to hurt you.'

Nate was on his feet before she finished apologising. 'You didn't. Again,' he commanded.

Over and over she threw him until her shoulder ached and burned. She took a moment to catch her breath and watched Neviah and Zeev prowling around each other in a circle. Neviah was tiny compared to his sturdy frame, but she didn't falter. She slipped out of his path as he lunged in an attempt to bring her down. With both of their eyes locked onto each other, it was difficult to tell who was the predator and who was prey.

By the time the sun came up, Nate had shown her how to sidestep, turn and shove her knee up into his groin and how to escape from a grab hold from the front.

'You did well,' he said. 'But you're out of breath far too soon. Before we go, I want you both to run around the courtyard.'

'What now?' Neviah said, bent over and panting.

'Go, before I decide on making it twice.'

They ran around the courtyard, to the sounds of warriors stirring from the barracks and Mirah's throat burned more than she ever thought it could. Nate and Zeev strolled over to a stone fountain positioned near the chasm. They watched their pathetic attempts at running whilst splashing water over their heads and down their necks.

Neviah groaned and slowed to a halt several paces from the fountain. 'I'm sure they enjoyed that.'

Mirah took the few paces to steady her breathing.

When they reached the fountain, Zeev said to Neviah, 'Same time tomorrow, then?'

He lifted his chin and Mirah suspected he was sniffing the air.

'Bring it,' Neviah said, scowling.

Nate ignored the tension between them as if it didn't bother him at all. He wiped his palms in his thighs and said, 'Drink. It's time to go.'

He dismissed Zeev and led them into the chasm. Instead of ascending up the shaft they went deeper into the mountain. The tunnel cut through the rock winding downwards before opening onto an enormous underground arena. She found no brilliance of lapis lazuli or gold, here charred scorch marks and bruised craters tortured the walls.

The Taphas women filed into the cavern. Bishnor and other giants sat like boulders in rows against a far wall. Mirah recognised some of the girls who had travelled with them lingering. The sisters, Ninsun and Nikurra, were standing near a torchlight suspended from the wall, its light shimmering off their dark satin skin and next to them to her dismay was Shayla, flicking absent lint from her shoulder.

With a vainglorious air and a salacious hip roll, the henna-haired woman approached Nate. She lifted her chin as she reached him and snapped, 'You're late.'

Mirah wasn't sure if she wanted to taste him or tear off his skin. Whatever her intentions, Nate didn't appear to care.

'You forget your place Esha,' he cautioned. 'You might oversee their training but this is my unit to command.'

That was something he'd neglected to mention the night before.

'You may begin,' he instructed her.

Esha strode away but Nate called her back. 'Your memory seems to have slipped whilst I've been gone,' he said, with an expectant glare.

Her face turned icy as a well-rehearsed, 'Thank you, Captain,' rolled off her tongue.

She bowed her head, relenting to his authority but everything about her told Mirah she was still standing tall on the inside.

'As I said, you may begin.'

Esha stepped into the arena and everyone paused. 'First a quick display and then we'll see what our new recruits are made of.'

She directed her gaze at a dark-haired woman with a long braid sliding over her shoulder. The woman stepped forward and bowed. She then pushed her arms out in front of her and balls of fire pulsed from her hands hitting the far wall.

Before Mirah could gather her thoughts, a whirlwind spun through the cavern, weaving its way in-between them. Mounds of earth and rock ripped from the ground and propelled through the air as the whirlwind dodged out of their path.

Wind and rock battled around the cavern with such speed, as tempting as it was to find cover, Mirah and the others froze. The whirlwind halted in front of Esha and lost momentum to reveal a slim, silvery-grey, haired woman standing in its place.

Without hesitating another silver-haired woman stepped forward and spears of ice shot through the air crashing against the walls spraying shards of ice everywhere. When they finished they stood together, their grey eyes and high cheekbones so similar Mirah wondered if they might be sisters.

Mirah, and the other new girls, patted down their windswept hair and brushed debris and melting ice from their clothes. To her dismay the Taphas women were immaculate. How they escaped the destruction unscathed, she couldn't comprehend.

Esha eyed them with a smirk of satisfaction and announced, 'Shemyaza descended from the clouds so that we the Taphas would not be kept in darkness. Through his unending generosity, he has opened our eyes to the knowledge hidden within. Tithes, it is an honour to be chosen and to learn the way of the Taphas. It's now time to choose your weapon.'

Mirah hadn't noticed the massive iron doors until they creaked open to reveal an array of amulets placed on an altar.

Leading them over, Esha ordered, 'Do not touch them until you have made your selection.'

All manner of gems; from fire oranges and reds of carnelians; to oil-black sardonyx with their red or white bandings; to polished agates, in aqua blues and greens and every other colour combination; even the rarest and highly sought after lapis lazuli; all of them carved and engraved with strange symbols and set into pendants, rings and armlets.

A jagged shard of amber on a golden wire caught Mirah's eye. The shape and the rough cut edges reminded her of her Ma's necklace, although hers had been green and fixed to a fine leather strap. Ninsun snatched it up and wound it around her neck before walking off unaware of Mirah's intention.

None of the amulets looked like weapons but Mirah felt this choosing was somehow important. She studied each amulet, not worried as others rushed in selecting their prize. In the end, she chose a ring with curling and twisting gold plaited wires spiralling around tiny golden globules, their patterning finished with an inlay of lapis lazuli.

She glanced over to see Neviah slipping on an armlet made of strands of plaited gold with an eye-shaped onyx stone.

'Now let's see what you can do,' Esha said, and they returned to the bruised cavern.

Nate had taken a seat at the far back behind the giants. In the shadows, his face was grim. Hold on to yourself, he had warned her.

'For those who haven't already done so, put on your amulets,' Esha instructed.

Mirah studied the embellished ring in her hand. An uneasiness swept over her as she considered what it might do.

'Now,' Esha commanded.

She looked to Nate. He gave a slight nod which she assumed meant to follow Esha's orders. She slipped on the ring and waited. She felt nothing and sighed in relief before reprimanding herself for ever fearing some unknown power would rise up and overtake her.

'Now, come and face towards this wall,' Esha directed.

The rest of the Taphas strategically placed themselves behind them.

'I want you to focus on your amulet. Let it direct you and then unleash what it offers against the wall. You first,' Esha said, pointing to Neviah.

Neviah stepped to the front. She closed her eyes and stood motionless. The Taphas glanced at each other as they waited. Neviah opened her eyes, let out a scream and threw fireballs from her fists at the wall.

'Fire Wielder,' Esha declared. 'Next,' she said, pointing to Ninsun who'd chosen the amber shard.

Mirah wondered what Ninsun would do and if she had reached the necklace first would she have done the same.

'That's some rush,' Neviah said, returning.

'How did you do it?' Mirah asked.

'I don't know, I thought of our families and how they had suffered and it just happened.'

A loud cracking sound as a rock shattered against the wall echoed around the cavern.

'Earth Wielder,' Esha announced. 'Next,' she said, to Ninkurra who now wore a lapis lazuli pendant.

A spiral of air rose before her and then sunk back into the ground.

'Air Wielder,' Esha announced.

From behind her, Shayla leaned over Mirah's shoulder. 'Maybe you'll be an Air Wielder,' she sneered in a low whisper. 'I'm sure the Captain would love your tickling breeze.'

'Shut up, Shayla,' Neviah spat as she pulled Mirah away. 'No one cares what you think.'

'Next,' Esha ordered beckoning Mirah.

She stepped forward and focused on the wall. All her being craved a glance at Nate for affirmation. Esha's impatience loomed heavy in overbearing waves so she forced her desire into submission and rubbed the ring, harmless on her finger.

Earlier, Nate had shown her strategies for defensive but this, what she was about to attempt was nothing other than pure unadulterated attack. She didn't know if she could bring herself to do it. Please don't let it be fire, she pleaded towards the ring.

‘Come on, little wind breather,’ Shayla sniggered.

Mirah shut off her mind and everyone else around her. She focused on the ring on her finger. She raised her hand and thrust it forward, half expecting to fail, before a spear of ice flew across the room. Instead of shattering into shards, the ice impaled itself into the rock.

‘Water Wielder,’ Esha said, raising her brow.

Shayla, now brandishing a sardonyx stone set in a gold bangle which coiled around her arm, had turned out to be another Fire Wielder. Mirah waited for the others to finish wondering where all this might lead.

Esha came and stood before them with her knuckles perched on her hips and feet placed well apart. ‘For now, you will only wield your power in the presence of the Taphas. If anyone disobeys, I will send them before Shemyaza. You are dismissed,’ Esha declared.

An hour later Mirah soaked her bruised and aching body in the warm watering pool in her room. Sumer had shown her how to remove a stone to let the water flow in and another to allow the water to flow out. She’d given her a soothing balm before leaving.

Mirah let the heat penetrate her aching shoulders and appraised the golden ring, holding it up to the light. Etched along the inside of the band were unfamiliar tiny symbols. Dipping her hand under the water, she felt a gentle pull against her finger as though the ring was drawing in power.

She’d known before the spear of ice formed what she would do. When she’d calmed herself and shut everything else out, she’d found she could sense every liquid molecule, in the air, the ground, even perspiring droplets from those waiting in the cavern. They called out to her, craving her attention. To select just a few had been difficult. How it worked or how she formed the ice, she had no clue.

I will open your eyes to powers yet unknown she’d heard it whisper.

✻ 9 ✻

Sumer arrived to escort them to the courtyard.

'Happy birthday,' Neviah said, exiting her chamber. She handed Mirah a braided bracelet. Three fine weaves of red, blue and green colours wound together. 'It's not much, but it's all I had to work with.'

'It's beautiful. How did you get it?'

Neviah glowed with mischievous indignation.

'Tell me you didn't cut up your garments?'

'If you ask me, they're lucky I stopped at three colours.'

Mirah slipped on the bracelet and Neviah knotted it.

'How did you know it was my birthday? I didn't even realise.'

'Zeev's comment yesterday. He said the summer solstice coming tomorrow must be enhancing my crabby mood. As if that has anything to do with it,' she snorted.

'Come, Nate gets impatient if he's kept waiting,' Sumer said.

'Like I care,' Neviah grumbled following her along the tunnel.

They passed silent chambers. Abela and Ayla had left to stay with the Azu and Dara was on her way to meet Chashmalim in the desert. If it weren't for Neviah her world would collapse.

Mirah admired the little weaved bracelet. 'Thank you, Nev, this means so much to me.'

'It's such a shame we won't get to dance and celebrate.'

Mirah caught up to Sumer. 'Do your people celebrate the summer solstice?'

'Not anymore. We only observe one festival now. Duranki. It's on winter solstice though, the day Shemyaza arrived on the mountain in his chariot to enlighten us all.'

'How do you celebrate?'

'No time for questions. Go,' Sumer said, pointing at the shaft. 'I have extra chores today.'

In the darkness of the shaft, Mirah thought about summer solstices and birthdays. If she'd been in Barakel, they would have lit fires, danced and celebrated the solstice blessing of the sun. Her Ma would have gifted her a crown of flowers for her eighteenth birthday as was the ancient custom of their clan.

Her heart sank quicker than their descent. She'd find no flowers, dancing or singing in celebration now, all that remained was an emptiness which no light could fill.

The darkness turned a darker shade after they stepped out of the chasm. Nate and Zeev were arguing. Looking up, they stopped before Mirah caught a word of what they said. Nate glared at Zeev and as they approached Zeev shrugged him off.

'This is not finished,' Zeev said. 'If you want to be an idiot so will I.' His countenance shifted to roguish amusement on sighting Neviah. 'My ray of sun, come again for seconds?'

Neviah held her tongue.

'It's definitely not over,' Nate grunted. 'Come,' he said to Mirah, glaring over his shoulder at Zeev.

When they'd moved closer to the centre of the courtyard Mirah asked, 'What was that about?'

'You.'

'Excuse me?'

'It doesn't matter. He was wrong.'

They sparred repeating the same defensive techniques from the previous day. Except for huffs and sighs when she didn't perform to his expectations, Nate stayed silent. A heaviness descended on him draining the strength out of her. What was Zeev wrong about?

After what seemed like the thousandth sigh she could hold her tongue no longer. 'How do you expect me to hold on to myself when you can't do the same?'

Before she could comprehend what happened he was behind her. His arm gripped her around her shoulders so tight he'd pushed her breath from her lungs. She gasped for air but couldn't breathe.

In the seconds he pinned her, she held onto his words, *it would be a shame not to see her light shine* but at that moment she wasn't sure if they held true. He squeezed tighter as though debating it himself. Heat fled up her neck burning across her mind, she was drowning in blood-red darkness.

'You'd better hold on to yourself better than that if you don't want to die,' he whispered in her ear and then released her.

Her body hunched over gasping for air.

Amidst her choking, Zeev dashed across the courtyard.

'What the bidu are you doing?' he roared.

'Teaching her a lesson,' Nate answered, his tone calm but forceful. 'One, I hope will one day save her life.'

'Are you all right?' Neviah asked, rubbing her palm over Mirah's shoulders.

'I'll be fine,' Mirah reassured her. 'I just need to catch my breath.' She glared at Nate through her hair.

He glared right back before turning towards the fountain. 'Three laps around the courtyard when you're ready.'

'We don't have to listen to him,' Neviah said.

'Yes, we do.'

She didn't understand why he'd become so driven to get his point across but she'd understood it perfectly well. If she had any hope of surviving, she'd take his lesson and learn from it. If he wanted three laps, she'd give him four.

Her lungs burned and so did his gaze as she lapped around the courtyard. He watched her every step, analyzing the way she moved, how he would shape and improve her performance. Whatever Zeev was cursing in his ear, he ignored. By the time she'd run the third lap he had her weighed up, and they both knew it.

On completing the final lap, he crossed her path as she neared.

His smile affirmed his confidence. 'I knew if there was any fight in you I'd find it. Drink.'

Mirah guzzled down the water.

'Today you were to begin your Taphas training. I'll tell them it's cancelled until tomorrow.'

If he expected her to ask him why he didn't show it and she had no intention of giving him the satisfaction of refusing to answer. Whatever fight he'd thought he'd seen in her was wrong. She had no desire to fight. The only desire she had was not to let him win.

‘Quick get dressed,’ Sumer said.

Mirah rested against the chamber wall absorbing its coolness against the evening heat. She watched Sumer rummaging through the garments, favouring a long white gown that clasped over one shoulder.

‘What does bidu mean?’

‘Where did you hear that?’

She would have missed Sumer’s alarm if she hadn’t been paying attention. Caution drove her, whatever bidu meant Sumer didn’t appreciate hearing it and betraying Zeev for saying it seemed like the wrong thing to do.

‘Sometimes men coming out of the barracks mutter it.’

Recognition bloomed on Sumer’s face. ‘They say Bidu is the name of the gatekeeper of the netherworld.’

Mirah pushed off the wall and came closer.

‘People forget the gatekeeper but no one forgets the netherworld. Makes no difference, either way, no one wants to go there.’

‘Where?’

‘The place of the dead, a tormenting pit within the bowels of the earth.’

That there was a place where the dead went was no surprise to her, her clan had called it Maon, a beautiful place of eternal rest high above the waters in the heavens. She wondered at these peoples’ morbid thoughts of the afterlife and considered if this was why Nate had been so determined to save Jabril.

‘Let’s not speak of such evil things. Put this on,’ she said, rushing back to the recess to get a pair of silver sandals.

Mirah lay the gown across her bed and took off her robe.

‘Why, what’s happening?’

‘You’ll see.’

Sumer helped her into the dress, clicking the silver clasp on her shoulder into place.

‘Your hair is still damp. I’ll have to braid it.’

When she’d finished, Sumer left Mirah standing in the middle of her chamber wondering what on earth was about to happen.

She contemplated going to find Neviah when a knock on her door made her jump.

The first thing she noticed was the lack of weapons as Nate stood before her. She had never seen him without his daggers and sword.

'Please come with me, I have something to show you,' he said and turned down the tunnel.

'What's going on?' she asked as she followed.

'You'll see.'

Why does everyone keep saying that and where was he taking her? The prospect of being presented before Shemyaza made her heart shudder.

He strode through tunnel after tunnel and she lost her bearings.

Without stopping, he said, 'I didn't mean to be so tough on you this morning.'

If this was supposed to be his attempt at an apology, he wasn't doing very well. She considered letting him stew but that would be pointless and besides, she needed him on her side.

'I get it.'

He stopped. 'You do?'

'You seem surprised?'

'I thought…' He picked up his pace. 'Never mind.'

The network of tunnels was so vast, she wondered if he was leading her in circles but then he paused by an entrance.

'After you,' he offered, his hand outstretched to guide her in.

Intricate obsidian glass sculptures filled the chamber. All kinds of glass flowers, trees and shrubs arranged into a splendid garden. She went to the closest flower. In its delicate petals, tiny pink particles glittered. The engravings in the glass so finely detailed. She touched a leaf and its prominent veins graced her finger.

The chamber was circular, and a pathway spread around a magnificent fountain stood in the centre. She studied the amazing masterpiece, with its passion flowers and vines rising up from its base, entwining with larger tubular flowers from which babbling water cascaded.

Mirah circled around the fountain taking everything in. She leaned over and examined the little glass gerbils, mongoose and lizards sat serene between the flowers and vines.

'This is beautiful.'

She gasped, noticing a hummingbird hovering in mid-air. She couldn't see what kept the bird in place or how it was even possible.

Nate stood as motionless as the obsidian glass.

'Why am I here?' He didn't move and his gaze disarmed her. 'Nate?'

'Sumer told me it is your birthday.'

She was speechless. With all that had happened, he'd brought her to this beautiful glass garden filled with flowers. He still wasn't moving, his gaze making her self-conscious. She stepped closer to the fountain and turned away from him, letting the water trickle over her hand.

'Thank you,' she whispered.

She sensed his presence close behind her. Did he want to reach out and hold her? Did she want him to?

For a moment the world fell away and part of her old self rose to the surface, the part untainted by fear and loss. At that moment, he wasn't a cruel deliverer, just a man who'd had the sense to do something nice for her.

He was a man, filled with masculinity who enthralled her and enticed her as much as he made her shy away. What did she really know about him? If she believed his repentance, then shouldn't she forgive him? Could she?

He had secrets more than she could number. He often spoke in what she considered half truths or said nothing at all.

Why? Why were Zeev and Nate arguing over her? If she asked Zeev would he tell her? She hadn't seen Nate kill any of her clan in Barakel. He'd kept her and the others safe from harm on his ship, been angered to the point of fury at the loss of Huldah, arranged Abela's healing from the Shaaph and secured safety for the girl who replaced Huldah. Even after her arrival, he still had a vested interest in her welfare. Was he truly trying to keep her safe and if so what was his agenda?

She sensed the pull and desired to lean back into him to feel the warmth of his safety, to test its truth but if she did what would he do?

'Look up,' he said.

With the beauty of the chamber, she hadn't noticed it had no roof. The stars twinkled in the night sky.

'Do you remember when I showed you the Star of Dignity? It's the brightest one over there,' he said, pointing it out. 'Out of all the stars in the heavens that one reminds me of you.'

His words held in the air and she couldn't help wonder how things might have been different if he'd been part of her clan.

'I have something for you,' he said, cutting through her confusion.

He reached over her head and she saw a golden star hanging from a chain as he lowered it. His hands brush against her skin and his breathing stirred the tiny hairs on the nape of her neck as he fixed its clasping.

'I hope you don't mind.'

She sensed his caution, his waiting for her to respond. She held up the exquisite star turning it in her hand. The star was small, simple and beautifully fashioned. He was making it impossible not to like him.

She swayed against the pulsing push and pull of space between them which compelled her to lean back. She wondered if it pushed him towards her. If they connected would he ask for what she was too afraid to give? She needed to get away, to put distance between them.

'I need to go.'

His breath on her neck was warm and heavy as he sighed.

'I'll show you back then.'

She hadn't dared take the chance to gauge his reaction as they strolled towards to her chamber though she suspected he was taking his time.

On reaching her door he said, 'I'll see you in the morning for training.'

She braved a quick peek and found him smiling. That victorious grin told her all she needed to know. He knew how he'd made her feel and enjoyed it.

'Thank you for my gift it's perfect.'

Her words came out faster than she intended, a faltering mess of confusion. She hurried into the safety of her chamber, rested her head against the door and listened as his footsteps padded away.

After their sparring, Nate once again postponed their Taphas training, and she hadn't decided if the delay should alarm or relieve her. She'd hardly finished eating when Neviah tapped on her door.

'Ready?' Neviah asked.

'Are you sure about this?'

'Of course, I'm sure. We'll never find a way out of here sat in our rooms and besides you heard what Sumer said.'

'We can go anywhere except where it's guarded,' Mirah conceded.

They trekked through the winding tunnels becoming more familiar with the layout. Mirah could feel the little golden star against her chest with each step. Now and then they arrived at rounded intersections with four exits. Each exit led into a long tunnel with other tunnels branching off of that. The network was a maze. They paused by an intersection near one of the tunnel entrances.

'What do you think that is?' Neviah asked, pointing to a small blue star painted on the wall.

Mirah brushed her hand over it. 'Let's go this way and see if there are any more.'

They followed the blue stars leading them deeper into the tunnel system. They noticed at each of the tunnel entrances other symbols painted on the walls. A sun, a leaf, three rippled lines, two vertical lines one black the other red, a winged beast and so many others.

The blue stars eventually led them to the lapis lazuli chamber filled with the golden stars. To their relief, Shemyaza's throne room stood empty.

'I think they are showing the way to places within the mountain,' Mirah said. 'If I'm right, then maybe one of the vertical lines will lead to the shaft.'

They tracked back to an intersection and found the black and red vertical lines.

'Shall we try black?' Neviah asked, pushing off into the tunnel.

Soon they stood at the top of the shaft leading to the warriors' courtyard peering down into the darkness.

Neviah quickened her steps as she swept back to the nearest intersection. 'I wonder where the red one leads?'

Mirah rushed to keep pace. 'Maybe we should explore the lower level?'

Part of her, she realised, as she followed Neviah, hoped she might bump into Nate. He'd never mentioned her birthday gift or her rapid retreat from the obsidian glass garden during their predawn training.

Numerous times she considered bringing it up but how could she explain her feelings when she didn't understand them herself. Somehow she had to get a grasp on her emotions. He has secrets, she reminded herself and agendas. He is smart, he is handsome, he is dangerous. More than ever she understood she needed to escape.

Neviah twisted and turned through intersections and tunnels until they spotted guards standing in front of a shaft rising higher into the mountain.

'Great,' Neviah grumbled.

'Let's go back.' She realised neither of them knew which symbol led to their rooms. 'If we return to the first shaft, I might find the way to our chambers.'

They returned by another route. Up ahead sunlight filtered across the tunnel floor. On nearing, they found a veranda which looked over a distant desert plain.

'We must be on another side of the mountain,' Neviah said.

Ripened oranges dangled from potted fruits trees and perfumed periwinkles adorned the veranda. Under a matching green canopy, a bench layered with enticing watermelon green cushions rested in the shade.

'Let's sit for a moment,' Mirah said. 'There's not a part of my body which doesn't ache.'

'Mine too.' Neviah sighed as she slumped onto the soft cushions.

They sat in silence enjoying the summery breeze, watching sand being teased from sand dunes into a swirling dance by the wind.

'We tried,' Mirah said, folding her knees and raising her legs up onto the bench.

'You give up too easy.'

'Well, even if we had found a way to escape what about Dara and the others? I would never leave without them.'

'We don't even know where Dara is. She may never return,' Neviah said, her eyes staring over the desert to some far off unseen place which held the mystery of the Chashmalim.

Mirah fiddled with a cushion, her finger tracing over its embroidered vines. 'There's nothing to go back to.'

Neviah's head snapped away from the sand dunes and she turned to Mirah. 'I can't believe you would say such a thing. What about—well you know?'

Mirah picked up the cushion, rested her chin on top of it and hugged it to her chest. She lowered her voice to a whisper. 'Gabe could be anywhere by now. Only death remained for him at Barakel.'

Neviah shifted around further in her seat to get a better view of her. 'You would forget him that easily?'

'Of course not. But what we did in the Taphas chamber, don't you want to find out more about wielding?'

'Not for the same reason you do,' Neviah snapped.

Mirah's head shot up. 'What's that supposed to mean?'

'I saw the way Esha, and the other Taphas women stared at you like you'd done something they'd never seen.'

'I threw ice. Like they showed us.'

'The ice didn't shatter against the wall though did it?' She glared at Mirah and then huffed. 'Well, I guess we'll find out soon enough, Zeev said we begin training tomorrow.'

Mirah leaned over to scratch an itch on her ankle. The golden star slipped out of her tunic, dangling in the air.

'What is that?' Neviah asked, staring at the swinging pendant.

She tucked the star inside her tunic. 'It's nothing, it's just a birthday gift.'

'From who?'

Mirah didn't answer.

Neviah's eyes widened, and she jumped up and fled across the veranda. Face red and welling with tears.

'You'll never leave,' she cried out, before rushing off back into the tunnels.

Stunned, Mirah sat contemplating why Neviah thought her ice impaling the wall was abnormal. How could she know?

Guilt descended on her like a dark creeping shadow. It threatened to reveal unspoken reasons why she desired to stay. No, Neviah was wrong. She leaped off the seat and sprinted through the tunnels following the black painted vertical lines towards the shaft. Neviah was nowhere in sight.

She turned a corner to find Shayla dead ahead of her. She considered turning back but something inside her screamed no. I won't let her stand in my way. Shayla, dressed in a pearl green, skin-hugging fabric sauntered towards her like a cat about to pounce on a butterfly.

'Have you seen Nev?'

'Maybe she's gone to make out with that guard,' she answered, adjusting the strap over her shoulder. She dropped her hand and teased her finger along the low cut line of her garment which exposed the curve of her breasts. 'I'm touched someone of her breeding doesn't try to rise above her station. I heard they gave such a public display.' She smirked and her wickedness spread across her face with a cat-like smile.

Mirah leaned in closer and snapped out, 'So you spread gossip about things you know nothing about?'

'Oh no, I don't have time for gossip.' Unfazed by the narrow distance between them, her haughty eyes stared at Mirah. 'I'm off to the garden to meet Nate.'

✻ 10 ✻

Silence lingered beside them as they made their way to the courtyard. Mirah had made several attempts to talk to her but Neviah refused to acknowledge her presence.

It had taken them two weeks to travel up the river, and that was with many oarsmen pushing them against its flow. On the other side of the mountain, desert plains expanded like a golden sea. How far did Neviah think they would get before capture or worse? No, she was being unreasonable and if silent sulking was all she'd offer, then Mirah would wait her out.

'What's wrong with you two?' Zeev asked, rolling up his sleeves.

Neviah wound her hair in a tight bun as though preparing for war. 'Nothing,' she hissed. She was spoiling for a fight, daring him to push her further.

He weighed up the distance between them and fixed his eyes on her. 'I've seen ice brinicles warmer than you,' he declared.

At the mention of ice, Mirah winced.

'Well anyway, I'll soon have your blood pumping.' He winked, willing her to attack him, 'Maybe the heat will take out your sting.'

Nate emerged through the gatehouse, his cloak billowing out behind him. Dawn was still an hour away and something about his athletic movement made Mirah wonder if he was just returning.

She'd assumed he lived inside the mountain but maybe he had somewhere else to stay. Wherever he'd been, he hadn't done much sleeping as he unhooked his cloak to reveal dark shadows under his stunning blue eyes.

'Ready?' he asked, his mind switching with faultless ease to the task at hand.

They paired off and Nate slid his arm gently around her neck, ready for her to break out of his hold.

'What's the matter?'

Her bottom lip quivered, and she pressed her lips together attempting to regain control.

'Where's your necklace?'

She couldn't speak. She couldn't explain that she'd taken the pendant off for fear of the chain breaking. She couldn't tell him about Neviah's accusations. 'I can't,' was all she could say.

His other forearm cleaved around her waistline as he drew her back against his body, holding her still for the briefest moment.

She desired to lean into him, to let him shoulder the weight of her burdens but Shayla's words pinched at the edge of her memory. She didn't even want to know if he'd held Shayla this way.

A waft of cool air swept up her spine as he let go and pivoted around to face her. He scrutinized her, searching for what ailed her. His cool blue gaze acknowledging her need for silence.

'Let's try defence from a dagger?'

Mirah's attention strayed to the sandy ground.

'Never take your eyes off your opponent,' he commanded, and with the softest touch, his hand lifted her chin. His eyes were stern, urgent but no sign of aggression but even so, as if trying to prove a point, the sharp tip of a blade pressed into her abdomen.

'They're not my enemies,' she reminded him.

'Maybe not, but they won't know that. You need to focus. Whatever this is snap out of it before it gets you killed.'

'Fine.' She stepped back from the dagger. 'Show me.'

He manoeuvred around her, coming at her from all directions, the blade shimmering in the fall of the moonlight. His precision with the dagger so controlled, never once did she think he'd cut her as she defended against his advances.

After over an hour of turning, dodging and stepping to the side of his blade, a glistening blue, watery cascade of sunlight reflected off the mountain and danced across the courtyard's floor.

'It's getting light,' Nate said. 'It's time to go.' He sheathed the dagger at his side. 'You need more practice. I'll come and find you later,' he announced before walking over to the fountain.

Neviah and Zeev joined them. 'They're not speaking,' Zeev said, cupping water in his hand and slurping.

Mirah sensed Nate's eyes on her but she refused to connect with his gaze.

'I don't need a babysitter,' Neviah said and stormed off towards the chasm and to the Taphas waiting inside.

Acknowledging her obvious unease, Nate said, 'I'll escort you to the Taphas chamber. I've arranged for Galia to oversee your training.'

⁂

The tall slim woman who had wielded water in the Taphas demonstration greeted them. Her silver hair swirled like waves over her shoulders enhancing calm grey eyes that revealed nothing within. Nate introduced Mirah and then left.

'My name is Galia. I'll be training you today. Follow me.'

Without waiting for a response she led Mirah back towards the tunnel she'd just come through. Neviah ignored her departure, preferring to watch a Taphas woman wield balls of fire against the far wall.

Galia swaggered out through the courtyard and under the gatehouse. Nate and Zeev were nowhere to be seen.

'Where are we going?' Mirah asked.

Without glancing back, she said, 'We need more water.'

In the outside plaza, men busied themselves setting up carts, whilst their horses munched on hay.

They crossed over and exited heading east. Galia led with silent footsteps through an affluent area of well-spaced clay brick towers, complete with their boundary walls. On the walls, an assortment of inlaid tinted glass shards, designed in a variety of mosaic patterns, sent a kaleidoscope of colourful reflections on the path.

Galia twisted and turned through the shimmering rainbow passageways until they came around on the eastern side of the mountain onto a carpet of luscious green grass.

'Just up here,' Galia said, leaning into the steady incline.

Beyond the ridge, a forest of conifers spread out before them, giving shade to numerous aqua, green terraced pools. All of them linked by small waterfalls and trickling shallow streams.

'Follow me.' Without pausing, Galia descended from the ridge and slowed when reaching the trees. 'I love that scent,' she said, inhaling pine and citrus perfumes. 'Not much further.'

Mirah didn't mind, the forest reminded her of home and she could have strolled through its leafy embrace all day.

Shaded from the scorching heat, she found the chirping birds both calming and stimulating. Three strange, red furry creatures with large amber eyes followed them, leaping from branch to branch as they went. Their chattering grew louder, and another larger than the three scurried along a branch towards them. The three bolted away from its advance.

Galia halted before a small raised pool. 'Freeze it.'

Mirah shifted on her feet. 'What?'

'Freeze the water.'

'I can't do that,' Mirah said, rubbing the ring on her finger.

Galia swirled her hand in the pool. 'How do you know what you can and cannot do? Until the other day, you couldn't form ice.'

'How does wielding work?'

'Wielding is a gift from Shemyaza. Now show me what you can do?'

Mirah dipped her finger into the pool and found it cool. She concentrated on the water, willing it to ice over. To her surprise, shards of ice formed spreading their icy white web across the pool.

Before she had a chance to grasp what she'd just done, Galia said, 'Good, and now this one.'

Galia led her onto the next pool, more voluminous than the first. By the time she had reached the lake, Mirah still had no real idea how she'd frozen several pools each one larger than the one before.

'Now I want you to create an ice path from here to the other side of the lake. Be careful of the fish. I don't want you killing them.'

Mirah stood before the lake assessing the water, the way it flowed and how to make a pathway from here to the other side.

You could freeze the whole lake if you wanted. Let me show you.

Unnerved by the strange voice in her head, she focused on the knowledge that Galia cared for the life forms hidden beneath the waters. She held her hand over the edge of the water, sensing the gentle pull of its current. A glassy pathway of ice crept out before her, crackling and grinding as it expanded across the lake.

'Good,' Galia said, stepping onto the ice.

A symphony of groans and whipping acoustics echoed up from underneath them as they crossed over to a small sheltered beach coupling the lakeshore.

'Now we are away from prying eyes let's find out what you can do. Concentrate on not freezing the water. Do it like this.'

Galia swirled her hands in the air and water spiralled up out of the lake, breaking off from the expanse. She guided the liquid to create the shape of an eagle which flapped its translucent wings. It rose high in the sky, soaring above them before swooping down over Mirah's head. Almost invisible, the eagle circled around them. Its form changing colour, as it flew past the towering windswept conifers behind them, up and then up into the clouds hovering in the deep blue sky.

Mirah watched in awe. 'That's amazing.'

The eagle swooped over her head.

'Stop gawking and wield.'

Taking the hint, she stepped up beside Galia and attempted to create a bird of her own. The shape was clumsy, something like the slush of melting ice, neither one form nor the other and difficult to manoeuvre through the air.

'Don't hold on to the water so tight,' Galia encouraged. 'Let each molecule bind together to create its form.'

Mirah relaxed her hold on the fluid and it collapsed, spraying them both with the memory of what it once held.

'Try again,' Galia said, as her eagle swooped over their heads.

Her second attempt lifted out of the water. It was more equally formed but still held a slushy texture. Galia's eagle swooped from above and as much as Mirah tried to lift her bird out of its way, watery talons punctured its liquid membrane and it fell to the ground with a splash.

As if sensing her dismay, Galia said, 'Don't worry it will come with practice.' She edged away from the lake towards the trees. 'Show me how you threw that ice spear yesterday.'

Mirah threw out her hand sending an unyielding spear of ice into the trunk of a conifer tree.

'Again.' Galia's censored grey eyes inspected Mirah's ring, her hands, the way she focused as each spear formed and flew through the air. 'Your technique is sloppy. You will need to work on it but still, I can't see how you do that.'

'What do you mean?'

'Sit, let's eat.'

Galia pulled a tin pot from a leather skin bag and filled it with water. Before Mirah realised what was happening, Galia had guided two small fish with whiskery barbels through the water. She picked them up, prepared them with a knife and set them in the tin. She rummaged in her bag and added basil leaves to the air bubbles now rising to the surface. Mirah watched in admiration.

'Wielding water has more to offer than fire or air,' she said, passing Mirah a handful of dates. 'Esha believes fire is the strongest of the elements but I know she is wrong. Fire is destructive, eating everything in its path but water can quench out their flames. If you're a strong enough Water Wielder, which I think you are, you will even be able to wash away Esha's flames.'

Galia prodded the fish with a stick which Mirah hadn't noticed she'd picked up.

'Air can be trickier to outmanoeuvre but I will show you some ways. I can show you how to construct ice walls, tsunamis, even freeze a man's blood to the core.'

Checking the fish cooked to her satisfaction, she pierced one with the stick and handed it to Mirah before preparing her own.

They ate in silence and Mirah considered how much she could trust her. Galia appeared to be as calm as small waves lapping a cooling embrace over heated sand but her muted grey eyes concealed the person held within.

When Mirah had finished, she traced little shapes with the stick in the sand. 'Why are you with me and not one of the others?'

'I'm the best Water Wielder we have, and the Captain requested me personally.'

I'm sure he did, Mirah thought to herself. She rushed to scratch out the sweeping inner curves and the deep-set eyes that replicated Nate's from the sand. 'What is the Captain like?'

'He commands from the front and would gladly sacrifice himself for any of us,' she said without hesitation.

She looked a few years shy of thirty, old enough to have been a Wielder for some time and wore a wavy, gold band and amethyst stone amulet on her arm.

Mirah returned to her doodling in the sand, careful not to draw anything resembling faces. 'Have you ever been to the front lines?'

'Yes, many times.'

'What's it like?'

'I remember the old ways before Shemyaza arrived. I was a child but I'll never forget laying awake at night fearing those beyond our borders. They always came under the cover of darkness, butchering with spiked wooden clubs any who stood in their path.'

Galia picked up the tin and bent down to the edge of the lake to rinse it. With her back towards Mirah, she said in a low whisper, 'My parents, my brother I lost them in those days.'

Crouching by the lake edge, silence swirled up around her and Mirah gave her the space to remember.

Galia stood and shook water droplets from the tin. 'The battles were blood-filled and ruthless and often. Shemyaza put a stop to all that. Now I am older and strong enough to protect what we have.'

Mirah tilted her head to face her. 'What do you have?'

'Peace. For the first time since any can remember we have peace in our lands and I will do what it takes to defend it.' Galia's gaze drifted to the ring on Mirah's finger. 'What made you choose that amulet?'

'I don't know. I guess the ring looked the least conspicuous compared to the rest.'

'Interesting,' she mused, before wiping her mouth and putting the tin back in her bag. She walked over and inspected the spears of ice impaled in the conifer tree. 'The way your ice penetrates through the wood; the same way it did with the rock. We've never seen this before.'

Her face lit up and her eyes widened as she brushed her fingers along the ice where it breached the now fractured wood.

'What do you mean?'

'Ice, it's good for piercing through soft materials, like flesh but—'

'Is there something wrong with me?'

'No, not at all. It's something new. I—'

'Galia,' Nate yelled.

They both looked over to find Nate ducking under a low branch as he exited the tree line.

'Wait here,' Galia said, and then she sprinted off towards him.

Mirah studied their interaction from a distance. Galia respected him that was obvious as he listened with interest to whatever she told him. He glanced over and she quickly turned and faced the lake.

One set of footprints shuffled in the sand but she didn't need to turn to know who was approaching.

'Galia tells me you did well,' he said, sitting beside her.

'Didn't she tell you I couldn't even form a bird?'

'It will take practice, just like your defensive training. Should we get started?'

'If I say no, will you force me?'

'Of course not. Although I could probably convince you.'

She heard the humour in his tone and turned to see him smiling.

'I'm too tired.'

He sat in silent contemplation and she distracted herself watching rings appear on the lake as a little fish surfaced.

'Do you want to talk about Neviah?'

'Not really.'

He sighed, and she understood that whatever his motive, he was trying to reach her. 'I took my necklace off because I didn't want to break it,' she confessed.

'I see. Well, you needn't worry. The linkage is stronger than it appears.'

She wondered what he saw and why he was sitting here beside her. 'Don't you have somewhere you need to be?'

Her stomach tightened at her question, without Neviah she was alone and what if he was just appeasing her and preferred to be with Shayla?

He let out a half chuckle. 'I have a multitude of things I should be doing but they can wait a little longer. Besides what sort of man would I be if I left you here by yourself?'

'I don't need your pity.'

'It's not pity,' he defended. 'Tell me, when you were in Barakel, besides healing, what did you like to do?'

She had to give him credit, he wasn't going to give up and let her stew in her own misery. To be fair, she didn't crave to stay there either. 'I liked to make pictures in the sand.'

He rose and went to the tree line and she heard snapping branches.

When he returned he stripped off the excess shoots with his dagger. 'Show me,' he said, offering her one of the branches.

She looked across the sand. 'It's too dry.'

'Aren't you a Water Wielder?' he challenged.

'I don't know how?'

'Well, with that I can't help you. I'm sure you'll figure it out.'

He set to stripping offshoots from the other branch. Mirah stared at the sun-dried sand. Until recently she had never sensed the water but she could feel its presence now. She wielded water to the surface, and the sand sank into a golden blank canvass. He smiled but didn't look up from his dagger.

'What would you like me to create?'

'Whatever is in your heart Mirah.'

She might not be able to wield an eagle like Galia but she knew she could paint one. Dipping the branch into the sand she outlined its form. Nate stepped further away and began a creation of his own.

For hours she sculpted the eagle, its wings spread wide in flight and she imagined it soaring high above the skies canopy, making its nest somewhere in the stars. When she traced out its talons, she imagined the eagle gripping hold of her, carrying her off to safety and her resting under the shade of its wing.

When she finished Nate came over. 'I should have known you'd be able to capture its beauty.'

He walked around, absorbing her creation and she couldn't help feeling satisfied by his look of admiration.

'What did you draw?' she asked, taking steps away from her achievement. She stopped in awe when she saw her portrait in the sand.

'Do you like it?'

'Is that how you see me?' she asked in shock.

Her long flowing hair rested in waves across her shoulders, the star pendant prominent on her neckline and the warmest smile expressed on her face.

'It's how I imagine you would look if things were different.'

Sadness overwhelmed her as she realised she'd never smile like that again.

'Don't cry,' he said, wiping her tears from her cheeks.

Grief bubbled up from her midsection and hitched in her throat. He drew her into a comforting embrace. She leaned her head on his shoulder and sobbed. She sobbed for the missing parts of herself, parts that never would be. As much as she knew his warm, strong body yearned to absorb all her grief, she held back something so deep she didn't dare risk opening.

'I'm sorry. I never meant to hurt you.'

When she could speak, she said, 'I'd like to return to my chamber.'

❊ 11 ❊

The following morning Mirah made her way to the courtyard alone. Neviah had not waited. Throughout the night one restless image haunted her. She hadn't seen it coming, the loss and the lingering shadow which remained.

It unnerved her how his sandy portrait captured her previous countenance. She'd spent so many days now just surviving, she hadn't given thought to the happiness she'd left behind.

Before stepping out of the chasm, she slackened her Taphas tunic and pulled the star pendant on its chain into view. She ignored Neviah and focused her attention on Nate as she crossed the courtyard.

If Neviah wanted to believe her reddened eyes resulted from her silent punishment and absence, she'd let her, the truth was much more abhorrent. Nate never asked if she was all right, he knew she wasn't, and she doubted she'd be able to hold herself together if he had.

She put everything she had left into training. If this was her life now, for her own survival she'd make the best of it and who knew, one day she might have a reason to smile. Nate didn't say a word other than to give her instructions and their sparring soon fell into a rhythm.

Just before dawn, he shouted over to Neviah and Zeev, 'That's enough for today.'

'What no running around the courtyard?' Neviah snapped.

He turned on her and with a voice so calm and deadly said, 'Two laps for you now.'

Neviah glared at him and Mirah hitched her breath. If Neviah didn't do as he instructed, she didn't dare think what would happen next.

Neviah glanced at Zeev.

He shrugged. 'Better get going.' His eyes expressed caution as he flicked a glance at Nate.

'I'll never let you beat me,' she yelled at Nate, and then began to run around the courtyard.

Nate strode over to the fountain. 'Coming?' he said over his shoulder.

Mirah caught up to him and he slurped and poured a handful of water over his head.

'You don't deserve to be avoided like that. She's supposed to be your friend.'

When Neviah completed her two laps she rushed past the fountain into the chasm.

'I don't think she feels that way anymore.'

'Well, I won't allow it. If she doesn't apologise, I'll stop her training.'

'Please don't.'

Zeev slurped water from his palm. 'I'll talk to her tomorrow.'

Nate snorted. 'That was her one and only chance.'

Galia exited the chasm. 'What did I miss?'

'Nothing,' Nate said and marched the other way.

⁂

Mirah's water bird lifted out of the lake, smaller than the day before but more equally formed. It had reached the height of the trees when Galia's eagle swooped causing Mirah to yelp and swerve her watery bird out of its way.

She didn't understand how, but she perceived the eagle's molecules circling, preparing for another dive. She flew her little bird up into the brilliant white clouds. If Gabe were here, he would have loved this.

Swooping and diving, the little water bird flew out of the eagle's path as though it was part of her. Even when sheltered within the clouds she sensed its fluttering wings, knowing when the eagle came in for another attack.

Her bird was tiny by comparison and after many failed attempts of escaping, she learned to turn and dodge it out of the eagle's talons with ease. She smiled at Galia and to her surprise, she smiled in return. Galia had a carefree manner and Mirah wondered if she got to know her how much she'd like her.

Galia lowered her eagle and made it perch on a fissured rock by the edge of the lake, holding its perfect form. 'Now bring yours beside mine and hold it steady.'

She lowered her bird onto the rock and tiptoed closer to observe it. 'It's beautiful. See the fine feathers. They look like crystal wings.'

Galia's eagle dissolved against the rock with a splash and she sat on the beach.

'Do you want to talk about what happened earlier?'

She was desperate to talk with someone, with Dara gone and Abela and Ayla with the Azu she had no one left to turn to. She wasn't sure how much she trusted Galia and still undecided if she could consider her a friend but she'd seen her with Nate yesterday and he appeared to trust her so she took the risk.

'Neviah and I had a disagreement. She hasn't been speaking to me for days.'

She wasn't certain if the perspiration running down her neck from under her hair was because of the heat, steadying the water bird or her nerves.

'About?'

'Nate gave me this necklace,' she said pulling out her chain.

Galia's eyebrow rose in surprise.

'It's nothing, it's just a birthday gift.'

The water bird disappeared with a splash on the rock and Mirah came and sat beside Galia.

'I tried to explain it to Neviah but she won't give me the time to listen. Anyway, this morning she made a rude comment and Nate punished her by forcing her to do laps. He said no one had the right to treat me that way. I'm prepared to wait her out, she will come around soon but it's just so hard, with what happened at Barakel and coming here into this strange land and learning how to wield magic and I just don't know who I can trust and I feel so alone.'

She knew she was rambling that her concerns were falling from her lips. Galia caught every word and listened until she ran out of breath.

'What?' she asked when she noticed Galia watching her with careful consideration.

'I don't know what to say. I never thought Nate would become so involved.'

Galia coughed into her hand and Mirah was sure she attempted to hide something. Did she think this was funny? She was about to get up and storm off when Galia spoke.

'I think you understand your friend very well. I'm sure, it's as you say, she will come around in time. Men don't understand this. I will speak to Nate if you wish and ask him to show Neviah some leniency.'

'Really?'

'Of course. Sometimes Nate can be a fool but he has never been cruel on purpose.'

'Thank you.'

Galia rose and brushed the sand from her clothes. 'Now that's settled, let's find out what else you can do.' She edged back towards the lake. 'Right, let's see how much water you can hold. Raise as much as you can into the air.'

'Seriously?' Mirah asked catching up to her.

'Yes, start in the middle of the lake.'

Finally, let's show them what you can do.

'Shh.'

'What?' Galia asked.

'Oh, nothing. I stood on a stone.'

Mirah kicked out a pebble by her footing and raised her arms concentrating on the centre of the lake. She could feel the ring pulsing on her finger and sensed each molecule of water waiting for her command. The water began to rise, receding from before her feet and gathering up into a swishing mountain.

'More, pull more,' Galia urged.

She closed her eyes and focused on linking each molecule with the next. The mountain of water grew higher. The strain of which pressed down on her, so heavy she longed to let it go.

'Just a little more.'

She could hardly hear Galia above the sound of pulsing water. The force of it calling her, urging her for more. She couldn't control the power, couldn't make it stop. Moisture seeped from her pores and rolled down her skin as though it craved to join the mountain of water rising from where the lake had once been.

'Mirah, that's enough.'

She felt a sharp tugging on her arm as Galia tried to lower it. She knew the conifers behind her bowed in the wind, their needle leaves drying and withering as they gave up their dew but she didn't know how to stop the surging force surrounding her. A force she no longer controlled.

'Mirah, please,' Galia cried, between coughing and wheezing.

Her head thumped to the beat of thudding footsteps. Warmth seeped into her mind, weaving along the throbbing watery veins under her delicate skin.

'What the bidu is going on here?' Nate hollered, and then darkness fell.

⁂

When Mirah gained consciousness, she lay across Nate's thighs with her head resting against his chest, his arms wrapped over her. From the lapping sounds of water, she realised she was still by the lake. She didn't move, didn't dare to open her eyes to see what she'd done.

'Is she alright?' Galia asked, her footsteps squelching in the wet sand as she approached and sat near them.

'She's still unconscious.' He sighed and shuffled his weight. 'Tell me what happened?' he asked, his voice calm but pressing.

'I don't know. She is exceptional. I've never seen anyone learn to wield water as fast and with as much control as she did. Yesterday we started with the basics, freezing and controlling the flow of water in the air. I got curious about the ice piercing through the Taphas chamber wall and asked her to show me again. Today she wielded a perfect water bird, and it outclassed my own.'

Galia paused and Mirah thought she had finished.

'I wanted to find the threshold of her ability. I'm sorry Nate. I pushed her to lift the water from the lake.'

'You did what?'

'She held the water, all of it and then I don't know. It was like it wasn't enough. She drew moisture from the trees, the ground, even our own flesh. If you hadn't come… I couldn't stop her. I couldn't break through.'

'And what about that?'

Mirah felt him move as though he jerked his head.

'I don't know how she did it. What are we going to do?'

What had she done? The discomfort of not knowing willed her to open her heavy eyelids to see what he surveyed.

'Do you want me to find another Wielder?' Galia asked.

'No, I'll take care of it.'

They were silent for a long while and Mirah leaned into the rise and fall of his firm chest. Her fatigue and the soft rhythm of him willing her back into slumber.

'Do you think she could assist us?' Galia asked.

'No.'

'With that kind of power, she could—'

'I'm not bringing her into this,' Nate snapped. His body tensed and his arms tightened around her.

Mirah held onto her consciousness a little longer. What was Galia asking of her and what was he objecting to?

Galia sighed. 'But she's already involved.'

'Not like that, she isn't. I won't risk it. Go back to the mountain.'

Galia shuffled then stood.

'Tell no one what you have seen,' he ordered. 'If anyone asks, do whatever you need to, to carve me some time.'

'Yes, Captain,' Galia said, before Mirah heard her footsteps retreating.

Mirah lay in his arms, slipping between wakefulness and rest. Her whole body trembled. She craved to slip into that place where she could hide and feel nothing, so she gave into it.

Sometime later, she stirred to the warmth of Nate's blue cloak wrapped around her. He was standing by the lake throwing stones into the moonlit water. Flickering silver highlights spread over the gentle current. She heard no plopping sounds as stones fell but a crack as though the stones bounced from rock instead.

'What is that?' her voiced cracked against the harsh, dryness in her throat.

He bent down filling a water skin and towering above him was a black shadow reaching up into the night.

'You tell me,' he said offering her water.

She sipped and then guzzled the liquid. Its icy embrace cooling her thirst. She tried to stand but dizziness and fatigue betrayed her.

He squatted on his haunches and seized a handful of sand. 'It appears you lifted the lake's rock bed as well.'

He let the sand drift through his fingers and then grabbed some more. His face was a portrait of confliction, one of awe and concern.

She placed her hand on his to get his attention. 'Did I hurt someone?'

She studied his eyes shielded by dark lashes, attempting to read what he'd say before he told her.

'No. Galia settled the surging waters as they fell.'

She let her shoulders drop and felt the pull of her muscles constricting against the ache in her neck. She glanced at the dark tower of rock protruding out of the lake.

'I know I lost control but I can tell by your frown, there's something else on your mind. What is it?'

'You're different.'

Her head snapped back to him. Whatever she'd expected, different, was furthest from her thoughts. 'What do you mean?'

'Wielders only wield one element of magic. You have to put the rock back.'

He shook the sand from his hands and rose to his feet.

'The rock bed?'

'Well, we can't have that hulking mound of rocks towering out of the lake. Someone will notice.'

'I can't.'

'You can and you will. Hiding this is the only way to protect yourself from the knowledge, I can assure you, you don't want others to know.' Reaching out his hand, he said, 'Come let me guide you.'

'I don't want to do this.'

'Please trust me. You have no choice.'

The urgency with which his eyes pinned her caused her to reach out to his offered hand.

'Take your time, nice and slow.' He pulled her up and came around behind her, steadying her as she swayed.

'But what if I lose control?'

'You're safe with me.' he stated firmly.

In his arms, she knew that in this strange place, if anyone who could protect her, it would be him. His strength and assurance embraced and held up her weakened frame.

She rubbed at the ring on her finger and with every ounce of energy willed it to do as she asked.

❋ 12 ❋

Ammo pressed his thumbs into his shoulders, rolled back his elbows and stretched out the knots riveting along his spine. Several neat mounds of coiled ropes, nestled like cobras on the ship's deck testified to his hours of hard labour.

A steady crowd of importers and exporters were setting up along the dock to broker their wares. The wind was soft and the water still.

Since he'd arrived in Anat two days ago, he'd heard of the attack and watched as they'd buried their dead. Still staked to a pole by the garrison was the Nephilim's rotting head. With Nephilim nearby, he was keen to move on, but it didn't look like they'd have the wind today.

He was about to scrape crusted salt from the carved lion head on the prow of his ship when he spotted Sojin. Something about the way he slinked around appeared odd.

Sojin slipped through the crowd unnoticed. He was following an old woman, leaning on a walking cane. She stopped to study lobsters crammed into a basket, pushed out her bottom lip and shuffled onwards. Sojin came towards her, brushed against her and as smooth as buffed ship's wax pocketed her brown purse.

'Ya darn rat,' Ammo said between clenched teeth.

He called out to one of his crew to take over and stormed across the gangplank.

Not long after, Ammo burst through the door into the tobacco haze of the Fertile Crescent. His green eyes scanned the inn. A path cleared as he made his way towards a young girl with red curly hair hurrying to pour him a beer.

'Don't worry yaself Honey, I ain't got time for no beer. Ain't touched that stuff in years.' He let out a low growl. 'Where are ya? Ya thieving hyena.'

The betrayal of creaking wood broke into the hush of stunned wayfarers and merchants seated on stools around cedar tables. Darting over to a table in the corner, Ammo spotted Sojin's boots.

'Get up,' Ammo ordered, holding his hand out for the elderly woman's purse.

'Sorry,' Sojin muttered under his breath.

He'd found Sojin stowed away on his ship three winters back. His mother and others had been taken in a raid when a war band of Nephilim had crossed over the Salmu sea.

Something in his gritty, hardened face had pulled Ammo to take action, and he'd spent the past few years instructing Sojin in the ways of the Acquisitioner's trade.

It wasn't going well. He had raw talent, and he was small for a fifteen-year-old which came in handy but he often got careless. Sojin would be lucky not to lose his hands on the Enforcer's block before long.

Ammo could be many things, a hired thug, bodyguard for the rich, he'd even taken a hostage or two for the right price but he had rules. Rules he stuck to no matter what; never take from your allies; never harm the fairer sex unless you have to, and most of all never get caught.

Ammo called the redhead over. 'Looks like I'll be sticking around for the night. Ya got a room?'

'Yes Sir,' she replied. 'I'll call Benhm to take your things.'

She turned to go but Ammo caught her hand.

'No need,' he grinned, 'I come as I am, no baggage.'

He resisted the temptation to tug her skirts as she scampered away. He'd see her later, of that, he was certain.

He studied Sojin now sitting at the table assessing other guests in the inn. His hazel eyes, shielded under a dark brown fringe were alert to every movement in the room as they darted from one person to the next. He'd fare better at a Scribehouse, he thought, although him being older, it would cost Ammo some serious silver. He decided to wait until morning and let Sojin choose, he owed him that.

'Your room is ready,' the redhead said. 'Would you like your food here or brought to your room?'

'He'll take his out back.' Ammo pushed out his chest and with an admiring gleam in his eyes said, 'As for me, my room will do fine.'

She scurried away to collect their meals.

Ammo leaned over to Sojin and tapped at his foot from under the table. 'Scram, ya Mugger, I'll see ya tomorrow.'

Sojin winked, tipped his rusty brown cap and made for the stable yard. The redhead returned with a tray filled with flatbread, mutton broth, pomegranates and figs and led Ammo up to his room.

⁂

The following morning Ammo whistled out the back door and Sojin soon emerged. His hair flattened on one side and lines streaked down the side of his face.

'Straw huh,' Ammo chuckled.

Sojin rubbed his cheek and scrambled into his coat. The inn was deserted. Now that the tobacco haze had evaporated he could see the inn wasn't such a bad place. As with everywhere these days it had a black line of rat grease skirting where the walls met the floor but there was no evidence of lice in the crevices at least.

He sniffed at the smell of baked oats wafting in from another room.

'I've decided ya would be better off at the Scribehouse,' Ammo declared.

Sojin's face paled. The Scribehouse stood in the northern quarter of the city. It was as old and dark as the mysteries it contained. Mysteries that the Clerics believed would one day defeat the Watchers and their horde of Nephilim. Ammo didn't believe script on clay could defeat anything but for a hefty price Clerics would take in an Apprentice.

He noted the dark etchings carved into the wooden table. They reminded him of twisting rivers outlined on his pigskin maps. Sojin sat there digging his fingernail into one of the rivers cascading off the table edge.

Ammo took a deep breath and exhaled. 'How many times have I told ya, we ain't no low life thieves? We are Acquisitioners. We only steal what we get paid to steal.'

Sojin raised his eyes and faced him. 'I won't stay. If you make me go, I won't stay.'

Ammo and Sojin stared at each other. It was the first time he'd seen Sojin attempting to make a stand. Finding it hard to keep a stern face, he let out a triumphant grin.

'Had ya going there, didn't I.'

'What?'

'Look, I just needed to get my point across.' He reached around and unclipped his belt. 'Take this.'

Sojin's eyes lit as he took the belt and its sheathed blade. He caressed his prize then strapped it on.

'If ya gonna get yaself caught, ya at least need something to defend yaself with. But ya have to promise me, no more thieving unless I say. Right?'

'I swear. I'll never do it again.'

'What did ya want the tokens for, anyway?'

'No reason. I was, well, you know, practising.'

⁂

They spent the day on Ammo's ship making preparations for departure. When sunset arrived, Ammo left and ventured out towards Tenby Market. The Town Square thrived with activity. Tinkers were selling their wares. Music jangled from carnivals and troupes competed for spectators' attention. The odour of cooked food and the foul stench of stale beer and sweat clung in the air.

The market was alive. Pickpockets threaded like veins through the crowds, mapping their routes towards narrow alleys. It wasn't hard for Ammo to mark the anomaly. In the chaos of the Town Square, stillness stuck out like a towering idol.

And there she was a tall slender woman standing by a merchant's tent filled with phoney jewels. She pretended to study a bracelet, but she stared right through it, at him. Tightening her hood, she stepped away, moving with fluid grace through the human ravines. She quickened her pace enough not to draw attention and slipped into a darkened side alley.

He suspected a trap as he followed and it didn't surprise him to find an arrow protruding from a crossbow, now levelled at his eye.

'Well this is interesting,' Ammo said, as he stepped back and raised his arms in fake surrender.

He scanned the alley for signs of others. It was empty and blocked off at the far end by a rickety wooden structure. She stood in a fighters' stance. A short dark cloak came to her thighs, not a cumbersome burden during a fight, Ammo supposed.

Dark tight pants, easy for movement and well worn soft leather boots made up her garments, no sack in sight to slow her down. Her lithe upper body pushed into steady legs. Not even a tremble in her crossbow arm. With one hand she pulled her dark hood back. Moonlight haloed over her long black hair, reflecting a spectrum of colours against a pale-skinned complexion. Her deep lavender eyes dilated. Alarmed, he reached for his blade only to remember he'd given it to Sojin.

'Chashmal,' he accused.

She dipped her head to the side but didn't answer.

'Well, whatever, I ain't got through life without adapting a few skills of me own.'

Chashmalim or not he wouldn't allow her into his head.

'That won't do you any good,' she said. Her eyes raised from the emerald ring he'd been rubbing with his thumb. 'I'm not who you think I am.' She lowered her voice, 'My name's Bina and I have a message for you.'

He didn't trust her but her lavender eyes, even in the darkness revealed a subtle ambient light that would never exist in a Chashmalim. Whoever she was, she looked exquisite. A mystery which appealed to his senses.

'What's the crossbow for then?'

'I assumed you might be,' she paused as if trying to find the right word, 'difficult.'

'So ya heard of me?'

'No, not exactly.'

Ammo chuckled to himself. 'Well, that's a first. Ya must have come a long way.'

She lowered the crossbow. 'Can we go somewhere, not so exposed?'

*

Several men sitting on the other side of the Fertile Crescent gave occasional glances in Ammo's direction.

'Do you know those men?' Bina asked, without even raising an eye towards them.

'No, but they know me, or at least they think they do.'

The redhead from last night busied herself preparing leather drinking vessels, focusing everywhere but in their direction. After a while, she scooted around the inn's tables with a beer in each hand. Placing one in front of Bina she turned towards Ammo. The vessel slipped from her hand, hit the edge of the table and fell into his lap.

He jumped out of his seat. 'Damn it, woman. These are my best silks.'

'I'm sorry,' she said, pulling a rag from her pocket and wiping the table. 'The beer slipped out of my hand.' Her smug smile revealed she was far from sorry. She leaned towards Bina. 'Don't let those long blonde locks or his generous physique fool you.' Then bending lower she whispered, 'I wouldn't bother yourself. He's a fast mover.' She turned tail and walked back towards the bar.

Bina smiled. 'You know some people, at least.'

'What she said, she didn't mean—' Ammo pulled the silk now stuck to his nether region from his skin. 'Well, ya know.'

Before his reputation slipped out the door on the whispering winds, he sat and decided to change the subject. 'Anyway, ya said, ya have a message for me? Well, here I am.'

'This filthy inn is not very private, maybe we should—'

'Go up to my room?'

Her eyes dilated, and she stared into an empty space. Ammo doubted she was reading the minds of people in the inn. He knew Chashmalim could transcend limits of space and time to communicate their thoughts with another. No, she was reading with someone else.

He slapped his hand on the table. 'Anyone in there?'

'Oh sorry,' she replied. 'I was admiring your ring. Tell me how you came to wear it?'

He dropped his hand under the table. 'No ya weren't.'

Her head tilted and for a fleeting moment, he wondered if she saw his chamber of imprisoned thoughts. It had been so long since he'd delved inside he couldn't remember everything in there but figured she at least wouldn't run away screaming.

'All right,' she confessed. 'I had to ensure you are who I thought you were.'

'And to do that ya were reading with someone else? Someone who knows me? Who? What did ya tell him?'

'I told him you think you're a legend in your own lifetime, dress like a peacock, and that you desire to mate with me.'

'Well, I can't argue with the last one. Who were ya talking to?'

'Meciel. He sent me here to collect you. He said, it's time.'

❊ 13 ❊

Mirah drifted in and out of sleep for two days before she arose and made her way to the courtyard. When she arrived Neviah and Zeev were sparring. She saw no sign of Nate.

Zeev looked up. 'Ah, glad you could join us.'

'Are you all right?' Neviah asked. 'They said you were ill. I would have visited but—'

'I'm fine,' Mirah cut over her. 'Where's Nate?'

'He's away. But don't worry. He's left me in charge of your training.'

Zeev grinned and Neviah groaned.

'Do one lap around the courtyard whilst I find his replacement.' Zeev jogged off towards the barracks.

She set off to the edge of the courtyard, surprised to find Neviah running by her side.

'I'm sorry Mirah. I've been a fool. I didn't mean what I said on the veranda.'

'Can we talk about it later?'

'Yes, of course.'

'Do you know where Nate has gone?'

'No. When I came down, Zeev said he was away and that you'd be joining later.'

Neviah gave her the once over, scanning for signs of what ailed her. 'I was worried when you didn't show for days. Are you sure you're all right?'

'I'm fine, Nev.'

Zeev returned with a mousy, brown-haired man. His serious chiselled face focused on them as he crossed the courtyard carrying two long wooden staffs.

'This is Eliah.' Zeev said. 'He'll be training you until Nate returns.'

Eliah weighed her up, assessing her medium height, the reach of her arms and the strength of her slender frame.

'Shall we begin?' he asked, handing her a staff. 'I thought we could start with these?'

Mirah took the staff and Eliah showed her how to grip it in the palms of her hands. His staff crashing against hers sent shock waves up through her arms. He was strong and ruthless, full of lean muscle but nowhere near as toned as Nate. With each clash of wood against wood, she considered how much Nate had been holding back.

'Good. Don't forget to duck when the staff swings for your head.'

She ducked and blocked and soon fell into a rhythm. The staff felt like something she could handle with practice and training. A weapon, though not as deadly as a dagger or a sword where she could defend against an attacker and at least give her time to escape.

Mirah watched Eliah as he swung his staff towards her and noticed how he dropped his guard now and then. She defended his blows and waited, then when he dropped his guard she swept her staff wide aiming for his right side. She'd been wrong. The strike took her off balance. Eliah pivoted bringing his staff across her left arm. The blow sent waves of pain ricocheting through her shoulder.

'Never underestimate your opponent,' Eliah said, his face stern and serious. 'I think we'll leave training there today.' He bowed and strode off to the barracks.

Mirah rubbed the back of her neck as she walked to the fountain. Her arm throbbed, and she knew she'd have a nasty bruise. If Eliah had taught her one thing, it was to never assume weakness in a rival.

'He's a good fighter,' Zeev said, arriving at the fountain. 'He'll do his best to get you as prepared as he can by the time Nate returns.'

'When will that be?'

'I don't know. A month maybe more.'

Mirah reeled inside. She ached to ask Zeev where Nate had gone but decided to wait and ask Galia.

As though she'd heard her name on the wind, Galia strolled out of the chasm.

'Glad you're finally up and awake,' she said, breezing towards them. 'I thought we'd try something different today.'

Galia smiled at Zeev who responded with a grin of his own. If Mirah didn't know better, she'd have suspected in Nate's absence they were conspiring against her.

Neviah muttered, 'I have to go. I'll catch up with you later.'

'What you're not even going to give me a wave goodbye?' Zeev called after her.

Neviah raised her hand but instead of a wave, she opted for a rude gesture.

'I'm in love,' Zeev said.

'You're always in love,' Galia mocked, and without waiting for a reply she slipped her arm under Mirah's. 'Come, I want to show you something.'

They passed through the city until they came to prodigious stone steps descending towards a small circular arena.

'It's a Diatheatre. We're early because I wanted to get the best seats.'

'What happens here?'

'Wait and see.'

They sat at the front in the centre and soon crowds of beautifully adorned women filed down over the steps. When they were all seated a man with a countenance as regal as his purple robes walked out onto the arena. Around benevolent hazel eyes, his skin creased and each crooked line on his face hid a multitude of mysteries which begged to spill forth their wisdom.

Silence swayed through the crowd and when it reached the centre of the arena, the man sang. His voice caused a symphony of immeasurable yearning as sorrow and joy wound its way amongst the crowd. Each note awakening visions of beauty and harmony; the splattering of rain on dry ground, floating pollen caught up in the air, new life, offering glimpses of who they could be. Memories both sharp and delightful, once hidden, now surfacing, revealing the shapings of their destinies.

Light filled Mirah's mind, her hand gripped the stone seating. It was the only reminder that she wasn't actually flying. She felt herself drifting into a realm where words have no meaning. A place where only expression exists. A place where dreams and despair collide and you gain understanding, for the briefest of moments before it releases you.

How long she had sat there, she didn't know. When she roused, the Diatheatre was empty, with only Galia sat beside her.

'How long?' she asked. She glanced into Galia's eyes and found them as glossy as her own.

'As long as you needed.'

'I've never heard anything like it.'

'No one has outside of this place.'

'His voice it sounds like… I don't know how to express it.'

'We call him the Fallen Star. How do you feel?'

'I feel strange, a mixture of heavy and weightless.'

'It's a strange feeling when the voice of your enemy becomes your saviour.'

Is that what this was? A glorious voice in the midst of everything strange and unfamiliar sending a healing balm to guide her through places unknown, to reach down into the void within her and create a new melody of her own.

'How come only women visited the Diatheatre?'

Galia chuckled. 'The men around here are too thick skinned to have their emotions pampered or so they'll tell you.'

Mirah contemplated what Gabe and his friends would have made of the Fallen Star's preternatural singing and concluded they would have accused her of being soft. She still missed him but somehow thoughts of Gabe no longer ripped inside her. The knowledge that he'd be all right cushioned her sense of loss.

'How often does he sing?'

'Every morning.'

'Do you think we could come again? Could we bring Neviah?'

'Of course. Come on, I'm starving, let's find something to eat.'

Galia bought oranges, and they sat by the edge of the river not far from Nate's ship. A longing, coiled tight in her stomach, opened its eyes.

Galia threw her an orange and asked, 'What do you want to do this afternoon? I wondered if you'd like to see the city.'

Mirah glanced up from peeling her orange. 'You're not attempting to distract me are you?'

With a tentative smile, Galia replied, 'I don't know what you mean.'

They sucked on the citrus juices and watched Nate's crew leaning over rubbing oil into the ship's deck. Galia flung her peel into the river and little fish came up to nibble and inspect it.

'We should discuss what happened at the lake. There's no point in avoiding it.'

Galia peered around before whispering, 'Not here.'

Mirah rose. 'I have questions.'

They strolled along the riverbank until they were far away from the crowds. Mirah recalled Galia and Nate's conversation after she'd lifted the lake's rock bed. She had so many questions and wanted to apologise if she'd hurt her but how much could she ask or say without Galia realising she'd been listening?

When they were a safe distance away she asked, 'Where is Nate?'

'Someone killed Zamani, he was Shemyaza's firstborn son. Shemyaza ordered Nate, Bishnor, Esha and others to find them and seek retribution.'

'Oh.'

It was all she could say. Inside, she battled a tangled web of emotions, their sinewy threads threating to immobilise her. Call it denial, she didn't care and told herself, he would come back.

'My sister, Arella, is with them.'

'I didn't know you had a sister. I thought when you told me about your family that you had been left alone. You must be distraught?'

'Not really. You saw her move like a tornado in the Taphas chamber. She's difficult to assault when she's whirling through the air.'

Mirah hopped over a slimy pebbled brook flowing towards the river. 'What about Nate?'

Galia skipped after her. 'Trust me, he has his own devices.'

'I thought you said Shemyaza brought peace?'

'He has within our borders but others still refuse to bend to his will. Nate believes in an old prophecy which says one day men will gather under thunder and then we'll descend into war but don't tell him I mentioned it. It's best to keep that to yourself.'

'Under thunder? What does that mean?'

'I don't know. I'm not sure anyone does.'

Mirah glanced around to check no one was nearby. 'Before he left, Nate said I was different, and nobody has ever wielded water and rock before. I've been thinking that the best way to protect myself is to understand how wielding works and what I can do. I don't want to shy away from it. Although I'll never use wielding in war, I'd like to help my friends if needed. Will you help me?'

'Are you sure?'

She was certain Shemyaza would expect her to wield this power. If she didn't gain control, it had the potential to hurt others and that was something she refused to allow. Mirah nodded.

'Then yes.'

They followed the river's flow away from the city and stopped at a river bend where riffles flowed over smoothened stones by the water's edge. Marsh reeds shrouded the area and gave a good view if any fishing boats came near.

'This is a good place,' Galia said. 'What I want you to focus on is controlling the rock and the water. First see if you can lift the smaller stones, balancing them one on another and then guide the water around them.'

Mirah calmed herself and focused on a tiny stone. She willed it to lift onto a dark red stone protruding out of the water.

'Good, now add another and focus on keeping them balanced. That's it. Now push the water and make it flow either side, not allowing it to touch the stones and hold the water at bay until the stones dry.'

'Really?' Mirah asked, raising her brow.

Galia came around to inspect her progress. 'When they're dry, add another stone. Find a large flat one. I want you to keep them balanced until I say let go.'

Mirah spotted a wide flat stone on the other side of the riffles and dragged it forward whilst holding the others stacked like a small tower. The stack wobbled when she gently wielded the flat stone into the air and balanced it on top of the others.

'I have an idea. See if you can force an airflow and knock down the stack?'

'But I can't wield air.'

'How do you know unless you try?'

She peered around, but all she saw was the river, the trees and marsh reeds. 'How do you grasp hold of air, exactly?'

Galia shrugged. 'Not sure.'

'Well, air wielding would be a lot easier if I could see it.' She looked again as though she was expecting the air to show its face and appear.

'Don't rely on your sight, feel it.'

Mirah focused on the breeze surrounding her and imagined its shape, the way the air curled and wisped. She didn't understand how air traversed this way and that but she somehow sensed a wisp and gripped it hold.

Air cleaved to air and gathered in strength, the wisp growing stronger and stronger. When she thought she had enough, she released her hold, and the air snapped forwards. The stones flew apart. The middle stone skipped across the surface of the river with such force it almost reached the other side.

'You know what this means?' Galia said, her eyes widening.

She stared at Galia's beaming face and her suspicion rose in defence.

'Fire,'

'No.'

'You have to at least try.'

Mirah faced away from her.

'Spoilsport.'

Mirah picked the up a large red stone, twisting it in her hand. 'What would happen if others found out?'

'I dread to think. Esha for sure would see you as a terrible threat. A potential rival for her position. She might make a move against you whilst she has the advantage against your inexperience. Most Wielders would prefer you standing beside them on the battlefield.'

'I told you I won't fight.' Mirah dropped the stone and water splashed over her dark leather pants.

'Someday you might not have a choice,' Galia muttered but Mirah still heard.

⁂

The day had been sweltering and Mirah wanted nothing more than to sink into her warm pool but as she returned to her chamber Neviah's door was ajar.

There was no getting around it, even if she darted past, her shadow would betray her. She peeked inside and found Neviah sat at a table eating.

Her room was similar to hers except decorated in shades of green with painted dragonflies and ladybirds on the plastered walls. She breathed in the aroma which smelt of smoked root vegetables and earthy herbs.

'Hungry?' Neviah asked and tossed her a flatbread.

Mirah crossed the room and slumped down on the edge of Neviah's bed. 'Your room is nice.'

'I'm getting used to it. The hot water in the pool is pleasant.' Neviah finished slurping her meal and offered her a cooled plum juice.

'Are you sure you are all right? What I said on the veranda the other day—I didn't mean it.'

'It's all right. I understand,' she said, taking a sip. 'How is your training?'

The bed sunk as Neviah sat beside her.

'I've grasped the basics. Ninsun and Ninkurra are kind but I can't stand being cooped up in the Taphas cavern with Shayla. What makes it worse is she's better than me. How about you?'

'Galia showed me how to create a water bird and on the east side of the mountain there are waterfalls cascading into many pools, I spend most of my time freezing them.'

'A water bird, how fascinating. Can you show me?'

'What now?'

Neviah nodded.

'But you heard what Esha said.'

'What harm can a water bird do here? She'll never know.'

Neviah lifted her hand and a small flame flickered on her palm. 'I've been practising each night. No one has come for me yet.'

'How does wielding fire work?'

Neviah closed her palm extinguishing the flame. 'I don't know.' She shimmied up the bed and rested her back against the wall. 'The fire just happens. Sometimes, I'm not sure if it's me doing it.'

'If I ask you something will you promise not to laugh or think I'm strange? I don't trust anyone else.'

Now she was here, Mirah wasn't sure how to phrase it. She'd recited and practised what to say but whatever way she'd framed it made her sound foolish. Fool or not, she had to know and Neviah was the only Wielder she trusted.

'The Fire. Have you ever heard it talking to you?' She could tell by Neviah's vacant expression that she hadn't. 'I mean not an actual voice speaking, more an impression of something and though you don't hear it you understand its meaning. It's hard to explain but when I was with Galia the other day, I sensed something urging me forward, faster than I was ready to go.'

'Maybe it's your fears playing tricks with your mind?'

Mirah glanced at the ring on her finger. 'Maybe. I guess you're right. I mean I haven't heard it since.'

Neviah stretched and leaned over placing her empty cup on a table beside her bed. 'I saw Abela today. She arrived with those vulgar looking Azu. One of the Earth Wielders dropped a rock and injured her ankle.'

Mirah looked up to see Neviah plumping up her pillow. 'How is Abela?'

'Now she's healed, her complexion looks rosy. Although I can't believe she enjoys wearing that ridiculous Azu frilly fashion wear. The light green suits her though.' She threw a pillow halfway down the bed, shifted forward onto her stomach and rested on her elbows. 'Abela said they are learning a strange language and spend most of their time mixing herbs.'

Neviah lay across her bed with her raised ankles swinging in the air. 'Do you ever wonder what would have happened to Huldah if she'd survived?'

'She probably would have wielded air and become a great spy. I keep asking about Dara but no one wants to talk about the Chashmalim. It seems if you mention them everyone becomes afraid and goes silent.'

Mirah told Neviah about Shayla and the nasty comments she'd made. As she spoke Neviah's legs stopped swinging and her lips pursed.

'I don't care what she says, Zeev's a good man.'

Mirah couldn't believe she'd complimented him. She'd never mentioned anything positive about any of them, not on the journey here and not since arriving.

As if Neviah hadn't noticed her shocked face she continued, 'And besides Shayla is nothing but a bitch and a liar. I wouldn't put it past her to have made up that story about meeting Nate in the garden.'

'Do you think so?' Mirah asked, struggling to read her eyes.

'He admires you.'

She resisted the temptation to clasp hold of her necklace. 'He's just helping us.'

'Yes well, you obviously don't see the way he admires you when you are sparring. I swear he would *help* you until his heart stops. The way his eyes linger over you. I wish someone from home had gazed at me that way. Do you realise, I don't know what it feels like to think about someone like that?' She let out a deep sigh. 'He's not trying to *help* us Mirah, he trying to save you. And as much as I see his determination, I still hate him for bringing us here and for everything else he's done. Sometimes, I want to hate you and have to remind myself that you haven't forgotten. But then, it's not like we're going home is it?'

'He said he was sorry for what happened at Barakel.'

There it was, the words were finally out. She expected Neviah to shriek, rage and pull on her braid, but instead, she lay still in silent contemplation.

'You know the girl you asked about, the one who replaced Huldah? He found a job for her in the kitchens.'

Neviah's mind ticked over and she had to remind herself to breathe.

'I will never trust him,' she said, after a long silence. 'There's something I'm not seeing. Sometimes I wonder if he hates this place as much as I do and then I remember what he's done. Mirah, please listen. Just because he desires you, doesn't mean he's right for you. I get it, he makes you feel safe, but that's not enough. Use his fondness for you against him. Allow him to train us and make us stronger. When the times is right we must be ready to escape. Aside from the obvious something strange is going on here and I can't put my finger on it yet.'

Mirah knew Neviah wouldn't let it go. She'd keep searching until she found the truth and when she did, she'd tell her. She also knew Neviah would never see beyond her blind hatred towards Nate.

'I want you to come somewhere with me. Galia will arrange it with the Taphas. There's someone I'd like you to hear.'

'Who?'

'They call him the Fallen Star.'

❊ 14 ❊

After journeying many days, jagged rock formations pierced up through the scorching sand. Like abandoned watchtowers, they loomed over a dry, cracked, riverbed. One that come autumn would flow and meet The Buranuna River to the south.

A behemoth of storm grey rock, shaped like a monstrous spine guarded the pass to the oasis. Thirty giants, twenty guardsmen and six Wielders converged near its entrance. Nate instructed Bishnor to organise several of the giants to take first watch.

The guardsmen along with the Wielders dismounted and led their camels through the pass to a clear turquoise pool. If any had questioned the absence of Water Wielders whilst crossing the desert plains, none dared voice it aloud.

After quenching his thirst, Nate sat in a slim slither of shade under a palm tree and contemplated his strategy for when they'd reach Anat. Men would die. He'd have to make a show, as Shemyaza had ordered but he needed to come up with a plan before Bishnor or Esha expected their orders.

Relieved that she was here, he watched Arella slipping off a pale blue veil, revealing braided silver-grey hair, a darker shade than her sister's. He couldn't remember who was older but looking at her, the way she moved with grace and wisdom, he assumed Arella was older than Galia if only by a couple of years. She leaned by the pool patting water along the side of her neck.

He felt Esha's presence, even before she strutted in front of him and blocked his view of the pool.

'How do you expect us to reach Anat without Water Wielders?' She fumed. Heat radiating off her like a shimmering mirage.

He'd commanded her to gather three Fire Wielders, one Earth and one Air without explaining their destination. If she'd known, she would have insisted Galia come along.

'We'll manage.'

She glowered at him, trying to work out his angle. 'I knew you were an idiot, but I never thought you'd be as foolish as this.'

Nate gave her a seductive smile infuriating her more. They still had several more days in the desert. He'd been foolish but he couldn't risk leaving Mirah without Galia to guide her.

'Maybe, I still like to see you sweat,' he said, faking a flirtatious gaze which flowed over the curves of her body. His eyes might have appeared hungry, but inside he suppressed the gag rising in the back of his throat.

Esha's long henna hair caught up in the breeze and her eyes snapped to his. He matched her glare, noting the swirling pools of amber fury threatening to scorch him to the bone.

'What are my orders?'

'I haven't decided yet.'

She stormed off.

After he'd eaten he searched out Bishnor and found him sitting on a smooth boulder, sharpening the edge of his sword. Zamani lay beside him running his barbed tongue over the remaining flesh and bones of an indistinguishable lizard. Nate preferred to ignore him, unsure if Zamani realised that Nate understood who this chimeric beast was.

'New blade?'

Bishnor never raised his head to see Nate's thin smile. He continued sliding the sword edge along the whetstone and then angled the blade, inspecting its sharpness.

'Blacksmith said he needed more time but if you ask me, this one is better than the one I lost.'

Nate gave a dismissive shrug, ordered him to rotate the giants on watch every two hours and to spread the word that from now on they'd be travelling at night.

They spent the afternoon resting under shade wherever they found it. Arella wielded a cooling breeze now and then. By early evening,

Esha gravitated towards Bishnor. By the sounds of their laughter, Nate supposed she had a new target in mind. It didn't surprise him.

He wondered if she'd ever suspect the beast laid beside Bishnor was Zamani in a chimeric form. Would Bishnor ever tell her? He dismissed the thought. Bishnor had more spite than to play fair.

Heat transmitted through the camel's heavy fur provided little warmth against the freezing nights. Each night as they travelled he yearned for sunrise only to regret its scorching approach. So did the desert rats as they abandoned their foraging quests to return to the safety of their shaded nests.

They avoided the heat of the day sheltering as best they could. He tried to push Mirah's abilities from his mind and focus on the task at hand. Untested and untrained, he knew Galia would do everything to protect her from exposure but knowing this didn't stop the gnawing ache.

Before dawn on the last day, the desert broke into marshland and they dismounted near a small river to the south of Anat. Nate ordered them to make camp. When dusk descended, he gave Arella a brown cloak and instructed her to scout ahead.

He took her to the side and whispered, 'When you reach Anat, tell them to leave enough men. I don't want the others becoming suspicious that they've received a forewarning.'

Arella made to the boundary of their camp before a whirlwind of air carried her away.

She returned a few hours later and reported to Nate who sat with Bishnor and Esha going over their plan of attack.

'Eight guard posts protect the city. Four to the south, two east, and two west. Their remaining men are stationed in a garrison near the bay.'

'How many?' Bishnor asked.

'Less than expected. I presume most were killed by Zamani and his forces.'

Her eyes darted upwards and to the left and Nate saw her lying tell. The others, too busy discussing the way forward didn't notice. Nate gave her a slight nod.

'Bishnor, you take the chimera and twenty of the giants and attack from the east.

Make for the garrison once you've taken out the guard posts.' Nate figured by keeping Bishnor and Zamani together it at least kept the carnage in one place. 'Esha, leave one Fire Wielder and Arella with me. Take the remaining Wielders and giants and come from the west. I'll bring the men up from the south. Do not wield fire to take out the guard posts. We don't want them raising the alarm before we arrive. Once we've secured the guard posts to the south, I'll send a signal to attack.'

Esha and Bishnor gathered their units and footsteps squelched in the marshy floodplains as they left. Zamani stalked ahead of them, his spikey tipped tail twitching in anticipation and his serrated edged fangs grinding with revenge.

'Thank you,' Nate said to Arella. 'What else?'

She glanced over to see those who remained busy checking their weapons and then sat. 'I spread the rumour of our impending arrival through the taverns and then followed as it swept throughout the city. They're not leaving.'

'Why not?'

'They've dug tunnels under their dwellings to hide their women and children.'

Nate cursed. 'When the fires begin, they'll be smoked out.'

'I can wield most of the smoke away.'

'Can you push their scent from the chimera as well?'

'I'll do my best,' Arella answered.

Rising, he said, 'Let's get this over with,' and beckoned the others to follow his lead.

Nate covered his head under the hood of his blue cloak and reached for his twin blades sheathed across his back. When they reached the first guard post, Arella pulled the air from the guards' lungs. Men clutched their throats unable to cry out, suffocated and dropped to their deaths. Quick and quiet they made their approach to the other three guard posts before Nate instructed the Fire Wielder to send a flare in the air.

They descended on the city of Anat from the south, east and west. Fire Wielders set alight everything in their path and death's amber glow lit up the city.

Zamani had taken flight, his golden wings soaring in the firelight before he dove with slaughtering strikes of vengeance on the men who'd defeated him before. Nate's men and giants slashed their way through the city.

Whenever Arella sensed tunnels under buildings, she encouraged fires to burn whilst pushing smoke high in the air until nothing but the sizzling heat of embers remained. She ran from one building to the next, forcing pure air into the tunnels beneath as she passed.

Nate didn't search men out but when they came at him or Arella, he gave them the one thing he could, a quick death with the edge of his curved blades. He made his way towards the garrison and found Bishnor and the giants, shields raised high to protect themselves from a hailstorm of arrows.

Metal clashed against metal. The aroma of blood and burning flesh sang through the surrounding air, mingling with the shrieks of dying men. The Earth Wielder arrived, and the ground shook beneath Nate's feet before the walls of the garrison collapsed.

Bishnor and the giants surged forward over the rubble and a wave of gigantic, muscled flesh tore into garrison soldiers who to their credit did not flee.

Nate spied Esha and yelled, 'Go to their ships, burn them all.'

Zamani swooped and grabbed his rotting head and followed after her.

Before sunrise, the attack was over with one building left standing amongst the debris and ash. Painted on its wall was a large flowering tree with all kinds of winged beasts surrounding it and some had human faces. The beasts were similar to Shemyaza's chimera but at the same time unfamiliar. He couldn't place the difference which unnerved him.

Nate hesitated before walking up to it. 'Send out your leader or we will burn you all.'

A door opened, and a man dressed in a white robe with a woollen weaved belt paused at the top of the steps.

'Come,' Nate said, walking towards him.

The aged man had a small hump deforming his shoulders. He surveyed his devastated city and the waiting giants and Wielders standing on the far edge of the stone plaza. He stumbled down the steps and staggered before Nate's feet.

'What is your name?'

With the back of his hand, the man wiped the sheen above his top lip.

'Danel,' he replied, in a whisper.

Nate understood the name meant, god judges. As he looked into the man's downturned, brown eyes he wondered which god the man served and if he judged wisely.

He lowered his head to the man's ear, 'I hope your god receives you. Tell me what is his name?'

'He has many unspoken names though some call him the Cloud Rider.'

'When you meet him, tell him, I had no choice.'

Danel's eyes flicked towards Nate's, a shadow of understanding whispered on his withered face.

'A quick death is all I can give you. I wish I could do more.'

Deep and enduring forgiveness emanated from Danel's gaze. Nate took a step back, he considered ways to show mercy but knew in his heart if he didn't kill him Bishnor would break Danel apart.

'Wait for him, his voice is like thunder,' the old man called out to those remaining inside the building.

Danel had answers, answers to questions Nate had been searching for but time had stretched as far as he could allow without raising suspicion. The man closed his eyes in silent affirmation.

'For the death of Zamani,' Nate shouted, 'and as a testimony to Shemyaza's power.' Nate swirled around and caught Zamani's eye before turning back to the old man.

He swung his blade, sliding it through the old man's neck with a clean break. Before his severed head hit the ground Nate turned to leave the city. He had to get away, not only because he hoped survivors hid beneath his feet but because with each moment he stayed, guilt and shame rose up to ensnare him.

'What about those left inside? Do you want me to burn them?' Esha asked.

Nate held in a breath. 'No. Shemyaza said to leave a remnant alive.

❊ 15 ❊

‘Today we’re going to try something different,’ Galia said. ‘To do so, we need to travel a greater distance, far from prying eyes.’

Her usual neutral grey eyes held a hint of excitement which reminded Mirah of a child about to receive a grand prize. It was early morning, and near to the lapis lazuli archway labourers had cleared the foundations of a derelict temple.

‘What god lived there?’ Mirah asked, passing sweat covered labourers wearing dusty leather skirts.

‘Don’t remember,’ Galia answered.

‘You approve of the temple’s destruction?’

‘They never served me well.’

Mirah thought she sensed subdued pain in Galia’s confession. She waited for her to continue.

‘They are building a new baking house. I think that will serve me better.’

They crossed through the city heading towards the river. Galia set a quick pace and Mirah rushed to keep up. Down by the river a reed boat big enough for two rested on the sand.

Galia pushed it into the water. ‘Get in. The quicker we arrive the more time we’ll have to practice.’

The boat sped through the water as Galia wielded a wave behind them.

They travelled until they were far from the city. Swaying fields of wheat shimmered golden in the distance. Galia wielded the reed boat to the river edge and then they dragged it up the bank. The wheat fields were as high as Mirah’s shoulders.

‘You’ll need to duck so your head doesn’t bob over the fields but this is the best camouflage I could muster,’ Galia said, sitting down. She rummaged in her bag and pulled out an apple.

'What are you expecting me to do?'

'Wield air, move yourself through the wheat field.'

'How?'

'How do you expect me to know, I wield water.'

Mirah stood at the threshold of the wheat field. For ages she watched the wheat leaning over against the breeze.

'What are you waiting for?' Galia asked, lying down. 'The sooner you grasp this the sooner we can find some entertainment.'

Mirah paced along the edge of the field, stepped inside the wheat and then back out. She wielded small stones into the air, brushed the breeze against Galia's hair but for all she tried she couldn't wield herself.

'Come on. This is disappointing and rather boring. I was hoping you would have learned this before Nate's return. I'd love for you to air wield him to the ground.'

'Really?'

'Of course, someone needs to knock his self-assured ass down.'

Mirah smiled to herself, facing away from Galia. She would love to see his face if she did and it would serve as justice for his absence.

'Are you sure you don't know how this works?'

'No clue. Just imagine he's standing on the other side of the wheat calling you?'

'Why would that bother me?'

Galia laughed from behind her. 'Well, if it didn't, you'd be the first pretty girl who didn't wonder what it would be like to be in his arms.'

'Have you?'

She nibbled the last of the apple core's flesh and discarded it over her shoulder. 'Never and before you ask I have my reasons.'

'Do you prefer women?'

'No. Come on, it can't be that difficult. Close your eyes, imagine. He's waiting on the other side of the wheat. His onyx hair tussled in the breeze, his gorgeous blue eyes searching, it's so hot he takes off his shirt. Think of his splendid physique ready to embrace you. If you reach him, he'll lower you to the floor, his body on you, moving. You're all he's ever wanted. He whispers your name as he caresses you and you want him to make you…'

Mirah shot through the air into the wheat field.

‘Close your mouth. Keep your head down,’ Galia called after her.

At first, the wheat whipped her face but after a while, she managed to part it just ahead of her. How could Galia know what she’d been thinking? Around and around she sped in exhilaration. She was free in those moments, outracing all that wished to apprehend her. Shouts of abandonment carried on the wind and she realised it was her. She wanted to go further, faster, but the wheat hedged her in.

‘There will be no wheat standing if you continue,’ Galia’s voice echoed on the breeze.

Mirah circled the wheat field once more and returned. ‘That’s the most thrilling experience I’ve ever had,’ she said, taking a breath.

‘You have obviously never been intimate.’

Mirah blushed. ‘What you said before and me taking off so fast, it had nothing to do with Nate.’

Galia chuckled. ‘Of course not. Had to say something to get you moving. I figured embarrassment would do the trick. Even so, I still want you to put him on his butt. He should be back in a couple weeks which gives you plenty of time to practice and gain control so he isn’t aware. Come on, I’m hungry. I know this nice little place to eat.’

On reaching the boat, Galia said, ‘You can wield us back. Balance the water and the air together. I doubt anyone will notice if you take it slow.’

The reed boat cut through the swell at an even pace. Steering took practice but by the time they reached the city, Mirah had almost stopped it zigzagging.

Galia led her to a large tower building with a seated courtyard.

‘The food here is excellent. I recommend the pigeon.’

The pigeon was delicious and Galia insisted they stuck around to listen to the musicians. She bought them beer and settled back to listen. Two men, one with a lyre and another with reed pipes began their ballad. The music was a rhythm of plucking notes and a haunting pipe melody. The lyre player began his song. His deep voice sounded flat compared to the Fallen Star, and he sang in a language unknown.

Mirah drifted into the rapture she’d experienced whilst flying through the wheat. She came out of her daydream and found people in the courtyard had moved closer to the entertainers, and the crowd swayed with the music’s rhythm.

'What's it like?'

Galia sipped her beer. 'What is what like?'

'Being with a man?' She shrugged. There was no one else to ask. Neviah didn't know and something Galia had said earlier had her interest peaked.

'My first was a disaster. A selfish lover. He was only concerned with his own needs. But then I was fortunate to learn that a true lover offers more than his flesh. A true lover is unafraid to give you all of himself, every essence of his being. There is nothing purer than that kind of joining. It is hot, ecstatic, intoxicating and you lose yourself in it, in each other. It's a moment you never wish to end and a moment you hold on to all your life.'

'How do you tell the difference before you… well, you know?'

'The one who ceases the arguments between your head and your heart. If you find that one, then you'll know.'

'That's so sweet,' Shayla sniggered. 'Missing your Captain are you Mirah?'

'Push off Princess,' Galia snapped raising her arm to reveal her amethyst amulet.

'Better set your sights lower,' Shayla said, before rolling her hips out of the courtyard.

'How did you know she was a Princess?'

'I didn't, I've never seen her before and don't you listen to her. The one who gives his heart to you would never look twice at her. You will become his anchor and he will become yours.'

After many weeks of training with Eliah, a network of bruises, ranging from deep shaded purples, musty greys and fading yellows covered Mirah's flesh. Not once did Eliah draw in close enough to touch her. He circled around swiping her with his staff whenever she dropped her guard.

Since attending the Diatheatre each morning to listen to the healing balm of Fallen Star, Neviah's spirits were lighter. Zeev jibed at her saying she was going soft. Mirah watched as Neviah feigned to the left before hitting him across the nose with her elbow, just to remind him how soft she really was. Zeev responded with a chuckle and gazed at her in admiration before lunging into another manoeuvre.

She left them to spend the day in the wheat fields and returned at dusk and in need of her soothing pool.

It was late when a small ball of ice materialised above her head.

From behind her chamber door, Galia suppressed a laugh. 'If you don't let me in, I'll melt it and drop it on your head.'

Mirah giggled as Galia entered her room smiling.

'I hoped to catch you awake. I couldn't wait to tell you there's going to be a celebration tomorrow evening. I wondered if you'd like to buy a new dress?'

'I've never purchased…. What I mean is, all I have ever owned is what myself and the others from my clan made.' She picked up her comb and brushed it through her hair. 'I don't have any silver.'

'Of course, you do. Hasn't anyone explained that you get paid for your service to Shemyaza?'

She paused the comb midway through her hair. 'You're teasing?'

Galia's smile turned into the widest grin. 'I know this wonderful place.'

Placing the comb onto her table, she asked. 'What are we celebrating?'

'Oh, you haven't heard? Nate and the others will return tomorrow. It seems their mission was a success.'

'How do you know? Is he all right?'

'He's fine. My sister became impatient. I bet she nagged him for days on the way back until he agreed to let her go on ahead.'

After Galia left, Mirah slipped into bed and knew sleep would not claim her.

❊ 16 ❊

'I can't wear this,' Mirah cried. 'What was I thinking.'

'Don't be silly,' Sumer said. 'You are beautiful.'

'But it's too revealing. I should never have listened to Galia.'

The dress was made of a palest green flowing silk, with a diaphanous tulle overlay embellished with silver and gold stars. The sleeves were cut longer than she'd seen other women of Hermonial wear but the translucent green sheer and its gold and silver embroidery worked well to hide most of her bruises. Except for the back where from the neckline to the waist the fabric was non-existent.

Galia had convinced her not to worry, ensuring her showing flesh was not an issue here but now stood in the dress, she couldn't help feeling self-conscious.

From a band of gold cut high around her neckline, a train trimmed in gold sent a shimmering galaxy of stars flowing down over her bare skin and trailed behind her.

'Stop worrying,' Sumer replied, whilst sorting through an assortment of jewels in a grainy, dark wooden box. 'Besides, everyone will dress in their finery tonight.' Sumer held up a silver comb with five little stars sprinkled with diamonds. 'This one will compliment your dress.'

She braided one side of Mirah's hair, shaping it around to the nape of her neck. Leaving the other side free, her curls and waves spread over her shoulder and down her back. Sumer slid in the comb and withdrew. 'Spectacular.'

'Can you help me with this?' Mirah asked, handing Sumer her star necklace.

They met the tithes in a waiting chamber. The circumference of the chamber had a ledge carved into the rock which provided seating with sunflower yellow cushions arranged upon it. She spied Abela and Ayla sat with Neviah and rushed over to them.

'It's so good to see you,' she said.

Sumer stated someone would announce them in turn and to make their way to the front and present themselves to Shemyaza.

'Great,' Neviah grumbled.

'It wasn't too horrific last time,' Mirah offered.

As she caught up with Abela and Ayla, the chamber emptied until she was alone. She didn't know what felt worse, presenting herself before Shemyaza or the waiting to see Nate. She was so lost in her thoughts and she didn't hear the announcer. Sumer rushed in and ushered her out.

'Keep your head high and don't forget to bow.'

Mirah held on to her star pendant, exited the waiting chamber and gasped.

Hovering overhead, rotating gilded orbs adorned the spacious cavern. Sunrays emanating from the spheres, spread streams of light swirling down the golden steps and across the room. It was spectacular. She stood stunned out of motion. One orb paused and held her in its spotlight and her dress sparkled to life.

Stillness settled over the guests as she descended the steps and walked through the cavern towards Shemyaza seated on the dais.

To his left, Bishnor's fire opal eyes prowled over her and when she came closer, he let out a low deep-throated purr.

To Shemyaza's right sat a beautiful woman, an alluring glossy, green pendant hung low, tantalising the plunging neckline of her gown. They were a trio of refinement adorned in a raiment of golden hues. Where was Nate, Mirah thought as she bowed.

Sheltered under the curls of her hair she was aware of Shemyaza shifting his superior posture.

'You are from Barakel? Is that correct?'

'Yes,' she answered, raising her head but not meeting his gaze.

He snapped his fingers. 'I expect you to look at me when I'm talking.'

He regarded her with a gleam of entitlement and a confident smile. 'I can see life in Hermonial is suiting you well.'

She didn't dare look away and tried to focus on the centre of his wide forehead and square plucked eyebrows. 'It is not what I expected.'

'Yes well, expectations can be rather disappointing but the unexpected is often the most thrilling, don't you agree?' He didn't wait for her to reply. 'Due to my sovereignty and generosity, you'll find a lot of what you didn't expect here.'

His voice sounded cool and alluring.

She tried to resist the sense of him gliding over her, permeating her essence, searching for weakness, like a pebble she was submerged in his slippery stream.

'Barakel? Isn't that where the girl with the gift of Chashmal came from?' Shemyaza asked, whilst rubbing his thumb and index finger along the sides of his chin.

'Dara, her name is Dara.'

The woman beside Shemyaza uncrossed her legs and said, 'If she is anywhere near as beautiful and as gifted as you, I'm sure she could one day be my replacement.'

Sadness filled the woman's dark eyes and Mirah wondered if the idea of Dara as a replacement encouraged her.

At the woman's interruption, Shemyaza pursed his lips, and he tapped his fingers on his throne.

'Dumah is my first wife.' Shemyaza explained. 'She is mourning the loss of our firstborn son Zamani but she has come here today to celebrate my victory and revenge.'

Watching his impatience, Mirah quickly said to Dumah, 'I'm sorry for your loss.'

Dumah blinked but said nothing more.

Bishnor shifted in his seat and Shemyaza gave him a sideward glance. It was the first time Shemyaza had broken eye contact and Mirah took a chance to draw a long breath.

Shemyaza offered her a righteous smile and then continued.

'Bishnor told me of the incident at Barakel. It's a shame your clan attacked without giving my sons time to explain. If any had survived, I would have sent word of how well you fit in here.' His fiery eyes flared with expectation and he let his words hang in the air. 'Anyhow,

I'm sure Bishnor would like to compensate you for your loss. How about the first dance?'

'That's not necessary,' Mirah said, a little too quickly.

'I must insist,' Bishnor said, darting up from his seat and towering over her.

A row of giants and men gathered facing and their dancing partners. Not knowing how to refuse him, Mirah followed Bishnor to the end of the line.

As the music started, she accepted his outstretched hand. Deep callouses ridged along his rough palm and she had no doubt as softly as he held her own, his hand had the power to crush bones.

He was nothing like Nate. Nate's power and strength not only exuded from his physique but also from within. Bishnor relied on brute strength alone. His hands were a solid anchor of dominance refusing to let her go.

In height, she reached just below pectorals which spread across his brawny chest. He enjoyed the hunt, she could tell. He led her with practised ease through the steps. Every step was a predatory dance of skill and brawn. He was aware of everyone in the room and they skirted around him, no one daring to cross the boundary he set, not even the other giants.

As she turned, she scanned the chamber looking for Nate. What would he think if he saw her dancing with Bishnor? She didn't understand their relationship, but she'd noticed the tension between them.

'You seem a little distracted?' Bishnor claimed, as he lowered his arm and guided her into a spin.

'I don't know the steps.'

His fire opal eyes travelled over her body, assessing the curve of her hips and the outline of her frame. 'You dance well. Don't try to follow the others, I will lead you.'

He swung his arm around her waist and lifted her high in a spinning turn. As he did so, he drew her close and inhaled. A low groan seeped from his mouth as though he scented his prize and found it pleasing. 'See,' he said, tactfully placing her down.

This time he didn't glare right through her and what she saw was hunger so repulsive she took a step back. Awareness spread across his feline face and he licked his lips.

They separated like the snap of a bowstring. The music ended and Bishnor bowed.

Without waiting for him to rise, she said, 'Thank you for the dance,' and rushed away.

She spied Galia and forced herself not to run towards her. To her relief, Bishnor returned to his seat.

'Here,' Galia said, offering her a drink. 'You look like you need one.'

'Thanks.' Mirah took a sip and choked.

'Fermented plums,' Galia chuckled. 'Burns a bit. We call it Toka.'

'You could have warned me.'

'What would be the fun in that?' Galia laughed. She glanced over at Bishnor now seated on the dais and a look of alarm graced her face. 'Come, let me introduce you to my sister.'

Mirah would have asked Galia what unnerved her but knew in her heart the answer, she had caught Bishnor's attention. She followed Galia across the room to where the Taphas gathered, among them, Neviah stood talking with Ninsun and Ninkurra.

'This is Arella. Arella meet Mirah,' Galia said.

In the golden orb light, Arella's sleek silver hair shone as radiant as her smile. 'My sister has told me so much about you,' Arella said. 'I'm sure we are going to be such close friends. And what a beautiful dress.'

'Thank you. It's nice to meet you.' Mirah cast her eyes around the chamber.

Galia leaned towards her. 'He's not here.'

'He's not coming to his own celebration?'

Galia shrugged.

Mirah spied Abela and Ayla talking with Neviah. 'Would you excuse me? I'd like to catch up with my friends?'

'Of course,' Galia replied.

As much as she tried to focus on Abela and Ayla and their talk of the Azu, she was too distracted. Zeev strutted over and before she could ask him when Nate would arrive, he'd asked Neviah to dance and to Mirah's surprise, she'd accepted.

She found herself wandering around with another Toka in her hand. She sipped and watched Neviah and Zeev dancing. If you could call it dancing, to her it looked an awful lot more like their sparring.

Music filled the room and the sounds of laughter grew louder with each cup of Toka.

She turned to see Shayla sauntering towards her, a small group of tithes following in her path. As she neared, Shayla feigned a slight trip and poured her drink over the front of Mirah's dress.

'Oh, I'm sorry,' Shayla lied, with not an ounce of remorse in her catty voice.

Giggles erupted from behind her. Horrified, Mirah glanced at the wet stain spreading across her gown. She pushed past Shayla and ran.

'Mirah wait,' Galia called after her.

By the time she'd reached the edge of the chamber, Galia and Arella were at her side.

'Come with us,' Arella said.

Galia held her hand leading her through the tunnels before turning off into a smaller chamber. It was the obsidian glass garden. Mirah gripped her pendant, tears threatening to escape.

'We'll have this sorted in no time,' Arella said.

Galia wielded water from the fountain and purged the staining from Mirah's dress. 'See. I told you water is more useful than fire.' She smiled.

'What's up with that girl?' Arella asked as she warmed air against the green silk.

'That girl is Shayla and I don't know why but she doesn't like me.'

'Hmm,' Galia murmured.

'She reminds me of Esha,' Arella said. 'Like calls to like.'

'Esha?' Mirah asked.

'When we first arrived here, Esha was another tithe,' Galia explained. 'She soon became the most powerful among us and rose to lead the Taphas, under Nate's command of course.'

Seeing Mirah's dress was dry, Arella lowered her hand. 'She was and still is the bane of our existence. Nothing will satisfy her until she's reached the top, and it doesn't matter who she treads over along the way.'

'Remind me not to get on her bad side,' Mirah said.

'Oh, I believe it's too late for that.'

She was about to ask Galia what she meant when a shadow emerged on the wall and expanded. Mirah lifted her head to find Nate standing in the entrance.

'Neviah told me what happened. Are you all right?'

She could only nod for fear of her voice breaking.

'Will you leave us?' Nate asked Galia and Arella.

Everything in the room dissolved into shadow including Galia and Arella as Nate stepped closer.

'I'm sorry, I wasn't here to protect you from that harpy. I knew the moment she stepped aboard my ship that girl would be trouble.'

Mirah broke into something which resembled a mixture of laughing and crying. She tried to gather her composure. Shayla was a new breed of nasty, but nothing compared to Nate's absence. Relief washed over her. He was here.

'I don't need protecting from Shayla,' she countered.

'You don't?'

'Water Wielder, remember. If Galia and Arella hadn't assisted, I could have sorted my dress, eventually.'

'The dress is certainly something,' he said, his blue eyes warming as they took it in. His gaze spotted her star pendant, and he smiled. 'I'd liked to have seen you dancing.'

'I'm glad you didn't.'

He frowned but to her relief decided not to press further.

'Will you come with me? I'd like to show you something?'

They descended through the shaft and followed a tunnel leading out the other side of the mountain.

'I come here when the moon is as full as it is tonight,' he said, leading her outside.

A path cut through a garden towards a stream. They followed it as it wound between mossy green banks. It was the most beautiful garden she'd ever beheld.

The stream was ice clear. Its bed covered in crystalline textures, inspiring a kaleidoscope of prismatic fractals that flickered and danced in the moonlight. The trees were in full blossom, beautiful flowers hung like delicate pendants in colours she never knew existed.

She swirled around taking in the view. The moonlight caressed a lavender carpet of flowers, their heads lowering as they passed.

'Even the flowers bow before you,' he said, in amazement.

She heard the rushing sound but nothing could prepare her for the water falling from the sky forming the most spectacular waterfall. Resplendent sprays caught the moonlight and spread out before her creating an arcing rainbow mist.

They sat on a bench underneath a fountain of cascading green foliage and drooping, rose-coloured catkins.

Nate took a catkin and twirled it in his fingers. 'I didn't want to celebrate. I'm not proud of what I've done.'

Mirah turned her gaze from the waterfall. The pain on his face made her heart ache.

'You need to understand. All I have ever known is Shemyaza. He has been good to me. When we were securing our borders, it made sense to defend our own but now things are different.'

Nate twirled the catkin. Whatever he thought about lured him into silence. After some time, he looked up. 'I truly am sorry about your family. I couldn't do anything to prevent it.'

She studied him and understood he meant it. 'Why don't you leave.'

'He will never let me go. If I attempted it, he'd send someone or something to find me. His reach is too powerful.' Nate's shoulders sank in defeat. 'Do you realise he is immortal? His sons are half immortal too.'

'That doesn't make any sense. How can someone be half immortal?'

'Their flesh can die but not their essence. When their flesh perishes, the essence of who they are returns to Shemyaza and he transfers their spirits into his chimera. The beasts below your room, one of them is Zamani.' Nate lowered his head.

'How is that possible?'

'He has powers more than you know. I didn't want to go to Anat but I couldn't refuse. I sent Arella ahead to warn them. We saved some at least.' Nate shifted his foot on the ground. 'You must think I'm weak?'

'No. I know what it's like to lose control over my life. There must be a way to break free from him. Something we can do?' She rested her palm over his clenched fist pressing into the bench. It twitched as she touched him but he didn't relax it.

'If there was, I would have found it by now. I'm sorry Mirah. All I can promise is I'll keep looking and if I find it, I'll take you out of here.'

She wielded two tiny hummingbirds from the waterfall and let them hover in front of them. Their tiny wings, so beautiful and fragile fluttered so fast they blurred.

'Only you could turn a weapon into something wonderful,' he said leaning closer.

'We will find a way,' she whispered.

She watched the little birds and her heart raced as fast as their beating wings. He wasn't her enemy. Although everything was still the same inside something within her changed.

'Will you dance with me?' he asked, standing up.

She reached for his hand and said, 'Yes.'

He placed his hand around her waist, pulling her against his chest. He nuzzled into her hair, breathing her in.

'I missed you,' he whispered.

They swayed to the rhythm of the waterfall's sprinkling beats and the moon as it flew by reflected on the gold and silver stars on Mirah's dress.

'I've gazed at a multitude of stars, reflecting their beauty on numerous oceans and not until now have I ever felt one gaze back,' he said, as their eyes met. 'Never have I dreamed I'd be able to reach out and touch one.'

Nate brushed his hand across her shoulder. She flinched and he tensed.

'What is that?' he asked peering at her skin through the sheer fabric.

'It's just a small bruise.'

'Eliah, he hurt you?' His face turned grim. 'I will have him cleaning the latrines for the rest of his service and that's after I've taught him a lesson or two.'

His brazen warrior strength rising to the surface told her exactly what he intended to do.

'You will do no such thing. At least Eliah never held back,' she challenged with a half smile. 'Over the past few weeks, I've learned one or two tricks of my own. I'm getting pretty good with a staff, you know.'

'Really? Well, we'll see about that.' His countenance shifted revealing a wicked grin.

When he teased her a spark flickered to life in his smiling eyes and lit up his handsome face. He pulled her closer, taunting her with the challenge of what was to come. The smile he gave her ignited a spark of her own.

They swayed under the moonlight and danced to their heartbeats, his arms wrapped around her, soothing the bruises and the deeper scars within. She didn't mind if he saw them, they made her; they made her stronger.

A draft swept up her skin, and she shivered.

'We should go,' he said with reluctance. 'It's getting late. I suppose I should take you back.'

When they reached the shaft, Nate asked, 'Do you remember what I said to you the first time we ascended into the mountain?'

'No.'

He placed his hands on her hips and tugged her towards him. His breath was warm against her cheek. Her heart beat so fast; she was sure he could hear it. In the darkness, his lips met hers, so gentle as though he was searching to capture a smile. She felt herself tipping into another existence. He slid his hand up the nape of her neck and threaded his fingers through her hair. His tongue brushing against her lips, exploring, tasting, offering her a part of himself. Not knowing what to do otherwise, she followed his leading. Her lips parted, and she opened herself up to his advance and he groaned.

Every time she'd ascended into this darkness, she'd wished it would end. Now she dreamed it never would.

'I'll never kiss and tell,' he whispered.

He stepped forward pushing her with his hips up against the lattice reed barrier, pressing himself closer. His lips travelling down the side of her neck with soft kisses caressing her skin. They brushed along her collarbone sending a tingling sensation into her core.

If she could see him she knew he'd be smiling, acknowledging he'd stroked a weak spot she never realised she had.

⁂ 17 ⁂

Mirah stepped out of the chasm to find Nate sparring with Zeev, and the descending moonlight shimmering on the staffs in their hands. As she walked across the courtyard, she studied his mastery, his anticipation of Zeev's advances and the way he swivelled and dodged out of Zeev's way.

She'd underestimated his flexibility and skill. He raised his arms defending against Zeev's swing. Their staffs clashed together and Nate shoved his arms out forcing Zeev to roll onto his heels. He hadn't even broken into a sweat.

Looking up a coy smile anointed his face. 'So, no holding back,' he challenged.

'I'll try not to swipe that smile from your face,' she countered, taking the staff from Zeev.

'Fighting talk, I love it.' Zeev chuckled, backing off to spar with Neviah.

They circled slowly around each other, assessing their stances and the positioning of their staffs.

'You think you can take me?' Nate asked, his eyes shining with the prospect.

'Definitely.'

'Then show me what you've got,' he said, bringing the staff across her body aiming for her ribs.

Mirah blocked. She manoeuvred against his blows, getting the sense of his speed, his style. He was faster and stronger than Eliah but she could tell he still held back.

He circled for another attack and she wielded the sand beneath his feet just enough to unsteady his balance before slamming her staff across his side.

‘Impressive,’ he said, knowing what she’d done. ‘I can tell in my absence you’ve been putting other talents to good use.’

She returned his coy smile, ‘You have no idea.’

The full force of his toned body came at her and she wielded herself through the air. Not enough to gain notice but enough to give her an edge against his speed.

As they sparred, she wrapped the air around herself and propelled out of his advances. She wielded the air against him, forcing him to flex his muscles and spend his strength against the pressure slowing him down. Sweat glistened on his brow and she resisted the temptation to use that against him as well.

With increased determination he studied her, weighing her up, and for the first time, she realised he saw her as a worthy opponent. If he’d guessed she’d wielded air, his fixed steady composure never revealed it.

Neviah and Zeev stopped to observe their whirling blocks and blows and to her relief, she held her ground.

Nate cast a playful eye, ‘I see what you’re doing.’

She shrugged. ‘A girl’s got to have her own advantages.’

She parted her lips and for a moment she thought he’d drop his staff and kiss her. Years of training calmed his focus, and he switched into his next manoeuvre. He was so fast. She pushed air against his approach and wielded the sand at his feet. He crashed to the ground, her staff poised over his groin.

‘Do you yield?’

He stared up at her in admiration. ‘Every time.’

‘If I hadn’t seen it. I never would have believed it,’ Zeev said, coming over. ‘Do you realise what you’ve done?’ he said to Mirah. ‘Nate, I will never let you forget this.’ Zeev bellowed out a laugh.

Nate groaned as he pushed up off the ground.

‘How did you do that?’ Neviah asked.

‘I overreached,’ Nate said, deflecting Neviah’s question. ‘I slipped on the sand and she took advantage,’

Mirah glanced at Zeev’s wrinkled brow as they returned to their sparring.

When they were a distance away Nate said, ‘You never cease to astound me. Air?’ he questioned, in disbelief.

In answer, she sent a cooling draft to alleviate his moistened brow.

'You did well to disguise it. Zeev you can trust. I'll explain to him later but you must be careful, there's few you can trust around here.'

Footsteps crossing the courtyard took Nate's attention as one of his guardsmen marched towards them.

'Shemyaza has requested your presence,' he said.

Nate dismissed the man. 'This can't be good,' he said, brushing the sand from his clothes. He glanced at the chasm and hesitated.

'Just go. Galia will be here soon. We've got into a routine of listening to the Fallen Star every morning.' She leaned on her staff, letting it take her weight.

'The what?'

'He's a singer.'

'Never heard of him. Is he any good?'

She swooned at the memory of his healing melodies. 'There are no words to describe him.'

'If he's competition, maybe I should check him out?'

Wicked images of Nate squeezed between the crowds of women flashed through her mind. 'Maybe you should.'

He busied himself contemplating for a moment before saying, 'I have to go. Shemyaza doesn't tolerate waiting.' He brushed his hand against hers before leaving.

⁂

They rushed through the awakening city whilst listening to The Fallen Star's voice as it crescendoed over the ridge of the Diatheatre. The only remaining spaces were on the back row. Mirah sat between Galia and Neviah and shut her eyes.

She could hear the rocks crying out in silence, see the wind bowing in reverence and sense the deep spring waters beneath her lifting their attention.

His voice, the sound in which galaxies were made, pitched into an explosion within her heart. She felt the shackles releasing, her doubts and fears fading under the embrace of the Fallen Star's graceful harmony. She became lost in the space between ending and beginning.

When she opened her eyes, all the women sat silent, and the Fallen Star's robes swished as he was leaving the arena.

'He sends fire through my veins,' Neviah said, 'purging everything that existed before.'

'I know,' Mirah agreed.

She closed her eyes and remembered the heat coursing through her body when Nate kissed her and how his hand brushed against her skin through the backless dress as they traversed the tunnels to her room.

On reaching her door, he'd guided her back against the wall and leaned his arm above her head. In the torchlight, she'd witnessed the passion and desire in his ice-blue eyes. With no hesitation, he'd tilted her head, leaned and crushed his capturing lips on hers.

He'd pressed his tongue against her lips and as she'd parted her mouth to receive him, his tongue delved in exploring. He'd savoured every moment, sliding his other hand down the curve of her waist, stopping over her hips, caressing and coaxing her shivers.

The heat of his body compressed against her made her flush. She'd turned away to catch her breath. Mirah, he'd whispered and as he breathed her name, she'd closed her eyes and surrendered.

'You look different?' Neviah observed.

'I've seen that look,' Galia said, revelation dawning. 'He's kissed you.'

Neviah's head swung up for confirmation. 'What was it like?'

Whatever motive piqued Neviah's interest had nothing to do with Nate. She tugged on her braid, conflicted about wanting to know about kissing and hating the man who had offered it. Somehow she needed to convince Neviah that he wasn't the monster she thought him to be.

'It was like the stars descended from the heavens, and though I couldn't see them, I sensed every star tingling against my skin. If he hadn't held me, I'm sure dizziness would have sent me plunging to my death down the mountain shaft.'

'He kissed you in pitch blackness inside the shaft?' Neviah asked. 'How romantic.'

'Romantic indeed. Nate is full of surprises,' Galia said. 'When Esha finds out she is going to burst into flames.'

'Why should Esha care?' Mirah asked.

'Open your eyes Mirah. His body is the image of toned perfection, sculpted over years of loyal service. He's the Captain of Shemyaza's forces. Everyone except Bishnor and his followers adore him, would lay down their lives for him without question, though he'd never ask. Every woman in this city wants those cool blue eyes upon them and Esha had his gaze once but then lost it.'

'They were together?'

'It was a long time ago. I shouldn't have said anything. Even though she'd deny it, I know she regrets him slipping from her grasp.'

'Did he love her?'

'What they had was not love.'

They strolled back through the city and Mirah pondered over what Galia had told her. It was naïve of her to think Nate hadn't been with women. He was older and hadn't lived a life as sheltered as hers. What did this mean for her, for them?

She hadn't considered his expectations or where they might lead. Did he even realise she was a virgin? Maybe she should tell him, give him a chance to escape, to find someone more experienced.

Lost in her thoughts she stumbled into the back of a stranger and shunted him forwards.

'I'm sorry,' she said, reaching her arms out to stop him falling.

A flaring of dark purple robes swished as he regained his balance. It was the Fallen Star.

'And what pray tell is causing you such a distraction?'

Except for his silk robe, he wore the same tasselled fringe skirt and sandals that men of higher status wore and his hair and beard were oiled in the same way but he didn't belong. An enigma though she couldn't fathom out why.

Up close secrets simmered in his light hazel eyes but before she discerned them he blinked and locked them away. He gave a sympathetic smile and waited for her to respond.

'You sound nothing like you do when you sing.'

He let out a low laugh and deeper smile lines spread across his skin. She would have thought him old but those eyes and the secrets they held betrayed a glimpse infinite youth.

'No one before has been brave enough to mention that.'

'I'm sorry. I didn't mean to cause offence?'

'No offence taken. In fact, it's rather refreshing. What is your name?'

'Mirah.'

'Mirah from Barakel?'

'You've heard of me?' she asked in surprise.

'I have my ways, as I assume you have yours?'

'I don't understand?'

He lifted a worn wrinkled hand as if to brush away her question.

'Don't worry yourself with those thoughts you were entertaining. Everything has a reason, in its own time and right season. And besides, you're more dignified than I ever imagined. There is no one, not even Esha who can compare.' He stepped into the crowd and disappeared. Mirah stood, mouth open wide, gaping.

Neviah pushed through the throng of people, holding out a shawl she'd purchased. 'Come, they have others,' she said, gripping her arm. 'What's wrong with you, you look like you've just seen Nate dancing with Shayla?'

Neviah dragged her over to a cart. The seller thrust an arraignment of coloured shawls with pineapple shaped tassels at her. To stop his urging, she picked one and handed over a piece of silver. Thoughts tumbled through her mind. She needed to get away, she needed space and time to process them.

She found Galia running her slender fingers over lavender coloured silk fabric.

'Do you mind if we don't train today? There's something I need to do.'

Galia eyed her with suspicion. 'Would you like me to find you later?'

'I'll make my own way back. If that's all right?'

Galia made her promise not to drift over the timber bridge into the west side of the city, saying some of the clientele visiting the drinking and pleasure houses were less than desirable, and then agreed.

She purchased a pear from another vendor and meandered through the city in search of a quieter place to sit. The empire Shemyaza was building looked wonderful. And even more so were the people as she passed by them.

Acknowledging reverent smiles, even a few salutes reminded her she dressed in her Taphas wear. She realised the people here were grateful for their protection.

A little boy, no more than eight, with curly brown hair sprinted over and placed a small wooden carving in her hand. He bowed, said something in a language she didn't recognise then skipped away.

She opened her hand to see a little wolf which reminded her of Nuri which led on to thoughts of Gabe. She wished he was here and hoped that wherever he'd gone, he kept safe.

As much as the people accepted her, she couldn't shift the feeling of being watched. She glanced to the mountain. Against its blue skin, the openings in its rock face looked like a multitude of eyes. She quickened her pace until obscured by the nearest building.

Her feet crunched over pine needles on the way to the lake. Instead of creating an ice path, she circled around it. After finding a shady spot under a withered conifer she sat and ate her pear.

She contemplated her meeting with the Fallen Star. How had he perceived her hidden thoughts and known she came from Barakel? Who was he? His cryptic message about times and seasons and reasons hinted at something like destiny. Was destiny possible? Was everything part of some cosmic plan?

She refused to entertain the idea. If events were foretold, then whoever foretold them would have known the fate of Barakel and could have done something to prevent it.

But how had the Fallen Star known what she was thinking? She considered if he had the power to read their minds and wondered if he did so whilst singing. If he did, then he could know the deepest innermost parts of her, possibly better than she understood herself. She felt torn between wanting to know more about him or avoiding him altogether. In the end, she resigned herself to the fact he didn't appear dangerous and had shown her nothing other than compassion.

Confusion taking its toll, she lay on the grass-covered in pine needles and watched small clouds crossing the sky. She took in their shapings, a bird, a bridge and a butterfly. Her eyes grew heavy, and she dozed.

When she roused, dusk had settled over the lake making the waters dark with soft silver ripples. The sky, the colour of purpura dye speckled with faint shining orbs. The breeze, warm and pure nestled around her and birds chirped as they settled in their nests in for the night.

She found Nate resting his forearms over his knees sitting beside her.

'I became worried when you never returned with the others.'

She propped herself up on her elbow. 'How did you find me?'

'Just a gut feeling?'

'What, no magic wielding powers of your own?'

'No, but I have other hidden talents,' he said, teasing her.

'Are you flirting with me?'

'Maybe. Would you like me to?' he asked tilting his head.

'I'd like to see your style.'

Mirah couldn't believe what she'd said. One minute she was fretting over her own inexperience and now she challenged him to what exactly she had no idea.

He took off his coat, folded it into a makeshift pillow and lay beside her. 'It's all right if you want to gaze over my body. I'm sure you must be finding it difficult to tear your eyes away.'

'I hadn't noticed,' she lied.

'Really? Maybe I should take off my shirt?' He made to sit up and reached over his shoulders, gripping his shirt.

'That's unnecessary. I get the picture, very well.'

He sniggered in victory and lay back down. 'I make you nervous?' he asked with concern.

'It's not that, it's just—'

'Are you worried about Esha? Galia told me she'd told you. I intended to explain to you myself. Our relationship, if you can call it that, was a long time ago. I was young, foolish and believe me, I got my fingers burnt.'

'It's not Esha, well not totally. It's just that, I've never… well, you know what I mean.'

'Ah, well I'd be lying if I said I wasn't tempted but it's a bit soon don't you think?'

Relief washed over her.

'And besides, I'm sure when temptation gets the better of you, you'll find a way to let me know.'

'You sound pretty confident about that.'

He laughed with genuine amusement and reached into a small pack. 'I thought you might be hungry.' He passed her a raisin flat cake. 'I stole them from Sumer.'

They watched the purpura coloured sky give way to darker purple streaks.

Nate, reached around her shoulder, drawing her closer. 'I'd rather not spoil this but there's something you need to know. Shemyaza is promoting Bishnor to Chieftain. He'll be leading Zamani's old war band from now on.'

'Isn't that better for you? I noticed you two don't get along.'

'We don't. It's a long story but in my youth, I blamed him for my mother's death. I'm not proud of my behaviour. The way I acted towards him was cruel.

I took advantage of every opportunity to belittle him and make him look foolish. He grew up despising me. Shemyaza's other sons watched on, thinking my ridicule would shape him and make him stronger. The truth is, I'm in part responsible for the monster he has become.

In later years he's become suspicious of my intentions. He's still under my command but I won't be able to keep him near me or intervene and manoeuvre him around some of Shemyaza's orders. With him off leading his own war band, it will be impossible to reign in any devastation he plans.'

Nate pulled on a strand of grass and twiddled it between his finger and thumb. 'He has a point to prove. Becoming a Chieftain, it wouldn't surprise me if one day he makes a challenge for my command. I thought you should know in case you—'

'Decided you weren't worth the risk? If you thought that, then you don't know me very well.'

'You need to understand, if it ever came to it, if he killed me, in our culture, he'd have the right as the victor to take everything dearest to me. I don't mean to sound presumptuous but you need to know.'

'Well then, if it comes to that, don't die.'

He dropped the grass strand and selected another one. 'There's more. Shemyaza is hosting a tournament to celebrate Bishnor's promotion. It will involve Wielders against Wielders.'

'Will I have to fight?'

'No. It's a display of the Taphas and the powers they wield. As long as you don't reveal your other abilities, you'll be fine.'

'Well, in that case, you'll be pleased to know, I have my abilities under my firm control.'

'I gathered from the ruse you played this morning. Nice tactics, though you could have warned me.'

'And miss the joy of seeing you fall flat on your butt. No way. Galia had me practising for weeks. She will be disappointed she missed it.'

'Well, it's time I sought my revenge,' he said, leaning over and pinning her down on the ground. 'Didn't see that coming, did you?'

She was about to say no when he kissed her.

⁂ 18 ⁂

Shemyaza insisted that the four gods who'd descended on the mountain with him, were to attend Bishnor's promotion to Chieftain. One god who Nate called Buzur resided beyond the Salmu Sea.

According to Nate, hot plains and lapis lazuli mines filled his empire. The wealth of which adorned the lapis boundary wall of Mount Hermonial. A recent attack on the Buzur's mines had delayed Shemyaza's plans for the ceremony.

In the days ahead of the tournament, Mirah saw no sign of the gods. The single testament to anything unusual was the cartloads of Sikaru, a favoured blend of beer. After delivery, workers wheeled heavy loaded wagons across the courtyard and they disappeared into the bowels of the mountain.

The ceremony was supposed to go ahead the next day and every time she'd asked Nate when the gods would be arriving, he'd chuckled and said, wait and see.

The thought of performing in a tournament intimidated her but competing under the watchful gaze of five gods, she found terrifying. Her one consolation, she'd had over a month to prepare. A month of taunting Nate in their sparring and spending most evenings with Galia, Arella and Neviah in the Taphas Cavern. Nate presumed she'd be paired against a Fire Wielder and had insisted Neviah and her train together. To her credit, Neviah never grumbled. She saw it as an opportunity to rise above Shayla.

In wielding fire against water they were equal. Neviah melted the onslaught of ice shards and spears hurled through the air and in turn, she quenched fiery bombs Neviah fired back.

She never dared to use her other abilities. Not that she didn't trust Neviah with her secrets but Neviah accusing her of being different still lingered in the back of her mind along with Nate's insistence that no one else should know.

They'd been in the Taphas cavern wielding for some time when Nate arrived.

'Do you mind if I steal her away? Seeing as tonight might be the last night of our lives?'

Galia chortled. 'Not if you intend to terrorise the poor girl with your pathetic attempt at humour.'

'I need to go anyway,' Neviah said. 'There's something I need to do.' She collected a cloak which Mirah assumed was Zeev's and left.

'So you're both leaving us here stranded?' Arella pouted.

His mouth twitched, giving away his straight face as he replied, 'There's plenty of tasks in preparation for tomorrow if you want me to give you orders?'

'Now that's funny.' Galia laughed, backing across the cavern beckoning Arella with her hand. 'We're going to the harbour, maybe we'll see you there.'

The evening warmth and desert sand clung in the northeast breeze creating a foggy sienna colouring in the sky. It made everything feel compact.

'I thought we could walk by the river,' Nate said, as they crossed under the lapis lazuli archway leading back into the city.

They strolled by the rubble of a derelict temple which even the labourers had abandoned for the evening. In the distance, Nate's ship resembled nothing more than a murky grey mass. The once glorious river now dimmed to a dull, milky beige.

'There will be no stars tonight,' he said, as their feet sunk in the sloping sandbar.

Mirah assessed the sky. 'I could draw the sand from the air if you'd like?'

'As tempting as that is, air wielding wouldn't go unnoticed.' He took her hand guiding her around sticky black bitumen stuck to the sand. Once they were past it, he didn't let go. 'I wanted to make sure you're prepared for tomorrow?'

'I'm not sure what to expect.'

With a gentle tug on her hand, he closed the space between them. 'Shemyaza will hold the tournament on the mountain top.'

She glanced back at the dark sapphire blue mountain and the sand whirled up in the sky, shrouding its lofty elevation. 'Does Shemyaza's ostentation know no bounds? I can't even say I find it surprising.'

She'd seen the plateau from afar when she'd first arrived in the city and remembered how the absence of its peak seemed unnatural. In its place, the shimmering, wobble of air had reminded her of a desert mirage.

She debated asking more about the tournament when he said, 'Can I make a suggestion?'

His face was nothing but calm and assuring as she tried to gauge any sense of apprehension so she nodded indicating for him to continue.

'Try not to send ice spears through the wall of the mountain. I'm certain Bishnor has already notified Shemyaza, but it's unwise to draw the other god's attention.'

'What are they like?'

'Shemyaza is the most powerful although you should never underestimate the others. It will be easier to explain when you see them. I'll ask Galia to enlighten you as they arrive.'

'You won't be with me?'

Nate stopped and picked up a stone from the sandy river bed. He threw it a great distance over the water before she saw it plop. Expanding circular waves emerged on the agitated surface and the river's flowing current responded by smoothing the ridges away.

'I'd prefer nothing more than to stand beside you but I can't take that risk. To show you favour will reveal to them my weakness.' He bent down and picked up another stone and stared out over the river as though deciding where best to aim it. 'If things didn't go their way, they'd use my affection towards you against me and in doing so may seek to cause you harm.'

'I thought inside Shemyaza's borders his empire was peaceful?'

'It is, mostly,' Nate said, throwing the stone in the water and shaking the sand from his hands.

They continued to stroll along the river until wooden beams rising out of the silt blocked their path.

Nate halted by the sandbank. 'When the gods meet on the mountain, they call it a Puhrum, it resembles an assembly or council and Shemyaza is their leader. But they have no allegiance to each other outside of the Puhrum. When their plan is complete, I suspect they'll turn on each other.'

'What is their plan?'

'To conquer the world.'

Laughter roared from a wooden structure built out over the water, Mirah spotted Zeev, Neviah, Galia and Arella lounging around a table in the corner.

'What is this place?' she asked.

'It's one of the better beer houses on the harbour. Shall we go inside?'

They entered through a mud-brick building filled with many of Nate's guards. Cedar incense attempted and failed to mask the scent of beer, sweat and wine. They squeezed through the crowded room with Nate dipping his head in acknowledgements to most of his men whilst Mirah dodged slops of beer raised in their hands.

To her relief, they exited the building out onto the timber structure set over the river. She reached the others to find blends of citronella perfumes wafting from overhead leafy green vines.

Zeev slapped two more clay jars on the table and poured honey-coloured beer from a jug.

'You took your time. I was wondering if I'd have this beer to myself,' he said, sliding one jar towards Nate. He passed the other to Mirah as she sat on a wooden bench.

Neviah and Mirah still wore their leather pants and deep blue Taphas shirts but Galia and Arella had changed into long flowing wrap-around garments. Galia wore white with an embroidered pink trim and Arella wore pastel green. Both had switched their leather boots for silver sandals which complemented their silvery grey hair. Only the amethyst stone set in a wavy, gold band wrapped around Galia's wrist and the dark blue sapphire pendant hovering above Arella's cleavage revealed they were Taphas.

Feeling a little self-conscious, Mirah said, 'If I'd know I was coming here, I'd have found something more suitable to wear.'

'Why bother,' Neviah responded, 'at least this isn't so revealing.'

Mirah shuffled her feet under the table. She didn't dare peek to see if Neviah had offended either Galia or Arella.

Over the past weeks, since listening to the Fallen Star, she'd seen the edges of Neviah's sharper tone soften. Apparently, it didn't apply to her sense of appropriate clothing.

'And besides,' Neviah continued, 'we've never seen Nate or Zeev wear anything other than their soldiers' garb. If they don't make an effort why should I?'

'Do you want to see my birthday suit?' Zeev asked, lifting his hand to undo his shirt. 'I've been told it appeals to the senses.'

'You do that here and I'll make you walk on hot coals,' she said, glaring at him to ensure he wouldn't dare.

'Elsewhere then,' he replied, as though it was just a matter of time.

'As much as I find your pitiful attempt at seduction entertaining, Zeev,' Nate said, 'I'd prefer not to have to come to your rescue.'

Nate unleashed a wicked grin which made Mirah's heart surge.

'We won't intervene,' Galia said. 'He could do with learning a few boundaries.'

Zeev slapped his thighs. 'Will no one save me from this fiery tornado?'

All together they responded, 'No.'

Amongst the laughter, Nate leaned over to Zeev and whispered, 'Brother, with that one, you're on your own.'

Zeev gawked at Neviah, her face now passive and amused studying him. Mirah could hear Zeev's unsaid words running through his mind, challenge accepted.

Zeev raised his jar of beer. 'To Mirah and Neviah and victory over their competitors.'

'What about us?' Galia asked, shoving against his shoulder.

'But you're not competing and besides your head's big enough.'

'You're not competing?' Mirah asked.

'Afraid not,' Arella said. 'If every Wielder competed, we'd be there all day.'

Galia glowered at Nate. 'We're supposed to stay on the sidelines ensuring the safety of everyone else.'

'Safety is important,' Nate responded. 'I had to choose the finest of Shemyaza's Wielders for such a prestigious task.'

'Flattery is such a lovely poison,' Arella said, wiping the edge of her lips. 'It makes me feel soft and gooey inside.'

Ignoring her sister, Galia asked Nate, 'So why is Esha competing?'

With his face turning more serious he answered, 'Everyone knows when it comes to fire wielding, Esha is the best. I'm hoping one of the Puhrum will take notice and whisk her away to a far-off continent on the pretence of her training their Wielders.'

Zeev grinned. 'That's ingenious. Did you come up with that plan all by yourself?'

'Further the better, if you ask me,' Neviah snorted. 'If she says once more that I need to be more like Shayla, I swear I will turn her earwax into boiling oil.'

'Whilst you're at it frizzle the ends of her hair,' Mirah said.

All the girls giggled at the thought.

Zeev leaned towards Nate. 'They're losing me now.'

Nate shrugged, and the girls laughed even more.

A while later, the tinkling of dice being thrown on wooden tables and cheers and groans from Nate's men filtered from the mud-brick building.

'I think we should go before they become too rowdy,' Nate said to Mirah. 'If I'm here, I'd have to intervene.'

She'd not touched her beer and as she rose from her seat, Zeev eyed it.

As they made their way back to the mountain, Nate scanned every crevice and darkened passageway. His hand often resting on the pommel of his sword as passers-by shuffled in the darkness.

Not until they returned to the courtyard did his shoulders relax, and he asked, 'Would you like to go to the garden?'

'I'm tired. Do you mind if we sit on the veranda?'

When they arrived she sat on the pink cushioned bench leaning up against the crystalline mountain.

Nate stood by the balustrade looking out over the city. 'I've always liked to come here and peer at the stars as they watch the city. I often come here and imagine what they're thinking. The changes they've seen over the aeons. It's a shame they're not out tonight. There's much more I could show you.'

'Before I arrived here, I'd never left Barakel's borders. I never realised the world was so large and immeasurable.'

'What was it like in Barakel?' he asked, in a gentle tone mixed with apprehension.

She picked up a cushion and hugged it to her chest. 'Well as you saw, we dwelt in rock shelters. We were self-sufficient for the most part, harvesting our crops and farming livestock. Living by the ocean brought a wealth of fish. Sea Bass is my favourite. We never traded with silver or bought extravagant garments and jewellery.'

Mirah lost herself in memories of sea breezes and fishermen hailing to one another from small boats bobbing on the water.

The last time her clan was all together had been at the initiation ceremony when Gabe, Tam and others placed their inky handprints on the cavern wall. Their imprints were all that remained of the men who'd lived at Barakel.

She suppressed the rising urge to think of Gabe, of where he would go and what type of man he would become.

'It rains for most of the year and also thunders. On the path leading from our shelters, a river flows from a ravine. I used to swim with my friends in one of the deepest rock pools. Cloud shadows crept along the water surface and we'd pretend they were leviathans rising from the deep to eat us. I didn't know then about sea monsters like the Dagani. I didn't know they were real. Our Ma's sat on the edge of the pool washing woollen and animal skin clothing. We lived with the landscape surrounding us, no cultivated gardens, evocative buildings, Diatheatres or canals erected as you have here. I lived a simple life, tending herbs and making poultices for my Ma.'

'Apart from the rain, it sounds very appealing. Better than the politics of this place.'

'Our winters were harsh. You have comforts here I could never have imagined. Until I came here, I'd never bathed in warm water.'

'And the wielding?'

Mirah twirled the gold and lapis lazuli ring on her finger. 'That too.' She took a deep breath and ran her fingers through her hair. 'What?' she asked, regarding Nate's adoring smile.

'The way you do that. The way you take a breath as though it somehow re-empowers you. I find it endearing.' He came and sat beside her. 'If I had the power to go back and change it, you know I would.'

Whatever he searched for in her eyes, he found and she felt it too.

'Everything has a reason,' she said. 'I don't profess to understand it but I know there's no going back.'

It wasn't the city and certainly not Shemyaza's vision for his empire or beyond.

She looked into his blue eyes and told him, 'This is my home now.'

❊ 19 ❊

Ammo watched Bina standing on his ship's bow looking out over the ocean. Her long black hair swayed in the wind like the flag above his crow's nest. Her hair, the only movement from her he could see.

The choppy swell pushing them up high and dropping them low didn't faze her. It appeared as if her feet were glued to the deck. He didn't know what to make of her. Either she'd spent her life at sea or she hid other talents behind her dilating lavender eyes.

She breezed around his ship like she owned it. Not pushy, ordering his men to do this or that, she hardly spoke a word but her presence spread before her, claiming the ground where she walked.

Where had Meciel found her? What was their connection? Questions, he'd asked over and over but she'd snort and say, you have your story and I have mine.

He'd offer to tell her everything about him, well most of everything, if telling her would loosen her tongue. But he'd known from the instant they'd met, even with torture she'd never utter a single word. A different tactic then?

Sojin crossed the deck and gave Bina a plate of spiced fish. In Sojin's presence, her eyes often softened. He studied them both whilst they ate, whatever they were saying, he'd grill Sojin about it later and make sure Sojin stopped with those ridiculous puppy dog eyes.

The wind beat against the sails. If it kept up, they'd reach Lithinos by the end of the week. Why Meciel had sent Bina to collect him, he'd find out soon enough.

'Sojin, will ya come and help with this,' Ammo called out.

Sojin beamed at Bina then rushed over and gripped hold of the rope.

'Wipe that darn smile off ya face,' Ammo grumbled. 'It's making me sick. Help me get this into the hold.'

They dragged the crate across the deck and lowered it through the hatch. In the storeroom and out of earshot, he launched into Sojin.

'What were ya talking about?'

Sojin picked at a callous on his palm. 'She said the food tasted awful.'

Ammo agreed. His cook had fallen ill when they'd docked at Anat and in their haste to leave, he'd grabbed the first man who offered to replace him.

'And?'

'What's with all the questions? I don't know, she just said stuff.'

'What stuff?'

Sojin shrugged. 'She mentioned the Nephilim's head stuck on the spike in Anat and said, if I ever needed to talk, I could go to her.'

Why did she bring that up, Ammo wondered? What did she know about Nephilim and why ask Sojin?

'I don't want ya talking to her about that. Not until I've got a grip on who she is.'

Sojin knew better than to argue and attempted to leave. Ammo paced across the storeroom, his body filling the doorway as he leaned against the doorframe.

His shoulders dropped as he shifted into a casual demeanour and asked, 'Did she ask anything about me?'

'No.'

He saw Sojin raise his questioning brows. He'd seen them before, every time he asked him to scram. So what if Sojin thought he found her appealing. She wouldn't be his first conquest or his last.

The single difference was Ammo had been questioning him for days and in Sojin's eyes, Bina was becoming a failed acquisition.

He realised he was acting like a lust-crazed fool and stepped aside. 'Go back on deck, I'll be up with ya soon.'

Sojin tipped his cap as he passed.

Ammo gently pulled him back by the shoulder. 'Sojin, one more thing. If ya ever want to talk about the Nephilim, I'm here for ya, always.'

❊

The next day Ammo changed tactics. He puffed out his chest, set his feet wide and called out to Bina.

'So, I hear ya think ya are smart enough to take me?' he challenged with his dagger raised glinting in the sun.

'Please,' Bina drawled.

His eyes widened as she swiped back her hair.

'Ya too afraid ya might miss,' he teased, 'or would ya prefer to kiss me instead?'

Bina swept across the deck in three paces. 'You will regret you ever asked.'

He was flat on his ass on the deck before he saw her move, the handle of his dagger spinning on the end of her finger.

Sojin cursed under his breath.

'I'll never kiss you,' she stated flatly and walked away.

His dagger twanged into the deck just missing his finger.

'I bet you'll never do that again?' Sojin said, reaching out his hand.

'Watch me,' Ammo grinned.

Lusty fool be darned, he didn't care. He hadn't had this much fun in years. She was a target worthy of conquest and for the first time, he wasn't sure if he'd win.

Before they reached the port of Lithinos, Bina had put him on his ass in several ingenious ways. It was all he could do to suppress his wincing every time he sat his bruised butt down.

❊

No one sailed to the shanty little seaport of Lithinos unless they came for the waiting crewmen on the docks. The crewmen circulated around for years, hooking up with one ship and then switching to another when they moored. Ammo had been here many times to select men willing and able to join his forces or build his ships.

The port consisted of timber storehouses, boarding shacks and a row of inns. Most of them filled with lice and other crawling things.

The moment he stepped off the gangplank, the smell of stale beer, stale sweat and stale food hit him, reminding him of home. He shrugged off the memories which chased him. He was so good at it often they never bothered to pursue him anymore.

'This place reeks. Does nobody here bathe?' Bina said, covering her nose with her cloak.

The crewmen waiting for work were sunbaked and covered in grime. Most of them laid out on the grass located between the ocean and the row of buildings. Ammo knew paid lookouts would yell when opportunity crested over the horizon.

He was about to lead them to the most favourable inn when Bina announced, 'They're over there.'

He marked Meciel with his shaggy cut silver hair seated in the shade under a huddle of trees.

'Sojin, get us something to eat, something that ain't still walking or ain't been dead for over a week.'

When he reached Meciel, he found him with two unarmed lads and a Nephilim's sword wrapped in swaddling in his lap. He realised the instant he got closer wherever Meciel had found them, these lads had survived an attack.

The smaller lad's hazel eyes reminded him of Sojin's. He even had a little rusty, coloured cap. Bina blinked at Meciel and set out scouting under the trees.

'We'll not be staying,' Meciel said.

That didn't surprise him. He knew Meciel wouldn't set foot in any of Lithinos' boarding houses.

'Where ya want to go?' he asked.

'Hermonial.'

Ammo didn't let the shock grace his face. He glanced at the lads. 'What about them?'

Meciel gave nothing away. 'Gabe is coming with us. Tam has other plans.'

He was just going to ask which one was Gabe when the smaller of the two stood up and said, 'I'm sorry, Gabe, I haven't changed my mind.' He shifted from foot to foot. 'I hope you find Mirah and she's all right. I promise I'll find Nuri and keep her safe.' Tam hovered unsure what to do next.

Gabe rose and gave him a bear hug. 'Don't do anything foolish. I'll return as soon as I can.'

Tam thanked Meciel and turned to walk away.

Ammo grabbed his arm and stopped him. 'Where ya going?'

Tam shrugged.

'Terra has been tracking Nuri,' Meciel said, shifting onto his knees and then rising. 'They're heading west.'

Ammo had no clue who Nuri was but he could see this shattered lad didn't stand a chance alone and undefended.

He unsheathed a dagger at his side. 'Take this,' he offered, 'just in case ya might need it.'

He watched Tam heading back across the docks before he spun and focused his attention on Gabe. He appeared to be around the same age as Sojin though much taller.

Gabe stared at him, his green eyes radiating a stubborn will which Ammo knew mirrored his own. Gabe glanced beyond him to Wind Weaver, clearly, he itched to leave. Fool, Ammo thought to himself.

'Sojin,' he yelled. 'We ain't staying.'

Sojin emerged and whatever he held in his hands, he dropped to the ground. It didn't surprise him to find Bina waiting on the deck when they returned.

He turned to Sojin, 'Take Gabe below and show him his cabin.'

He waited until darkness shrouded his ship and his crew had settled for the night. 'Well?' he asked Meciel who had perched on a barrel.

'The lads were from Barakel. Shemyaza must have found me somehow. He knew I would be guarding the prophecy, and he sent his hordes to destroy him. There is nothing left.'

'So, it's over? Building up ya forces for the Cloud Rider?'

He already started calculating a new plan. A new strategy and a new income.

'It's not over yet.'

'Well, if he's gone, who ya gonna get to lead em?'

'Gabe.'

'Ya can't be serious.'

It wasn't often he had no quick comeback. He understood the men he'd recruited. Not even believing it himself, he sold them Meciel's prophecy of the Cloud Rider's saviour. They'd revolt if he walked Gabe into their camp and even he probably wouldn't come out alive.

'I been building ya forces for years and ya expect me to hand em over to a kid?'

Meciel stroked his beard, plotting his next move. 'We need to stop in Nanshe.'

'Why the hell do ya want to go there?'

'Shemyaza took Gabe's sister. He won't focus on the Cloud Rider's chosen path until he's found her.'

Ammo bristled. 'So what, ya gonna walk into Hermonial? Do ya realise how insane that sounds?'

Meciel raised his eyes from under his bushy eyebrows. 'I promised to help him.'

'I never took ya for a fool.' He knew his words sounded condescending but Meciel didn't flinch. 'What did he do in Barakel? Tell me he at least has some skills?'

'Apprentice carpenter.'

Ammo rolled his eyes.

'I need you to train him,' Meciel said, lowering his feet onto the deck.

Ammo blew his fringe from his perspiring forehead. 'This is gonna cost ya.'

'More than you realise.' Meciel sighed.

He could have suggested for Bina to train Gabe. It would have been worth it, to work out how she moved so fast but then he thought, why forfeit the silver.

The following morning, he stuck a sword in Gabe's hand. The kid looked like he expected the blade to come alive and torture him. What had he done to deserve this Ammo grumbled to himself, knowing full well he'd done plenty.

He spent the morning showing Gabe the basics. This kid appeared determined, he had to give him that. If he could temper his frustration, he might actually learn something.

'Who is Nuri?' Ammo asked, bringing his sword in for another parry.

Gabe lunged forward and thrust his hands into Ammo's chest, sending him reeling backwards.

Thunder clapped overhead and Ammo caught Meciel's smile.

❊ 20 ❊

To reach the plateau they'd ascended in small groups up through not one but three shafts. On the level above Mirah's chamber, she caught sight of men in dark robes hunched over desks, pressing reeds into clay tablets in a voluminous airy room.

'What are they doing?' she asked Arella.

'They are the Sanu and this is the Edubba, house of the scribes. They record Shemyaza's good works.'

From the way Arella spoke with a subtle hint of sarcasm, Mirah assumed recordings of Shemyaza's works, good or bad, would bend in his favour.

The next level was of exquisite design. A mosaic of aqua green tiles paved the tunnel floors and intricate murals covered smooth white plaster walls. As she passed them she caught glimpses of winged horses and lions and other strange creatures, all of them delightful and nothing like the ferocity of the chimeric beasts she often heard roaring from below her chamber.

As the final shaft rose into the sunlight, it took a moment for her eyes to adjust. She blinked and blinked again at the sight she saw.

'Amazing isn't it,' Galia said, strolling towards her.

'I don't know what to say,' Mirah said, stepping away from the platform whilst taking in the view.

A wall of crystal rock, rising three or four times her height surrounded the wide plateau. In its glacial fortifications, she could see her anxious reflection. Carved into the rock to her left, were five thrones with engraved wings spreading high above them.

Ahead, Bishnor and six other giants waited by a sunken pool. The pool had steps leading down into the purest blue water she had ever seen. But the most shocking was the lofty, shimmering doorway rising high into the sky. How had she had never seen it from the ground?

'It's the Isten Baba - the first gate,' Galia answered, to her unspoken question.

She understood now why Nate avoided answering when she'd asked when the gods would arrive. How could anyone find the words to explain a portal joining the gods' world to their own?

'Quick, let's get the best seats before Esha and the other Taphas arrive,' Galia said, leading her to smaller seating cut into the crystal rock on the opposite side of the plateau from the thrones.

Neviah emerged from the shaft her face deadpan with no hint of astonishment as she strode across the plateau.

'I swear if someone doesn't cut that tongue out of shitty Shayla, I will explode,' she said, flopping down beside her.

'What did she say?'

'She said my freckles bring out the sluttiness in my eyes.' Noticing the Isten Baba, Neviah gasped. 'What is that?'

Dropping her voice into feigned boredom as though nothing unusual stood before them, Mirah said, 'It's only a gateway to the heavens.'

'It makes you feel insignificant, doesn't it?'

Mirah caught a flash of Esha's dark henna hair and dropped her gaze to the ground. She sensed Esha's eyes smouldering over her as she walked to the centre of the plateau. It was the first time Mirah had been in her presence since knowing her history with Nate.

Esha called everyone to attention and Mirah focused on the snaky long braid coiled over her shoulder.

'As leader of the Taphas, I shall provide a display to show the Puhrum what you aspire to become. Our newest recruits will follow after. I'll call you in pairs and you will each compete, one against another. There will be two parallel lines chalked across the plateau. It's your task to prevent your opponent from crossing the line closest to you. Remember, you're here to impress the Puhrum. Do not let me down.'

Next to arrive were several men carrying long, curled, brown kudu horns. They positioned themselves on either side of the Isten Baba.

A few moments later, two members of the Azu emerged with a man wearing a black turban and a long black sash hanging over grey robes. Miniscule wrinkles like dried out plant roots spread over his hands and face. Aged he might be but Mirah spotted nothing frail about him. He advanced towards the pool giving a slight bow towards Bishnor.

She first saw the shine on his boots and the pommel of his sword when Nate entered the plateau. He escorted Shemyaza's wife Dumah to her seat.

'Just because he brushes up well doesn't mean you can trust him,' Neviah said, low enough for only Mirah to hear.

She had to agree, he looked splendid. He made his way over to Esha and stood with his back towards her. She didn't mind, he'd already warned her that for her own safety he'd pay her no attention. What she didn't appreciate was Esha leaning in closer as though she couldn't hear whatever he said.

Mirah jumped in her seat when the deep warbling sounds of the kudu horns blasted over the plateau announcing Shemyaza's arrival. She'd expected him to adorn himself in fine clothing, jewels and a crown, not the plain purple garment wrapped around him, held in place by a belt and sheathed sword.

In the daylight, she noticed his well oiled dark hair and braided beard. She saw no signs of his wings as the kudu horns silenced.

He took determined steps straight to the Isten Baba and with outstretched arms, his voice rumbled like torrential rain when he announced, 'Ati me peta babka.'

The clover-blue shimmer over the gateway flared brighter and then dissolved to reveal ominous black steps leading up into the sky.

In turn, each of the gods descended the stairway. The kudu horns blasting as they crossed over the threshold onto the plateau. They greeted Shemyaza, glancing their immortal eyes over everyone in attendance before seating themselves on their thrones. Galia spoke in hushed whispers as each one arrived wearing the same purple robes as Shemyaza.

'That's Usemi,' Galia said.

Whether it was the subtle shifting of sunlight or caused by his slick motion, Mirah couldn't tell but his skin shimmered, switching between light tan and pale green. He reminded her of a lizard basking in the sun with bold, golden eyes set over wide spreading, slim lips. He was smaller than Shemyaza and looked like he'd popped out of a crevice compared to Shargaz who came next.

Shargaz's hulking, chubby stature appeared to compress by the time he sat on his throne. He stroked reddened, spiderlike fingers through an even redder beard. Galia informed her that Shargaz was the Supreme Smiter, responsible for metallurgy and a keen advocate for war.

Buzur was so pale-skinned, Mirah wondered if he'd never been in the sunlight. His eyes were the same colour and size as the imposing ruby gemstone he offered to Shemyaza. She supposed the ruby was compensation for the ceremonial delay. He stopped and spoke to Shemyaza. Whatever he said caused Shemyaza's fiery eyes to harden.

The god's descent through the portal was a long, drawn-out affair and Mirah shifted on her seat. She glanced sideways towards Nate to see if he observed her reactions but he faced forward, tense and alert. She slipped her hand into Neviah's and squeezed it. The kudu horns announced the final god crossing over the threshold.

The last to descend was Ditallu and to Mirah's surprise, she was female. Her hair, cropped short and as white as chilled ice, gleamed in the sunlight.

'She is the Belit-Seri,' Galia said, 'Lady of the Wilderness. Beautiful isn't she?'

Mirah couldn't deny her beauty. She wore her purple robes longer than the others. The back flowing over the plateau behind her as she took graceful steps to her throne.

Shemyaza closed the portal before seating himself on the central throne. Usemi and Shargaz to his left and Buzur and Ditallu on his right. No one stirred, absorbed in the triumph of the five gods that beheld them.

The black turbaned man came and bowed low before Shemyaza.

'He is the Sangu Mah,' Galia said. 'He will preside over the ceremony. I have to go now and prepare for the tournament.'

Shemyaza signalled with a jut of his chin for the ceremony to begin.

The Sangu Mah slipped out a clay tablet from beneath his robe as his sandals padded over to the pool. He stepped down into the water and little waves and ripples lapped against his grey robe.

He submerged up to his armpits. His black sash floating like two far-reaching tentacles on the blue water.

Bishnor came out from behind the six other giants dressed in an orange loincloth. A long scar lashed over his right thigh and scattered over his entire body were a motley of smaller scars.

'What is he doing?' Mirah gasped.

Ninkurra leaned over Neviah and said, 'It's called immersion. We have something similar but not as grand an occasion as this.'

'I didn't mean the ceremony,' Mirah said, watching Bishnor unhook the loincloth from over his hips and letting it drop to the floor. He stood stark naked. A demarcation line separated his tan skin from the white flesh of his buttocks.

'Oh that,' Ninkurra said, brushing away his nakedness like she'd seen it before. 'Didn't anyone tell you, the ceremony is symbolic of death and rebirth? He can't take anything in the pool with him.'

They forgot to mention that, she thought, staring over at Nate. With his back to the gods, she caught his sly glance and even though he didn't show it, she knew later she'd wipe the hidden grin off his face.

Bishnor entered the pool, the water reaching his hips. Two of the giants followed in after him. He stopped before the Sangu Mah who raised the clay tablet closer to his eyes and spoke in a foreign tongue.

Watching the Sangu Mah became a sombre affair and dragged on for ages. Mirah had no clue what he was saying, but she picked up the rhythm and beats of the language, enough to know when the Sangu Mah was drawing to a close.

The two giants held their hands across Bishnor's shoulders and he fell back into the water. He didn't struggle as they held him under. Mirah wondered if the death part wasn't as symbolic as Ninkurra had suggested until he burst up out of the water.

He emerged from the pool, his right arm from his shoulder to his wrist now covered with small oily black pictographs and geometric symbols. On exiting, another giant gave Bishnor a robe, and he thudded across the plateau and kneeled before Shemyaza.

Shemyaza rose and glided the sword at his side from its sheath.

'This sword is fashioned from anbar found only beyond this world.' He sliced the double-edged sword over Bishnor's chest. 'With blood, you shall honour it as you honour me as Chieftain.' Shemyaza offered the sword to Bishnor. 'Its name is Zabar.'

Bishnor rose and when he turned droplets of blood trickled through the hairs on his chest. Raising the sword above his head caused the giants to roar in approval.

After the servants had delivered refreshments to the gods, Esha came and bowed to Shemyaza.

'This is Esha, my most faithful and powerful Wielder,' Shemyaza said to the Puhrum. He gestured for her to begin.

Buzur and Shargaz leaned forward as Esha stepped back wielding fire into her hands. She thrust her palms upward, sending a ring of fire into the sky and then wielded the ring to the ground encircling the fire around her. She stroked the flames into a spinning column, feeding it more fire until the column grew higher.

She gracefully pivoted and wielded the column of fire around the plateau, her arms moving in perfect symmetry as she split the column in two as it expanded. The columns paused, one at each end of the plateau and she stretched the perpetual fire up and over to form an arc of flames over her head. Holding the arc in position, she wielded fireballs in each palm and released them with great speed, one aimed at Shemyaza, the other at Usemi. Neither of them flinched as the fireballs sped through the air, halting in front of their satisfied faces.

'How wonderful,' Usemi said, 'such precision.'

Esha wielded the fireballs back towards her and split the fireballs in half again and again until she wielded more than a dozen in the air.

The fireballs zoomed in an aerial display with such force and speed it became difficult for Mirah to track them as they spun and shot through the air.

'It's impressive,' Shargaz agreed, 'but in battle how much damage can your Wielders achieve?'

'You may have few in numbers,' Shemyaza replied, gesturing to the Taphas seated opposite him, 'but as you can see, I'm building an army.'

Esha wielded the fireballs up into the flaming arc above her head. She drew the fire columns closer and raised them into the air, spreading out the flames over the plateau.

The sky turned into a blanket of molten lava, the heat of which becoming insufferable. She dropped her hands and thousands of globules of molten lava cascaded towards them.

Everyone except the gods ducked in response. Esha smirked and when Mirah was sure she was going to burn alive, the lava evaporated.

Buzur rubbed his pale-skinned hands together. 'I've never seen a Fire Wielder strong enough to sustain the power of turning flames into lava.'

His red eyes lingered on the small opal and sapphire amulet dangling from her neck as though trying to decipher its power.

'You are dismissed Esha,' Shemyaza said.

Mirah didn't miss the gloating hidden behind Shemyaza's slim smile.

Two Wielders rushed across the plateau and marked out chalk lines. Galia, Arella and several other Wielders positioned themselves around the plateau.

'And now a tournament from my newest Wielders,' Shemyaza announced. He turned to Shargaz and said, 'A far stronger strategy than wielding swords, don't you agree?'

'I have another suggestion,' Buzur cut in. 'As you know the pitiful attack on my mines delayed your ceremony. I've brought gifts which are in need of disposing. I thought they will compensate.'

'How intriguing,' Ditallu said. 'A far more entertaining display, I'm sure.'

The other gods agreed and Shemyaza adjusted his purple garments as he stood to open the Isten Baba.

'What's going on?' Neviah asked.

Mirah shrugged, 'I have no idea.'

She looked to Nate and found his eyes fixed and stony. The telling sign of his white knuckles gripping his sword pommel unnerved her. She caught sight of Esha, her face beaming as she gave instructions to Galia who in turn spoke to Arella. They both glanced over at Nate and he closed his eyes briefly. Whatever he signalled, they understood, their eyes turning as expressionless as his.

By the time she returned her focus to Shemyaza, the Isten Baba had re-opened. Buzur's guards herded shackled men down the blackened stairway and led them onto the plateau. Dark bruises and untreated wounds aside, the prisoners didn't appear too injured. Their ragged clothes revealing they were just beginning to shed weight.

The shackled men surveyed the scene, weighing up the danger, and searching out potential escape routes. They assessed the gods seated on their thrones and cursed. Esha stepped forward beckoning Galia and Arella to her side and awaited instructions.

'We've already seen what she can do,' Buzur said, pointing to Esha. 'That would hardly be a fair competition.'

Shargaz twisted on his throne and made a strange clicking sound through his teeth. 'As you said, Shemyaza, it's supposed to be a tournament for your latest recruits. Let Esha pick the best three of your more recent additions. After all, we don't want the tournament to end too soon.'

'Excellent,' Ditallu agreed.

'As you wish,' Shemyaza replied, gesturing for Esha to choose.

Esha scanned the Wielders. 'Shayla, Neviah and Mirah, step forward.'

As they crossed the plateau, Esha slipped a scheming smile at Nate. 'You heard what Shargaz said, he doesn't want this over too quickly. This is a display of your powers as Wielders. Impress Shemyaza before you kill them.'

Panic hit Mirah's body hard, her heart thumping against a hollow ache within. 'You expect us to murder them?'

Air refused to fill her lungs, and she didn't know if she'd first collapse or start choking. She thought she'd understood when Nate explained his trapped and powerless feelings. How was she going to escape this?

'Of course, you will kill them. They are criminals.'

'I won't do it.'

Esha curled her lip. 'No one refuses Shemyaza. If he doesn't destroy you first, I'll burn you to ash myself.'

❊ 21 ❊

Nate clamped unsaid curses between his tongue and teeth. He wanted to strangle Esha as she sauntered towards him, her slick smile revealing she knew how much Mirah meant to him. He'd be damned if he'd let her know she'd gotten under his skin. Instead, he relaxed and unclenched his clammy fists.

'Problems?'

'Nothing I can't handle,' Esha responded.

Her sense of victory made him want to vomit. He braved a glance at Mirah and found her whispering in Neviah's ear.

Shackles clinked to the ground and Buzur's guards dragged the rebel's chains to the edge of the plateau. The rebels worked the blood flow back into their wrists, rubbing and shaking their hands.

Did Mirah understand, these were fighting men? They'd come at her fast hoping to obliterate their competition. Would she attack? He doubted it.

Years of once adoring and then loathing Shemyaza spread out before him. He'd never hated Shemyaza more than he did right now. Resigned to the fact he could do nothing else, he prayed to the old gods, Anu, Enlil and the nameless Cloud Rider. Calling out silently for any of them to intervene.

'How are they going to defend themselves with no weapons?' asked Usemi. 'It seems hardly fair and rather boring.'

Buzur instructed his guards to unsheathe their daggers and place them on the ground as a Rock Wielder chalked a wide circle on the plateau.

'If you step over the line, you will be dead before your foot touches the floor,' Shemyaza said to the captives. 'Pick up the weapons.'

Unhurried they collected the daggers and spread out, keeping inside the line of the circle. Among the rebels, Nate spied a tall lanky lad with freckled cheeks. He was young compared to the others, maybe seventeen or eighteen. His grip on the dagger loose and unskilled. Had no one shown him how to use one?

The lad stared at Mirah, his face a mask of misery. When they spotted him, Neviah gripped Mirah's arm. They recognised him. How? And what was he doing here?

Mirah and Neviah followed Shayla into the centre of the plateau. They formed into a huddle, their backs together in a protective formation.

The rebels didn't wait for Shemyaza to give the command. One of the sturdier men rushed forward, dagger positioned to shunt it into Neviah's ribs. She responded by hurling a brutal fireball straight at his legs, knocking him to the floor. He rolled over dousing the flames from his pants. She would fight back at least.

The rebels paced around the edge of the circle, moving inward reducing the distance between them. If Mirah and the others didn't wield a defence the rebels would soon surge and attempt to overpower them.

With everyone's eyes on the centre of the plateau, he edged around the chalk line to get closer to Mirah. Shemyaza be damned if she didn't fight back he'd intervene.

Except for the lanky one, the rebels in unison doubled over, their complexions withering. Mirah was drawing the moisture from the pores of their skin, not sufficient to injure them but enough to send them a warning.

He was certain if she had the mind to, she could draw every drop of moisture from the rebel's bodies. By the lake, he'd witnessed her almost drain the life out of Galia.

In desperation, the rebels launched their daggers. They clashed with shards of ice blocking their advances. The daggers fell from the air, the rebels lunging after them. Relief swept through him. At least she wouldn't let them harm her.

Sinuous curling flames that flexed like fingers spread out from Shayla. On reaching the ground they charged across the plateau like forked lightning hitting their targets with a crack.

Several of the men didn't rise and the smell of charred flesh brought Nate's memories back to Barakel. The remaining rebels surged forward and chaos ensued. Shayla whirled lethal fireballs into stomachs, shoulders and heads, men burst into flames, falling to the ground.

Blood trickled down Neviah's arm from a small gash, her face now furious. Nate had no doubt if she had the opportunity to fight against the men and giants who'd attacked Barakel, she wouldn't hesitate in destroying them. He couldn't help wonder if he'd still be one of her targets.

With tactical skill she held the ground against the rebels, defending with combustible fireballs at any who approached her or Mirah. How long could this continue before Shemyaza tired or became suspicious?

A rebel flashed towards Mirah, Nate was about to step over the chalk but a thick barrier of ice surrounded the man. Nate heard the rebel's dagger chipping at the ice as he stole a glance at the immersion pool, the water two-thirds gone.

A stray bolt of fire flew into spectating Wielders. It was quickly extinguished by Arella smothering the flames, and the Azu took care of the injured.

Three rebels remained. The one behind the ice wall, a brutish dirty blonde and the freckled lanky kid.

To his shock, Mirah rushed over to the lanky one. She blocked his pitiful jabs with the dagger. He wasn't even trying to hurt her. In between thrusts and blocks, they exchanged a few words, too low and too fast for him to hear.

The blonde brute crouched, blade in hand, ready to strike if Neviah lost her focus. He'd seen that glare in her eyes before, whenever Zeev got on her bad side. She'd take the brute down when he came for her.

With no one left to fight, Shayla put her hands on the ice wall, melting the ice. The trapped rebel burst through the wall and met with a fiery death. She rounded towards the blonde brute. Nate recognised the battle frenzied glaze. She was losing control.

A firebolt blasted into the brute and he dropped to the floor, a smouldering pile of flesh.

'You're welcome,' Shayla snapped at Neviah.

Intent on seeking glory, Shayla sized up the lanky kid. Tears welled in Mirah's eyes. This kid's life was over. She blinked them away and shrilled an agonising scream. The lanky kid rose in the air and she wielded him over the side of the mountain.

The Wielders gasped. Buzur and Shargaz jumped up from their thrones.

'Water and air. How is this possible?' Shargaz yelled.

Nate studied the gods' faces, all of them stunned, including Shemyaza.

Bishnor rushed forward. 'As Chieftain, I claim her as my bride,' he announced.

Years of avoiding confrontation dissolved from Nate. A rage hotter than a Wielder's flame burned in his chest. He knew defying Shemyaza's will was dangerous but he didn't care. He couldn't allow this to happen.

He hollered, 'I challenge his request.'

Bishnor snarled.

Ditallu's gaze was a little admiring as she said, 'Fascinating… how these humans still have the capacity to sometimes surprise us.'

'Indeed,' Shemyaza said, staring at Nate.

'I don't give a damn about him,' Buzur said, giving Nate a dismissive wave. 'I've never understood what you see in that human and to rank him above your own blood.' He pointed to Mirah. 'What about her and that power?'

Shemyaza raised his voice. 'I'll not have you interrogate my leadership or my motives. Nate's loyalty is without question.' He held up his hand, warning Buzur to stay silent.

Nate examined the other gods to see if any would come to Buzur's aid. The gods revealed no allegiances and Buzur backed off and obeyed.

'Mirah is a matter for us to discuss later. However,' Shemyaza continued. 'I will not have my sons fighting and certainly not over a woman and I do not hold with rape. If there is any choice between them, it will be hers.'

'How diplomatic,' Usemi said.

'Diplomacy is an art,' Shemyaza reminded them.

'But think of the power from her offspring,' Shargaz said. 'If she were mine, I'd consider wedding her myself.'

The way his eyes feasted on Mirah made Nate want to plunge his sword through Shargaz's chest.

'I said, these are not matters to discuss now.' Shemyaza rose from his throne. 'The ceremony is over. Everyone, except Mirah, leave now.'

Mirah stood motionless in the centre of the plateau. Had she heard what they'd said? Nate joined her resting his hands on her shoulders.

'I'm sorry,' she said, with her eyes fixed on the ground. 'I couldn't let Shayla kill him.'

He lowered and tilted his head attempting to see her face shielded under her hair. 'You knew him?'

'His name is Eran, he's from Barakel.'

Nate had already guessed she hadn't just wielded him over the mountain but had also saved him from the fall. 'Did you hear Shemyaza?'

'I heard.'

'And Bishnor?'

'That as well.' She raised her head to meet his gaze. 'We are powerless against them, aren't we? I understand now.'

With small reassuring, tender strokes, he massaged her shoulders. 'Listen. Shemyaza is more interested in your wielding. He doesn't care about things like marriage.'

She blinked. 'What about offspring? I'm sure he cares about that?'

Nate swallowed. She had a point. Would Shemyaza consider her as another wife? The plateau had emptied, only Neviah and Galia were waiting by the shaft.

'I have to go. Please don't be afraid. You're too valuable for them to hurt you.' He kissed her on the forehead and whispered into her hair, 'I love you.' There was no point in hiding it now.

⁂

When they were halfway down the first shaft, Galia's voice cut through the darkness. 'Do you want to talk about it?'

'No.'

They stayed silent the rest of the way until Nate broke off and left for his chamber. He'd not been there long when someone knocked on the door.

Zeev entered and Nate paused his pacing. 'Galia?'

'She is worried.'

Nate let out a deep sigh. He expected before nightfall everyone within the mountain will have heard.

'So Mirah can wield other elements?'

Nate ignored him.

'What the bidu happened? I've sent guards out to search for the body.'

'You won't find him.' Seeing Zeev's confusion, he explained. 'It wasn't an accident. She did it to save him.'

'Why would she do such a thing?' Zeev asked slumping down in a chair.

'He's from Barakel.'

Nate returned to pacing, back and forth across his chamber.

'If you don't stop that, you're going to mark a groove in the floor. Come and sit down.'

'I can't. If I stop moving, I can't control the urge not to break something.'

Zeev studied his boots whilst processing his thoughts and trying to piece everything together.

'Is he the one Shemyaza sent you after? I mean if he was skilled enough to escape the slaughter at Buzur's mines?'

Nate hadn't considered that. The kid was not even a fighter. 'I don't see how he'd be a threat to Shemyaza. Will you ask Eliah to use discretion and continue searching? There aren't many places a stranger can hide.'

'And if he finds him?'

'Direct him to my other quarters.'

'You'd reveal your quarters for a stranger?'

Nate sighed. 'It's not for him.'

His fists were clenched so tight, he flexed his fingers and clicked his knuckles. He marched over to the table finding his beer jug empty.

'What do you think Bishnor will do?'

Nate thumped his fists onto the table. 'I can't talk about him now.'

Seeing Nate needed to be alone, Zeev rose to leave.

Nate looked up. 'When you find Eliah, will you go with him? I'd go myself but I can't leave.'

'We'll find him,' Zeev said, closing the door as he left.

Left alone, he chewed over the angles Shemyaza might play. Even after his challenge against Bishnor, Shemyaza still believed him to be trustworthy and still considered him his son. He could use this to gain leverage. He wasn't surprised Buzur didn't accept Shemyaza's favour towards him, he had difficulty understanding it himself.

Would Shemyaza consider Shargaz's suggestion to wed Mirah himself? Nate didn't know, but he knew Shemyaza had a talent for manipulating people's decisions.

Even though Shemyaza had said it was her choice, he might find her wielding too tempting. His art of diplomacy always meant getting his own way. And what about Mirah? He understood the powerless feeling of being forced to make choices. Of picking the lesser of two evils.

Doubts crept into him. Is that all he was to her? He didn't want her to choose him that way. On the plateau, he'd told her he loved her and meant it. Somehow, he'd always imagined love would take longer and not sneak up on him unawares.

Sumer arrived with food and set it on his table.

'Have they descended yet?'

'Sorry,' Sumer answered, fidgeting with her clothing. 'Would you like me to stay?'

Nate shook his head. 'I'd rather be alone.'

He baulked at the food after she left. The thought of losing Mirah became so overpowering he exited his chamber.

The tunnels appeared darker, more constricting. He soon reached the shaft leading to the plateau. The guards stationed there didn't dare say a word. They'd heard.

He growled under his breath, ignored them and leaned towards the shaft. Looking into the darkness was pointless, and he knew it. The impossible void absorbed everything even the sound of the wind. He couldn't stay here. He roamed back through the tunnels, ending up outside Mirah's chamber. Should he go in?

Desperation overwhelmed him. He opened the door and inhaled her delicate scent filling the room.

One of the chimera below her chamber let out a series of shallow roars which sounded strangely like laughing. Zamani, he realised. Not wanting to pry, he sat on the silks covering her bed and waited.

After some time, he spied a small carved wolf on the bedside table and wondered how she had come by it because no wolves existed in Hermonial.

In the enveloping darkness, moonlight shone through the opening subduing the shadows. He stood up and paced around.

Mirah finally entered her room and to avoid alarming her he said, 'I hope you don't mind me—'

She swayed, and he rushed to catch her. Lifting her, he placed her gently on her bed. He didn't want to leave so he nuzzled down beside her, cradled her in his arms and breathed her in.

Locked within her were so many answers. Answers he knew she was too depleted to reveal.

As she drifted into the realm of heavy sleep, he studied her dark twitching lashes, her endearing freckle on the rim of her ear, and the faint scar above her brow and committed them to memory.

She was here.

He released the gnawing fear he'd kept suppressed. Fear he'd refused to acknowledge as if its acknowledgement would make it real.

She was still here.

Shemyaza hadn't sent her through the Isten Baba portal.

✳ 22 ✳

Mirah moved and a sharp pang lanced through her head. She instinctively reached for her brow. Nate tensed but remained seated on the other side of her chamber. Distant. Why was he sat over there?

She remembered the warmth, the closeness of his touch as he'd held her. The way her body melded into his, the safety and assurance exuding from him, washing over her in soothing waves.

'You should eat,' he said, indicating to a tray of delicious fruits on the table.

His withdrawn tone unnerved her.

'What's going on?' she asked sitting up.

'It's late. A little after midday.'

'That's not what I meant.'

She tried to read him as he sat upright, rigid, his dark wavy hair uncombed, his shirt creased. She presumed he hadn't left her chamber but something had changed. If he thought she was no longer worth his consideration, then why was he still here?

His eyes flicked to the hole in the rock at the sound of a chimera snarling outside and then returned to hers. Whatever he saw made him grimace. Well, this wasn't advancing as she expected. She'd dreamed of opening her eyes and him gently kissing her forehead.

'You can leave if you want. You don't have to stay.'

He got up and wandered slowly to the door. Her heart felt like it would crack open.

With his back towards her, he paused. 'I can't. I need to know.'

'About Shemyaza, the wielding or us?'

With his hand on the latch, he didn't turn. 'All of it.'

Why wouldn't he face her? Did his confession of love shame him? Was it a lie to keep her from folding? She knew deep inside a betrayal like that would break her. A nauseous awakening compelled her to make sense of her reasoning.

'After you left, they questioned where I came from. They asked about my parents. I told them they were dead. They asked about siblings and I said, I'd had a brother but he'd gone too.'

It wasn't a total lie, and she'd been glad they hadn't pressed her further.

To her relief, they didn't ask about Eran and she'd assumed they thought she'd killed the rebel as requested.

'Shemyaza asked if I knew someone called Meciel. I'd never heard of him and told him so.

Shargaz demanded another wielding demonstration.

Buzur pressed to know what other elements I could wield.

I didn't see the point in hiding it. I suspected they wouldn't let me go until they knew. I informed them I wielded water, earth and air.

Ditallu enquired about my wielding amulet. I told her, I'd picked the ring because it was the simplest of them all.

They discussed between them my potential for wielding fire and I explained that was something I couldn't do. They pushed and tested my abilities until I collapsed in complete exhaustion.'

Nate still hadn't turned. She yearned to see his face, to gauge his reactions, to find out why he wouldn't look at her.

'When I could no longer stand, they made me sit on the floor. I tried to understand what they were saying, but they spoke in a foreign tongue. They appeared to be debating and arguing.

Then Shemyaza opened the Isten Baba, and the gods left us alone. After he closed the portal, Shemyaza allowed me to sit on an empty throne beside him. He said it was time for my choosing. He explained that if I willed it, I didn't have to choose at all.'

She paused, hoping Nate would turn. He didn't move. 'I told him that, I choose you.'

Nate let go of the latch, his hand poised ready to snatch it again at any moment.

'Was I mistaken?' Mirah asked.

'Do you think I'm just the safer option?'

'What? Of course not.'

'Are you sure?'

'How could you think such a thing?' she asked, her voice rising higher.

He turned, and the sunlight caught the relief washing over his face.

'Mirah,' he said.

He almost crashed into her pushing her back on the bed. His body settling on hers, shielding, protecting and claiming.

When his lips met hers, she desired to let her body meld into him. His kiss was passionate, gaining sincerity, awaking in her sensations she never realised existed. Her body responded, aching, betraying her for the pleasure it sought. If he didn't stop kissing her soon, she knew she'd yield into its craving.

As if sensing they were about to cross over a threshold, he rolled onto his back. For a long while, they stayed silent except for their small panting breaths.

'I'd thought I'd lost you,' he breathed.

She cuddled into him, watching the rise and fall of his chest.

'I thought maybe you'd consider joining with the stepson of your enemy a step too far. Or that Shemyaza would manipulate you into accepting Bishnor or take you for his own. I don't think I could have survived if you'd chosen one of them.'

She took his hand and gave it a gentle squeeze. 'What happens now?'

He gave her a sinful grin. 'I guess we plan for a wedding before Shemyaza changes his mind.'

Part 2

⁂ 23 ⁂

As Mirah waited, she sensed the surrounding air, thick and muggy. She peered at the stars most of them blotted away by the dense cloud.

'Do you ever have storms here?'

'Not this time of year,' Nate answered.

'I sense one coming.'

She hated being summoned to the plateau but Shemyaza now insisted on observing her progress. She glanced again to the Isten Baba, its clover blue shimmer still separating them from the realm beyond.

Weeks had turned into months. Ditallu was arranging her wedding dress. A gift she insisted on providing and after months of hearing hints about its design, she still hadn't seen it.

'How long will he make us wait this time?' Neviah asked.

Nate shrugged.

Whatever Neviah thought of their wedding, she kept to herself though she had plenty to say about being ordered to the plateau.

'I'm sure he makes us come here to watch us suffer. Why should I be indebted to Shayla? She took the blonde rebels life for her own glory it had nothing to do with me. And now she wants me to thank her for saving my life! I won't do it.'

Ropes pulling taut announced the platforms ascension. Mirah's stomach folded over. Shemyaza wasn't the only one interested in her wielding. Bishnor exited the shaft and strode onto the plateau, his new sword swinging on his hip. He rolled his tongue over his top lip and his coveting gaze roamed over her body.

'Has he danced with you yet?' His fire opal eyes flashed with desire and he stroked his brutish hand down the length of his sword. With a satisfied smile, he lumbered across the plateau and sat on Shemyaza's throne. 'Thought not.'

Nate ignored him, refusing to succumb to his goading. She was amazed at his patience.

'I hope Abela and Ayla return in time for the wedding,' Mirah said.

Nate smiled, he knew any mention of their wedding infuriated Bishnor. 'The village is not far. If the fever continues, I'll send my own men to escort them. Don't worry they'll be here in time.'

Mirah hadn't yet found the courage to ask Shemyaza about inviting Dara. She didn't even know if the Chashmalim would allow her to leave her training in the desert fortress.

'Have you decided on the flowers?' he asked knowing full well she had.

She almost laughed.

Sumer had stepped up her maternal fussing and taken it upon herself to organise most of the wedding. Mirah didn't mind. She took joy in seeing her come alive when she showed her an array of flowers, advising her on which ones were the best.

Bishnor rose from the throne and went to the portal. It shimmered and evaporated.

There were no Kudu horns announcing his arrival. Shemyaza exited the portal and its clover blue membrane shivered back into place.

Bishnor and Shemyaza's unspoken communication reeked of secrets they'd never reveal. Shemyaza assessed Nate and dipped his head in approval. He stretched his extraordinary golden wings high and then folded them.

When he focused on her, Mirah wanted to wield herself over the mountain and would have considered it, if not for Neviah and Nate standing beside her.

'Mirah you look as beautiful as ever. I hope I didn't keep you waiting though I'm sure you don't mind. If you excel today, I have a small gift for you.'

She didn't give a damn about the gift, his displeasure concerned her more.

Each time he'd ordered her to wield for him, she'd hidden her developing skills as much she dared without raising suspicion. It wasn't the only thing she held back. When she'd wielded Eran over the mountain, she'd been sure she'd heard a distant echo laughing.

Shemyaza came and stroked her hand and ice covered her skin. His immortal eyes glowered and she wondered if he realised how every part of her recoiled at his touch.

'After I delivered you from Barakel and realised your uniqueness, I chose to give you a gift beyond measure. Now you must honour me and fulfil your pledge. Let's begin.'

He took his place on the central throne and waved his hand.

She swallowed. God or not, he was insane if he believed he'd delivered her from Barakel. She'd not asked for a gift, never pledged anything and he acted like she should be grateful.

Neviah gave it her all and Mirah responded with just enough. Not once did she penetrate the rock with an ice spear blaming that first time in the Taphas chamber on some kind of fluke shot.

Midway through forming an ice dagger, Shemyaza commanded them to stop and rose from his throne.

'I know you can do better. We'll commence in a few days which will give me time to consider developing your motivation.'

⁂

The following morning, she rushed to wash in her bathing pool before dressing in her Taphas wear. She'd dreamt of a thousand terrible ways Shemyaza contemplated her motivation, beginning with dreaded beasts like the Dagani or Zamani and ending with Bishnor.

As they walked to the shaft, Neviah pulled on her braid.

'Are you all right?' Mirah asked.

'I'm fine,' she bit back. 'I just don't see why Nate insists on us rising an hour earlier than before.'

'He's worried.'

They paused by the shaft. Mirah peered into the dark void, waiting for the platform to appear.

'Why should he worry?' Neviah continued. 'If we had it in mind to, we could annihilate him.'

Mirah whipped her head up as she swung around. 'You don't mean that?'

Neviah shifted on her hips. 'I'm not saying I would but if we chose to we could.'

When the darkness in the shaft absorbed them Mirah broke the silence. 'I think after what happened on the plateau, Nate understands we won't kill anyone. It terrifies him.'

'Well, he's wrong.'

'Why?'

'Because those rebels weren't my enemies.'

Mirah wished she could see Neviah's face. She was always so readable but in the darkness, she couldn't gauge her responses. Whatever impact the Fallen Star previously had on her, the incident on the plateau had undone. Neviah still refused Mirah's invitations to hear him sing.

'I still see them,' Neviah said, her voice softening.

Mirah knew who she meant. Every time she closed her eyes the rebels, wide-eyed and burning seared into her memory and clashed with returning images of Barakel.

She hadn't known Bishnor's name then, but it was him who'd led the giants into their shelter. The bloodlust in his eyes showed her his intention. She'd seen the bodies being dragged across the ground and stacked ready for igniting before Nate and his men ushered them towards his ship.

Eran, it seemed had a talent for escaping. Nate didn't believe he was still in Hermonial. When he'd asked, she told him Eran was a friend from Barakel. She wished she'd had time to find out how he'd survived and why he'd been with rebels at the Buzur's mines. All he'd managed to tell her was a rumour that Gabe boarded a ship at Lithinos. How he'd got there or where he planned to go, Eran didn't know.

'I see them too,' Mirah yielded.

She didn't tell her Nate came to her room each night and comforted her until she fell asleep or how much he'd become her shelter and sanctuary, her antidote. It didn't seem fair.

When they reached the courtyard, Zeev was grinning and ready to spar. Mirah narrowed her eyes and his face dropped.

Neviah paused. 'I know I've said it before but thank you again for saving Eran. I know you took a risk.' She grabbed hold of her braid, tightening it at the end, and said, 'Let's do this.'

Mirah followed her, feeling a little whiplashed.

Neviah strode over to Zeev. 'Can you show me how to shunt a dagger in between the ribs?'

'Really?' he asked, his deep brown eyes weighing up her agenda.

'Yes, so I know how to do it if you ever gawk at me with that ridiculous expression again.'

'If you don't like getting out of bed so early, I could always join you?'

'If you feel like being burned alive, try it.'

He gave her a sword. 'Maybe one day I will,' he pledged, bringing his sword down against hers.

Nate rolled his eyes. He held out Mirah's staff, and she took it readying herself for his attack. He feigned to the right, slid under her staff, grabbed her hold and winked. 'I thought we'd try a new tactic. One where you defend against physical ambush.'

'You just want to embrace me.'

'Can you blame me?'

'No wielding?'

He'd made her agree beforehand after reminding her he'd seen Wielders' power fail.

'No wielding,' he confirmed.

His movements were fast and raw. Each time she tried to block his approach he manoeuvred around her staff coming up inside it, holding her for longer than needed. Teasing aside, Mirah could see her own failing. She needed to work out how to keep him at bay.

'Watch his feet,' Zeev shouted over.

'Thanks,' Nate shouted back, dryly.

She studied his footsteps until she saw a pattern in his movements.

'Trust Zeev to open his generous mouth. I was enjoying that,' Nate mumbled as he failed to catch her once again.

'You're supposed to be training me,' she accused.

'I would have told you in the end,' he said, coming up and wrapping his arm around her waist. 'I just couldn't resist it.'

She went to push him off.

'You're too captivating. I can't let you go.'

⁂

Galia dawdled around vendor after vendor holding up pastel fabrics with intricate gold and silver embroidered designs. 'What about this one?'

'It's as beautiful as the last one,' Mirah replied.

Galia strolled off insisting they might have something better elsewhere.

After so much walking in the midday heat, Mirah's feet were swelling in her boots. 'If you don't choose something soon, I'll pick for you,' she pressed.

'I like the first one best,' Galia said, lowering the lush green silk. 'The cream one with the woven, silver birds on the seam. It will go well with my hair.'

After returning and purchasing the fabric, she left Mirah with a slight bounce in her steps to meet a dressmaker on the other side of the city.

With Nate busy completing drills and inspecting his men, she found herself wandering. She walked to the river and paddled in the water.

Some labourers nearby chanted to a rhythm whilst rubbing a beeswax coating onto oars. Her feet soothed, she weaved through the city until she stood outside the doors of the Azu. She was deliberating knocking when an Azu with a burgundy chord entwined in her braided hair came out.

On seeing Mirah asked, 'Can I help you?'

Although she'd seen them a few times, she still found it difficult not to stare at her cone-shaped head.

'I was wondering when Abela and Ayla will return?'

'They returned this morning but they're not here. I believe they're assisting a woman suffering from toothworm.'

Whatever toothworm was it didn't sound pleasant.

'Do you know where they are?'

The Azu pointed behind her. 'If you follow the canal past Mammetum's temple ruins, you'll come to the cities old quarter. They should be somewhere down there.'

'Thank you,' Mirah said, thinking the Azu had been most accommodating compared to the few she'd met before. Maybe things would be different since Shemyaza had announced Nate's official proposal.

She wandered around narrow dusty tracks hoping to see Abela or Ayla. The old quarter housed a series of smaller dwellings, most of them squarish, compared to the circular towers nearer the mountain. There were no courtyards, upper levels or ornamental glass decorating their walls.

She reached several children wearing brown weaved tunics playing with wooden beads on the path. A girl with an oval face and a wide smile set over a prominent chin ambled towards her. Her dark, bouncing, curls settled on her shoulders as she stopped.

'Are you a Wielder?'

'I am,' Mirah smiled.

Her large brown, almond-shaped eyes gleamed. 'How does it work?'

Instead of explaining what she didn't understand, she decided to try and show her. She'd never wielded water from a distance but thought to try guiding a small bubble of water from the canal near Mammentum's temple. When it came into view, she relaxed. Later she'd ask Galia about the distance Water Wielders could wield from.

More children with expectant faces gathered as she wielded the bubble of water into the shape of a small frog.

The children gasped as the frog hopped around in the air. They chased it, leaping and laughing, with their little arms raising to catch it.

'Thank you,' the girl said, watching the others play.

She was older, on the cusp of adolescence and Mirah presumed some of the younger children were her siblings.

'My name is Mirah. What is yours?'

'I'm Haia.'

'I don't suppose you've noticed anyone dressed like the Azu? I'm looking for my friends.'

She shook her head. 'Could you teach me how to do that?' she asked, watching the little frog still leaping around.

'I'm sorry it's not possible.'

The girl's face dropped.

'Maybe when you're older,' Mirah said, trying to ease her disappointment. She regretted her words the moment she spoke them. She didn't want Haia anywhere near Shemyaza or Bishnor or most of the other Wielders.

'I have to go now and see if I can find my friends,' Mirah said.

Haia trotted off, gathered the children, and they retired to their beads. A sadness overcame Mirah as she remembered how naïve she'd been playing stones with others at Barakel.

She wandered on until reaching a small brook banked against the edge of the city. On its far side, several cedar trees created long sinister shadows over the ground. She was about to retrace her steps when someone stepped out from behind a tree.

'Gabe!'

She leaped over the brook and sprinted towards him, crushing her body against his. Emotions which had no language poured out of her with every emerging tear.

'Easy,' he said, stepping back to prevent himself from falling.

She never thought she'd see his mischievous grin again. 'What are you doing here? Did Eran tell you where to find me?'

'Eran's alive?'

'You haven't seen him?' she asked wiping her tears.

'Geez. Eran. When I returned, I only found Tam.'

'Tam's alive?'

'Can we talk about him later?'

She considered asking about Ma but knew in her heart if she'd survived he'd have already said. 'I can't believe you're here.'

Relief washed over her. He looked older, nearly a foot taller, his brown hair cut shorter. His face was more tanned with a slight hardening that never existed before. Perspiration glistened on his forehead and his bog-stained cloak hung loose off his shoulders.

'You must be sweltering?' She contemplated wielding air and cooling him but decided against it. She could explain that later. 'There's a brook back there.'

'I'm not thirsty,' he said, glancing behind her.

Months worth of dirt covered his dark pants. It seemed strange to see a dagger sheathed at his side. He'd never carried a weapon until now.

'You look different,' Mirah said.

'So do you.' He reached over tugging on her Taphas shirt. 'What are you wearing?'

'It's kind of normal around here. How did you know how to find me?'

His eyes scanned across the brook making sure no one regarded them. 'Come, we don't have much time,' he said, clutching her hand pulling her into the trees.

She followed him for a few steps but then paused. 'Where are we going?'

'I need to get you out of here. Somewhere safer.'

'I can't leave.'

He tugged on her hand and she dug her heels into the dusty soil.

'I'm not leaving. Neviah, Abela and Ayla are here and I'm… I'm getting married.'

'What?' he asked. The shock halting him in his tracks.

'I'm not being forced if that's what you thinking. I'm sure if you come and meet him, you'd like him. He can arrange somewhere for you to stay. No one else needs to know you are here.'

'Can you even hear yourself?'

His tone hardened in a way she'd never heard him speak before.

'Do you realise how ridiculous you sound? You're only seventeen.'

'Eighteen,' she corrected him.

She couldn't place his expression. Was he angry? A deep pang surged through her at his sharp accusations. She snapped at him, 'You have no idea what I've been through. Don't judge me.'

'Have you given yourself to him?'

She flinched, her hands tightening. 'Not that it's your business but no.'

'Then we're leaving. I will return and get the others once you're safe.'

She took a pensive stride towards him. 'I told you, I'm not going.'

'How can you even consider joining yourself with a Nephilim? Do you know what they are? They're disgusting murderous hybrids,' he said, curling his lip.

'Do you mean the giants? I'm not marrying one of them. Not everyone here is like that.'

He spotted the ring on her finger and blanched. 'Do you understand how that works?'

'Of course,' she answered.

'Then why? What have they done to you?' His focus darted behind her for the briefest moment, checking again that no one was watching. 'I can't stay. I took a terrible risk sneaking here. If someone finds me—'

'Please come with me,' she begged, grabbing hold of his arm.

'Meciel warned me you might refuse to leave, and I didn't believe him.'

He turned deathly pale, and she cringed with revulsion at the pain she caused him.

Regret poured from his moistened green eyes. He grabbed her arm and placed his hand on her forehead. 'I'm sorry.'

'What are you doing?' She tried to push him away, but he was much stronger.

Forcing his hand over her forehead, he uttered, 'Galah.'

A flashing heat seared through her mind and she shoved his arm aside. He let her go so she could step away.

'What have you done?'

'I've taken the veil from your eyes, Mirah. You need to see the truth.'

She searched around trying to determine if anything looked different but everything appeared the same.

He backed up a step. 'I'll return at the same time in three days. I hope you change your mind.'

'You're walking out on me? She reached out to him. 'Gabe, why are you doing this?'

'Because you leave me no choice.'

❊ 24 ❊

Mirah hesitated under the cedar trees. Part of her longed to chase after Gabe, to convince him and to beg him to stay but he'd bolted too fast and not even looked back.

One moment her hopes had come alive and the next they shattered. She knew Neviah would grab Abela and Ayla and run but what about Nate, would he come with her? Everyone would be in danger when Shemyaza came for him.

Galia, Arella and Zeev flashed through her mind. They were her friends. She didn't want to leave them. She rubbed her fingers over her forehead to soothe the oncoming ache. He'd given her three days to decide what she would do. Three days to come up with a plan to try and persuade him to change his mind.

She crossed over the brook into the old quarter and cast her eyes to the inky darkness sweeping across the sky. The wind promised an unleashing of torrential rain. A flash of light snapped against the blackened clouds, forcing them to submit and descend lower.

The children playing with the beads had scattered. She hurried along the dimming pathways past the rustic mud-brick houses. The old quarter was abandoned, and she considered if the people thought the coming storm an omen of some kind.

Near the canal, dread wept like the rain itself on the women's faces. She would have put their desperation down to the suspect omen if it were not for their clenched expressions slathered with ruin.

Widows—though conquered husbands laboured at their side, barren—though coerced children gripped their skirts.

It wasn't just the defeated gods' temples brought to ruin, under their lush clothing, shattered shells remained. Everyone unique though unified by a muted wail of agonising grief.

The wind howled and would have extinguished their dreams if they hadn't died long ago. How had she not seen this before? She curled her fists and fled.

By the time she reached the Diatheatre, her face paled ashen. Her breathing as stuttered as the rain. There were no spectra of women smiling in an array of coloured gowns. The once safe haven now as empty as the expanding void inside. She sat on the well-worn steps, too afraid to go back outside.

What had Gabe done to her? She lifted her knees and hugged them tight against her body. Sometime later the Fallen Star sat by her side.

'I see someone has removed the veil.'

She cast her gaze over his empathetic frown. 'What's happening?'

'Shemyaza glamoured the city. The truth is what you see now.'

'How is that possible? Their faces, the people, they are broken.'

'Perhaps the question you should ask is why?'

She caught the heaviness in his eyes before he explained. 'Shemyaza's empire is built on a lie. If the people here don't submit, then he fills their minds with deception, conditioning them to serve him. They are nothing more than slaves. You already comprehend what happens to those beyond his borders.'

Mirah unfolded her legs and rubbed her hands over the back of her knees, pushing the blood flow into her calves. 'Why don't they fight back or leave?'

'Most don't know any different and those who once did, can't remember.'

'But I'm friends with people who remember. People who are not deluded.'

The Fallen Star's brows pulled together, and he fixed his gaze on hers. 'As you know, he has other ways of controlling them.'

She closed her eyes and brushed her thumb in smoothing rotations over her palm, her index finger grazing over her amulet. Her mind flashed to Nate sitting in the garden when he'd said, *if there was a way, I would have found it.* She looked up to the Fallen Star for answers, maybe he knew something they didn't.

The Fallen Star stared at her ring. 'Do you understand what that is? How it functions?'

'Not really. I mean, I know how to wield but not how it works.'

'You've seen the Isten Baba?'

'Yes. It's a portal through which the gods walk.'

The Fallen Star scoffed. 'They are not gods. Although they attempt to claim the title. The Isten Baba is the first gate from which they descended on the mountain from another realm. It's not the only gate.

In the unseen realm, time doesn't dictate like here.' He drifted, imagining things undefinable and then blinked. 'There are other beings in that realm who for reasons I'm not at liberty to explain can't cross over. The amulet you're wearing is a link between you and a being from the other realm. The Wielder has no power.'

'I thought the amulet had given me power of my own.'

'No. The Wielder using the amulet channels another being's power into this world.'

'What sort of beings?'

'They are malevolent, some of them serve Shemyaza. They have no flesh and desire a body of their own.'

Alarmed, she sat up straighter, a tightening rip in her belly seared at the sudden movement. 'Do any of the Wielders know?'

'Possibly. I suspect some may have heard their voices.'

Whatever this being was, it had been using her. She sensed its taint creep across her flesh. Her skin prickled as if in warning against her destruction. She grabbed her finger to wrench off the ring.

The Fallen Star reached over and placed his hand across hers. 'I wouldn't do that right now. Not if you're planning on returning to the mountain.'

'Does it know, this being, my thoughts and my feelings? Does it have a name?'

'It perceives what you allow it. As for its name, there are many. I don't know who is linked to that ring.'

'Does Nate know about this?'

The Fallen Star patted her hand. 'I'm sorry.'

Her voice picked up speed as panic erupted. 'Why didn't he tell me that everything I see is an illusion?' She swallowed the bile rising in her throat. 'Why didn't he tell me about this?' She shook off his hand and lifted her own to show him the ring.

'That's something you'll need to ask him.'

'How did you find out about this?'

'I once came from that realm.'

Mirah jumped up from her seating.

'I'm not like them,' he said, quickly. 'Whilst I'm here, I try to ease people's pain and suffering.'

A growl tore across the sky and Mirah raised her hands over her ears shielding against the thunder's lament.

'The storm is a good sign. As I said to you before, everything has its time and its season. Your journey, as difficult as it has been will one day strengthen you. You should go now before someone wonders where you are.'

He was right, Nate would finish with his men soon. She thanked the Fallen Star and left. She'd figure out what to say to Nate on the way.

As she neared the mountain, the heavens unloaded torrential rain. Her clothes clung and sagged against her skin. Keeping to less travelled roads, she saw no one and was glad, she didn't think she could bear to see their tormented faces.

Would Nate be the same? What would she do when she faced him?

Gabe had taken the veil from her eyes, only to submerge her in what felt like an ocean of fire. She tried to keep above its waves but the closer she came to the mountain the hotter its heat burned her airways. She was going under. Time felt irrelevant, frozen in the space between unknowing and knowing. A place where she began fading.

She drifted across the deserted courtyard and shivered in the darkened shaft. Her plans to search out Nate's chamber shifted as she decided to change out of her wet clothes first. She still didn't know what she'd say to him.

❊

She'd finished changing when he tapped on her door and entered.

'What's the matter?' he asked, concern rising on his face.

Her stomach lurched and tried to escape her. 'Did you know about the glamour?' she shrieked.

He rushed towards her.

'Don't touch me. Did you know?'

'Yes.'

'Why?' She couldn't bring herself to say anymore.

'We can't discuss this here.'

Rain drenched her clothing as they crossed back over the courtyard.

Nate passed her his cloak. 'Please take it,' he urged.

Darkness had arrived early because of the storm. He led her through the deserted city coming to one of the rustic tower homes. Guilt and relief flowed through her. Nate still looked the same.

As soon as he entered the building, he stripped to the waist, dropping his wet clothes on the floor. His blue eyes never left hers as he redressed. She pleaded with herself that he had a good explanation.

The rain pelted against the reed thatched roof almost drowning out the sound of his voice.

'You're safe here,' he reassured her.

Under different circumstances, she'd have asked why he had this place. Not that she could see much in the dim light. She stayed silent, waiting. The only sound, except for the rain was water dripping from his sodden cloak still wrapped around her, as they pattered onto the wooden beamed floor.

He left the room and returned with a woollen blanket. 'You need to remove those soaking clothes.'

She ignored his offer, refusing to uncross her arms clamped over her breast. Not daring to force her, he lay the blanket on the back of a chair.

'How could I explain to you what you couldn't see?'

Mirah conceded to herself his answer made some sense. If she were in his position, how could she have explained it? Relief crept to the edge of her senses but she held it at bay, not able to give in to it yet.

'How did you break through Shemyaza's glamour?'

She wasn't ready to expose Gabe and diverted his question with another. 'Do you know about the beings orchestrating the wielding?'

'How do you know about that?'

The sharpness of his tone took her off guard, and she blurted out, 'The Fallen Star seems to be the only one in Hermonial who tells the truth.'

Nate's shoulders sank, and he reached for her. 'I didn't want to frighten you.'

She took a step back. 'So you promised to keep me safe by lying?'

'I didn't lie.'

No, he hadn't lied. He hadn't mentioned anything at all.

'You let that Beast use me? You allowed that Beast's power to surge through me. You said you'd keep me safe.' She shuddered at the repulsion heaving through her. Couldn't he see the damage he'd done? 'Tell me, Nate, where does the truth go when it's unspoken?'

The tears welling in his blue eyes made them glassy. His voice dipped low, and he surrendered, 'I never wanted any of this for you.'

'Neither did I,' she snapped and dashed out the door into the rain.

His footsteps squelched behind her, following from a short distance away. When she crossed under the lapis lazuli archway, they silenced.

❊ 25 ❊

The next morning Sumer came to her room. As soon as Mirah saw the shadows under her weary eyes, she realised Nate had spoken to her.

Did she know about the glamour and the wielding? She was old enough to remember before Shemyaza's arrival. If she knew then probably so did Zeev and what of Galia and Arella? Did they know about the beasts wielding their power?

'I'm fine. I'm not hungry. Leave me alone,' she said, before slamming her door.

After she heard Sumer's footsteps pad down the tunnel, she peeked out of her chamber and left to speak to Neviah. She had an idea she wanted to test, but they needed to be far from the mountain.

She slipped into Neviah's room and shut the door. 'I'm not going to training. Will you meet me by the river later? There's something we have to discuss?'

'What's wrong?'

'I can't talk about it now. Please, just stick to your routine. I don't want anyone to become suspicious.'

'What about Nate?'

'Tell him, I'm unwell.'

For the next few hours, she stayed in her room fretting that he might knock on her door.

❊

When she approached the river, Neviah stood up and wiped the sand from her clothing.

'What's going on? Nate looked as terrible this morning as you do. He stormed off into the city when I told him you were sick.'

'Everything here is a lie.'

'I know that.'

'No, you don't. There's something I want to try but I'm uncertain it will work. Come, it's more private by those marshes.'

'You're acting strange,' Neviah said as she followed. 'What is this all about?'

Satisfied the marshes hid them from view, Mirah said, 'Gabe was here.'

'What do you mean was?' she asked, scanning her eyes around as if she expected to see him. 'Where is he?'

'He did something to shift a veil from my eyes. I'd like to see if I can show you.' Mirah reached over and touched Neviah's forehead and whispered, 'Galah.'

After several attempts, she flopped down onto the sand. 'I don't understand why it isn't working. I'm sure I have the word right.'

'Mirah, what is going on?'

She recalled how Gabe had done it. They were arguing his voice more forceful. She wondered if instead of asking she should seek to be more commanding.

'Let me try again?' With every ounce of might she possessed, she demanded the glamour to shift from Neviah's eyes.

'What was that?'

She grabbed Neviah's arm and led her along the river. 'Look at them,' she said, pointing to men digging for worms in the silt.

Neviah squinted and after a moment her eyes snapped to Mirah's.

'It's called a glamour. Everything we believed is a lie. Gabe said he'll be back the day after tomorrow to take us home.'

'What about Nate?'

Mirah closed her eyes and rubbed her hand across her brow. 'He's not coming.'

'I thought you loved him?'

'I do.'

'Then I don't understand?'

'There are other things, more complicated things which I'm not ready to explain. For now, we need to keep our routine, not raise suspicion and find a way to reach Abela and Ayla.'

In case they became separated, Mirah explained where to meet Gabe. Three days seemed an awful long time.

Keep to your routine, she'd told herself over and over as they made their way to training the next morning. Would Nate see right through her, realise her intentions? She hadn't seen him since storming off into the rain.

Last night was an endless purging of conflicting thoughts and emotions. She felt violated knowing an unnamed being used her and touched up against her soul. The Beast's voice had been silent since the lake and it had relieved her to ignore it, hoping she'd somehow been mistaken.

Maybe she was being too hard on Nate and she needed to take responsibility for her own denial? If she talked to him, would he come, could she risk it?

No, he'd known for sure about the wielding. He'd allowed that Beast to use and defile her. As much as she loved him, she couldn't forgive him for the betrayal.

Every essence of her being recoiled against the knowledge of their impending separation. Her plans accusing her of her own treachery against herself, against him, against their love. On and on her meditations surged through the night as she sat, arms locked around her knees, rocking herself in an attempt to pacify them.

When she arrived in the courtyard the following morning, Eliah's grim face revealed that Nate had confronted him about her bruises. She pushed thoughts of where Nate was or what he was doing to the side.

Zeev had his head bowed, finding the dust on his boots very interesting. She crossed towards them and whispered to Neviah to act normal.

They'd been sparring for a while when Eliah said, 'Your technique has become sloppy in my absence. You need to focus.'

'Yesterday, I was unwell. I'm still recovering.'

'Maybe you should visit the Azu?'

'I plan to go after,' she replied. The first part of their plan clicking into place.

'Then we'll leave training for today. It's good to see you again.'

‘Thank you for your assistance. I hope Nate wasn’t too severe with you?’

Eliah shrugged. ‘I cleaned the latrines for a week. I’m guessing it could have been worse.’ He smiled a knowing smile.

Eliah never discussed his history or what he thought of this place. It was likely that if Zeev and Nate trusted him, they’d probably taken him into their confidence. Either way, she liked him and was glad she’d seen him before leaving. ‘It’s good to see you as well,’ she said, passing him her staff.

When she reached the Azu, the door was ajar. She stepped over the threshold and a mixture of pungent herb scents wafted around the small room.

A formidable bronze statue of a seated cone-headed woman dominated the space. She sat with her arms across her chest, a string of golden amulets covering her neck and a row of pleated frills adorned her legs. Whichever way Mirah rotated around her, the statue’s penetrating eyes followed. Whoever she was, she gave Mirah an uneasy feeling which made her pity the sculptured dog reclining at her feet.

‘Can I help you?’ said a rounded figured Azu.

‘I have a headache.’

She turned and over her shoulder said, ‘Follow me.’

The Azu led her into a cedar panelled antechamber. Mirah studied a perplexing cuneiform script inscribed all over the wood as she waited. On the far wall, rows of clay jars and pots in varied shapes and sizes were organised along with small terracotta figurines with hands holding various body parts.

‘Sit,’ the Azu said, her cone-head nodding to a chair.

She selected a few jars, scooped their contents into a clay bowl and set the bowl over hot coals. The Azu ignored her, preferring to chant over the burning contents.

Mirah found the aroma appealing. ‘What are the ingredients?’

‘Goose blood, fat and the rind of its gizzard,’ she announced without looking up.

She regretted asking. At home, she would have made tea from blue vervain or rosemary and sage.

The Azu removed the clay bowl and its contents from the coals. 'It will take a moment to cool,' she said, stretching for another jar.

'Is Abela or Ayla here?'

'Ayla is making poultices.'

'Could I speak to her?'

The Azu place down the jar and left the antechamber. She returned a moment later and announced, 'She will be here soon.' Returning to her labour she scooped out a reddish cedar wood resin from the jar.

On arrival, Ayla regarded the Azu's preparations. Her brow furrowed. 'Headache?'

'You have no idea.'

When the contents had cooled to the Azu's satisfaction, she ground them with added herbs and mixed them into the cedar resin. It formed a thick gooey ointment which she rubbed over Mirah's forehead.

'Thank you,' Mirah said.

The Azu scraped the remaining ointment into a small pot. 'Weddings can be so stressful. Here,' she said, handing Mirah the pot. 'I'm sure Ayla can see you out.'

When they were alone, Mirah tapped her fingers to her tacky forehead. 'I was expecting herbal tea.'

'They have strange ways around here.'

Mirah's eyes flicked to the door, and she softened her voice, 'I need to talk to you, somewhere private.'

'Is it about the wedding?'

'Yes and no.'

'There's a quiet garden out the back.'

Every herb and plant she knew and others she didn't recognise filled the garden. They paused by a lily covered pond, the cast of their shadows encouraging the golden fish to rise to the surface, searching for food.

Satisfied no one was nearby, Mirah poured out everything in whispers. When she finished Ayla let out a long breath.

'Will you come?' Mirah asked.

'Of course and so will Abela.'

'Do you know where Mammetum's ruined temple is?'

Ayla nodded.

'Then meet us there tomorrow at midday.'

Standing by the exit of the Azu's complex, Ayla took her hand. 'You've made the right choice,' she reassured her.

On her way to meet Neviah, she bumped into Galia.

'I was coming to find you. Zeev told me you'd gone to the Azu. Are you ill?'

She waved the small pot in her hand. 'I feel better now.'

In the truth, the ointment was working. It not only relieved the headache but soothed some of her anxiety as well.

'We've missed the Fallen Star. He's already stopped singing. I don't suppose you feel like shopping? I've seen the most precious sandals.'

'To be honest, I just want to bathe in my pool.'

Galia's dark eyebrows lowered, the beats of her mind silently ticking.

'I'll catch up with you later,' Mirah said, rushing off, the pain of seeing Galia heavy on her heart.

If she didn't find a way to warn her or Arella about the wielding, then she was no different from Nate. But how? How could she tell them without risking their plans to escape?

When she reached the mountain, Nate leaned against the archway of the lapis boundary wall. He stared at the sticky residue on her forehead and grimaced.

'I know you're not ready to talk to me but I thought you should know, that lad you saved, Eran, Bishnor has found him.'

'Where? Is he all right? Can I speak to him?'

'Bishnor took him into the bowels of the mountain before I could intervene.'

Her voice came out sharp and urgent. 'You have to help him. Get him out of there.'

'I'm working on it.'

She leaned up against the archway. She couldn't take anymore. 'Don't,' she said, lifting her arm out to stop him as he edged closer.

'I love you Mirah. I'm trying to protect you. Don't look away from me,' he pleaded.

With her raised arm shaking, she rested her head back against the cooling gemstone covered stone and shut her eyes. If she didn't stop swaying, she knew she would faint.

'I'm sorry. Please, don't hold it against me. Let me help you.'

He came nearer. The warmth of his breath caressed her cheek, but he didn't touch her. She couldn't move. If she allowed his support, she'd crumble.

She sensed his hesitation, saw the shadow of his movement crossing her eyelids as he shuffled favouring one foot over the other. Love pangs beat within her chest, their sharpness crying out for him to ease away the pain.

Something changed.

Her heartbeats slowed. A calmness overcame her not quite cold but distant, unrecognisable. She opened her eyes.

'If you want to help me help Eran.'

She pushed off the archway and crossed the courtyard into the chasm.

⁂

Later that evening Neviah entered Mirah's chamber. 'Have you eaten?' she asked.

Mirah didn't answer.

'I have food in my room.'

She returned a moment later with cheese, flatbread and some grapes.

'You need to eat. For tomorrow,' she said, in a low secretive whisper.

She meant well so Mirah didn't protest. The hollow of her stomach grumbled in agreement as she swallowed a tiny bit of cheese.

Neviah leaned by the opening in the mountainside. 'Those beasts are not in the arena,' she said, filling the sound of emptiness.

She'd already known, their silence confirming they'd gone somewhere but where or why, she didn't dare to focus on that now.

She paused pushing her food around her plate. 'Eran is here. He's their prisoner, somewhere under the mountain.'

Neviah didn't turn from the opening. She unfolded an arm and tugged on her hair braid. 'It changes nothing. We stick to the plan.'

If she'd had the energy, she would have argued for the impossible knowing they'd never reach him.

'Do you know with everything going on, you've not told me how Gabe found us?'

'I don't know. Our meeting was brief. He said he'd explain later.'

She retreated from the opening and studied her. 'Why haven't you confided in Nate? Even though I still don't trust him, I know he'd come with you if you asked.'

'I can't talk about him now.' She blinked slowly, pushing back the moisture in the corner of her eyes.

Neviah wrapped her hands around her shoulders and her voice cracked as she said, 'I don't want to leave Zeev behind. I kind of like him.'

Mirah wasn't sure if her admittance was to herself or her. 'I know,' was all she could reply.

'We should sleep,' Neviah said, preparing to leave.

Mirah hadn't even realised the stars blossomed in the sky until now. She twisted away from them and waited for a new nightmare to begin.

⁂

The following morning, she heard Neviah's rapid footsteps echoing in the tunnel before she opened her door and shot inside her room.

'I'm not sure Zeev believed a word I said when I told him I was ill. What if he's in the courtyard or follows us when we leave?'

'Nev, calm down. Did you see Galia?'

'No. It's strange, she never appeared and when I asked Zeev, he said Nate had her running an errand.'

Mirah wanted to ask more about Galia's curious assignment but realised Neviah was already flustered and inquiring further would only make her worse. She'd slept little for the past three nights and had no energy left to carry Neviah through this, she didn't have the resources to support herself.

'We have one chance. All we can do is stick to the plan and hope for the best. Ready?' she asked, opening the door. She took one glance around her room and left.

To her relief, they saw no one as they traversed the tunnels to the shaft. When they reached the bottom and crossed to the chasm, Mirah said, 'Remember if anyone asks, we're going to the Azu.'

Neviah nodded. 'I hope Zeev isn't around.'

She inhaled a deep breath, and they stepped into the light. She would have sworn Neviah didn't take another breath until she crossed under the lapis lazuli archway.

They were midway to the Diatheatre when Neviah interrupted her surveillance of the street ahead.

'Are you sure about this? It seems risky stopping to say goodbye to the Fallen Star. I mean how long before Nate realises we've left?'

'I have to do this. There's something I need to explain to him. I'll tell you later after we are safe.'

Neviah stopped in her tracks. 'I don't like secrets. I think you should tell me now.'

Mirah couldn't tell her about her plans to ask the Fallen Star to warn Galia. She'd been too afraid to disclose the horror to Neviah just yet.

Seeing Neviah would not to budge, she walked off. 'I'll meet you by the brook as soon as I can.'

She rounded the street corner and froze. Nate raced over the top of the Diatheatre steps against the flow of women leaving.

What was he doing there? The thought of him seeking retribution because of the Fallen Star's confession sent a muted shrill deep into her core. How could she have been so foolish to give Nate his name?

Neviah grabbed her arm, pulling her behind a building. 'This way,' she urged. 'Run,' she snapped, her words penetrating Mirah's clouding brain.

He'd looked so wounded and exhausted that Mirah had to remind herself of what he'd done. How he'd let that Beast debase and defile her. She cringed at the prospect of its power surging through her.

With every step she paced, she couldn't identify if her ragged breath was from running or anxiety

❊ 26 ❊

Gabe curled his toes inside his mud crusted boots. Like a motionless bronze idol, he fixed his gaze across the brook, still nothing. Would Mirah come? How long would he wait before sneaking into the cursed city to find her? Alone, he somewhat regretted declining Meciel and Bina's offers to assist him. This was his risk to take and his alone.

He glanced at the majestic crystal blue mountain reigning over the mud huts and resplendent buildings beyond. He'd listened to every detail Meciel shared about the war beyond the heavens and Shemyaza's descent on the mountain. At the sight of it, every strange word Meciel taught him fled from his mind and so did the power that came with them. If she didn't come the chains of defeat soon would.

The blazing sun seared remnants of the storm away, leaving an elixir of mildew harassing the air. He resisted the urge to rub the sting in his eyes, every time he'd closed them the dreaded memory of her pleading cries surfaced. Who was this man she'd given her heart to? What had he done to her? He knew if he saw him, he'd kill him.

A haggard woman strolled to the brook to draw water. Gabe willed her to leave. If she saw Mirah with possibly the others, he'd have no choice but to intervene. What if Mirah came to refuse him? To try again to beg him to stay?

Ammo would have known what to do. Underneath his swagger stood a champion who'd coached him on how to survive, not just with the skills of an Acquisitioner but how to endure on the inside as well. He'd warned Gabe she might react this way, but he'd refused to believe it until now.

The woman filled her water skin and shuffled back into the city. She'd not long gone out of view when he stiffened, his legs almost buckling.

Mirah looked terrible. He wasn't guilty. He'd achieved what he'd needed to open her eyes. Neviah, Abela and Ayla were with her. As the girls crossed the brook, Gabe scanned behind them, checking they weren't being followed.

'I'm glad you came.' He wanted to embrace them all, most of all Mirah and ask her to forgive him for his harsh words but instead, he said, 'Talk later, keep moving.' He urged them onward as they moved through the trees foreboding shadows.

Neviah kept pace with him through the brown grass whipping at their hips. Mirah stayed a short distance behind with Abela and Ayla but he couldn't risk stopping or slowing down.

After some hours they entered the boggy marshes, and he slowed his pace. The pungent scent of decay clung to their clothes and seeped into his nostrils.

He stopped on a muddy elevation rising up over the sodden ground. Cracked eggshells, feathers and gloopy bird droppings decorated the mound. Crouched and sheltered within the frayed reeds, he passed around his water skin. Still, no one spoke as they gulped the water and tried to catch their breath.

They'd been moving for some time when flattened marsh reeds cut out a pathway and he retraced his steps down to the river. The small fishing boat, to his relief, still bobbed on the marshy water.

'Hurry,' he said, as he picked up two oars.

He rowed to the far side of the river and let the current draw them downstream. Often, between the currents' distractions, he chanced glances at Mirah, aware he still showed no sign of relief that she'd come. The others sat with hesitant expressions waiting to ask for news of Barakel.

'Damn,' he muttered as they rounded a bend in the river to find a sizeable barge, heavy laden with cedar rowing towards them. 'Quick, hide yourselves under there,' he said and pointed to a fishing net in the middle of the boat. He lay his cloak over them, shielding them as best as he could.

'Do you think they will see us?' Abela whispered.

'You don't need to worry about them,' he reassured her. 'It's who they might tell if you're seen.' He listened to their shallow breaths as the barge passed. Without their eyes upon him, he relayed their deepest fears. 'No one except Tam remained alive at Barakel.'

Some might have accused him of being a coward but Ayla's gentle voice broke the silence. She offered nothing other than appreciation when she said, 'Thank you.'

When the barge was a safe distance away, he searched up and down the river. 'You can come out now. The river is clear.'

A fishy odour wafted towards him. If it were not for the seriousness of the situation, he'd have bellowed a laugh.

Their hair clung to their perspiring foreheads, and they were tangled in netting entwined around them.

He watched as Mirah unknotted fish net from her ankle. All he wanted was to speak to her alone.

❊ 27 ❊

They reached a small encampment sheltered in a wood the following evening. An old man with bushy eyebrows and a matching silver-white beard leaned over a fire pot whilst stirring an aromatic stew. Mirah thought he appeared more troubled with the concoction brewing than their hurried breach through the tree line.

Next to him sat a woman with a crossbow in her lap. She had glorious long black hair flowing to her waist and the most unusual lavender coloured eyes. She looked to be around thirty without a blemish on her pale skin.

Gabe gestured with his hand and said, 'This is Meciel and Bina.'

'I'm overjoyed you joined us,' Meciel said, his voice deep and round. He glanced up at Gabe with a slight hint of reverence.

'This is my sister, Mirah and our friends, Neviah, Abela and Ayla.'

'Come, you must be hungry,' Meciel said. 'I've made a stew. I hope you like it. It's my secret recipe.'

Gabe and Bina groaned simultaneously.

'Say you love the food,' Bina said, 'or we'll never hear the end of it.'

The long journey and the warmth of the stew lulled them into sluggish silence.

When they'd finished, Gabe delved into a sack pulling out ragged cloaks and shared them around. He dug deeper and gave sets of leather pants and long-sleeved tunics to Abela and Ayla. 'I have others if you prefer them?' he asked, glancing at Mirah and Neviah.

They both declined, favouring their Taphas clothing.

Gabe shrugged. 'Rest. We don't have much time before we need to be moving.' Facing Mirah he said, 'I'm glad you're here.'

She had so much to ask him. She still hadn't told Neviah about wielding but she knew that to do so she needed to speak to her alone.

Too exhausted for anything else, she slipped the ring from her finger, tucked it into her boot and watched Gabe until her eyes drifted.

She caught the sulphur scent before she saw the Beast's haunting apparition and the matted fur flinching over its wide chest. It rose on its hind legs. The sound of its pointy snout sniffing out her scent made her recoil. She ducked behind a conifer. Was she at the lake? Saliva dripped from its sharp fangs.

Come back. You are mistaken. Let me show you.

The Beast's head snapped in her direction. Its nostrils flaring.

Mirah ran. Thudding footsteps and claws scraping against the rocks behind her. On and on she raced, thick ferns whipping her legs, slowing her down. The distance between them shortening. The wisps of her hair sticking to perspiration on her skin. She couldn't outrun it. Long hooked claws ripped into her shoulder when the Beast lunged, knocking her to the ground.

Mirah screamed.

Gabe shook her shoulder. 'It's just a nightmare.'

She peered into the darkness and made out a few concerned faces. The Beast knew she was fleeing. She stared at Gabe's agonised face. 'We need to go. Now.'

He didn't hesitate, didn't try to reassure her it wasn't real.

The moon sat low in the sky, providing enough light for them to see a few paces ahead. They travelled west away from the river. If she'd known where they were going she'd have gone onward and quickened their pace.

Slowing to a halt, Gabe said, 'Wait here. There is a village up ahead. We don't have time to circle it.'

Bina shot off. She assumed to check the perimeter.

'How much further?' Neviah asked Gabe.

'After we reach the other side of the village, it's a two-week journey to our ship. We would have come up the river, but we assumed they'd have lookouts. Crossing land is the safest option.'

'How on earth did you find us?' Ayla asked.

'I found a sword abandoned on the beach. The sword belonged to a Nephilim, someone called Bishnor. Meciel told me about Shemyaza.'

Bina returned, her hand waving them forward.

They crept over the dusty ground. Small dark, round mud huts rose like omens ahead of them. Their inhabitants enticed into slumber. They made their way through the village without a sound.

After trekking some distance, the sun rose from behind. The landscape changing into dusty plains. The warm pink sky spread over the horizon as far as Mirah could see. They had no ground cover, or food, the water skin Gabe held was nearly empty.

She could feel the ring pressing against her shin. Would dehydration force her to wield water?

On the skyline, a dark shadow flew towards them.

'What is that?' Mirah asked.

Gabe lifted his hand, shielding his eyes against the sunlight. 'Don't be frightened. This is Terra. She may appear beastly but she isn't.'

Terra glided to the ground. Gabe reached up and stroked her leathery shoulder. She dipped her head, nuzzling him with her snout, pushing him backwards. Above warm golden eyes, a maroon crest sat like a crown. Terra snorted and Mirah and the others took an instinctive step back.

'He had the same reaction,' Meciel confided. 'It took him weeks to get to know her. I'm sure it won't take you girls as long,' he challenged.

As the heat of the day rose, Terra soared above them, circling and wafting small gusty breezes as she passed.

'Terra,' Meciel call out.

She descended, cocked her head to the side as though she were listening, then lifted into the air and flew away. Up ahead a small formation of rocks protruded from the ground.

Gabe surveyed the hazy horizon. Satisfied they weren't being followed, he said, 'Take a rest.'

Terra returned and dropped a whole sweet lemon tree with the roots still attached.

'She's a good hunter,' Meciel said.

'I'm glad she is,' Gabe said, picking lemons off the branches and passing them around. 'If she wasn't we'd be dead by now.'

Sweet lemons replenished their thirst as they sucked out their juicy moisture, one after another.

'It's not safe here. We're too out in the open,' Gabe said, rising from the rock.

They followed his leading. Bina and Gabe at the front and Meciel following at their rear.

Mirah fell back next to Meciel. 'How come Gabe appears in charge?'

'He's not the boy you once knew,' Meciel answered, whilst adjusting the sleeves on his grey robes. 'He's had a difficult journey. One that has changed him.' His attention turned to tightening his belt and when satisfied, he continued, 'He hasn't said much. He's too focused on getting you all to safety.' He looked at her with sympathy. 'Give him time to adjust.'

She was about to walk over to the others when Meciel's hand graced her arm. With immeasurable wisdom, he said, 'If you allow pain to burrow deep enough it will grow roots.'

'Excuse me?'

'It's all right to grieve for him, you know.'

The gentle reassurance in his voice soothed her. He gave no judgement, just the offer of a listening ear if needed. She wondered if he sang if he'd sound like the Fallen Star.

'You remind me of someone.'

Meciel raised one of his bushy eyebrows and the lines on his brow deepened.

'I don't know his name but your voice and the way he sang… We called him the Fallen Star.'

Meciel let out a low chuckle. 'Why doesn't that surprise me even over there, he always sought the drama.'

Mirah's jaw dropped. 'Does Gabe know where you come from?'

'He knows I'm different, but he's been too fixated on finding you. It's the only thing he's thought about. Maybe soon I will explain but not yet. I've been waiting for a chance to ask you, six of you were taken. Where are the others?'

'How do you know about that?'

'I was there but didn't reach you in time.'

'If you had, they would have executed you.'

'Maybe, maybe not.'

Mirah watched as the others walked ahead, it wasn't only Huldah and Dara who were missing but now the heavy weight of Eran as well.

'We tried to escape and one of Shemyaza's monsters killed Huldah. They took Dara to the Chashmalim.'

Meciel closed his eyes and folded his hands together covering his mouth. When he opened them he glanced at the white band of flesh around her finger.

'You should tell Nev about her amulet soon.'

'We need to be further away from Hermonial. She has a wicked temper. If anyone is following us, they'd hear her scream.'

❊ 28 ❊

An abundance of lightheaded women leaving the Diatheatre parted before him as Nate bounded down the steps towards the Fallen Star.

They'd met before, Nate had sought him out after Mirah revealed her fascination with his singing. He'd been around gods long enough to know the Fallen Star was no ordinary singer. The power veiled behind his eyes was immortal.

Nate considered him an ally after the Fallen Star confessed his intentions and divulged where he came from.

'I need you to speak to Mirah. She's hurting. She won't talk to me. She won't let me explain.' His words tumbled from him. Urgent. He didn't care.

'I warned you nothing stays hidden forever. You didn't listen and now you're too late. Her brother, the one chosen by the Cloud Rider, he came for her.'

The world folded, crushing him. 'Which way did she go?'

'She left by the brook bordering the old quarter.'

Nate turned to flee.

The Fallen Star called after him. 'He has an army and a power like thunder. You will require leverage.'

Nate bolted up the steps. He didn't slow until reaching the mountain.

'Where's Zeev?' he snapped at the closest sparring guards.

An upright guardsman pointed his sword over to the barracks.

Zeev jumped up when Nate burst through the door, his eyes widening before regaining his composure. Nate jerked his head gesturing for him to follow.

'What's going on?', he asked, as Nate halted in the courtyard away from listening ears.

'Mirah, she's gone. Can you check on Neviah, see if she's still here? She might know something. I'm going to find Galia and Arella. Meet me here as soon as you can.'

Zeev returned a short while later shaking his head at Nate and the others waiting in the courtyard. Neviah leaving hadn't surprised him.

He led them over to a weapons storeroom and asked Arella to keep watch by the door. Zeev swept dust off one of the crates and perched against it whilst Nate fought the urge to race straight to the old quarter knowing his delay widened the distance between them.

'I'm going after her but I need your assistance before I leave.'

'Nate,' Galia urged. 'You should let her go. Why bring them back, just to be trapped here with the rest of us. At least they have a chance at freedom.'

'Do you really think Shemyaza will allow her to leave, knowing what she can do? Besides, I'm not bringing her back.' He exhaled a weighty breath. 'Do you remember the prophecy about men gathering under thunder? In Anat, I learned that thunder is the Cloud Rider's chosen one. It's Mirah's brother. This is our chance. He could defeat Shemyaza.'

Zeev picked at splinters on the crate. 'I don't believe in old fables. Who the bidu is the Cloud Rider anyway? We've never even seen him.'

'Zeev,' Nate barked. 'I lack leverage. The Fallen Star said Mirah's brother has an army. The lad Mirah saved is under the mountain, his name is Eran. I need you to help me get him out.'

'Wasn't all her family dead? What army?' Zeev asked.

Nate rubbed the back of his neck. 'I don't know any more than that.'

'You're not coming back, are you?' Galia accused, as she weighed up his intentions.

Nate nodded in affirmation.

'Then, I'll come with you,' she declared.

He dipped his head in appreciation before turning to Arella.

She turned from the doorway. 'Zeev should go with you. I'll keep Sumer safe.'

Shifting off the crate, Zeev asked, 'What's your plan?'

'I want you to change the guard rotations and clear the route down through the mountain, keep them distracted long enough for us to get

Eran. Galia, can you gather supplies and our weapons? Meet us by the brook past the old quarter. Arella you stay with me.'

Zeev went to leave but hesitated.

'Go,' Arella said. 'I won't let any harm befall your mother, I promise.'

After Galia and Zeev left, Nate said, 'I don't trust Shemyaza not to come after you or Sumer after we've gone.'

'I'll take her to Anat.'

'You heard what Danel said when we were in Anat?' he asked surprised.

She gave a half shrug. 'No, but by your blanched face, I knew he'd revealed something. Hopefully, I can find some supporters still there.'

'Thank you,' he said, as he moved closer to the door. 'Let's do this.'

They entered the chasm and darted into the tunnel leading into the bowels of the mountain. Moisture slid down glossy, green algae walls dripping into deep-cut channels on either side of the pathway. The only sound was the collected water trickling past them towards one of the pools in the gardens.

At intervals between shadow and darkness, someone had fixed small burning torches to the walls. Arella smothered their flames as they passed.

The tunnel sloped and spiralled downwards, deeper under the mountain. The further they travelled the cooler it became. When they reached the bottom, it opened into a small circular chamber. They stood listening, neither daring to speak. Nate circled the chamber, pausing at each entrance. One, he knew led to another exit but of the three remaining, which one?

'If you don't tell me who else survived at Barakel,' a voice growled out of the darkness, 'I'll break your other arm and then hack off your fingers, one by one until you do.'

Nate rested his hand over his dagger sheathed at his side. He hoped Zeev had removed the guards stationed in the tunnel.

'I was knocked unconscious,' an inflamed voice protested. 'When I came around everyone was dead.'

Nate and Arella halted outside the cell. He listened to the sounds coming from within and after detecting their positions he nudged Arella's hand and opened the door.

Dank musty air engulfed him mixed with sweat and torture. A hulking brute of a man had Eran prostrate on the floor with Eran's arm twisted over a rusted anvil. Nate recognised the guard by the scar above his ginger eyebrow but hadn't known he'd allied with Bishnor.

In three paces he towered over the stooping guard. 'I need to speak to the prisoner.'

The guard dug his knee deeper in-between Eran's shoulders and gripped tighter on Eran's arm.

'That's an order,' Nate growled.

Without his focus straying the guard lifted his knee.

'As you—'

He never got the last words out. He doubled over choking, clutching his throat searching for the air he'd never find. Then keeled over, dead.

Chains clinked as Nate loosed Eran's shackles.

'Mirah sends her blessing,' he said, hoping the lad wouldn't put up a fight.

They left the cell and crept back to the chamber.

Arella unhooked one of the torches. 'Not that she needs it but look after Galia.' She swept over to Nate, rose on her tiptoes and kissed his cheek. 'This is not goodbye,' she whispered, and with the torchlight illuminating the slippery green tunnel roof, she left.

Nate ignored Eran's quick evaluation, and said, 'Let's go and stay quiet.'

Zeev and Galia were sheltering within the cedar's cooling shadows when they reached the brook. He hadn't explained to Eran, who they were or where they were taking him. Eran, to his credit, held his broken arm, kept moving and didn't ask. Nate figured he'd weighed up his options and with the mention of Mirah decided to stick around. For his silence, Nate was grateful because talking would slow them down.

Zeev pointed to footprints in the ground. 'By the look of them, there are four females and a male.'

Nate guessed the other tracks were Abela and Ayla but it surprised him that Mirah's brother came alone. He set a fast pace through the marsh reeds whipping at his legs until the tracks ended by the river edge.

Zeev scratched the back of his head. 'We've lost them.'

Nate crouched, focusing on the footprints pressed into the silt. 'They would have gone downstream for sure. The river mouth is too guarded. They probably crossed over going west,' he reasoned. 'It's what I would do.'

Galia stepped up to the river edge. 'Then we follow on the other side until we pick up their tracks.' She waved her hand and froze a path over the river.

Eran's eyes widened, but he never said a word. Nate calculated after he'd seen Neviah and Mirah wielding fire and water on the mountain, an ice path probably didn't faze him much.

They'd hidden the fishing boat in the boggy marsh reeds.

Nate spotted their tracks. 'Galia, for the next few miles can you camouflage our footprints and theirs as well?'

A wet path followed behind them, the depression of their footsteps sinking in the soil. When they reached a small village of goat herders, they halted. The inhabitants seeing who they were, agreed to let them rest in one of their mud huts. When questioned, they had seen no one passing through.

Nate pushed back the reeds screening the mud hut entrance and squinted at the gloom eclipsing the dusty plains. 'I'll take first watch.'

He waited until Zeev and Galia were sleeping and nudged Eran in the leg. He shot up sitting on his straw mat, cradling his arm.

'When they awake, we'll reset your arm. That's if you ever want to use it again.'

'How come you don't know where Mirah is going?' Eran asked, crossing his legs.

How perceptive, Nate thought. 'I know where, just not the exact route they have taken,' he lied. 'We're supposed to catch up to them before they arrive.'

To his relief, Eran seemed satisfied with his answer. Nate shifted his shoulder blades against the hard wood surrounding the mud hut's entrance.

'What do you know of Mirah's brother?' he asked, focusing back into the gloom.

'Gabe?'

'Yes. Mirah thought he was dead.'

Eran cleared his throat. 'He wasn't there when they attacked us. I searched for him the next day but when I got to the cave, it was empty and when I returned to Barakel, he'd gone. I tried to follow but… I'm not as good at tracking as you.'

So Eran didn't realise he'd been at Barakel. It didn't surprise him to hear Mirah knew Gabe hadn't been there. It hurt that after they'd become so close she still hadn't told him.

'What is Gabe like?'

'He's my best friend. He's funny, kind and loves adventure. At first, I made friends with him because I longed to get closer to Mirah but after a while—'

Nate cleared his throat.

'I didn't mean to… I mean,' Eran stuttered as Nate glared at him. 'I saw on the mountain what you felt for her. The way she stared at you when you edged closer to the chalk line. At home, most of us felt the same way.'

'Most?' he asked, leaning slightly into the room.

Eran didn't dare elaborate. Smart, Nate thought. Why this sudden surge of anger? Was he jealous? He attempted to relax his jaw, blinked and refocused on the gloom.

'How old is Gabe?'

'He's a year younger than Mirah.'

Younger? How could he be younger?

'Get some rest,' he said, holding back a snarl.

In the darkness, Nate contemplated everything he'd learned. How could someone so young come to their rescue? If he fought like Eran, they didn't stand a chance. He wondered if Mirah would have fallen for this lanky kid if he hadn't taken her away?

It seemed like every star peered into his conscience and when they could face him no more they slipped away. Daylight broke with a haze of peach and golden streaks blending on the horizon. Nate was still sat on the ground with his elbows resting on his knees pondering over Gabe.

'You didn't wake me,' Zeev groaned.

Nate rose. 'Let's set his arm and keep moving.'

When they reached the dusty plains, the tracks fizzled out.

'We go straight ahead. It's the shortest route to the sea,' Nate said, marching on.

Galia rushed up beside him. 'Are you ever going to tell me why she fled?'

'Wielding. You understand the power behind it but it doesn't appear to bother you?'

'I squished thoughts of Shemyaza out of my head long ago,' she said, looking down.

She doesn't know, he realised. Not making the same mistake again, he told her about the beings in the other realm. He wondered if he'd lose her too as she contemplated his revelation. He tried to read her expression but her grey eyes revealed nothing.

'I don't like it,' she eventually said, 'but what difference does it make if wielding comes from one source or another? I can't imagine living without it now. Is that why she left because of wielding?'

'She didn't agree with your reasoning. She said it defiled her.'

'But that doesn't make sense.'

He couldn't bring himself to confess the rest. How Mirah had accused him of lying and breaking a promise. How devastation wrecked him when she pushed him aside.

'It's different for her,' Galia conceded. 'Her connection to the wielding is stronger. I'll talk to her when we find them.'

And then what? The shift in tone when Mirah asked where unspoken truth went screamed of defeat. He'd never heard such desperate pleading.

❊ 29 ❊

They'd been tripping over twisted roots and ducking under gnarled branches for most of the afternoon. Gabe peered skyward, sighed and pressed on, rushing towards the diminishing light ahead and fleeing from the darkness creeping behind.

Each time he glanced over his shoulder he expected blue cloaks to appear amongst the slender trees. He could only tell when Terra flew overhead by the rustling of leaves. Her silence both calmed and unnerved him.

Two more days and they'd reach Nanshe. Where would they go after? Gabe didn't know, but he assumed Ammo had enough places to lie low. And what then? All he'd cared about was finding Mirah.

Every day on the ship's deck he'd sweated and parried. Ammo's intentions were to train him for war but he'd had no care for that. So what if Ammo spent years raising an army, and they expected him to lead it? They were wrong.

He took every swing and blow, worked until his wrists throbbed. He'd even bested Ammo a few times towards the end. If it helped rescue Mirah, he'd do anything. He'd kill anyone who tried to stop him.

He'd not been ready to witness the subjugation and the horror the people endured as he scouted the city. It had terrified him to think of Mirah a prisoner, the pain and the suffering she experienced. Maybe when this was over he'd return, not to lead an army but to do his part, help those people, pay retribution for Barakel and his Ma. But not until Mirah was safe.

He kept his focus forward, refusing to acknowledge everyone's exhaustion. As if in answer to their silent prayers the trees parted and gave way to a small clearing. Shrouded within a veil of trees, he finally agreed to let them rest.

Someone had dragged two fallen tree trunks into the clearing and ash from a long-dead fire was littered with small bones. He didn't like the look of it and hoped if anyone intended on returning, they'd have made it back by now.

Bina dipped under the trees and returned with wood. A fire blazed soon after and they sat on the logs, each of them contemplating their own thoughts.

When he'd first seen Mirah by the brook, she was healthy with a light-hearted spring in her steps. She didn't look that way now. She sat with the others; the firelight flickering over her face, exaggerating the desolate shadows under her eyes. Her high cheekbones were more prominent, a hint of her cheeks drawing in. She was wasting away and not just on the outside.

A movement in the dusk covered tree line caught his attention. His head snapped in its direction. A tall broad-shouldered man with ice-blue eyes fixed on murder stood with a long dagger poised at Eran's throat.

'Do not move,' he commanded.

❊ 30 ❊

Nate understood the risk and expected them to attack. By using Eran, he hoped they'd at least give him long enough to explain. He scanned his opponents sat in a small wooded clearing, weighing up their threat. He knew for certain, the dark brown-haired lad, with a face like thunder, was Mirah's brother. Sitting opposite her, his sharp eyes flicked at the distance between himself, Mirah and Nate. He spied two others he didn't recognise.

A resplendent silver-haired man, whose aged face showed no fear, his potential undetectable. Nate's instincts kicked in and he knew not to underestimate him.

The other was a woman. Moonlight, haloed in a silver shining ring on her dark hair. He could tell by her lithe frame and posture, the way her immovable glare assessed him as an opponent, she'd be deadly in combat.

Her eyes dilated and a tug of fear whipped through him. What was a Chashmalim doing with them? She could drop him to the ground without even moving. Why hadn't she killed him already?

Mirah rose. The chain of her necklace reflecting in the firelight comforted him, she hadn't removed it. Eran fidgeted and Nate tightened his grip on Eran's shoulder, pulling him closer to his chest. The dagger pressing firm against his skin.

'Don't move or I'll slice my blade across your neck,' he growled.

It was for this reason he'd asked Zeev and Galia to hold back. He didn't want a fight. If Mirah moved towards him, he'd let Eran go.

'I came to speak to him,' Nate said, jerking his elbow towards Gabe. 'If you listen to what I have to say, I swear I'll release him.'

'Go on,' Gabe said, slowly rising.

For someone so young, his voice sounded deep and Nate imagined if he roared it probably would sound like thunder.

'I know who you are.'

Gabe squared off his shoulders. 'Well, that puts me at a disadvantage. Who the heck are you?'

'My name is Nate, stepson of Shemyaza.'

'Tell me then, Nate,' Gabe sneered. 'Why shouldn't we just kill you?'

'Ask Mirah,' he answered, without even daring to take his focus off Gabe.

He'd wounded her so much she'd run from him and he wasn't sure she'd ever forgive him but he knew, she wouldn't want him harmed. If she did, then he'd let them.

'Don't hurt him,' Mirah said.

Cold and cut off, her tone relieved and chilled him.

Gabe weighed up Mirah, his eyes questioning hers. Is this the one? He cast his gaze back to Nate. 'What did you come here to say?'

'I heard you're the chosen of the Cloud Rider. I want to serve you if you'll let me?'

'We don't need your service,' Gabe scoffed. 'Now do as you promised and this time,' he emphasised, 'I'll let you leave.'

Meciel made a low cough. 'We need him. He knows what goes on inside the mountain. He knows Shemyaza.'

'He could be a spy,' Gabe said, still unmoving.

'A spy he may be,' Neviah said, 'but I know he loves Mirah and would do anything to protect her.'

Gabe spent ages considering his options, stopping briefly to talk to Meciel before conferring with Mirah, their muffled voices too low for him to hear. It didn't go unnoticed that Bina had placed herself between them. She scanned the tree line and with a slight lift of her brows focused back on him.

'Tie his hands,' Gabe said to Bina.

Nate dropped the dagger on the ground and held out his wrists.

As soon as he'd freed Eran, he blurted out, 'He's not alone, there are two others.'

'They aren't waiting to ambush.' Nate defended. 'If you allow it, they will come and surrender.'

Zeev and Galia stepped out from shadows and dropped their weapons to the ground.

Wrists bound, Nate studied their interactions. Bina weighed up Galia, eyeing her amulet. Galia gave Mirah a warm smile and Mirah ran to her embracing her with a hug. Zeev grinned at Neviah who sat up straighter. Abela and Ayla sat close together looking up at Meciel as he spoke.

Gabe also assessed them and Nate saw in his eyes the same notion he knew was in his own. If they survived each other, then maybe they had a chance.

With their hands bound, Nate, and the others were made to sit by the fire.

'That went well,' Zeev muttered.

Gallia twisted her wrists against the binding. 'They took my amulet. How can you possibly say that?'

Nate ignored them. He watched Mirah standing with Neviah over by the edge of the clearing. She took a deep breath and wiped the back of her hand across her brow.

His mind flashed to when he'd first seen her do this on his ship. How she carried the weight of her friends' burdens close to her heart. How it moved him to find out more about her. He struggled against the desire to go over and support her. She hadn't even acknowledged him since he'd sat down.

He'd often seen Neviah's temper but nothing compared to the fury blazing now. As he wondered the cause of it, Neviah stormed off. He noted how quickly Bina jumped up to chase after her. She made it halfway across the clearing in one leap, her steps well-paced and surefooted until she faded into the tree line. Abela and Ayla were now preparing bedrolls and Mirah came to help them. Meciel was talking to Eran. Gabe sat next to them listening but never glanced away from him for long.

Why had the Cloud Rider chosen him? He wouldn't dare ask Zeev or Galia what they thought. He knew they'd be thinking the same. He must have been staring because Gabe locked eyes on him. He'd expected to see hatred but what he saw was something else, something which didn't have a name.

Eran spoke catching Gabe's attention. He smiled and said, 'It seems you're becoming a bit of an expert at escaping. Sojin is going to love you.'

⁂

The next day they crossed over farmland. The day after they reached Nanshe Bay. Salty air drifted up from the ocean as they trekked through the settlement.

All that remained of Nanshe's temple was its foundations and some newer buildings testified to the temple bricks reuse. The golden shrine which once shimmered over Nanshe was absent and smelted with the rest of the old gods' shrines. Their gold now dispersed like a galaxy of stars in Shemyaza's throne room.

Nanshe's Dream Diviners had not left. On the temple foundations, a large oxblood coloured tent with painted gold fish and pelicans billowed in the breeze.

Zeev's head jerked in the Diviner's direction. 'Had any dreams lately?'

'Not any whilst sleeping,' Nate replied, watching the Diviners offering fish and barley bread to women and children congregating nearby.

One of Nanshe's Diviners rushed over. Her dark hair tied in a bun tight against her head. She had no jewels or lavish clothing just long flowing hessian robes.

'You long journey, yes? Come, we may help you.'

She glanced at their bound wrists, compassion rising in her eyes and followed them, pestering Gabe.

'Come, I help you. Give you and prisoners food for long journey.'

'Leave us,' Gabe said.

The Diviner pestered on. 'I tell you your dreams, yes? How you go on your journey.'

Zeev stretched up tilting his head back. 'I have a dream,' he called out.

'What are you doing?' Nate asked.

He shrugged his shoulder. 'I'm bored with this endless walking.'

The Diviner checked out Gabe's reaction, seeing he made none, she dropped back beside Zeev.

Zeev raised his voice so everyone could hear him. 'In my dream, there is a woman. She burns with fire,' he said seductively. 'But every time I reach out to touch her, she turns cold.'

The Diviner walked beside him contemplating.

'Really?' Nate asked, in exasperation.

Zeev let out a half smile. 'What? It's true.'

'If she not resist the inescapable, how she know what the inescapable is?' the Diviner chanted.

Zeev frowned and stared at the Diviner expecting more. 'I don't get it?'

Nate chuckled. 'Well, that will teach you. Good luck working it out.'

The Diviner withdrew as they continued towards the harbour.

From up ahead, Nate caught Mirah turning her head towards Neviah. He wished he could see their faces. He missed her laughing. As much as he didn't want to admit it, he even missed Neviah's temper.

Mirah's arm looped under Gabe's. The bond between them strong, revealing itself more and more as the distance between them and Hermonial grew. Apart from the slightest moments, a quick smile, or the briefest laughter, Gabe's guard never faltered, and he was at least thankful for that.

Along the harbour men shouted directions and guided pulleys and ropes, lowering crates of salted fish onto transport vessels. From here they distributed fish around the continent. Men on fishing boats organised their nets readying themselves to catch another haul of fish.

The arm of the ocean stretched its way along the borders of Nanshe. Its rolling waves harassed gigantic boulders which created a protective seawall curving around the narrow mouth of the gulf. Sea spray settled on the slippery wooden beamed walkway secured to the lowest level of boulders and to their left wooden piers cut across the waters.

They were heading for the ship docked on the furthest pier. Clever, Nate reasoned, from there it would be the fastest way to escape.

On the far side of the gangplank, a man blew his blonde fringe from his eyes. Taking in his lavish silks and the embellished gold rings on most of his fingers, someone less aware might consider him a flamboyant high born. Nate didn't think so. Whoever this robust man was, his striking green eyes didn't miss a trick. He spied their bound wrists the instant he saw them. Standing beside him a brown capped lad grinned.

'Ya been gone so long. I thought ya got yaself killed.'

Gabe crossed the gangplank, Mirah and the other girls following. Meciel and Bina waited behind him. Did they expect him to run?

'I believe you owe me some silver,' Gabe said, patting him on the shoulder. 'This is Neviah, Abela and Ayla and this is Mirah, my sister.'

'I'm pleased to finally meet ya. My name is Ammo. Ya probably heard of me?'

Bina groaned from behind him. Ammo lifted his head and smirked at her.

'This is Sojin,' Ammo announced to the girls. 'Come. Welcome aboard Wind Weaver. Ya must be hungry and in need of resting.'

Gabe assisted the girls onto the deck and asked Sojin to show them to their quarters. Nate almost laughed as Sojin stood taller, not knowing which girl to stare at first as he led them away. Mirah never looked back.

'I see ya brought me guests?' Ammo said, nodding his head towards the gangplank.

'The dark-haired one calls himself Nate,' Gabe pointed out. 'He's the son of Shemyaza.'

That got Ammo's attention, and he flashed Nate a discerning stare. Nate knew Gabe was goading him and held the correction to stepson on his tongue.

'He was Mirah's betrothed,' Gabe dug deeper.

Nate picked up the emphasis on was. What had Mirah told him?

'The other two are Zeev, his second and Galia, a Water Wielder.'

Ammo instinctively scanned her for an amulet. So he knew about Wielders, Nate reasoned.

'Go,' Bina said and ushered them up the gangplank.

'Why ain't ya killed em?' Ammo asked.

'I'm still undecided.'

Gabe and Ammo escorted them below deck to an empty storeroom with no porthole.

As they walked away, Ammo grumbled, 'The winds have turned against us.'

More than you know, Nate thought.

Galia sat on the only crate in the storeroom. 'What do we do now?' she asked, rubbing the vacant space on her wrist where her golden amulet had once been.

'We wait,' Nate answered, sitting down on the wooden decking.

Zeev searched around for something useful. It didn't take him long; the storeroom was bare except for the crate and an empty barrel. Giving up his search, he asked, 'What do you make of them? Gabe doesn't look like he can lead an army.'

'He keeps strange company. I'll give him that. I suspect Meciel is from beyond the portal.'

'You think there are other gods?' Galia asked.

Nate brought his legs up to his chest and rested his hands on his knees. 'After Mirah wielded Eran from the plateau, Shemyaza asked her if she knew someone named Meciel. She told me she'd never heard of him but if he was near Barakel. If that's where Gabe met him. It would make sense why Shemyaza ordered its destruction.

I can't figure out Bina.' He paused and rubbed the bridge of his nose. 'At first, I suspected she might be Chashmalim but now I'm not sure. Ammo is seasoned, if anyone's preparing an army, it's most likely him. One thing I know, as young as Gabe is, they expect him to command them.'

Zeev came and sat beside him, stretching out his long legs. 'I wonder if Shemyaza knows we've gone?'

'Neither of you need to worry. As soon as we got Eran out of the mountain, Arella left taking Sumer straight to Anat.'

'I wish she were here,' Galia said, waving her hand like a fan. 'We could do with some air.'

She was right. The air stifled them and the sun's heat wasn't even high overhead yet.

'We should rest,' Nate said, laying down.

⁂

The sway when the ship turned woke him and the air cooled the further they cut through the swell. How long Nate slept, he didn't know. He gathered it must be early evening. The door lock clicked and the lad Gabe had called Sojin entered.

'Water,' he said, placing a pail down.

Nate assumed he was Ammo's son but when he spoke he had a different accent. He tried to place it thinking, somewhere south beyond the Salmu sea. Somewhere in Buzur's territory. Wherever he came from his assessment of them screamed confidence.

'You're from Niggisu?'

'Not anymore,' Sojin answered. He focused on Galia, 'You need to come with me.'

Nate took a protective step forward and warned Sojin, 'If they hurt her—'

'Mirah will never allow it,' Galia interrupted. She rose and accompanied Sojin out of the storeroom.

The light filtering through the crack under the door soon dissipated into darkness.

Zeev yelled, 'If you don't let us out, I will piss all over your ship.'

Still, no one came.

Nate estimated they'd been sailing for at least another day before Gabe and Ammo returned. Gabe walked over and leaned against the empty barrel and Ammo's large frame loomed by the door.

'Tell us what you know?' Gabe asked.

Nate saw no reason to hide it. He shared about his life with Shemyaza, the instability within his Puhrum, the other four gods and where their portals were stationed. He told them about the number of giants, the chimera, the Wielders and the Chashmalim. How many of his men would follow him if he asked? He imparted everything they needed to know to protect Mirah.

Gabe's brows bumped into a scowl. 'So you followed, knowing you'd lead Shemyaza right to her?'

'Of course not.' Nate said, through gritted teeth. 'If his interest was in me alone, I never would have risked it. You have to understand Shemyaza will never let her go. She's unique. Her ability to wield water, earth and air is powerful, it's like nothing we've ever seen and the other gods know about it. He'll never risk one of them finding her and using her against him.'

Gabe shifted against the barrel. 'So why would Shemyaza inform them she's left?'

'Our wedding,' he confessed. 'They'll become suspicious when it doesn't happen. You need me.'

Ammo tapped his finger on the doorframe. 'We don't need ya? We have our own forces.'

Nate stared at him. 'Whatever strength you think you have, it won't be enough.' He let his words hang in the air. 'Those who will come against you were once under my command. I trained them. I know their tactics and besides, Shemyaza won't want me harmed.' He turned to Gabe. 'I may be the only person who can stand between them and Mirah.'

He didn't see the point in highlighting that if Bishnor got his chance he'd probably kill him. Or that he wasn't even sure how Shemyaza would respond now he'd broken free from his grasp.

Gabe lifted off the barrel. 'You can go on deck.' As he crossed the storeroom, he added, 'If you try anything, Ammo will slit your throats, if Bina doesn't kill you first.'

'Can I speak to Mirah?'

'That's for her to decide,' Gabe said, turning into the corridor.

❊ 31 ❊

'You're going to have to come out and face him sooner or later,' Neviah said, entering the cabin.

Mirah ignored her and continued focusing on the endless ocean spanning out from the porthole. For all she knew Shemyaza's Dagani could be lurking out there.

The surge and swell dipped and rose with her own adrift feelings. Wherever they were, the waters were choppy, the sky overcast, and the sea muted grey.

Neviah sat on the edge of the silk-covered bed. Whoever Ammo was, he had an elaborate taste. A small spot of light reflected off the wood near the porthole and to her dismay, Mirah realised Neviah still wore her silver and onyx armlet.

'Where are Abela and Ayla?' Mirah asked.

'They've gone to assist the cook.'

That didn't surprise her. Three days they'd been sailing, and the food tasted awful. She should help. These people Gabe called his friends had come to save them. She should offer her service and help them though she didn't have the energy.

'Will you tell Galia, I'd like to speak with her?'

'Of course, I'll get her now.' When Neviah arrived at the door, she hesitated but whatever held her thoughts, she kept to herself.

Galia appeared a few moments later and sat on her bed.

Mirah turned from the porthole. 'Tell me what you know about your wielding?' she asked, looking down at the empty space where Galia's amulet had been.

'Nate told me wielding is not a gift from Shemyaza but from something else.'

Nate had told her? So she hadn't known before, Mirah concluded. 'You miss wielding, don't you? The power it gave you.'

'Yes. It's awful being surrounded by all this water and not being able to sense it.'

Mirah understood the vacant, exposed feeling of losing the power and abilities once relied on. 'You wouldn't miss it if you knew the source from which it comes. Have you never heard its voice?'

'No. There's no connection other than with the water I'm wielding.'

'The Beast, it chases me in my sleep. I try to keep my eyes open. When I'm awake, I can mostly shut it out.'

Galia reached over and clasped her hand. 'I'm sorry, Mirah. I didn't realise what you were going through.'

'What's it like on deck?' she asked, absorbing the comforting warmth from Galia's hand.

Galia tutted. 'There're plenty of oversized personalities up there. For the sake of a far more terrible enemy, they seem to have put their differences aside. Although watching Nate spar with Gabe, I wonder how long their tolerance will last.'

'What?' Mirah asked, pulling away from her and swinging her legs off the bed.

Galia kept her tone cool and steady. 'We can't afford to lapse with our training. But if you ask me they've both got a point to prove.'

'I need fresh air,' Mirah said, rising. 'Will you walk up with me? I don't think I can face it alone.'

Galia smiled and Mirah knew she'd fallen into her trap.

A hive of activity spread over the deck. Ammo's ship was imposing but as she walked onto the deck, it didn't seem large enough.

Crewmen were in the rigging adjusting the sails and those not working sat in small huddles playing dice. It certainly lived up to its name, Wind Weaver, she realised as it cut through the swell at great speed.

She spotted Zeev standing with his back to her. Sojin was showing Eran and Neviah how to sneak up behind him and pickpocket something hidden underneath Zeev's blue cloak. Ammo stood nearby, re-braiding a frayed rope, evaluating Eran's technique. He clamped his teeth in disapproval.

'I can hear ya,' he yelled over.

'But—'

'Stop ya whining, it's ya arm that's injured, not ya footwork. If ya want to sneak up on someone ya gonna have to be quieter than that.'

Eran rolled his eyes.

'I saw that,' Ammo grunted.

Meciel and Nate sat further away watching Bina throw daggers into a round wooden shield tied to the ship's bow. Here and there between its dents and splits, flecks of green paint remained. The emblem which once before existed was as indistinguishable as the distant bleak horizon.

The whole set up appeared unwise because if she missed the dagger would go overboard. She flicked her wrist, and the dagger landed with a thud in the centre of the target. Mirah discerned those chances were slim.

She sensed Nate's awareness of her but he never came rushing over and she appreciated him giving her space.

'I'm all right now,' she said to Galia. 'I need to speak with my brother.'

Gabe leaned against the side of the ship, his eyes cast over the ocean.

She came up beside him and after a moment asked, 'What are you thinking?'

'I imagined us starting over somewhere new, somewhere safe. But I see now, for Shemyaza it will never be over. Nate told me about the power you wield. They're not going to let you go.'

She'd expected as much. Since leaving, she'd heard the Beast. At first, it tried tempting her into returning and when that didn't work it switched to taunting her that she'd never escape.

'It's not me,' she corrected him. 'It's not my power.'

Gabe reached over and she rested her head on his shoulder.

'Years ago Meciel instructed Ammo to gather forces. Meciel wants me to lead them. He insists I'm some kind of saviour. How ridiculous is that? It seems we are pawns in a war that's not of our choosing.'

'How did you meet them?' she asked, brushing strands of windswept hair away from her face.

'Do you remember the hermit? The one who lingered on the edge of our borders. Turns out that's Meciel. He's strange but there's no darkness in him. He uses an unusual language to move things around.

It was Meciel who taught me how to remove the veil from your eyes. I'm sorry I forced you but it was the only way to make you see.'

She wrapped her arm around his waist. 'It wasn't easy making the adjustment but I'm glad you did it.'

She glanced over to Meciel slurping stew.

Gabe followed her gaze. 'He slips off often. I followed him once, but he just sat down and closed his eyes for hours. I got bored. He thinks I don't know what he is but I've kind of figured it out. Apparently, he's been watching over us since we were children. Anyway, thugs who stole Nuri, threw me into a boar pit and Meciel helped me get out.'

Mirah rummaged in a pouch tied to her waist. Here take this, she said, passing him the little wolf carving.

Gabe held the wolf up turning it around inspecting its shaggy coat carved into the wood. 'It looks like her.'

'It comforted me when I felt the most alone. I'm sorry about Nuri. I know how much she means to you.'

'I'll get her back, as soon as this is over,' he said, pocketing the wolf in his cloak.

'What happens now?'

'We're going to Chaba Misgab to meet with Ammo's forces. It's the safest place I can think of.'

She heard the clashing of blades and turned to find Nate and Zeev sparring. Eran and Sojin were close by copying their moves.

She watched the determination on Nate's face and remembered how he'd encouraged her to develop her technique, knowing that one day it might save her. She pushed away memories of the last day they'd trained and how he'd favoured embracing her instead.

'I'm amazed you've allowed them their swords?'

'If I'd known how good they were; I wouldn't have considered it. Ammo's not too keen.'

'Why then?'

'He may be the son of our enemy but I can see he'd do anything to protect you. Ammo made me train for months from morning to evening. I practised knowing I might need it to help you but I'm not as good as Nate.'

'Galia told me you'd been sparring. I understand how you feel.'

'You trained?' he asked surprised.

'Nate insisted. I've learned a few skills of my own. I'm not the weakling you remember, not anymore.'

'Well, in that case, you'll have to show me,' he said, nudging her shoulder.

She chuckled. 'Challenge accepted but it will have to be later. I want to help Abela and Ayla. Do you know where they are?'

Gabe led her to a hatch which opened onto a wooden staircase. The galley was at the end of a narrow passageway.

'I'll leave you to it,' Gabe said and turned to go.

'What can I do to help?' she asked when entering.

Abela and Ayla glanced up from chopping vegetables.

'There are some onions over there,' Abela said, pointing to a red reed basket.

The galley filled with the odour of braised meat boiling in a huge pot.

'Glad to see you're up and about,' Ayla said, looking up from slicing carrots.

Mirah surveyed the kitchen. 'Where's the cook?'

'He's up on deck somewhere,' Abela said. 'We refuse to let him in here.'

'How did you learn how to do this?' she asked, placing onions on the counter and picking up a knife.

'We begged Meciel to show us then turfed him out too,' Ayla grinned.

'He wasn't so easy to persuade though,' Abela added, and they both laughed at the memory.

They diced and chopped and stirred and Mirah felt herself relaxing.

The scent of the stew wafted onto the deck and everyone including Ammo's crew came in one by one. Abela and Ayla ladled the stew into wooden bowls whilst Mirah gave out the flatbread.

Her stomach hollowed when Nate arrived and she dropped his flatbread when she passed it to him. She'd need to speak to him soon.

After they'd eaten, everyone except the two men on lookout in the crow's nest sat on the deck sipping beer.

Sojin taught Eran how to play a game using small pebbles on an inked pigskin. Sojin's eyes missed nothing as he played. The game was unfamiliar and as often as Sojin tried explaining the rules to Eran, she couldn't work it out either.

Neviah and Zeev slunk off near the stern of the ship and Meciel had already gone below. Galia and Bina sat further away talking. She wondered how they were getting along. Mirah still hadn't spoken much to Bina although she'd watched in admiration how her elegance and grace matched her prowess.

The sun dipped over the horizon and she didn't want to retire below and face the Beast she knew would come for her in her dreams.

'How long before we arrive at Chaba Misgab?' she asked Ammo.

'If the winds stay as they are another few weeks.' Seeing her shoulders sag, he explained, 'It ain't all by sea though, it will take around three or four days to reach their encampment.'

'How many men do you have?' she asked.

He glanced at Gabe, his face turning a little sour. 'Numbers ain't our problem. We need more weapons.'

'With what Nate has told us,' Gabe said, 'Ammo thinks we should attack Shargaz first.'

'It makes sense. They have the metal and the weapons. We'd be taking out their supplies to Shemyaza's forces and supplying our own. We're gonna have to make a start somewhere,' Ammo challenged.

Gabe sniffed. 'I said, I don't like it.'

Their voices rose, cutting over each other arguing.

Mirah retreated and peered over the side of the ship at the waves dancing with the moonlight.

They were going into war because of her. She needed to stop this. If she returned to Shemyaza and pleaded with him, promised to stay, could she avert this? She tensed, aware of Nate coming up behind her.

'I know what you're thinking. He'd welcome you back but your returning won't protect those you love.'

He leaned his elbow on the side of the ship and faced her. Unable to look him in the eyes, she focused on the merging of the ocean and the dimming sky.

'Mirah, do you understand? Shemyaza believes Gabe is a threat. He will hunt him and destroy him. I don't relish the idea of going up against Shargaz but Ammo is right. They won't expect it. We'll have an advantage and if we succeed, a better chance against the others and with one less fake god to worry about. It will make Shemyaza cautious and give us more time.'

His words rang true. He'd been Shemyaza's Captain and had spent years strategising every possible course of action.

'You don't need to be a part of this,' she said, noticing his hands. His knuckles were white, and she knew he was resisting the urge to touch her. 'When we get to Chaba Misgab, you should take Galia and Zeev and flee. This is not your fight.'

'I can't let you go. I'd bleed out before I left you.'

She tensed and focused on the ocean and to the stars, she hadn't noticed emerge in glittering protest.

'It's over there,' Nate said, pointing to the Star of Dignity.

That he remembered caught her breath. It felt so long ago when they'd watched the stars from aboard his ship.

'Mirah, please listen, I came for you because I love you,' he declared, reaching out towards her.

She clasped her hands together.

'I'm sorry. Tell me what I need to do?'

'There's nothing you can do.' Her voice shuddered in her throat and she gasped for air. Tears welled in her eyes and rolled down her face. 'By not telling me, you allowed that thing to— You broke something in me. I don't know how to fix it.'

He swallowed, and she looked into his eyes. The moonlight exposed the glistening moisture in them. 'It's over,' she said and fled across the deck to the echo of him calling after her.

'You never told me about Gabe.'

She flew through the hatch and down into her cabin.

As much as her heart rallied against her she knew what they'd had, was over.

✼ 32 ✼

Nate cursed and followed after her. Bina, standing with her hands on hips and feet spread far apart stopped him in his tracks. He'd not meant to accuse her about Gabe. He didn't even care that she hadn't told him.

'Let her go,' Bina demanded.

His focus shifted beyond her. Everyone on deck watched him, judging. Gabe and Ammo hands poised over their daggers. Apart from Neviah and Galia chasing after Mirah, no one moved.

He strode over to Zeev standing on the ship's bow. Zeev tried to pass him his beer, but he ignored it. Neither speaking, they watched the waves breaking. How long he'd stood there he didn't know.

His clothes dampened as the sea mist crept in and enveloped him. On the horizon it looked like a god had rubbed out the world, ready to start again on a gleaming white canvass.

Footsteps padded up behind him, he whirled, realising Zeev had already gone.

'Keeping things hidden always earns deceptive wages,' Meciel proclaimed. 'If you put it right, you can still reap the reward.'

'I don't know how?' Nate said, rubbing his face.

Meciel laid his hand on Nate's shoulder. 'You'll know when you see it.'

'You know them, Shemyaza and the others?'

Meciel nodded.

'If one of them captures her, and she's not wed, then you know what they'll do.'

'Then you had better be prepared,' Meciel said, fading into the misty shadows.

Meciel was right. He needed to focus on Ammo's plan against Shargaz. He had his own score to settle. If it were not for Shargaz suggesting Esha pick three Wielders, none of them would have found out about Mirah. He'd wait for her until eternity is over. Until then he wouldn't push her. He'd wait until she found her way back to him.

After a week the winds turned against them. They lowered the sails to prevent drifting backwards. Ammo spent most of his time on the deck with essential crew members to keep watch.

Nate wondered what action Shemyaza planned. He was sure Shemyaza would send Bishnor. He'd search all the coastal areas until he picked up their trail in Nanshe. Nate hoped he was correct and Bishnor wouldn't expect them to go south. He scanned the horizon for distant galleys and was relieved to still find none.

Ahead he could see the constellation of Enki, among them the Celestial Scorpion. He knew their names, Girtab, Lishi, Nabu, and more and the two stars forming the scorpion's sting, Sharur and Shargaz.

He almost jumped when Ammo asked, 'Tell me more about Shargaz.'

'You're following his star. You seem to know where he is.'

Ammo awarded a half smile. 'Tomorrow, if we have the winds, we'll head west for a little detour.'

'How have you hidden your forces so close to his borders?'

Ammo beckoned him to follow. 'We have Meciel to thank for that,' he said over his shoulder, 'but I guess, ya being with Shemyaza, ya know all about glamours.' He stopped towards the stern of the ship and sat on an upturned boat. 'So what about Shargaz?'

Nate sat down. 'Shargaz is known as the Supreme Smiter and not just for his talents with metallurgy. He has a head for war and revels in it.' He picked at a rope knot and tightened it. 'It will be wiser to sneak in and steal what we can.'

'That ain't gonna work,' he said, plucking at the cuff on his silk shirt.

'Why not?'

'Ya haven't seen the size of my forces,' Ammo said, pushing back his shoulders. 'We need his steel. I guess we'll work out the rest when we meet him.'

Nate let his fingers slack on the knot. 'You have no plan?'

'It ain't my plan to make but I'll guide Gabe as best I can. Ya know how to kill a scorpion?' He traced out a circle on his thigh and prodded his finger dead centre. 'Ya make em sting emselves in the back.'

The only fire they had came from Neviah and even though she still wore her amulet, if she still wielded, she'd be no match against Shargaz.

'You believe in Gabe then? That he's chosen by the Cloud Rider?'

'Meciel believes, and that's good enough for me.' He rose. 'I saw ya sparring with Gabe. I know ya held back on account of Mirah. If ya want to help her help him. I taught him as best I can. With ya technique, he might stand a chance.'

'You want me to train him?' he asked, in surprise. 'He'd never agree.'

'Wouldn't ya do anything for Mirah if ya had the opportunity?'

The next day the wind changed. They travelled south until midday and then turned west. Nate surveyed Gabe and Ammo parrying with swords which had seen better days. Ammo wielded his sword well. If he was up against most of Nate's guardsmen he'd out skill them but Ammo was right, he'd taught Gabe as much as he could.

'Here try this,' Nate said, offering his sword to Gabe. 'Can I borrow yours?' he asked Zeev.

'Sure, this should be interesting,' he chuckled, unsheathing his sword.

Their blades clashed, and they parried. Gabe's muscles flexed well against the strain but his inexperience shone through.

Between the ringing of blades, Ammo shouted, 'I'll take ya bets.'

Raucous cheers erupted and crew members ventured closer.

'Gabe has no chance,' Zeev said to Galia. 'Do you want to wager some silver.'

'You men are all the same,' she replied, strutting off to sit with the girls.

'You leave your left side too open,' Nate observed. 'Hold the weapon higher, like this.'

Gabe lifted the sword but as they fought on, sweat ran down his forehead. He wiped the drips away and the distraction cost him. Nate slammed Zeev's blade across Gabe's crossguard. Gabe lost his grip, and the sword dropped to the deck.

'You'd be dead doing that on the battlefield. If your eyes sting, learn to ignore it. Now let's start again.'

When they finished, Nate's shirt stuck to his skin. Gabe's face was flushed as red as Mirah's hair. Nate could have killed him more times than he could remember. How was this boy, balancing on the cusp of manhood, ever going to defeat Shargaz or Shemyaza when he couldn't even defeat another man?

'Tomorrow, we'll do it again,' Gabe said, walking off to wash from a water barrel.

Zeev came over laughing. 'You keep this up and by the time we reach Chaba Misgab, I'll be a rich man.' He held out his palm full of silver and small round tokens.

'You're unbelievable.'

Nate spied Ammo crouched over counting his winnings. Ammo snickered at him from under his blonde fringe.

He wanted Gabe trained that was understandable, but he'd still taken the opportunity to make a wager as well. Ammo and Zeev were so similar and despite everything, he realised he liked him.

Zeev jerked his chin in Gabe's direction. 'He nearly had you a few times.'

'I had to at least let him think he had a chance.'

'Have you done that to me?' Zeev asked, following him to the barrel of water.

'Of course,' Nate laughed.

'You're an idiot,' Zeev grinned.

Later that evening, Mirah thanked Nate and then walked away.

The bond they shared had been his bridge away from Shemyaza, now he'd crossed it, would the bridge shatter beneath his feet? Would time erase the memory of the smiles she gave?

He desired to run his fingers through her hair, to feel her tender lips on his. He missed her touch, her scent, the way she smiled at him but most of all he missed the way her eyes lingered on his, filled with expectations and promises of where their love would lead them. He saw none of that in her eyes now and it gutted him.

Casting a glance over the ship he saw Galia sat talking to Bina. They were often speaking in low whispers and he wondered what captured their interest. Too deep in conversation, neither of them noticed as he neared.

'You don't like me?' he heard Galia ask.

'It's not that I don't like you. It's that I don't like what you do.'

'But I'm no different from you.'

'My power is my own not borrowed from a fallen one.'

Nate let out a small cough, and they glanced up. Bina stood up and left.

'What was that about?'

Rising, Galia said, 'I was trying to convince her to give my amulet back.'

'Oh.'

'What powers was she on about?'

'Don't know, don't care,' Galia said and strode off as well.

What was it with the women on this ship and their insistence on walking away from him? He'd be glad when they reached the shore. Maybe firmer ground would firm up their heads.

After several more days, they arrived at Chaba Misgab. They were about a quarter of a league from the seashore when he felt the air ripple. The empty shingle bay, backed by red cliffs, transformed into a full-blown harbour. Slender galley ships overwhelmed the wooden docks. There must be at least a hundred ships he calculated.

'One hundred and thirty-four, five including Wind Weaver,' Ammo said, watching him take in the impressive view. 'Although as ya can see mine ain't no warship.'

'How did you manage it?'

'I've been doing this a long time ya know. My men built the galleys here and every one of em is trained in warfare. For each galley, there's a hundred and seventy oarsmen and space on board each galley for four hundred men.'

'I thought you said your forces are camped another few days from the coast?'

'They are. These ain't included with em. Meciel will take ya to the encampment.'

'You're not coming?'

'Someone's got to lead em,' he said, nodding to the harbour

The knowledge that Ammo was leaving them jarred him.

'I added my own special design,' Ammo said, pointing to a long length of bronze protruding from the galley's keel below the waterline. 'I call it a ramrod.'

Compared to Shemyaza's warships the galleys were smaller but their slim design and light construction would give them the speed Shemyaza's ships lacked.

With Wind Weaver moored, Meciel took the lead and disembarked.

Gabe stepped on the gangplank and Ammo caught hold of his shirt. 'Ya look after my forces, ya hear me. Ya lead em well.'

Gabe reached over and grabbed his arm. 'Thank you. For helping me find Mirah and for this,' he said, as his gaze drifted over the galleys in the harbour.

Nate saw genuine appreciation mixed with doubt leak from Gabe's eyes. He waited to say thank you to Ammo as the others spanned over the harbour front heading for a dirt track chiselled into the cliffs.

'Hey Bina,' Ammo called after her, 'Ain't ya gonna even bless me with a goodbye kiss. This might be ya last chance,' he teased.

He sketched a bow as she paced back towards him. His eyes were hungry and filled with risk and taking chances. 'I've been waiting for this my whole life,' he said to Nate.

She cut across the harbour, her lavender glare boring into Ammo with a ferocity that made Zeev and Neviah's bantering look tame.

'Maybe I should go,' Nate said.

'No wait, ya got to watch this. This is gonna be a vision of a lifetime.'

Bina, on reaching them stopped a few paces before Ammo. Her glare a fixture of cool composure. 'I told you if you ever asked again, I'd knock you back on your ass.'

Ammo waited expectantly. She parted her lips and exhaled a small gust of air. He flew backwards into a water barrel, landing on his butt several feet behind Nate. Water slurped over the barrel ridge drenching him and his silk clothing.

Nate caught the slimmest victory smile as Bina pivoted and walked off.

'Did ya see that?' Ammo said. Raising his voice louder, he announced to everyone within hearing, 'She finally blew me a kiss.'

Bina groaned. She was impressive. The way she curled the air was different to how the Air Wielders worked. She wore no jewels, and he wondered if she hid another kind of amulet.

Ammo swept his soaking hair from his face and peeled his silks away from his chest.

'I wanted to say thank you for bringing Gabe back to Mirah.'

'Ah don't worry yaself about that. I ain't never had what ya had but I can see how much it cost ya. I'm sorry it didn't work out for ya. If we'd had time, I think we'd be great friends, ya know.'

He rose and shook the water from his hair. 'I could have used a man with ya skills as an Acquisitioner. Maybe who knows if we survive?'

'I hope to see you again at the scorpion's nest,' Nate said.

When he reached the track leading up through the cliff, he surveyed Ammo's galleys. They rocked together on the lapping sea, nudging each other as the current swelled. The galleys reminded him of cockroaches swarming out of their burrows to escape a deluge.

He left to the sound of seabirds squawking their battle cries overhead, to catch up with the others. He followed their dusty footprints up the track and found Zeev, Meciel and Gabe standing outside a timber hut. It was the first in row upon row of timber huts which from the number of men milling around, housed the crew and the forces for Ammo's galleys.

Gabe was feeding fish to a beast. Nate wasn't sure if it was some type of bird or reptile or both, whatever it was, it was huge.

'This is Terra,' Gabe said, as Nate approached. 'She belongs to Meciel.'

Terra snorted and Gabe threw her another fish. Nate studied her conical razor-sharp teeth as her jaws opened to gulp down the fish. He noted the lethal hooked talons and wondered how she'd fare against Shemyaza's chimera. 'What is it?'

'She's a Dactyr,' Meciel answered. 'She fell out of her nest and I reared her when her mother refused.'

'She's upset because Meciel sent her ahead of us,' Gabe added.

'Where are the girls?' Nate asked.

'They've already gone inside to wash up,' Zeev said, nodding to a timber hut behind him. 'They picked the room on the right, we're on the left.'

A row of wooden beds, three on each side and covered in woollen blankets filled the room. Someone had left fruit, cheese and flatbread on a table. A small barrel of beer stood in the corner.

The beer was the first thing Zeev spied when he entered and flopped down on the bed nearest to it. 'That Ammo's done well getting those galleys.'

'He's an Acquisitioner,' Meciel said, appearing in the room.

'An Acqui what?' Zeev asked.

'He gets things accomplished, things no one else will take the trouble to.'

'Shame he's leaving. I'd like to have shared a beer with him.'

Meciel leaned his staff against the wall. 'He doesn't drink.' He laid down on one of the beds, drew the blanket tight to his neck and turned over.

Zeev raised his brows at Nate and shrugged.

Nate took the bed closest to the exit. He lay on his back, arms folded behind his head and closed his eyes. He listened to Zeev munching on grapes and pouring himself a beer over the sounds of men outside singing, laughing and throwing dice.

'You want one?'

'I'm too tired,' he answered, and pulled the blanket up to his chin. Compared to Hermonial the temperature chilled him. He was asleep before Gabe entered.

A loud shrilling scream woke him. He rushed out the exit, still clothed, to meet Gabe coming from outside. In the darkness they both searched for the girl's door and heard Galia utter, 'It's a nightmare. You're all right. There's nothing here.'

Gabe's wide eyes shone whiter than salt rock, and he knew they mirrored his own.

'I don't know how to help her,' Gabe whispered.

'We do so by destroying the portals and killing them all,' Nate replied.

❊ 33 ❊

Mirah sat in the wooden hut's doorway waiting. She'd woken up, and found the others gone, she presumed to gather supplies.

Armed men with loaded sacks hefted over their shoulders glanced her way as they trekked towards the harbour. She pulled the blanket tighter and wondered if they realised this was her fault.

Sunrays burst from behind the clouds and the ocean changed from muted grey to aqua green. A golden bridge of sunlight rested on the water, its broad pathway diminishing as it stretched towards the horizon, leading nowhere. Over the cliff edge, galleys were already leaving, their blue sails flapping in the wind under a silver-blue sky.

Against the flow of men squashing together along the dirt track, she spotted Ayla with her head bowed low coming towards her.

'Where have you been?' she asked when Ayla reached her.

'I walked with Abela down to Ammo's ship. We discussed it last night. It made sense for them to have a healer and besides, Abela didn't want to separate from Sojin.'

Revelation gripped her, she'd been so absorbed in her own world, focusing on Gabe and avoiding Nate, she hadn't noticed anyone else.

'Are you all right?'

'It feels strange. We've never been separated before but it's the right choice. They will need her. Eran said he'd keep an eye on her.'

'Eran's gone too?'

'It seems Sojin is pretty popular.'

Mirah regretted she hadn't taken the time to get to know him better. Terra swept overhead and landed a few feet away just before Meciel and Gabe rounded one of the timber huts.

Gabe adjusted the sack on his shoulder. 'Ready?'

'Where is everyone?' she asked, looking around.

'They're coming,' he said.

As she rose, the others emerged.

'I thought you'd like this,' Nate said, passing her one of two wooden staffs.

Did he expect her to spar? Of course, he did. He wouldn't let their separation deter him from ensuring she was prepared to defend herself or even fight. Would she fight? She pushed those thoughts into the ever-expanding vacuum of darkness within. She wasn't ready to consider that yet.

The staff was black with a fine grain. She swung it around testing its weight. Slightly heavier but she could sense the staff's sturdiness and strength.

'I found you a new cloak,' Galia said.

It was deep blue, Hermonial colours and matched the ones the others now wore. She shrugged off the blanket favouring the cloak and its warming embrace. 'Where on earth did you find this?'

'That Ammo takes care of everything,' Galia chuckled.

Gabe headed between two timber huts which opened onto a track drawing them further inland. The others fell in behind him.

Catching up to Meciel, Galia asked, 'Where is Bina?'

'I instructed her earlier this morning to go with Ammo.'

Nate roared with laughter.

'What's so funny?' Galia asked.

'Oh nothing,' he chuckled to himself.

'Well, clearly there is something?'

'Let's hope Ammo makes it around the coastline alive,' he said, quickening his pace to catch up to Gabe.

The further inland they travelled the darker the overcast sky became. In the distance, a canopy of dull grey clouds loomed, imprisoning the sun behind their barricade. Mirah was about to mention it might rain when the first patters dripped onto her cloak.

The wind soon hissed towards them bringing sheets of drenching rain. It reminded her of the climate in Barakel. She pulled her hood tight under her chin, focused on the cloak in front of her and plodded on through the pouring rain.

By nightfall, the rainfall ceased. She sat by a fire drying her clothes wondering how she'd stay awake. Nate sat on the opposite side.

He sized up everything going on in the camp except her although he watched her from his periphery.

Part of her ached to reach out to him, to stop his pain and to feel his warmth and comforting embrace shielding her from her fears. She missed the wild strength of him and the way he'd always made her feel safe but that was before.

She'd never tell him how much she struggled to let go of their dreams. The torture he'd suffer by knowing was pointless.

Or how she often wondered what it would have been like to have had him, to understand the gift of joining. Would she have been able to fix what he'd broken in her if she'd known? But those were different dreams, dreams which will never be real. What remained were reflections of, what-ifs and maybes.

Last night the Beast had chased her through the streets of Nanshe. She'd run into the Dream Diviner's tent and taken refuge. The Beast circled around, sniffing and snarling whilst she'd held her breath.

I hear your heart thudding, I smell your fear, the Beast accused.

When its claws shredded the tent fabric, she'd screamed. Galia had been there instead of Nate.

She stared into the fire's flames and wondered if the Beast somehow followed her. Did it know she'd been in Nanshe? No, it couldn't, the Beast was trapped in the other realm.

But if Shemyaza had tracked them to Nanshe? Then the Beast might know. And if trackers were in Nanshe, then the Beast had revealed their location.

If her suspicion was true, then this was something she could use. As much as the Beast terrified her she needed to know for certain. She walked over to her bedroll, ready to face the Beast and find out what it knew.

The morning arrived too quick, and the Beast hadn't come at all. It should have relieved her, but she woke up anxious.

Nate came and handed her a bowl of Meciel's stew. 'Are you all right?'

She took a long savouring sip. 'I think they've reached Nanshe. The Beast, it chases me in my nightmares.'

Nate frowned as he listened to her explain what she'd dreamed. He stared in horror at the fading white line around her finger.

'I wish I knew how to break the connection and free you from its grip.'

'If what I suspect is correct, at least we know where they are.'

'But it's not worth the cost.'

He rose and beat his bedroll into his sack. Yes, the cost had been too great Mirah thought to herself.

They travelled until sunrise over grassy fields dotted with white granite stones.

Neviah groaned at Zeev. 'If you say one more time how you've stubbed your toe, I'm going to melt you.'

Zeev held up his hands in mock defence, his widespread grin challenging Neviah's own. It would have been funny if Mirah hadn't realised Neviah still considered using her amulet.

She squinted at a wall of green swishing treetops reaching up to catch hold the ascending sun. Terra glided over them, a silhouette against the sun's rays.

'The camp is on the other side of that forest,' Meciel said.

✻ 34 ✻

Covered in tacky resin, cobwebs, and crawling bugs, they picked up a river and followed its flow. It had taken all day to trek through the cedar forest. The first sign they were reaching its edge was the increasing number of fractured tree stumps.

'We'll stop here,' Gabe said.

He examined the sloping fields and the far side of the valley. On the opposite hillside, a thick wall of cloud concealed where he assumed the encampment lay.

He spied Nate giving Zeev a knowing glance and didn't care. He marched to the river, splashed water on his face and refilled his water skin. How the heck was he going to lead these forces? He'd have to fake it. He hoped whatever Meciel saw in him, those men on the other side of the valley saw as well.

Defeated, he sat on a hacked stump, ignoring the splinters and studied the little-carved wolf. He hoped Tam had found Nuri by now.

Dusty black boots arrived in his vision.

'I remember the first time I took command,' Nate said.

He lifted his head to find him sitting down on a stump opposite. 'How did it go?'

'I thought I would shit my pants.'

'And?'

'My training won over. You'll be fine but if you sit here like a child waiting for the darkness to shroud you, those men in the encampment will know. You must march over there and make a statement.'

Gabe had no clue about strategy or organising forces but what he knew or so Meciel kept telling him was a voice like thunder. A voice given to him by the Cloud Rider. He waited for Nate to return to the others and then he returned to them as well.

'If you're rested. We need to get moving. I want to reach the encampment before nightfall.'

After hiking up the valley it took several paces to breach through the wall of cloud surrounding the encampment and when they were through, Gabe wasn't the only one to inhale a sharp breath.

The encampment was a scarred, dun-coloured wasteland with numerous pitched black tents, the size and scale of which he couldn't discern.

'This way,' Meciel said, leading them towards the heaving presence of a high towering timber structure set in the middle of the encampment.

They weaved through the maze of blackened tents and pitch ropes. Banners and standards pitched outside the tents divided the encampment into various tribes. The first banner Gabe noted was an adder biting the heel of a rearing horse on a green background.

Men with hardened faces, sat on weathered tree stumps, sharpening bronze sickles, axes and hoes. Gabe cursed to himself. If this was all they had then they were in trouble.

Shouts and cries brought others out of parted tent flaps to watch their procession through the camp. They passed a banner with a crimson lion, its head raised over legs tucked under its body.

Men bowed to Meciel and gave lingering glances over the females. They checked out Nate and Zeev and their weapons, marking them as not from this region. Then they fixed their eyes on Gabe.

As each man weighed their travelling party, they recognised who he was supposed to be. Not by his achievements, he gathered, but by the process of elimination. He didn't let his eyes linger long enough to gauge their reactions. He concentrated on the timber structure ahead, willing it to open its jaws and devour him whole.

Inside two men sat on the far side of a cedar table. By the amount of the cracks along its grains, the fate of which had seen better days. A third man leaned against a hearth positioned behind them.

Gabe resisted the urge not to swallow against the dry heat and smoky air as he, Meciel and the girls sat down. Nate and Zeev came and stood guard behind them. He was aware of them scanning the room for threats and checking the exits. There were none apart from the door which they'd just come through. He knew they'd already assessed the three men's weapons, their battered swords at their sides, a few rusted daggers and their potential threat.

He noted all three wore the adder biting the horse's heel sigil and wondered if the leaders from the other tribes would arrive soon. Meciel made their introductions.

'I am in charge,' said the pudgy man by the hearth, slurring through his dark, braided beard. 'My name is Kesel and these are Tur and Avar.'

Gabe caught Kesel's unsaid inference. Behind him, Nate bristled as Kesel claimed his right to continue his rule along with the two sitting in front of him. Avar cut Gabe a stare which reeked of disdain.

Out of the three, only Tur stood out among them. His face was clean-shaven, his dark brown hair cut short, tattoos spread across his neckline and lowered beneath his shirt. Of the three, Tur's physique alone was honed for war and his ice-blue focus bored into Gabe searching out his weakness.

'Where's Ammo?' Kesel growled out.

'I sent him with the galleys,' Gabe answered. His voice wobbled. If he didn't get control of himself everything would go to shit.

Avar swung in his seat towards Meciel. 'Why would you allow him to order such a thing?'

Gabe sensed Nate behind him tensing rigid.

'I don't need to explain myself to you,' Gabe said, his voice going deeper.

Kesel strode from the hearth. 'No, maybe not,' he snapped at Gabe. His knuckles hit the table as he leaned in-between Tur and Avar. 'But you do have to explain yourself to me.'

Gabe forced down his compulsion to lean away from the reek of tobacco and stale beer. 'You're not in charge here anymore. You're dismissed.'

The words shot out of Gabe's mouth. He didn't care. He hadn't liked the man from the moment their eyes met.

Kesel's face turned almost as green as his sigil. 'You think those men out there,' he sneered, 'the ones, I've been training all these years will follow you?'

'I have my own War Chiefs and they're a darn sight more capable than you,' Gabe said, squaring off his shoulders. 'I know what you're thinking, that I'm young and easy to push around. You're wrong. You're just a fat, lazy beer guzzler.' His tone turned incredulous. 'I bet you haven't done an ounce of exercise in years.'

Kesel and Avar had half unsheathed their swords when Nate and Zeev pinned them on the cedar table, their daggers poised at the back of their necks.

'Don't move,' Nate warned Kesel, puncturing his skin with the tip of his dagger. A small trickle of blood ran over the grime on his neck.

'Meciel, can you ask Terra to escort them from the encampment?' Gabe said. 'The far side of the forest should be far enough. I wouldn't want them spreading poisonous lies amongst my men.'

Meciel rose and left the building.

'I'll gut you,' Kesel snarled.

'You can't do this,' Avar whined.

'What about you?' Gabe asked Tur, who hadn't flinched or said a word.

His ice-blue eyes savoured the challenge and his flawless assessment of them took everyone in. 'I'm here for the war.'

'Good answer,' Gabe replied. 'You can stay as long as you keep your mouth shut.'

He hardly believed it as Tur offered his hand to shake on their agreement.

Nate and Zeev disarmed Kesel and Avar and bound their wrists.

'Accompany them to the edge of the encampment, let Terra take over from there,' Gabe ordered. Focusing on Tur, he said, 'Go and tell the other War Chiefs that Nate will meet them at dawn.'

When Tur rose he towered a good head height over Nate. He didn't smile but gave him an acknowledging nod. It unnerved Gabe how easily Tur discerned them. He hoped for Tur's loyalty because without it he didn't know if even Nate could bring him down.

By the time Nate and Zeev reached the door, Gabe felt his muscles trembling.

From behind he heard Zeev say, 'Meet Terra, if you cause a fuss or stop before reaching the other side of the forest, she's been given permission to eat you,' and then they shoved Kesel and Avar outside.

Neviah stared at him in disbelief. 'What just happened?'

'I think it's called a coup,' Galia answered.

'Fat, lazy beer guzzler?' Mirah questioned.

Gabe sniggered. 'It was the first thing I could think of.'

He was pacing by the time he heard Nate and Zeev laughing as they returned.

'Well that didn't go as expected,' Zeev said, flopping down in a chair.

'Consider yourselves promoted,' Gabe said. 'Nate you are now my official Captain and Zeev you are still his second. I figure some of us around here should know what the heck we're doing.'

He caught the respect in Nate's eyes as he said, 'As you wish.'

'Good, because soon we're to start moving these forces. We've got a false god and a portal to destroy.'

✻ 35 ✻

A square blockade of galleys cut through the ocean to the rhythm of beating oar drums. Damn, he was good. Nobody else could have pulled this off. Meciel knew it too.

By the time Ammo reached twenty-one, he'd built up a formidable reputation. And if the price fit the task… well, Meciel paid him well.

He'd chosen odd jobs on the side, in-between building ships and recruiting the men. Jobs that Meciel definitely wouldn't approve. He reckoned he always had his reputation to upkeep. The silver kept coming, and he'd stopped listening to Meciel's stories about the Cloud Rider years ago but darn they appeared to be coming true.

The wind gusted, catching sun-bleached blue sails. Perspiring seamen leaned on redundant oars gulping water during their moment of reprieve.

Before reaching Shargaz's main harbour, they aimed to offload most of the men onto land. They'd attack from the sea and the shoreline. He planned to use his own galleys as a barricade, raid storehouses for steel and salvage any of Shargaza's galleys which remained. Once loaded the galleys would return to Chaba Misgab, but the men would stay and cross by land and meet up with Meciel in Isriq.

Ammo found Bina standing at the bow of the ship. Sea spray wetting the deck. He sniffed the salty breeze.

'There's something strange in the air,' she said.

On the horizon, a thick white canvass of sea mist crawled towards them. He sensed nothing, but he'd learned enough about Bina to never doubt her.

'Sojin,' he yelled, 'Get up in the nest.'

A gust of wind caught Bina's long hair and its black tendrils whipped across his face.

'Whatever's out there, we'll find out soon enough,' he said.

Bina's eyes hardened as Sojin made quick work climbing the mast to the crow's nest. 'They shouldn't be here. They're no older than boys.'

He'd considered leaving Sojin, Eran and Abela in the safety of Chaba Misgab's harbour but was anywhere safe anymore?

'They're better off with me,' he replied.

Bina shifted her footing and her eyes dilated. It still unnerved him. Even after he'd seen them dilate many times on their journey to join Meciel.

'Gabe has taken control of your forces. Meciel said it went as expected.'

Her lavender eyes returned to normal, and he exhaled a deep breath.

He swiped his fringe from his eyes. 'Well darn it, maybe there's hope for us yet.'

Sojin hollered from the crow's nest. 'Ships.'

He squinted at the dark shadow rowing out of the mist. 'How many?'

'One, oh hang on there's two. They're making right for us.'

'Stay there until ya see their colours, then get ya ass back here.'

Ammo never liked the waiting. The lull between victory or defeat felt never-ending. By the speed they sliced through the swell, ally or enemy, he estimated, they'd be on them by midday.

His galleys diverted into a phalanx formation, their ramrods hidden under the waters. Their turning brought the tide against them causing a strong current to drag against the galleys' hulls. The oarsmen's straining faces revealed how much they fought against it.

'They're dark blue,' Sojin shouted.

He could tell by Eran's paling complexion he knew and so did Ammo. The ships belonged to Shemyaza.

When his boots hit the deck, Ammo said to Sojin, 'Get below and take Eran with ya.'

Sojin hesitated.

'Now! There ain't nothing ya can do, stay with Abela,' he ordered. He licked his finger and held it to the surging wind. 'Pull down the sails,' he yelled at his crew, 'and bring me to the right of our galleys.'

From there he'd gain a better view of the action. The thud boomed first and then the sound of cracking wood. His lead galley rose from the sea amidst a plume of water and split in half. The galley crew flew from the deck into the ocean.

Ammo cursed loud and ferocious. He sprinted to the side of his ship and saw a flash of red dip below the waves. The ocean rippled in its wake and he tracked its movements.

A scaly, flat head, shaped like an anvil breached the surface, its gnashing jaws snapping around a struggling man. Its eely body coiled and crushed his bones before dragging him under the sea.

Ammo, still reeling, heard Bina snap, 'I can't do anything from here.'

She strutted over to an oarsman, grabbed a spear laid near his feet and climbed onto the side of Ammo's ship.

'What are ya doing? Ya think ya can spear that beast from here?'

'No,' she replied and lifted off from the ship, black-tipped, grey wings spreading wide.

'Darn,' he muttered to himself.

Another of his galleys splintered in half. One of Shemyaza's ships headed straight towards them. The other veering right.

Bina circled above and then she dove. A shrill cry reverberated across the ocean and a gush of musty, yellow liquid spread over the waters as she jammed the spear into whatever lurked beneath before ascending again.

She flew towards Ammo at great speed and descended in the sea's direction. He leaned over the side and watched her drive the spear into the serpent. She dragged the spear along its flesh. The serpent's back split wide open, revealing black chunks of vertebrae along its spine.

'You're welcome,' she said, and then shot into the air.

Ammo heard whizzing and looked up to see fireballs and ice shards flying overhead.

'Shields,' he yelled.

Several of his galleys erupted into flames. If his men escaped into the water, they'd be fated against the serpents circling below. How many he couldn't guess. Smoke billowed from the galleys, along with the scent of men's burning flesh.

'If ya want to live, ram that ship,' his voice bellowed over the commotion.

If they heard him, he couldn't tell although the galleys surged on through the swell. His men fired a volley of arrows which burst into flames mid air. The thought of Fire Wielders out on the open sea sent him livid.

He spat out windswept ash. 'Hold fire on ya arrows.'

Bina returned to his side. 'I've taken out two. The last one fled but at least I've slowed it down.'

'How are we gonna stop their Wielders? They're cutting through my galleys faster than it will take to reach em.' He rubbed the green gem on his finger.

'There are no Chashmalim on their ships,' Bina reassured him.

He shot passed her and vaulted onto the bow.

A red-haired giant standing on the ship veering right glared at him. Dismissing him soon after, his burning amber eyes scanned over Wind Weaver, searching. Beside him, a woman with braided henna coloured hair wielded fire in her hands but didn't attack.

'They're not here, leave them,' the giant ordered his crew.

The woman stroked the flames and smirked at Ammo. He felt the pull of the challenge. If she hadn't been his enemy, he'd have grinned and given her a cocky wink. The giant and his ship veered away, leaving Shemyaza's other ship to continue its attack.

An ice spear slammed into the bow, shattering, sending ice everywhere.

'I've had enough of this,' he said, picking up an ice shard and popping it in his mouth. 'Get me closer.'

The oarsmen rowing the galley nearest to Shemyaza's ship doubled over gasping for air.

Bina raised her arms and shouted, 'Gadah.' She turned to Ammo, 'Hurry, I can't hold them forever.'

One of Ammo's galleys rammed into the side of Shemyaza's remaining ship. Its bronze rod smashing into its hull. A huge bubble of air resisted the surging water but not for long.

'Move,' Ammo yelled.

Dagger in hand, he ran and hurdled from one galley to the next until reaching the galley with its ramrod still thrust through Shemyaza's ship.

He unsheathed his sword as men rushed forward with him ready to assault Shemyaza's Wielders, guards and crew.

With Bina suppressing their powers, it was a fair fight.

Ammo plunged his dagger into the first Wielder, her warm blood gushing over his wrist. He swung his sword through the next spraying blood over his silk shirt.

Between the bawling and bellowing, blades clashed, clinking steel against steel. Blood spray lubricated the ship's deck in its oily life force. He swallowed, forcing the salty tang from his throat.

Swords, daggers and deep blue cloaks became a blur. A pear-shaped mace whirled at his head. He ducked, pivoted and thrust his blade into the man's ribs. His dagger jarred against bone. The man died before his body thumped onto the deck. His eyes wide, his death stare leading him to the world beyond.

When the fighting ceased around twenty guards and several Wielders surrendered.

'Take their amulets,' Ammo ordered one of his men.

The Wielders dropped a variety of jewels into a sack.

Shemyaza's ship listed, taking on water. The bow submerged, waves gushing up the deck.

'Abandon ship,' he hollered.

On reaching Wind Weaver, he flicked his head, spraying off excess water and checked his arm. The gash was long but not deep. He hadn't known of it until he'd dived into the salty sea and swam. It stung but not as much as his split lip.

Bina threw him a towel, and he rubbed the remaining moisture from his hair. Black blood clung to her tunic reminding him of bog mud and a slight sheen embraced her brow.

'Never seen ya sweat before,' he teased.

She stumbled forward.

On instinct, he outstretched his hand but the resistance in her eyes made him stop. 'Are ya all right?'

'What about them?' she asked, staring at Shemyaza's Wielders.

'They are powerless,' he said, holding up the sack. 'Let em swim.'

He marched across the deck towards the stern. 'Sojin,' he yelled, 'bring Abela, bring supplies.'

Two of his crew were already untying the covering on the small reed boat.

'Lower this overboard,' he commanded.

Sojin emerged with Abela and Eran.

'Abela, do ya think ya can help the men?'

She observed the devastation, taking in the sight of men swimming from burning and sinking ships and the galley's crewmen using oars to push the dead away. He wondered what memories stirred within her.

'I'll do what I can,' she replied.

'Good. Sojin ya and Eran go with her. Move from galley to galley, patch em up and move on.'

Ammo surveyed his fleet. He guessed Shemyaza's Wielders destroyed at least eight galleys. Not counting the survivors still in the ocean, he estimated he'd lost a good few thousand men.

He hadn't touched a beer in years and shuddered, remembering the last time and what it cost him. He resisted the urge to drink now. Bina caught up with him.

'Darn, for a while there, I thought Shemyaza's Wielders were gonna ruin my reputation.'

She let out a shallow groan but even for her, it was a poor attempt.

'I'm not sure if ya are up to it but when ya are strong enough, ya should warn Meciel. Whoever that giant is, he didn't care about us. I'm guessing Shemyaza sent him after Mirah.'

'I'll update him at sundown.'

He'd expected as much. Whatever power she held, it wasn't limitless, and she'd never admit her weakened state.

'Ya know, ya gonna have to tell me sooner or later. I assumed ya was just playing hard to get but darn, who, what are ya?'

Bina bristled and walked off.

'This changes nothing between us ya know,' he called after her, knowing full well it changed everything.

'Oh, trust me I know.'

❊ 36 ❊

Blue patches of sky snatched at silver-edged clouds drifting westward and the sun's rays frolicked with smoke spiralling up from the camp's morning cook pots.

Mirah and Neviah were on the roof of the timber Command Centre watching Nate and Zeev and several War Chiefs. For three nights she'd waited for the Beast to enter her dreams but it still declined to reveal itself or any trackers' location.

'Do you remember when we sat on the veranda in Hermonial?' Neviah asked. 'We're not the same anymore. Are we?'

Meciel had taken Gabe off somewhere at dawn. She didn't say it but they weren't the same and neither was he.

Tur, now promoted to War Chief after Kesel's removal, had returned to introduce Nate and Zeev to the other tribes.

She could see them standing in a sandy arena which reminded her of the garrison courtyard at Hermonial. Even from here Nate stood majestic. He wandered with Tur, who stood a foot taller to his left and Zeev on his right towards the row of War Chiefs. Mirah didn't recognise their sigils but she could detect their distinctive colours of reds, purples, yellows and greens.

Nate stopped to speak to every War Chief. She wondered what he said as they straightened their shoulders and acknowledged his command.

His confidence and ability to take the lead already forming strong bonds. Her heart tugged knowing he'd broken theirs.

'Of course, if he wasn't handsome, it wouldn't be so difficult.' Neviah sighed.

'What?' she asked, as her head whipped around.

'Look at him. I've tried to ignore his ridiculous flirting but I don't know anymore.'

Mirah realised she was looking at Zeev. 'You desire him?'

'What if some of us don't survive? I don't want to die not experiencing what it feels like.' She stole her gaze from away from Zeev. 'Did you ever—'

'No. Can we talk about something else?'

They were silent for some time.

The War Chiefs below dispersed, and Nate dug his boot in the dust. Before long, tribesmen arrived and paired off. Nate and Zeev circled around, assessing their techniques, offering advice where needed.

'We should teach them how it's done,' Neviah said.

Mirah caught the gleam in her eyes. 'You're right, come on.'

Zeev's face was a panorama of amusement, Nate's not so much as they strolled between the sparring men. They took up their place amongst the sweat and dust kicked up by the tribesmen.

Neviah had grabbed Nate's staff and held it ready. 'Let's show them how to win this war,' she said, wielding her staff low across Mirah's thighs.

Mirah dropped one end of her staff to the ground and used it to swing her body up and over Neviah's staff.

'Nice.' Neviah grunted as wood hit against wood.

They sparred until their lungs burned and dusty eyes itched. It felt good having a staff in her hands, to focus on sparring and nothing else. They finished to a solo clapping and Zeev coming at them with a water skin under his arm.

'Thanks,' Neviah said, taking a swig.

'Now you're warmed up, all hot and sweaty, are you ready for the real action?' Zeev said, reaching his hand over the pommel of his sword.

'Come to my room later,' Neviah said, before rushing off.

Zeev swung around to Nate, his eyes probing for answers, questioning what he'd heard and then shot off after Neviah.

'You did well,' Nate said, stepping closer.

'So did you. We were watching from the rooftop.'

She pushed the end of the staff out with her foot and observed his slight hesitation as he noted it now positioned between them.

'What Gabe did, removing Kesel and Avar, I didn't see that coming,' he said, moving sideways.

She pivoted. 'As far as leading goes, he couldn't have found a better Captain.'

'Mirah, I, can we—'

'I need to help Galia and Ayla with something,' she said, edging backwards.

Her voice quivered. With a slow blink, she shoved the well of tears down deep. Would she ever find the space to cry them out?

Without breaking into a run, she headed back to the Command Centre but when she reached it she kept going.

She followed a trail down through the valley until she came to the river and collapsed onto the mossy grass. Under the sound of gurgling water, she let her tears flow and even though she no longer sensed their particles, each teardrop ripped from her soul.

She lay on the moss and stared into nothing for a long while. If her Ma was here, she'd show her how to get through this.

She sensed the shadow first and opened her eyes to discover Galia standing over her.

'I thought I'd find you here. I always search out water when I'm low.' She wandered to the river. 'Even though I can't feel it, I still find it soothing. Don't you ever miss it?'

'I sometimes miss flying water birds and children's faces lighting up when chasing watery frogs.'

Galia let the water flow through her fingers, swishing her palm against its flow. The wind stilled, and the trees became motionless, leaving only the river to gurgle its tune.

'I lost my beloved. He was Zeev's older brother. In the desert, I couldn't reach him in time.'

'Oh Galia, I'm sorry. Why didn't you tell me?'

'Until now I didn't think you'd understand.'

Galia flicked the water from her hand and came and sat beside her.

'I came so close,' Mirah said. 'My heart, a wide open gulf drawing him to me. I didn't comprehend the fear I know now. His betrayal… it would have been kinder to have killed me at Barakel.' She sniffed and wiped her cheeks. 'It's like an emptiness but I know it's far from that. Does it ever go away?'

'In time, it changes into something else.'

'Meciel said, if I allow the pain to grow deep enough, it will grow roots. I feel them burrowing. My flesh is tearing and I don't know how to stop it. What should I do?'

'I don't claim to understand what you're experiencing. I don't have a connection to whatever power surges through my amulet like you. Nate doesn't understand it either. All I do know is, if I had a second chance, I wouldn't hesitate.'

Neither spoke for a long time.

She missed the birdsong, though she heard it, it didn't sound the same. Sorrow and anguish sang in their melody and mimicked her own. Chirping little echoes reminding her of intoxicating smiles and snatched dreams.

'We should return,' Galia broke into the silence.

'You go. I need a little more time.'

After Galia retreated, Mirah went to the river and lowered her hand into the frozen water, letting it wrap around her fingers. She waded out until the current pulled around her waist. Bending her knees, she submerged herself and let the water wash over her, not to cause harm but to cleanse.

Her mind jumbled back through images of her past. Her Ma's curly red hair framing her smiling face, Gabe setting his inky hand on the rock shelter wall, Nate's raven black hair and cool blue eyes shining under the starlight, Huldah's last breath, images flooded through her mind, one after another, images of Shemyaza and the Beast, faster and faster.

Her lungs cried out for air and her bones rattled under her icy skin. A little longer she begged herself.

Then she saw him, the Fallen Star, the creases around his hazel eyes and merciful smile. *Everything has a reason, in its own time and right season.* She rushed out of the river and raced back to the camp. Deep inside she knew, she knew the reason.

Thunder rumbled across the sky bringing Mirah back to herself. She sprinted through the valley, thunder cracking behind her. She reached the Command Centre and with wet hair clinging to her face, she burst through his door.

'Nate.'

He leaped from his bed, scanning her for injuries. Water dripped onto the floor. She couldn't move.

'Nate,' she pleaded.

She felt her wet clothes soaking into his. His firm body, shielding her from a threat he couldn't see. He brushed hair from her face and searched her for understanding.

'Kiss me.'

His lips crushed against hers, passion and months of yearning drove him. He poured all of his being into her like it was his last chance. The force of him causing her to gasp. He pulled his head back, his gaze taking her in. She saw the flaming spark of desire and the heat of it ignited her own. In that moment she came alive.

He nuzzled into her hair and she heard him breathe her in. 'I thought I'd lost you,' he whispered and guided her lips back to his.

She wrapped her arms around his neck drawing him closer. She couldn't get him close enough.

'I need you,' she pleaded.

His kisses caressed her neck and then smoothed over her collarbone. He realised what he did, how touching her there made her shudder and want release. His self-assurance purged through her apprehension. Invisible stars entwined around her, their light, dancing steps spreading over her skin. Her head swooned, and she shivered.

'You need to remove those wet clothes.'

'I don't want you to stop.'

Nate moaned. 'Not here, not like this.'

She studied him searching for a gap in his resistance. His eyes filled with love and yearning. Whatever fixed his determination clawed to escape, to set him free, to not resist her but he held on. She knew that for whatever reason he wouldn't change his mind.

Nate lifted his white shirt draped over the chair. 'Put this on.'

He turned away to give her privacy. When she was standing in nothing but his huge shirt, he folded his cloak around her. 'Come,' he said, leading her to the bed. His lips gently caressed her neck as he stroked her hair. 'I love you,' he whispered. 'Go to sleep.'

⁂

Where are you? the Beast sneered.

Mirah saw through the beast's eyes, a bird's-eye view of galleys on the ocean. Then it swerved through fire and ice shooting across the sky, Wielders. Galleys burning, dark objects floating in the water, bodies.

Trapped behind the Beast's view she couldn't help them. It lowered its gaze, pausing over Wind Weaver, eyes scanning.

I know you're here, it tormented.

Ammo ran across his ship and leaped over the side.

The Beast snorted.

Mirah's breathing became ragged.

What was Ammo doing? She wanted to beg the Beast to turn back its gaze.

'No,' she cried out.

She awoke to find Nate leaning over her, his hand gently shaking her shoulder.

'Ammo's galleys are being attacked,' she said, through heavy breaths. 'They know we're here.' She pushed off the bed. 'I have to tell Gabe.'

Her clothes and boots were still damp as she hurried to put them on. She found Gabe's room empty and rushed downstairs to the command room.

'Where's Gabe?' she asked Galia.

'He's not back yet. I couldn't sleep.'

Galia watched as Nate came and wrapped his arms around Mirah's waist. With her eyebrow raising slightly, she said, 'I've made tea.'

When Gabe returned with Meciel, exhaustion harassed him. She felt guilty burdening him with more.

'What about Shemyaza?' Mirah asked after she'd told them.

'He doesn't know where you are,' Meciel said.

She would have been pacing if Nate hadn't kept her hold. 'But I saw—'

'What you saw was a hunting party,' Meciel said. 'Ammo destroyed one of their ships. The other, when they realised we weren't with them left to continue searching.'

'He's right,' Nate said, giving her waist a gentle squeeze. 'If they thought, they were in any way connected they'd have interrogated them before leaving.'

She could sense Nate's mind racing, shifting his strategies into play.

He turned to Gabe and said, 'They're too close. We need to be moving and we must split the forces. I'll instruct Zeev to lead half the men, to keep with the planned raid on Shargaz's mines, the rest we'll take with us.'

'We leave at first light,' Gabe said, rising. 'I'll be on the roof if anyone needs me.'

Galia followed him and she heard their muffled voices lowering in the corridor the further along they went.

Nate kissed her brow. 'I have to help Zeev and raise the War Chiefs.'

He hadn't asked her anything about her change of heart and she yearned to explain. 'Go,' she said.

Left alone, she asked Meciel, 'Before you go can you clarify how the Beast can see?'

He paused by the door. 'There is a veil between our worlds. Those in the other realm are not omnipresent. They can't be everywhere at once. I believe it tracked whoever is tracking you, to get a glimpse of where you are.'

'What does it want?'

'You already know the answer.'

⁂

Mirah stepped onto the Command Centre roof. She found Gabe sitting on the ledge next to Terra watching the buzz of activity going on in the encampment. The torchlights and campfires competed with the darkness making the tents and the men below barely visible.

Terra's head hung low and cocked to the side, her golden eyes watching her as she approached.

'She doesn't frighten you?' Mirah asked.

'She reminds me of Nuri,' he said, massaging her leathery shoulder.

Terra shifted, her talons scraped against the wood and she let out an indignant snort.

Mirah drew closer and asked, 'What were you thinking?'

'I was remembering when I used to play practice sticks with Eran and Tam, fighting off leviathans or invading armies. It's not a game anymore.'

Men weaving through the tents called out in the darkness and she peered into the gloom, eyes straining to view them. 'What's your plan?'

'Meciel said he can close the portal. He wants me to destroy Shargaz. Since they took you, he's been teaching me their language. It's strange, I can't explain it, but it feels alive when I speak it. The more I believe the more it seems to work. He's convinced my words are stronger than any sword.'

She sensed his conflicted emotions. He stood on a crossroads between the relief of having her with him and the uncertainty of what lay ahead. But deeper still she recognised his unshakable determination and knew it would win through.

'What do you think?' he asked with concern.

'We stick together; we stick to your plan.'

He smiled and she realised as much as he didn't want this he was doing this for her. Everything within her wanted to tell him they should run, hide, maybe they could outsmart them if only for a while.

'Before, how did Meciel learn about the attack on Ammo's galleys?'

'Bina. I see what you're considering, I've already tried it. And before you ask, I don't understand how their communication works either.' He pulled her into an embrace. 'I'll never let anyone separate us again.'

She wondered if Meciel communicated with the Fallen Star and if they did what the Fallen Star had told him of her time in Hermonial. Whatever Meciel knew, he kept well guarded and that didn't surprise her. He'd been a mystery at Barakel and she didn't think she'd ever unravel the extent of who and what he was.

'I have something for you. I meant to give this to you earlier, but I didn't want to let it go.' He lifted the green shard of their Ma's necklace from his cloak.

Mirah clasped her hand around his. She understood how much he clung to the shard and the memory of their Ma. 'You keep it.'

'But it's yours.'

'Not anymore.'

⁂

They departed for Isriq the following day to the sound of horses' hoof beats and marching footsteps. Tribes were arranged according to their standards, and the Crimson Lion's banner led the procession. The Brown Ox, Yellow Cross Swords and many others followed. The largest tribe with the Green Adder banner taking up the rear.

They rode through a grassy valley and met with a rushing river flowing from the basin of a mountain range. As they travelled, the path narrowed and irregular granite boulders made way for slender waterfalls.

Hedging them in were lofty snow-crested mountains with shady conifers surrounding their base. Eagles screeched, protecting their nests. Terra ignored them, soaring high in the hazy blue sky.

Ahead, Neviah shifted in her saddle. Mirah tapped her bay horse's ribs and trotted up beside her.

'What's the matter with you?' she asked. 'I know it's been a while, but it's not like we haven't ridden horses before.'

'If I'd known we'd be riding today, I wouldn't have done what I did last night.'

'Oh,' Mirah said, her face blushing. 'Did you take a tonic?'

'Of course, I did. I'm not an idiot.' Neviah glared at her from across her dapple grey pony.

'When Zeev breaks off to the mines. You should go with him.'

'Are you sure?' Neviah asked, her shoulders relaxing.

'Stay with him. You should be happy.'

'I don't know about that,' Neviah grumbled, shifting again.

They stopped by a lake before nightfall. Nate and Zeev left to make sure the War Chiefs organised lookouts over the camp.

He'd ordered that no fires be lit but the high moon reflected its silvery ambience on the lake. The motion of shimmering water reminded her of Galia's hair.

The tribesmen went to the lake to wash and swim. She sat some distance away and watched Neviah splashing water at Ayla and for a moment they were all back in Barakel. In-between splashes Neviah often looked over the camp searching for Zeev.

Knowing Neviah and Ayla were going to the mines instead of Isriq lifted her spirits. She hoped, at least in the mines, amongst the smelting iron ore and its gases, Neviah wouldn't risk wielding fire. Ayla had argued at first, saying she wanted to stay near Meciel and keep track of Abela. She'd relented when Nate explained those at the mines would need a healer.

Nate and Zeev sauntered over, stripped to the waist and waded into the water. Refined for war, every muscled curvature a testament to their strength.

Zeev grabbed Neviah and pulled her under. He was formidable but nowhere near like Nate. Masculinity drooled off Nate in droves as he stood facing over the lake.

'You should come in,' Ayla said, wading out of the water.

'It's too crowded.'

Covered in horse sweat, she'd spent most of the day swishing away horse flies and her face stung with the never-ending nips from midges.

Ayla rummaged around in her sack and threw a small pot over to Mirah. 'Salve, for the bites.'

She sniffed at the creamy salve. 'This smells awful. What is it?'

'Petrified spines of sea urchin. It will sooth away the sting.'

She debated whether to use the salve as Ayla searched for dry clothes. Neviah shrieked in excitement as Zeev chased her through the water.

'I'm going to change,' Ayla said.

Mirah settled on her bedroll listening to the others playing in the water. Soon the camp noise turned into low murmurs, snoring and cautious footsteps.

The fresh grassy scent, the gentle lapping of the lake and the people surrounding her, ready to take back what belonged to them filled her with hope. Nate lay down, and she rested in his embrace. She drew her staff closer to prevent someone from tripping over it and closed her eyes.

'You are nothing more than a shadow,' she told the Beast.

❊ 37 ❊

Nate and Gabe stood before the War Chiefs. Zeev had marched out before sunrise leading tribesmen under the standards of the Brown Ox, the Grey Wolf and the Green Adder with him.

The three tribes combined amounted to four thousand men. Nate hoped it would be enough. He'd watched them leaving armed with farming sickles, hoes and axes. Those more fortunate carried wooden shields, spears, slings and swords. He understood now why Ammo insisted on attacking Shargaz's mines. They needed its steel.

The War Chiefs waited for Gabe to begin. Earlier, Nate sent three men to scout out Isriq. They'd returned early that morning to report on a well-defended city and that Shargaz built his residence within a dormant volcano. They didn't risk straying too close and had no idea about the portal.

Nate had already briefed Gabe on the wisest tactical strategy and advised him that the War Chiefs needed to hear it from him.

Gabe paced in front of them. He was young and inexperienced but nothing about him stood out as a fraud.

With a stick, Gabe drew two circles in the sand. 'This is Isriq city, and that is the volcano,' he said pointing to each circle. To the War Chief with the Red Lion sigil, he said, 'You are to come up between Isriq city and the west side of the volcano. I need you to hold the ground.' He sketched a line in the sand between the circles to emphasise the position. 'Do not go into the city. I don't want innocent citizens harmed. You're to prevent Shargaz's forces stationed in the city from crossing towards the volcano.'

Sliding the stick to the south of the city, he directed his attention to the War Chief with the Yellow Crossed Swords sigil, 'You will come from the south. I expect Shargaz's forces to attack our men positioned between the city and the volcano. Instruct your men to come up behind and block them.'

Turning to the War Chief wearing the Eagle over the Burdened Blue Sky sigil, he said, 'You come from the east and focus your attack on the volcano.' He slid the stick to the circle representing the volcano. 'I will meet you there.'

'What about the north?' the Yellow Cross Swords War Chief asked.

'Leave the north to me,' Gabe answered. 'I will be leaving soon to enter the city. Before you follow send scouts ahead to take out any patrols. Charge tomorrow at nightfall. Any questions?'

The War Chiefs shook their heads.

'Good, then let's start this war.'

Whatever Gabe thought of himself, Nate heard his authority and the War Chiefs he directed, determined it as well.

Nate had wanted to sneak ahead himself and spy out Isriq but he couldn't bring himself to leave Mirah behind. He had no clue what caused her to return to him. When she'd ran into his room, seeing no blood, he'd thought the worst, that someone had ravished her.

She'd felt so small, so cold and shivering. Kiss me, was the last thing he'd expected to hear fall from her lips.

He loved the feeling of her embracing him, reacting to him, her unspoken communication escaping in those little sounds, anticipating what was to come. He'd craved to discover every part of her, learn how she touched and moved against him.

When she'd pleaded, he fought against the fear he might still lose her and the throbbing ache raging against him. She deserved more than a rotting timber Command Centre. Deep inside he knew this wasn't their time.

⁂

The city of Isriq lay on the far side of the mountain range. Disguised as merchants, they had a day to trek through the pass and sneak into the city before the War Chiefs marched.

Nate and Gabe led the horse whilst Mirah, Meciel and Galia rode in the cart.

In the mountain pass, out of the corner of his eye, he often saw the shimmer of sunlight reflecting off steel. If his assumptions were correct Shargaz's sentries should be preoccupied, most likely drunk and attended to by women paid enough to traipse outside the city. After all, who was foolish enough to march an army against the Supreme Smiter?

He counted eight guard posts and hoped the scouts did their job well. If they didn't, their men would become trapped inside the mountain pass. He hated the idea but could see no other way to get the men through.

They reached the edge of the city at sunset. In the diminishing light, black volcanic rock out of which their habitations were made, submitted beneath a tremendous white idol rising over the city. From here he couldn't quite make out its form through it reared on hind legs and wielded an indistinguishable weapon with particular menace.

Pulling off the track, they hid their cart and freed the horse. They crept under the camouflage of pine trees, coming up on the west side of the city.

After assessing the dyed fabrics drying in the small courtyard, he figured the nearest building belonged to a weaver. He barged through the door, sword raised and nearly vomited at the stench.

An elderly woman with gnarled hands holding up her linen fringed skirt halted with her knee half lifted in the air. She stood in a pail, crunching dried beetles under her feet. He noted her spindle legs dyed crimson up to her shins. The stench, he realised came from another pail, piss he assumed.

'This is your lucky day,' Nate said swallowing.

An old man with wispy, white hair jumped up from a loom.

'Do not move,' Nate warned.

The man froze.

Nate glanced around the room. 'Anyone else?'

The old man looked at his wife.

'Sit,' he said, to the woman, pointing his sword towards a stool by the table. 'You as well, over there,' he ordered the old man. He backed to the doorway and raised his hand to call over the others. With everyone inside, he closed the door.

'We won't hurt you,' Mirah reassured them. 'We need somewhere to stay until tomorrow.'

'Is that stew?' Meciel asked, sniffing the air.

How he couldn't smell the overwhelming odour of piss was beyond him.

The woman nodded, her wise eyes widening.

'I love a good stew,' Meciel said and lifted up the ladle.

With the number of weapons everyone carried, the old man and his wife didn't create a fuss.

'Galia can you get rid of that,' he asked, nodding to the offensive pail.

After they'd eaten, Nate slipped out. He tightened the hood of his cloak and slid through the darkness. Every step he took from Mirah tugged against him. The pressure to rush ahead and return sooner clashed against his training and he willed himself to listen to caution.

He kept to the volcano's south side, it would be closest when the legions arrived. The stink of shit hit his senses before reaching the cesspit. He'd have groaned if not for revealing his position, everything about this place reeked. He followed the slurry which led to the volcano, its sides a jagged formation of sharp-edged black rock.

Thick sludge seeped out an old iron grate. After a quick survey, he clutched the bars and heaved. One bar snapped off in his hand. He paused, waiting for guards to raise the alarm. When he heard nothing, he gripped the edge of the grate's frame and pulled again.

The grate ground against the rock and he searched for any sign someone overheard him. He was about to abandon the grate and move on when it loosed and came free. After wiping rusty hands onto his pants, he hunched over and entered a low bearing tunnel. So foul was the stench, he drew his cloak over his nose.

The tunnel led straight forward, sloping upwards. He stepped over intermittent piles of slurry sliding from smaller outlets. It was so disgusting even the vermin didn't dare trespass.

When he reached another grate, he could go no further. Without making a sound, he peered through the grill. He estimated he was around two thirds up the height of the volcano.

To his relief, he saw no molten lava, instead lights from oil lamps lit up chambers carved out of the crater's igneous rock.

The portal stood in the centre of the crater on a raised dais. It fanned out in an inky green glowing circle.

Surrounding the portal were three chimeric sentries. In the shimmering light, they glowed a vibrant, bluish-green. Crustaceous plated armour segments made up their torsos and protruding from their midsections, wings folded like a shroud across their ridged spines.

One scurried, claws scraping over the dais and stopped at the edge. Its tail arching up and over, its swollen barb dripping with venom. The barb turned and twitched as though testing the air for predators.

Nate observed two black eyes set on the top of its crustaceous head shining in the moonlight. The chimera's mandibles snapped opened and closed. Their clicking sounds making him shiver. He instinctively leaned back, hiding deeper in the tunnel's shadow.

He tracked back to the Weaver's hut. Galia gagged when he entered.

'There's a washtub outside,' the old woman said, passing him a white weaved sheet. 'When you're undressed, pass me your clothes.'

'I have my own clothes,' Nate said, reaching for his sack.

'Then leave your boots,' the old man added.

He raised a questioning brow at Gabe.

Gabe scrunched his nose. 'I suggest you do what they say before I turf you out the door myself.'

His boots were cleaned when he returned. 'Well, I can see everyone has become acquainted. What happened?'

'Meciel has a unique understanding of people,' Gabe said. 'Whilst you scouted, he calmed their fears but more to the point, what happened to you?'

He explained everything he'd seen and about the grate blocking their path.

'Leave that to me,' Meciel said.

'I don't suppose you saw any sign of Shargaz?' Gabe asked, drumming his fingers on the table.

'No, though I saw three of his chimera, similar to scorpions but with wings and they're about the size of a horse. Their pincers could slice a man in half.'

The old man placed a tray of drinks, which looked a lot like dreaded red beetle juice, onto the table. 'Shargaz resides in his chambers under the portal.'

All eyes fell on him.

'I'm delivering fabrics there tomorrow. If you'd asked I would have told you.'

Galia laughed and said to Nate. 'Well, that will teach you. I'm so relieved we don't have to trudge through that stench.'

'Tell us what you know?' Nate asked.

The old man's jowls flapped until morning. The overseer of Shargaz's concubines had instructed him to bring fabric later that evening.

They spent the day resting until an hour before the old man was due to deliver his merchandise. Gabe and Galia were outside helping the old man and his wife fill their cart with an array of various shades of red fabrics. Mirah stood to help them.

'Wait,' Nate said. He knew she'd refuse, but he had to try. Now they were here, and he'd seen the volcano, the thought of her being captured overwhelmed him. At least with the old couple, she'd have somewhere safer to stay. 'Will you wait here? I'll come back for you when the attack is over.'

'I can't.'

'But it's too dangerous. Once we're inside it will be like stepping into a cage. If Shargaz somehow gets hold of you—' He dare not hide the truth from her now. 'If we fail and Shargaz takes you prisoner, you heard what he said, he'll force you to wed him and one day he'll use you to wield for him against Shemyaza.'

'Gabe will take care of him.'

'Mirah, please. Listen.' He tried to make her see the urgency in his eyes.

'I'm going,' she said, shrugging him off and rushing to those waiting outside.

How the bidu was he going to protect her? She didn't understand. She said she'd never fight. She wouldn't even wield.

He dropped to his knees. 'Cloud Rider. I don't know who you are, I don't even know your true name but if you're listening. I'll do anything you want, just keep her safe.'

Meciel rested his hand on Nate's shoulder. 'Your supplication will not return to you empty, now get up. The battle is in the Cloud Rider's will.'

Nate rose, he considered chasing after her and trying again but instead, he checked the daggers in both sides of his boots and the other attached to his belt. He adjusted his sword at his side and sheathed his two curved blades across his back.

'We're ready,' Galia said, hesitating at the door.

Meciel reached into the pouch inside his cloak. 'Bina said you might need this.' He placed her amulet in her hand.

'I don't understand?'

'Even an enemy can be used to save you,' he said and walked out the door.

❊ 38 ❊

The chilled night air whipped around outside and Mirah soaked up the others' warmth as they lay huddled together under the Weaver's fabrics. If she wasn't so scared she might have fallen asleep. Instead, she listened for the sound of steel against steel.

The Weaver stopped the cart, and she heard his soft slipper footsteps padding along the side of the cart towards the rear. He hefted rolls of fabric onto his shoulder and after ensuring the remaining fabric still concealed them, huffed and walked away. She kept her breaths shallow and waited.

Nate brushed his finger over her lips. The last time she'd seen such fixed determination was on Shemyaza's plateau. She knew in her heart he'd have stepped into the ring if needed. She knew he'd do the same now.

Then it came.

The thudding assault of their tribemens' footsteps charging into the crater. They climbed out of the cart. Nate had been right. Shargaz hadn't prepared for anyone either stupid or brave enough to storm his volcano.

'I'll need my strength for the portal,' Meciel said, 'but I'll hold off their Air Wielders as long as I can.'

Meciel and Gabe ran for the portal.

Wielders, she'd spent so much time trying to forget, she hadn't allowed herself to think about their presence here.

Their tribesmen filled out around the crater and took up their positions. The world paused as everyone waited for the charge of Shargaz's giants, Wielders and men. She realised they were like peas in a bowl of Meciel's stew waiting to be picked off.

Arrows whirled overhead, their bronze tips searching out their prize. She braced for impact only to realise they turned to ash and metal clinked against rock.

Shargaz's guardsmen swarmed out of the volcano's chambers like ants from a smoked out nest. She caught the flashes of their red tunics clashing against their own, wearing the eagle sigil of blue. From the other side of the crater, giants flooded out of a chasm and like a stampeding herd of horses, they crashed into their wall of tribesmen.

Nate never left her side. His curved blades dispatching any who dared to cross his path. They dodged wielded rock and ice shards. Where was their fire? Nate's strategy entailed keeping her moving, to keep her distanced from the dais where they knew Shargaz would make his stand.

In the midst of the frenzy, scraping of claws scuttled over the rock bed. Every step the chimera took rattled her bones. It dashed across the crater, yellow venom dripping from its raised barb. Its primal rage and guillotine pincers carved a path right towards them. If it were not for sheer terror, she would have fled.

'Go, I'll take care of this,' Galia said.

Mirah followed Nate's fury as he cut down Shargaz's men.

Men hollered and screamed, fell with grievous injuries, then their silence, slacking into nothingness.

Blood oozed from a face wound on a roaring man who broke through Nate's defences. She raised her staff to block his lunging sword. Her staff shuddered up her arm.

The man's sword clunked to the ground a distance away. He had a dagger ready quicker than she took a breath and came at her again. She brought her staff up between his legs. The pop made her cringe as he buckled over.

When she looked, Nate had been drawn further away. Before she could shorten the distance, red-coated men blocked her path.

A fireball exploded at Nate's feet. He jumped from its burning flames. One, two, three more explosions, the gap between them widening.

Mirah parried two men who charged at her. She winced at the crunch of bone as the first man's thigh crushed against her staff.

A gush of breath forced out of the other when her staff punched into his chest.

She reeled against the chaos, the last breaths, the stench of slick blood and opened bowels overpowering her. She tightened clammy hands around her staff and fought against the terror knocking her thoughts to the side.

Give me a chance to redeem myself.

'No,' she screamed.

You forgave him, the Beast accused.

Shargaz emerged midway up the volcano a distance behind Nate, his flabby face assessing the carnage below.

His wings spread wide. He lifted off the side of the volcano and glided towards the portal. A spiny scorpion tail with a pointed spike arced over his body between his wings.

Thunder cracked overhead. Through the blur of reds and blues and giants slashing at men, she couldn't see Gabe or the dais.

Another fireball descended in front of Nate. Esha strode into view and a lead weight pinned Mirah's feet to the ground. Esha toyed with him, using her fire to push him further away.

The sound of Mirah's heartbeat thudded in her chest. The surrounding men retreated, grinning. She presumed to give her a better view. Was Esha going to kill him? She felt the grab on her clothes around the back of her neck and spun around. Bishnor lifted her off the floor.

'I told you I'd have you,' he snarled.

She beat her staff across his ribs and he threw his head back and laughed. 'What no ring?'

She spat in his face.

He wiped his cheek with his finger and slid his tongue over the slob. 'Oh, I'm going to have fun with you but first, I've got a brother to slay.'

She found her feet on the ground but he didn't let her go.

'Nate,' Bishnor roared.

Nate ran towards her, another fireball stopped him in his tracks. When Bishnor knew he had Nate's full attention, he brushed his calloused palm over her breast.

'I'll come for you later.' He sneered and then licked his tongue up the side of her face. 'Keep her busy but don't harm her,' he said, shoving her into his closest men.

Violence burned in Bishnor's eyes, he drew his sword and lumbered over to Nate.

The men she'd been fighting backed away to join the fight elsewhere and Bishnor's men surrounded her. They wouldn't dare harm her. Instead, they taunted, harassed and blocked her path enough to stop her running.

Esha smirked and stroked the fire in her hands. Her eyes flicking between Mirah and Nate. She realised what Esha was thinking. *I'm going to watch you see him suffer and then die.*

Bishnor circled and stalked his prey. The rage in his fiery opal eyes weighing up his opponent, waiting for the sudden movement of Nate's attack. He towered over him and she knew if Bishnor caught hold of him it would be over.

Bishnor, sword raised, lunged and slashed. Nate dashed out of its way. He was faster, more agile, compared to Bishnor's strength and brawn. They circled once more.

Bishnor reached forward, grabbed one of Nate's curved blades and yanked it away. He flicked the blood dripping from his hand over Nate's boots. Nate retreated and blinked sweat out of his eyes. How long could this go on?

It would be a shame to see him die.

Like a skilful archer, the Beast's words hit out at their target, cutting into her heart.

Bishnor swung his sword for Nate's head.

'No.' Mirah screamed.

Nate dodged and rose out of its way.

'Hear that? I will skewer you and then her,' Bishnor growled.

Colour drained from Nate's face. He ran at Bishnor, dropping onto his thigh and slid across the rock. His remaining curved blade sliced into Bishnor's calf. He sprang to his feet, ready to strike again, blood seeping from the grazing on his thigh.

'Is that all you have?' Bishnor gloated.

Nate limped, favouring his other leg.

Bishnor rotated around him, assessing his target.

The ground under her trembled. Thunder echoed through the volcano to the crack of lightning striking somewhere near the dais.

'You think I never saw through your years of manipulation?' Bishnor growled. 'How you did just enough to deflect any suspicion. All these years you flaunted Shemyaza's favour.' Bishnor heaved in the back of his throat and spat on the floor. 'It was mine, and you stole it. And here I am to take it back.' He sheathed his sword and rose both his arms out to his sides. 'Unless you can stop me,' he goaded.

'You talk too much.'

A dagger flew from Nate's palm, smooth and swift. It pierced into Bishnor's shoulder missing his heart. Bishnor yanked it out and laughed.

Granite, grey clouds stretched across the sky, darkening the crater. Thunder roared again and again and again.

The sides of the volcano shook. Rocks split apart, falling, shattering everywhere. Lightning struck the ground all around.

Bishnor seized the opportunity and lunged at Nate. He grabbed him by the throat, lifting him high and knocking the other curved blade from his hand.

Shadow descended on Mirah.

I won't harm you. I never betrayed you.

'I said, shut up, you filthy liar.'

Bishnor's men, hedging her in, laughed.

'Get out of my way,' she demanded.

They defended their line. She raised her staff.

You foolish child.

Nate's skin turned deep red, the edges of his mouth going blue. 'I'm sorry,' he mouthed.

'Stop! I'll come.' Mirah screamed. 'If you let him live, I'll come.'

'Oh, you'll come, won't she Nate,' Bishnor said, the smile on his face turning carnal.

Nate closed his eyes, waiting for the inevitable and in that moment, she saw a world where he didn't exist.

Bishnor pinned her with a stare. His lips peeled back, his broad ridged nose scrunching. He determined to watch her witness Nate's end. She saw the glint of Bishnor's unsheathed knife rising and the wrath in his eyes. This was it, he was going to kill him. He raised the knife ready to plunge it into Nate's heart.

Mirah sank to her knees and slid her hand into her boot. She felt the power as she slipped the ring on her finger. The Beast let out a victorious groan, darkness surrounded her, searching for a way to seep in through her mouth, her nose, her skin.

Together we can take on the world.

'No. You are nothing more than a shadow. Get back.'

It tested her, pushing against her resolve.

'You're not in control anymore,' she said.

She ripped the ground in front of her open, peeling back the rock as it cracked apart. The whole volcano shuddered. Ice flew through the air and speared into Bishnor's heart.

Nate gasped for breath.

A blossom of red spread across Bishnor's tunic, blood trickled out of his mouth into his beard. Bishnor froze. His fire opal eyes zeroing in on her. He blinked, and she watched the black slits of his pupils expand, turning his eyes solid black.

Nate, still gripped in Bishnor's hand, lifted his leg, taking a dagger strapped to his boot. He plunged the dagger into the side of Bishnor's neck.

Nate dropped to the floor.

Bishnor crashed down beside him.

Mirah knew Bishnor was already dead.

'If you don't want to be next, you'd better move,' she snapped at the men still blocking her path.

She ran for Nate. Esha stepped forward, fire flaming in her hands. Mirah felt someone brush up beside her.

'I'll take care of her,' Galia said. 'Go to Nate.'

Nate tried to stand.

'Wait, catch your breath,' Mirah urged.

Anyone who came within their periphery, she pulled the air from their lungs until they collapsed.

She kissed him gently, surrounded him within an ice wall and then screamed at everyone fighting in the crater. 'Drop your weapons or you die.'

Her loud shrill reverberated around the crater. The world paused.

She ignored Nate behind her begging her to set him free. Those who still held their weapons, she purged, filling their lungs with their own blood. Shargaz's giants, men and Wielders fell to the ground.

Inside the crater, those who remained standing, hushed, and she heard the clashing of steel outside.

Like a wave washing over the city, the sound silenced.

She melted the ice wall, Nate threw his arms around her and she breathed him in.

Two towering columns of fire whipped down from the sky.

Where was Gabe?

❊ 39 ❊

Terra screeched overhead.

Gabe followed her shadow sweeping across the rock bed as he and Meciel ran towards the dais.

'Rua, lahat,' he roared following after her.

Arrows disintegrated and bronze tips rained from the sky.

Terra swooped down onto one of the chimera standing guard. Her talons crunching through the crustaceous shell on its tail. The chimera's snapping pincers tried to pierce her wings as she beat them in readiness to take to the air.

She ascended, lifting the chimera with her and heaved it over the ridge of the volcano. Still gripped in her talons, its tail ripped from its armoured body and struck the floor, twitching, as she descended for another.

The two remaining chimera scurried to the edge of the dais, their pincers patrolling the air.

'Chaziz,' Gabe boomed.

Lightning flashed from the sky. It arced over one of the chimera striking its spine. The chimera juddered, its body splitting open.

Behind him, hacking and thrashing, blubbering and choking, the cries of victory and men falling echoed around the death arena.

'Reserve your strength. Wait for Shargaz,' Meciel ordered, shooting past him to the portal. 'Let Terra deal with the chimera.'

Terra landed on the rock bed. She folded her leathery wings. Her neck extended, jaws snapping at the remaining chimera.

Gabe searched over the fighting to see if he could spot Mirah. He spied her standing next to Nate who wielded his curved blades with blinding fury.

Meciel stopped at the portal and thrust his hand into the inky green membrane. The words he spoke were indecipherable. Gabe could only pick up 'Atar' repeated over and over. Meciel's arm swayed around as he traced out the script to destroy the portal.

The portal's glow dimmed, the edges shrinking against his chanting. It was taking too long.

Shargaz landed on the dais. Gabe had never seen such a grotesque being. Red ochre membrane stretched between the skeletal limbs on his wide spread wings. Arching over his flabby torso, a scorpion tail hung above his head. Gabe stared in disgust. There was nothing godly about this being.

'Meciel, it's nice of you to pay me a visit. Who is my dessert?' Shargaz asked.

As he spoke his voice integrated with a series of rapid percussive clicks. The sound of which reminded Gabe of leaping beetles near his home.

Meciel ignored him. Shargaz focused on Gabe, edging closer, covering some of the distance between them. Gabe would have stepped back but Terra's talons and the chimera's claws scraped close behind him.

Doubt fell on him, taut, like a noose strangling. It told him to weaken his knees, his bladder, to listen to his stomach churning, to run. He was no saviour, just a boy pretending at manhood and nothing more than Meciel's distraction. For what? To destroy a portal which Shargaz would no doubt rebuild once he'd slaughtered him.

'If you continue, Meciel. I will kill him.'

Shargaz's voice clicked with malicious intent and Gabe's knees wobbled.

'Gabe, remember what I told you. Guard your mind.'

He didn't need his mind to conjure images of leviathans, the monster standing before him was real, not covered in impenetrable scaly armour but adorned with loathing and murder.

He couldn't move, if it weren't for his heart beating against his ribcage, he'd have thought his essence had fled.

He tried to summon up a memory, something to fight the fear. There was nothing that could have prepared him for this reality.

Move, you idiot, he begged himself.

Mirah screaming from somewhere on the far side of the crater shattered everything. Enraged he broadened his shoulders. Fake it, Gabe told himself.

Shargaz herded him back towards his chimera. Why was he being so cautious?

He licked his ruddy lips, 'Before I kill you, boy, tell me your name?'

'Thunder,' Gabe barked.

Recognition flared in Shargaz's dark eyes and then dissipated.

Gabe mumbled under his breath, 'Raash, anam, raam.'

Swirling clouds masked the sky, thunder rumbled and the ground beneath them shook.

Shargaz laughed and unsheathed his sword. 'Shemyaza has his Wielders but I prefer to do this a more intimate way.'

The barb on his tail aimed at Gabe.

He expected Shargaz to advance but his gaze lingered over the battle raging and he smiled. The beard shaping his chubby face reminded Gabe of mandibles. He realised Shargaz was stalling. Every moment another of his men perished and Shargaz revelled in their demise.

Anger bellowed up from within and forced him to act.

'Pacach,' Gabe commanded.

Shargaz froze. 'What are these pitiful tricks? You think you can shackle me?'

As he realised he couldn't move, his voice ascended higher, somewhere between confusion and hatred.

Gabe glanced over at Meciel. He'd dropped to his knees, the portal still half open. He needed more time. The distraction cost him.

One of Shargaz's sons, a gigantic Nephilim, bound onto the dais. In two strides, he swung an axe at Gabe's head. Gabe swerved but the tip of the axe caught his ear. He felt the warmth trickle down the side of his neck, pooling on his shoulder.

'Chaziz,' he called.

A lightning bolt surged from the sky and gripped the Nephilim's shoulder. Lightning coursed through his flesh, his axe seared to his hand, blood vessels bursting in his eyes. The Nephilim's scream made no sound. Blood seeped out of his ears and met with the web of branching scars spreading up his neck. The lightning snapped in retreat, the Nephilim fell to the ground.

Gabe swallowed the sharp tang licking his throat along with the memory of his clan burning at Barakel.

'Call your Nephilim off,' Gabe ordered Shargaz.

Bina flew across the dais towards Meciel.

As his mind registered she had wings a chain whipped around his ankles, and he crashed onto the serrated rock covering the dais. The air punched from his lungs. His shoulder popped from its socket and he screamed.

Another Nephilim dragged him from the dais. The flesh on Gabe's back ripped open, every part of his back searing in pain. His muscles cramping against the chain cutting into his ankles. He leaned forward, grabbed hold of the chain and dug his heels into the rock bed. He tried to conserve his energy for Shargaz. It was pointless. If he didn't take out this Nephilim, he'd be dead.

'Lahat,' he cried, and flames engulfed the Nephilim.

Out of the corner of his eye, he saw the barb on Shargaz's tail. Shargaz was free. His tail whipped down to sting him. Gabe rolled, the stinger piercing into the rock bed where he'd just been. Yellow venom oozed out of the hole and dripped from Shargaz's shattered barb. Gabe scrambled away on his hands and feet like a crab.

'Ani thrd ash mn e shmin u thakl athk,' he roared at Shargaz.

Shargaz halted his attack and looked up in shock. Two columns of golden fire spiralled down from the heavens wrapping their blazing flames around Shargaz's wrists. He writhed and pulled against his tethering. His face contorted in anguish.

'Raash,' Gabe breathed.

He couldn't stand and was too exhausted to say it louder. The volcanic rock bed cracked. 'Raam, Raash,' he said, over and over again.

Thunder rumbled over the volcano and the crater vibrated. Rock severed from its foundations. A void in the ground opening. Shargaz thrashed against his fiery lashings.

'Let me stay. I'll serve you,' he begged.

'Niphal,' Gabe uttered and Shargaz fell to the ground.

'I know how you can defeat Shemyaza,' Shargaz whined.

The ends of the fire columns dropped from the sky into the gash in the rock bed dragging Shargaz under the ground. His pitched, panicked wailing reverberated in Gabe's ears as he fell deeper into the chasm that would be his prison.

'Atar,' Gabe ordered with the slither of strength he had left.

The rock bed closed over sealing Shargaz inside.

Heat surged through Gabe's head and he collapsed on the dais. The butt of his dagger's handle dug into his waist and Terra nudged his side with her snout. He heard footsteps, a distant voice, he knew he should remember, calling his name.

He hadn't noticed the cold until his mouth gaped open.

❊ 40 ❊

'Gabe!'

By the time Mirah reached the dais, Abela knelt at his side.

'He's still breathing,' she reassured her. 'He has a dislocated shoulder and his back…'

She didn't finish. What could she say?

Mirah yearned to touch him but hesitated.

The flesh on his back was stripped bare with loose bits of skin still attached. Blood seeped through his shredded clothing and leaked from his ears and his nose.

Mirah moved closer, careful not to touch him. 'Gabe, it's me. I'm here.'

Gabe didn't stir.

Nate yelled to the closest tribesmen, 'Bring that cart.'

It amazed her that the cart was undamaged although the little bay pony had not fared as well.

A chaos of questions broke out on the dais. She hadn't notice Ammo until he demanded to know the whereabouts of Bina. Blood and snot covered his face. She saw no signs of injury other than a split lip and a cheekbone, so swollen, his eye would soon shut for sure.

Nate's voice raised above the others, 'Where's Shargaz?'

Voices erupted, Gabe groaned, Terra snorted.

Everything became too loud.

'Stop,' Meciel called over them.

He was pale, burdened. Whatever had taken place on the dais had drained him to the core

'What happened?' Mirah asked.

Meciel trembled, and Ammo rushed and grabbed him to prevent his fall. He leaned into Ammo and a moment later Sojin appeared with his staff.

'Shargaz is gone,' Meciel said. 'Gabe imprisoned him deep underground in the Abzu.' Meciel tightened his grip on Ammo's shoulder and positioned his staff to support his weight. 'I tried, but constraining the Air Wielders' whilst destroying the portal... it was taking too long. Bina came to assist me. We were close but then something gripped her from the other realm.'

Ammo glanced in the portal's direction. Nothing remained except shattered debris covering the dais. A chimera, wings torn and missing its head lay lifeless on the edge of the dais. Terra stood beside it. A few deep gashes on her thigh.

'Where is she?' Ammo asked.

Meciel's head sagged.

'Ya have to get her back,' he urged.

'The portal collapsed the moment she disappeared. I'm sorry.' The tears in Meciel's eyes wept with devastation.

Mirah heard the wheels of the cart rumbling forward. She glanced up to see tribesmen dragging bodies out of the cart's path as it rolled towards them.

The gathering of reusable weapons and looting of corpses had begun. Carrion birds as black as night, invisible if not for the shine on their beaks, settled their wings on the ridge of the volcano waiting to take their feed.

'Ammo,' Nate said. 'You need to focus, help me get Gabe onto the cart.'

The glaze in Ammo's uninjured eye sharpened.

'Sojin, Eran, help Meciel,' Ammo replied.

Moving Gabe became a four-man affair. After Sojin and Eran assisted Meciel, they returned to support Gabe's legs. As much as Nate and Ammo tried, they couldn't lift him without the wounds on his back splitting further apart.

Gabe never stirred as they lay him in the cart. Abela jumped in beside him and assured Mirah that he was still alive.

Nate wiped his bloody hands in the weaver's fabric and asked, 'Has anyone seen Galia?'

No one had seen her.

Mirah's stomach churned. 'Abela, will you go with Gabe and the others into the city? I'll come and find you wherever the healers are.'

Ammo organised tribesmen to push the cart and as it rolled away the Crimson Lion War Chief arrived. Nate instructed him to meet them in the city by the healers after the War Chiefs had taken care of the wounded and secured Shargaz's surrendered forces.

'What do you want us to do with the fallen?' the War Chief asked.

'From clay they came and to clay they will return. Bury the dead as is custom so they'll not come back as ghosts.'

The War Chief went to do as commanded and Nate called after him. 'Not the giants, they must burn.'

The stench of opened bladders, bowels, and disembowelled stomach remains tainted the air. The volcanic rock poached the heat from the slain, their blood abandoning them to flow into fissures in the scorched rock.

They searched amongst the living and the lifeless and found Galia sat on the ground with her head resting in her hands. In front of her, Esha's whole body including the smirk on her face was frozen in stone.

'She wielded lava over her head. I was freezing it and it fell,' Galia said.

Esha looked like an idol raising her hands to a god of fire and brimstone.

'Are you hurt?' Mirah asked, assessing the blood on her clothes.

'Just a few gashes and bruises.'

She offered Galia her hand. 'Then let's catch up with the others.'

The healers in the city were known as the Gula. They'd set Gabe's shoulder by the time she arrived. With no cone-heads in sight, they worked efficiently tending to his wounds.

As they left Abela offered to help with the injured. She paused by the door. 'I don't suppose you've heard from Ayla and those at the mines?

Mirah shook her head.

'Gabe will recover,' she assured her.

'Thank you,' Mirah replied.

She sat by Gabe's bedside for hours, gazing at the sunlight on his face, trying to avoid glancing at the blood seeping through the bandages.

Somewhere in the distance the triumphant sound of horns blowing and dulcet cries of victory carried on the wind.

‘I guess I faked it pretty well if we’re still alive,’ he groaned. ‘Is everyone all right?’

‘Everyone here is fine,’ she reassured him.

She didn’t see the point in burdening him with news of Bina. Exhaustion harassed him, and no one had any ideas on how to get her back. She decided to let Meciel explain.

‘I expect you’ll be comparing scrapes with Nate for weeks. I had to force him to sit still for the healers attending his thigh before he limped off into the city with Ammo and the others to take command.’

Gabe’s eyelids were slipping closed. She suggested he rest but he never heard her.

Mirah found Abela and the Gula busy treating the injured. She set to work following Abela’s guidance. She was no longer a healer and the poultices and potions were unfamiliar.

Later that evening, Nate asked her to walk with him. They strolled through the volcanic rock city and he told her what he’d learned. How the glamour over Isriq collapsed as soon as Shargaz was sealed in the Abzu. How the giants fled and the guards and Wielders allied with Shargaz either fled with them or surrendered.

They were coming to the edge of the city.

‘I want to ask you something?’ he said.

‘Go on.’

‘All this time, you’ve said you’d never fight but today, what you went through, are you all right?’

Even though he didn’t say the words, she understood what he meant.

She had taken lives, crossed over a threshold with no return. She wasn’t proud of it. They were destroying everyone around her, people she loved, people who were fighting for their freedom. She knew in her heart if she hadn’t stepped in many more would have died.

‘The shadow… I mean the Beast. It didn’t force me if that’s what you’re thinking?’

His shoulders relaxed.

‘It doesn’t control me. I made my own choice to save these people and those I love.’

Nate didn’t offer pity. He understood her sacrifice.

An image of Bishnor flashed through her mind. At the moment before his eyes turned black she witnessed the hatred and the promise. He'd come for her once Shemyaza transformed him into one of his chimera.

'What do you think Shemyaza will do?' she asked.

'Can we worry about him later? There's something I want to show you. They said it wasn't far.'

He led her away from the city and along a well-trodden dirt track. They climbed up the spiralling track until they reached the top of the hillside. From here she could see over the volcano, to the dim torch lights of the city and the sun's glowing arc as it settled under the horizon.

'Down here,' he said.

A path went over the hillside, leading onto a small plateau cut into the hill. On the grassy banks, a purple carpet of lavenders and violets dipped their heads in the perfumed breeze. Nate strolled to the far side of the plateau and sat down, his legs dangling over the edge.

'Come here, you have to see this.'

She sat beside him. What was she supposed to be looking at? The view was pretty, full of green swishing trees, their branches darkening through the lack of the sun.

'Wait,' he said pulling her down to lie beside him. 'Look up there.'

Stars blossomed one by one until they filled the sky.

'Over there,' he pointed. 'There you are.'

She followed his direction, spying the bright star glistening brighter than the rest. The heavens felt infinite and unbound.

'We've had word that the attack on the mines was a success. Neviah and Ayla are all right but Zeev was injured.'

'How bad is he hurt?'

'Enough to suffer Neviah as a nursemaid,' he chuckled.

Mirah smiled at the thought. She wasn't decided on who she should pity more.

Nate shifted on to his side to relive his injured thigh. 'What you did today with the ice wall, it was foolish, you could have been hurt. Promise me you will never separate us again.'

'You were wounded.'

'I don't care. Promise me.'

She brushed her lips against his. Tenderly he kissed her. Each kiss, a sacred moment strengthening their bond. She opened the keys to her heart and let him in. He understood, the invisible connection between them pulling taut.

She felt the weight of him pressing down on her and the grazing of his stubble on her chin. His passion rising, calling out to her. All her femininity cried out to him, begging him to come and claim her.

'I want you,' he groaned. He paused, motionless and then rolled back beside her.

'I don't want you to stop,' she said, tugging on his tunic.

'Are you sure?'

'Yes.'

'But we have no contract.'

'Then we'll write it on our hearts.'

She leaned closer to kiss him.

'Wait. I have something for you. I wanted to wait until we could—' He rummaged around inside his cloak. 'Will you have me?' he asked, unfolding his hand to reveal a gold wedding band.

She knew the reason; she'd known in that moment when she immersed herself in the river.

She put her doubts to the side. He hadn't betrayed her. He'd been as bound as everyone else. The only way to truly have him was after he'd cut his ties to Shemyaza.

Love required freedom, if not free then it became something else, something twisted.

She realised now, love was never a remedy for her insecurity, fears and pain. It burns freely and never for selfish gain. It burns like unquenchable flames which river floodwaters can never sweep away.

This was love, and this was freedom. This was now their time. He was free and so was she to enter a new season. Whatever came after would be their choosing.

He slipped on the ring and declared. 'I am yours and you are mine.'

The passion and hunger in his eyes as he came to claim her, made her shudder. She looked in his eyes and promised she'd never let Shemyaza enslave him again.

❊

Beyond her hearing, the Beast laughed and smiled at the Taphas ring still on her finger.

End of Book One

Character List

Barakel

Abela (breathing)	Ayla's twin sister. Tithe sent to Shemyaza. Azu Healer.
Ayla (oak tree)	Abela's twin sister. Tithe sent to Shemyaza. Azu Healer.
Dara (pearl of wisdom)	Tithe sent to Shemyaza. Chashmalim.
Eran (watchful)	Gabe's friend.
Gabe (man of El)	Brother of Mirah.
Huldah (quick as a weasel)	Tithe sent to Shemyaza.
Mirah (var. Amira – Princess)	Sister of Gabe. Tithe sent to Shemyaza. Elemental Wielder.
Nuri (unk)	Gabe's hound.
Neviah (Prophetess/seer)	Mirah's best friend. Tithe sent to Shemyaza. Fire Wielder.
Tam (complete)	Gabe's friend.

Hermonial

Bishnor (Bish = bad)	Chieftain son of Shemyaza. Giant/Nephilim.
Dumah (silence)	Shemyaza's wife. Mother of Zamani.
Eliah (unk)	One of Nate's soldiers.
Fallen Star (the)	Singer in the Diatheatre.
Haia (God of Stores)	A young girl.
Nate (he gives)	Stepson of Shemyaza. Captain of Shemyaza's guard.
Sangu Mah (unk)	High Priest.
Sanu (to tell)	Scribes from the Edubba.

Sumer (land of civilised kings)	Zeev's mother. Nate's old nursemaid.
Zamani (lightning)	Firstborn son of Shemyaza.
Zeev (wolf)	Nate's best friend and second in command.

Immortals

Beast/Shadow (unk)	Being from the other realm.
Buzur (god of deep mines/ god who solves secrets)	Conquered territory beyond the Salmu Sea.
Ditallu (ashes)	Conquered the ice city of Ankida. Known as Belit-Seri (Lady of the Wilderness).
Shargaz (Supreme Smiter)	Conquered territory of Isriq.
Shemyaza (infamous rebellion /I have seen)	Conquered Hermonial and the surrounding territories. Self-proclaimed god from the other realm. Leader of the other immortals.
Usemi (changed/turned into)	Conquered Lacash territory.

Wielders

Arella (messenger of God) in Hermonial.	Air Wielder. Galia's sister. Resides
Esha (fire)	Fire Wielder. Resides in Hermonial.
Galia (born of the waves)	Water Wielder. Arella's sister. Resides in Hermonial.
Ninkurra (goddess of pastures)	Air Wielder. Warrior protector of Shayla. Tithe from Ana Sepiya. Sister of Ninsun.
Ninsun (cow goddess)	Earth Wielder. Warrior protector of Shayla. Tithe from Ana Sepiya. Sister of Ninkurra.

Shayla (Shay = a gift)	Fire Wielder. Tithe from Ana Sepiya.

Other

Azu (physician)	Healers in Hermonial.
Ammo (unk)	An Acquistioner. Adopted Sojin.
Bina (wise/understanding)	Companion of Meciel.
Danel (judge. var.)	Leader in Anat.
Jabril (finds strength in God)	Nate's crewman.
Kesel (stupid fool)	War Chief at Chaba Misgab.
Lestas (unk)	Thief. Hails from Radad.
Meciel (unk)	Hermit from near Barakel.
Sojin (unk)	Apprentice Acquisitioner. Adopted by Ammo.
Terra (earth/ground)	A Dactyr belonging to Meciel.
Tur (to search out/follow)	War Chief at Chaba Misgab.

Acknowledgements

Writing this book has been an epic journey of discovery and I'd like to thank the following people:

My mum who started me on my path. If you hadn't asked me to join you on that writing course, I never would have visualized Ammo.

My daughters, Tasha and Rachel, for losing their mother for the year and their endless support and feedback.

My Professor, Anthony Caleshu, for his commitment, patience and assistance in realising my ideas.

To all my family and friends who have patiently waited for my mind to return to the real world.

Cover designed by: Maria Spada
https://www.facebook.com/maria.spada.10004

About the Author

Cully Mack received her BA in English Literature and Creative Writing and her MA in Creative Writing at Plymouth University. She resides in England with Leo her loyal four-legged companion who knows more about Gabe, Mirah, (and the rest of the characters mingling in Cully's head) than any dog should.

Some days he woofed, *are you forgetting my walk?* Other days he spent forever in sun speckled forests whilst Cully argued with characters who insisted on their own paths. Most days he tilted his head, *we've been over this a thousand times.* Now his amber gaze watches—judges, *what about Nuri?* Cully isn't sure why he's so uptight. It's not like he doesn't know what happens in book two…

For A Voice That Thunders Series updates, see Cully's pages:
Facebook:
https://www.facebook.com/CullyMack/
https://www.facebook.com/groups/2308034742648180/
Goodreads:
www.goodreads.com/author/show/19033629.Cully_Mack

For Cully Mack's books go to Amazon:
https://www.amazon.com/Cully-Mack/e/B07QBLXZLT/ref=dp_byline_cont_ebooks_1

For newsletter sign up email: CullyMack@outlook.com

A Scream That Shatters

(Voice That Thunders Series book two)

They'd all been told. If Shemyaza's Wielders and Nephilim perished it was up to them to ensure he died. Of the five sent into Isriq only he remained. His fellow brothers in anguish fled like bolting rabbits, never to return.

So he watched and waited. Waited for the opportune moment.

Hidden in plain sight. No one here knew his burdens, his torment, his face.

His mind regurgitated the horror, the threats. The glee as Shemyaza drank their pain. Dagger pushed in hand, promoted. Assassin was now his name. Never take another's life his father always said.

And here he was ready to ambush, watching and waiting for the opportune moment.

Why?

A promise. He knew it was a lie but a slim chance, it could save them…

No one noticed as he prowled, smashing his terracotta figurine against the floor. No one noticed as his dagger almost slipped from his belt.

He saw them all seated high, saw the adoration of the crowds. Saw the one marked by Shemyaza for destruction.

Liquor breath quelled his doubts. He exited the inn into the celebrations, searching, waiting.

He'd never know if Shemyaza kept his promise but still, he might...

One thing he knew—his last words. It was insisted he say them.

Shemyaza requires your heart.

Printed by Amazon Italia Logistica S.r.l.
Torrazza Piemonte (TO), Italy

13100236R00189